Blaine turned her attention back to the door as she heard voices.

"She's somebody—" a voice drifted through the crack in the door "—important, I bet."

"So what's she doing downtown at a women's free clinic?" another more twangy voice asked. "They said she wouldn't tell the nurse at the desk anything but that she needed to see a doctor."

Blaine moved closer to the door, knowing that if she let them shut her inside the room she would be alone with her problem and the worry might overwhelm her once more. If she really was pregnant, she wasn't sure how she'd deal with carrying a child knowing her husband didn't want one.

**"In a remarkably moving story, Thomas examines these very different lives and creates characters readers truly care about."**
—*Romantic Times* on
*The Widows of Wichita County*

*Also by JODI THOMAS*

THE WIDOWS OF WICHITA COUNTY

*Look for Jodi Thomas's next book
Available August 2005*

# JODI THOMAS

## FINDING
## MARY BLAINE

MIRA®

ISBN 0-7783-2064-2

FINDING MARY BLAINE

Copyright © 2004 by Jodi Kouralats.

www.MIRABooks.com

Printed in U.S.A.

# FINDING
## MARY BLAINE

# One

Blaine Anderson pulled the linen drape away from a wall of windows in her bedroom. A chill brushed over her, soft as breath. Early spring hesitated, she thought, waiting for the last exhale of winter, just as she always hesitated, waiting to live.

She'd learned long ago that with any joy came the knowledge it wouldn't last. Before she'd started school, her parents gave her birthday parties. First came the excitement with the gifts, friends attending, and the cake with candles, then came the fights her parents always had afterward. Blaine quickly learned the lesson. With the highs came the lows.

She looked out over the waking city of Austin. The warmth of the newborn sun couldn't burn away the chill she felt floating on the air. Like an invisible cloud, change drifted near. But Blaine wasn't a warrior who'd ride out to face it. She was a coward who'd hide and hope it wouldn't find her nestled into the urban hills of her hometown.

She always liked the way Austin, Texas, welcomed spring's anticipation—like an aging adolescent who clings to his music long after the days of high school are gone.

Blaine stared out from the third-floor balcony of their town house. She loved the rolling hills, the blending of new and old. A college town. The state capital. A small town stretched into a metropolis where power and politics danced while history and promise played.

A part of Blaine wished she could be Rapunzel hiding away in a tower, letting only her love climb up. Crowds frightened her. Even the traffic set her nerves on edge. If she'd had her choice, she'd have been a small-town librarian not a big-city archivist. She would have worked with children, stocked books and spent her days curled into a chair reading, not doing research for companies who would probably never read her reports.

But Mark's work was here and, in truth, he'd blown their budget to buy a town house with balconies and garden space so she wouldn't feel cramped. The place, though part of a huge complex, was quiet and gated for security. Normally, Blaine found peace here, but the past few weeks hadn't been quite normal with morning runs to the bathroom and restless nights of worry. It was time to face her fears. This was one problem she couldn't simply ignore until it went away.

Something was wrong deep inside her and she'd have to go out to find answers.

Her smile didn't reach her eyes as she thought of how people in general frightened her but having to share her worries with strangers bordered on terrifying. Except for marrying Mark, she felt as if she'd lived alone all her life. Her mother, once Blaine's father left, had worked nights. By grade school, Blaine let herself in every afternoon, made her own dinner and only rolled over in bed when she heard her mother come home around midnight. She often sat her dolls at the kitchen table so she wouldn't have to eat alone.

Blaine crossed to the dresser and lifted her keys, then glanced back, making sure everything in the room was in order. Perfect. Every room of her house was a show-room of modern design and contemporary art.

Blaine walked down the stairs thinking that living with Mark was probably the closest thing to living alone. Most days she felt as though she had all the advantages of a husband with little of the bother. Even from the first, they'd both respected one another's privacy. Both only children, raised by almost absent parents, they'd fit perfectly as a match.

She heard the shower as she walked past the spare bedroom where he'd been sleeping while working nights. No matter how late he worked, Mark rose at dawn and ran two miles before getting ready for work. He was a man of order, no highs or lows in his nature. Even the dining-room table, now covered with his work, had an order about it.

When she crossed to the kitchen, she knew his juice glass waited in the sink for her to move it to the dish-washer. In the ten years they'd been married, the details of their life had settled into a balance. If Mark decided to run for an office on the Railroad Commission, there would be another shifting. She'd have to accompany him more in public, maybe even do a little entertaining, but he'd promised, win or lose, they'd take a long vacation after the election and when they returned, he'd make any transition seamless, if possible.

Blaine loved that Mark was so driven by goals. She was proud of him. It hadn't been easy for a kid from a town the size of a dust spot on the map, with a career-drunk father, to climb all the way to partner in one of the most powerful law firms in Austin. She loved listen-ing to his plans, watching his dreams unfold.

Blaine could never be a dreamer. She was a watcher of people and of life. The players like Mark had to have an audience. He needed someone in his corner, someone he could count on, and she loved being that person even though he seldom looked back. But they both knew, when he did, she'd be standing right there.

As she crossed to the sink, she stumbled over Tres. The huge old calico pushed her foot with one paw and rolled over.

"'Morning.'' Blaine knelt to scratch the cat's ears. "Found a new place to get in the way?'' It had been a constant amazement to Blaine how the cat never managed to sleep in any of the baskets she'd bought for her. "Glad you weren't here when Papa came by or he might have flattened you into a rug.''

Tres purred. Blaine smiled thinking of how Mark hated being called the cat's papa. He'd complained about the animal since she'd brought Tres home six years ago. The kitten had been half-starved, living behind a Dumpster in the alley near work. For the first few months Mark swore she'd brought home a rat. Even now, he didn't quite get the concept that one lives with a cat, never owns one.

Tres, for a trash-eating kitten, had quickly become a very particular cat. She only ate her cat food if Blaine scrambled an egg with bacon bits and mixed it in with the food. Blaine knew she spoiled the animal, but with the help of the microwave she could have Tres's breakfast ready within a few minutes.

Grabbing an egg she bumped the refrigerator door closed with her hip and reached for the cat-food box in the broom closet. She always scrambled the egg in an old blue bowl that didn't match any set of dishes. It took the microwave heat well and Blaine told herself blue was Tres's favorite color.

She smiled, thinking of how she had to bite her lip

when Mark pulled the same bowl from the cabinet for midnight ice cream. If he'd never noticed it was Tres's breakfast bowl, she wasn't about to tell him.

When she straightened from serving the cat food, she took the pen lying beside the phone and scribbled out a note to Mark. For a long moment, she stared at it, wondering if she should have said less…or maybe more.

She could feel the invisible balance of their life together shifting. One piece of paper, not even an ounce in weight, might sway the scales. The ideal life. The perfect couple. After this day it all might crumble.

She dropped the note beside Mark's keys, grabbed her jacket and ran out, suddenly in a hurry to turn over the hand fate dealt her.

# *Two*

Blaine stared at her reflection in the window of the private waiting area. An automatic sprinkler outside the clinic had hopelessly streaked the glass, blurring the view and whitewashing her likeness into a ghost. Not quite there, not quite gone.

The effort from fighting the morning traffic into downtown only added to the feeling of panic she tried to ignore. But she could no longer walk around the problem, watching it grow even as she ignored it.

Placing her hand on the sill, she wished the spring's warmth could somehow pass into her. She felt frozen inside. The bleak kind of cold folks get when they forget to care if they live or die. Her mother's words from years ago drifted back to Blaine, "You'll never be anything but a little mouse, Mary Blaine. You're a mouse of a girl and you'll be a mouse of a woman."

Once, her mother had even told her that Blaine had been the reason her father left. "No one can love the weak," she'd shouted. "Folks only tolerate the meek." Yet when her mother raged, Blaine always hid, never facing her, proving her mother right.

Blaine pressed her hand against the glass, needing bravery now to face what the doctor might tell her today...what she'd have to tell Mark tonight. Her mother was wrong, she thought, I've just been storing up courage all my life.

The alley view did nothing to ease the sorrow lodged in her soul. Rusty Dumpsters, trash, worthless boxes, wooden crates. An old tin shed ran along by the alley too rickety to hold more than lawn equipment and looking as out of place among the brick buildings as Blaine felt she did in the free clinic. At thirty-two, she looked as if she could still be in her mid-twenties, but panic rapidly aged her toward senility today. After ten years of calm, trouble had found her. It grew inside her even as she denied it.

She watched a man carrying a brown paper grocery bag stroll into the shed. He came out a moment later and looked around, then disappeared once more.

Blaine turned her attention back to the door as she heard voices.

"She's somebody," a voice drifted through the crack in the door. "Important, I bet."

"So what's she doing downtown at a women's free clinic?" Another, more twangy, voice asked. "They said she wouldn't tell the nurse at the desk anything but that she needed to see a doctor."

Blaine moved closer to the door, knowing that if she let them shut her inside the room, she would be alone with her problem and the worry might overwhelm her once more. If she really was pregnant, she wasn't sure how she'd deal with carrying a child knowing her husband didn't want one.

Mark had his plan. She wasn't sure she could face him and kill his dream. Children were a someday goal to Mark. He'd had to live with the burden of being an unwanted child and he'd sworn many times that he'd rather have no children than bring one unplanned into the world. He still had the belt scars across one shoulder where his father beat him while swearing that Mark's birth had ruined his life.

"I don't know why she's here, but she's rich." The first young woman's whispered tone traveled from the hallway. "Maybe she's checking us out, planning to do volunteer work or make a sizable donation. It wouldn't be the first time. Just 'cause we don't see them, don't mean Austin ain't full of folks with deep pockets. Some might want to help."

Glancing through the slit in the door, Blaine noticed two women wearing white standing a few feet away. Their backs were turned to her, but they both seemed young and as thin as she fought to stay.

A baby would change her thinness. Blaine touched her waist. A baby would change everything. Mark might never leave her, but she hated the thought of him staying and resenting her. How many times in their marriage had he questioned whether anyone should bring new life into what he always called "this mad world"?

"You notice her clothes?" One girl giggled from just beyond Blaine's door. "She's wearing a month's pay. I'd die for an outfit like that. It's classic."

Blaine grinned, thinking she'd worn her plainest, oldest pantsuit today. Both her shirt and trousers were baggy, holdovers from ten pounds ago before she'd dieted from slim to fashionably thin. She wanted to pass unnoticed through the doors of the clinic, hoping to have questions answered and tests run before she talked to her husband. She wished she could circle unnoticed through life for a while, but she had not even made it through a clinic without people talking about her.

The door opened and the voice had a face. "Excuse me." A young woman entered dressed like a nurse, but

Blaine would bet there was no degree behind the uniform.

"You'll need to put these on." She held out a gown and paper slippers while she leaned her head toward a corner of the room that had been blocked off by what looked like an old shower curtain. "And we'll have to ask you to take off all your jewelry. I'm not sure what kind of tests the doctor will want to run."

Blaine slipped the wedding rings from her left finger as though removing a trinket and not thousands of dollars' worth of gold. "Would you keep these safe?" she asked the girl, knowing her chances of walking out with the rings were better if she gave them to an employee. "Sindi?" Blaine read the name tag dangling from the girl's waist.

"Sure." The girl slipped the ring into her vest pocket. "My desk is just next door. I won't let them out of my sight." She seemed pleased Blaine trusted her. "I'll put your coat at my station too, if you like. Things have a way of walking off around this place."

Blaine handed the girl her fur-trimmed jacket, made more to show off the highlights of her hair than for any warmth. She couldn't help but notice Sindi naturally had almost the same color curls, brushing her shoulders just as Blaine's did. Blaine no longer remembered her natural color. It had been almost twenty years since she had first bleached her hair and began her journey to become someone else.

"Bet your husband will want you coming home with this." The girl petted the coat as if it were alive.

Blaine wanted to answer that she was not sure he would notice if she came home at all. He had paid little attention when she ordered the fur, only saying "Happy Birthday" while he wrote the check. That had been the week he'd argued his first case before the Texas Supreme Court. He'd rambled on about his strategy all through her birthday dinner.

She realized Mark never asked about her hair color. The transformation had been complete by the time she met him in college. For all she knew, he thought her a blonde. They'd both gotten what they wanted that May. He'd been accepted to law school and she'd slipped on his engagement ring. The only comment she could ever remember him making came the night he asked her to marry him. He'd said something about her being a knockout blonde who wasn't saddled with any kids and that spelled perfection in his book.

Shouts rumbled from somewhere down the hallway.

"I'll be right back." The girl's blue eyes danced with excitement. "Go ahead and change. Remember, the gown opens in the front. It'll be a while before a doctor will get to you. We're running short-staffed today. Half the town's out with the flu and it hit us extra hard this week. Seems like everyone with kids called in sick. I guess I'm lucky to live alone and have no one passing germs to me.'

Yelling echoed into the room once more.

"Is something wrong?" Blaine couldn't make out words from the angry voices. They came from the crowded waiting room where she'd sat for over an hour trying not to touch anything.

"No. We can handle it. Being short-staffed is nothing new." Sindi wrinkled her eyebrows. "Oh, you mean about the noise. Probably just someone upset over waiting. Or a drunk or someone high on drugs wanting meds. The doctors don't like to call the cops unless we have to. Usually with the police comes the press and with all the nuts out there today, a place like this doesn't need publicity. We've got our own security. They'll pull Frank in and he'll take care of the problem. He may have a bad leg, but he can put the fear of the devil in most folks.''

Sindi offered a pat on Blaine's arm. ''You've nothing to worry about. You're about as far as you can get from the noise. Nobody's coming way back here to cause trouble.''

Blaine nodded, remembering the guard she'd seen standing in the parking lot lighting a cigarette when she'd walked in. Though this clinic was advertised as a full-service facility for women, she guessed the abortions they did were controversial and, being in this neighborhood, probably brought in all types. Downtown Austin brimmed with druggies and the homeless, she'd seen them often enough on the streets.

The girl hurried out. Blaine turned back to the window as she set aside the gown and slippers. Maybe she wasn't pregnant. A doctor had told her years ago the odds were against it ever happening and Mark had accepted the news with a single nod, eliminating children from his plan without comment.

But something was wrong inside her and had been for three months. If not pregnancy, then what? She didn't want to think of the possibility of cancer. Even saying the word put form to her greatest fear.

She shrugged, thinking this was one more question she wished she had a mother to ask. But her mom, already ill with cancer, had left her with a neighbor one afternoon swearing she would return soon. She hadn't even glanced back when Blaine yelled goodbye. Six hours later, when the police knocked on the neighbor's door, they'd told Blaine simply that her mother wouldn't be returning.

Maybe that was the real reason Blaine feared having a baby. Maybe she was afraid she would be no better at parenting than her mother had been. In truth, that may have been the reason she never pressed Mark about children. Neither of them had examples to build on. Her mother had thought she was pregnant a month before they found the cancer. She'd fought it for six months without even once explaining anything to Blaine.

Thoughts of going back to her office and forgetting today's nightmare for a while longer drifted through Blaine's mind. She liked the tiny space she'd been given in the basement of the old downtown library building that now housed the Travis County records. Though she wandered in unnoticed by the library staff most days, she had a place to go and work waiting for her.

Only, today she knew that if she went to work she'd only spend the day worrying. She had to find out. She'd made it this far, she could face the answer.

The sound of a lawn mower from somewhere beyond the window blended with the voices arguing down the hallway. Sparrows played in the shrubs just below the window. They hopped from branch to branch scolding the approaching mower.

The engine roared as a man riding the mower neared the building. He adjusted the brim of a baseball cap with oily fingers as he glanced first in one direction, then the other. When he raised his head and shoved back the tattered blue cap, Blaine met his gaze. Angry gray eyes, cold as stone, stared at her as if he saw nothing alive beyond the glass.

A cry caught in her throat at the hate smoldering in the tombstone-colored stare. He'd been the man she'd seen carrying the grocery bag earlier.

He lowered slightly, depositing something beneath the

window where she stood. The blue brim of his cap now hid his eyes. Then he rode away, not bothering to mow the rest of the grass. When he reached the shed, he jumped from the machine and hurried away.

Blaine almost tapped on the window to point out his error, but she guessed no one would care about the patch of grass out back of a clinic. Her daily routine overflowed with unimportant details, almost as if somewhere in life's scheme she'd been assigned to see after things no one else wanted to bother with.

But not today, she thought. Today the details would shatter her world. Worry had slowly destroyed the calm of her life until she could stand the uncertainty of it no longer. Today she'd know one way or the other. Cancer, or a baby, either would destroy her life.

Sparrows chirped outside, still calling an alarm.

"Fly away," Blaine whispered, leaning close to the glass. "Fly away."

A moment later a rolling blast hit her full force, knocking Blaine through the window with cannon might. At first, all she saw, all she thought was that she might crush the birds. Then a deafening avalanche tumbled over her like death's black cloud and she flew with plaster, brick and birds through the air.

She landed amid the alley trash and rolled, no more than a doll tossed among the rubble. Boards, bricks, papers blanketed her as dust filled her lungs and fire flickered in her hair. She staggered through the smoke heading nowhere but away.

Blaine fought to scream, but the air was on fire. As she labored to breathe, flames slid down her throat. The air burned again as she coughed it up. She crawled away not caring that the trash scraped her knees and ripped her clothes. Her ears rang, disorienting her, as panic throbbed along with blood.

Reason told her a bomb had just exploded, as she'd seen a hundred times in movies. But was it only the first of many? There was no time to think. Another volley of bricks might kill her. She had to hide. Survival took over.

She scrambled for shelter, instinct short-circuiting all thought. Across the alley she slammed against a brick wall of an abandoned warehouse. Mindlessly, Blaine moved hand over hand along the wall until she found an indentation in the brick. She placed her back against the building and tried to see beyond the smoke. Nothing. Slowly, she slid down, covering her head with her hands as trash tumbled over her and a falling brick hit her head.

Like a friend from old, the need to hide took command. She balled further into herself. Everything would pass if she could disappear as she had years ago when her parents' fights started. The smell of burnt hair stung her nostrils as boards piled atop her, bruising her, burning her, protecting her.

Blaine covered her ears and blocked out the sounds around her as she tried not to breathe. Don't think of the noise or the pain. Drift away, she told herself over and over. Drift away.

In the faraway world beyond her hiding place, sirens wailed, people rushed, water sizzled, but, burrowed into her cave, Blaine closed out everything, even the pain. She nestled farther into the space between the bricks, hiding away from the world.

Squeezing her eyes tight, she pushed all trouble aside as she had when she'd been a child hiding beneath blankets in the hall closet. She pushed aside the panic, the noise, the smells. The throbbing in her head eased to a dull ache. She couldn't tell if she was falling asleep or passing out from the pain. It didn't matter. She drifted away.

# Three

When Blaine awoke, fear kept her still. All was silent around her. Slowly, she made out the sound of water dripping. The air smelled cool and flavored with the odor of a campfire, or more precisely of the trash burning in a huge barrel in her grandmother's backyard. Darkness pressed against her, so thick she couldn't tell if her eyes were open. Her leg throbbed with a dull ache, her hands and face crackled with tiny scabs when she moved, and her throat felt raw, as if she'd swallowed slivers of glass while she slept. The pounding in her head had concentrated at one spot just above her hairline.

Slowly, she crawled from her hiding place and retraced her steps. Pale moonlight washed across the alley now littered with parts of the building she had been standing in hours before. Water leaked from huge hoses left on the grass, but the smell of a fire dominated the air. The building was black. Dead now.

She moved out into the open, trying to make sense of what had happened. Boards blocked the space where windows had been. The bush and sparrows were gone. A red light blinked at the corner of the building, flashing an eerie strobe against the clinic's exposed bones.

Blaine felt she'd passed out in Austin and awoken in a war zone.

"Hey, lady! Get out of there!"

She looked around, but could find no form to the order.

"No one is supposed to be back here." The man moved from the blackness, his steps faltered as he dragged one foot noisily across the rubble. "This is a crime scene and I'm the only one who's supposed to be near here." He tapped a silver badge on his chest that looked more like a name tag than anything official. "Folks died here today. Have a little respect."

When she did not move, his gloved hand grabbed her arm and yanked.

Blaine stumbled, losing her shoe in the roots of fire hoses as she tried to match his limping strides.

"You'll have to sleep it off somewhere else," a man yelled from inches behind her. "You're the third drunk tonight who wandered off Sixth Street and tried to scavenge among the rubble." He tightened his grip. "I've had a hard day of it. The next one I find in here may get more than just an escort off the property. I'd like to get my hands on that blasted idiot who laid dynamite at the back of the clinic. He's made one hell of a day for me."

"But..." Blaine tried to explain. Words couldn't cut their way up her throat.

She let the man hurry her along until they were on the broken sidewalk in front of what once had been the clinic. Yellow tape roped off the area, as if anyone would want to enter. In the streetlight she noticed his badge had the name Frank Parker printed across it.

"You're the clinic's guard," she whispered, trying not to hurt her throat any more than she had to.

"Yeah." He straightened. "And I think I may have seen the man who did this. He'd better pray the cops catch him before I do. He just destroyed the best job I ever had. I work twenty-four hours straight and they're laying me off come sunup.''

She swallowed, her throat too dry to say anything else.

"Don't come back." He shoved her toward the street. "Or you'll be sorry." His threat sounded hollow with exhaustion.

She wanted to scream that he was the one who would be sorry if he ever laid a hand on her again. She was the wife of one of the most powerful lawyers in Austin. She'd had dinner with the governor last week. She was somebody.

But it was too much effort to force words. It was easier to be nobody for a while. Plus, in her state, if he guessed who she was, he might call the press. If her choice was between being mistaken for a drunk or her name being flashed across the front page as being injured in a welfare-clinic bombing, she'd take the drunk.

She glanced down. Covered by a layer of ash, and standing in the poor light, she looked like a person of the street. Untying the scarf at her neck, she used the hundred-dollar silk as a rag to wipe her face, then tied her hair back in a knot. Her salon-straightened hair felt as if it had been fried with a bad perm. A few places were extra crispy, but she was suddenly too exhausted to care. All she could think of was that in a minute she'd wake up and this nightmare would be over.

Blaine walked up Congress Avenue heading toward the lights of the capitol. She'd driven these streets all her life and could tell what time it was by the type of people who were out. Business hours—suits and convention goers, shoppers and panhandlers. Evening—diners and daters, meeting for happy hour and extending into dinner. The midnight hours—freaks and hard drunks mingled with druggies and college students who wouldn't make it up for the next day's classes. But sometime, after three and before dawn, the small town that exploded into a city slept in peace to the snoring sound of a street sweeper.

When Blaine had been in college, she used to run down the center of Lamar Boulevard during this lonely time of night. She'd felt like the last person alive.

The sidewalk was cool on her bare foot as she limped along with no destination. She had no money, no ID. Her wallet had been in the pocket of the jacket she'd handed over. There was no hurry. She'd left Mark a note telling him where she'd gone, half hoping he might find it and ask why. But she doubted he would even see it. He had moved into the spare bedroom a few weeks ago, claiming he needed to concentrate on a case he was preparing for. Concentration meant not bothering to tell her when he came in or left. He'd done it before, several times, and each time it was longer before he moved back in with her.

Work consumed him until there was no time for her, for them. It was so important that he be nothing like his father that Mark left few minutes in the day unplanned.

On the outside she and Mark were the perfect couple. He'd made partner younger than anyone ever had in the almost hundred-year history of the firm. His father had celebrated early and been too drunk to board the flight to Austin.

Mark had simply taken her hand and told Blaine it didn't matter. They celebrated alone. And though he held her tightly that night, she couldn't help but wonder if her presence even mattered.

Blaine thought she wanted things to remain as they were, but lately she felt like one of the sparrows she had seen in the bush. Dancing from branch to branch, knowing something was about to happen, but afraid to fly away. If Mark decided to go into politics, he'd need a more outgoing wife. They'd no longer be the perfect match.

She touched her belly feeling nothing. Surely if she'd been pregnant, she would have felt something, even if it was early. The fear that it might be a tumor growing inside her made her hand shake slightly. "Thirty-four," she whispered to herself. Her mother and grandmother both took their last breath during that year of their life.

A cab passed, honking at her for no reason. She stumbled on the heel of her one shoe and landed against a construction wall covered with paper. Blaine leaned down to pull off the shoe and felt the warm thickness of her own blood at her ankle.

There wasn't enough light to see her injury. She limped half a block before she found a bus stop occupied by a few sleeping homeless. She sat between two bag ladies while she examined her leg. A deep scratch oozed blood along her calf, wetting one side of her trousers from knee to ankle.

"We have to leave soon, Mary," a bundle of rags in the darkened corner of the bus stop mumbled. A pink nose appeared, then a tanned face made of wrinkles and a smile.

"I'm not Mary," Blaine answered kindly, remembering that her mother had often called her Mary Blaine when she was angry. When her mother died, Blaine had shed her first name as easily as she shed her past.

"Well, you be careful out here." The little woman grinned as though passing on great knowledge. "I worry about you, Mary.'

Blaine realized for the first time in her life she wasn't afraid of being mugged. She had nothing. She was nobody. "I will be," she whispered and smiled back at the woman.

"They're feeding pancakes at the shelter today," the bundle added. "We want to get there early, Mary. Wouldn't do to miss that. I've heard they sometimes have sausage links, but I ain't never seen none."

Blaine felt sorry for the woman. "Thank you." She smiled again, wishing she had money to buy the old woman a real breakfast. "But I'm not Mary."

"Shut up, will you." A head poked out from beneath the larger bundle of rags. A black woman whose age wasn't written easily across her face, added, "It won't hurt you none to be Mary, miss, if that's what she wants. She gets a kick out of making up names for folks. Calls a lot of them Mary. It must be a name that got stuck in what little mind she's got left."

Blaine saw the woman's point.

"You only got one shoe," the smaller bundle of rags said as she dug in one of her bags. "I can fix that, my dear."

She handed Blaine a pair of white slippers while mumbling about the price of getting shoes that fit properly. "Your feet have been growing like weeds these days." She patted Blaine's arm and snuggled back into her blanket.

When they fell back into silence, Blaine caught herself smiling. She'd never been in more of a mess in her life.

A clock on a wall across the street at a twenty-four-hour copy place told Blaine it was almost six. If she walked toward the capitol and down a few blocks, she could reach the parking garage Mark used. Maybe she could catch him before he went into work and get him to take her home.

He'd be upset that she was hurt and he'd ask a hundred questions, but he'd take her home and insist on doctoring the cut. He was the one person she knew who was more afraid of germs than she.

She walked slowly through the shadows as the city began to awake. It crossed her mind that Mark might want her to go to the police. But what could she tell them? That she'd seen a man mowing the lawn in the back of a clinic she never should have been at in the first place. The thought of having to face questions she couldn't answer frightened her.

When she reached the law offices, all the windows were still dark. If her luck held, no one would see her looking like this but Mark.

She slipped into a blackened doorway between the parking lot and the employee entrance to the law offices. Her throat hurt so badly, she wasn't sure she could yell Mark's name when he passed, but maybe he'd hear her whisper.

A secretary hurried in carrying a box of doughnuts. Her keys rattled against the door as if she was frightened to be arriving so early in the shadows.

Blaine remained very still, not wanting to scare her if she became aware of someone near.

Next came a large man swinging a briefcase like a weapon. When he was within ten feet of her, Blaine recognized him as Harry Winslow, one of the senior partners. His gray hair looked as if he forgot to comb it but, even in the shadows, he appeared powerful and controlled.

Blaine thought of calling out. He would help her. She could go inside and have coffee and doughnuts until Mark arrived. Only, the thought of having to answer questions about why she was at the clinic stopped her. She'd tell Mark first. He had a right to know. Then they'd face the problem together and find out what was wrong with her.

Just as Harry Winslow's key connected with the door, a thin shadow moved toward him.

Blaine opened her mouth to scream a warning.

But before sound could climb up her throat, Winslow turned and faced the man. "About time you contacted me, Jimmy!" he snapped.

"Mission accomplished." The thin man tapped his ball cap.

"You got the wife?"

The thin man nodded once.

"Thank God we didn't have to take out Anderson. I like that boy, but I sent Shorty to watch his apartment just in case you didn't get the job done."

"I did what I had to," the thin man grumbled. "Have I ever not done the work?"

Winslow huffed. "Messy. Couldn't you think of a quieter way?"

Blaine couldn't move. Couldn't breathe. Surely they weren't talking about the bombing…about her.

"I did the job, didn't I? You said quickly, not quietly. Had the sticks in my truck, didn't see no way that would be faster. I still got some cleanup to do with the witness." The thin man took time to spit before continuing. "A few adjustments under the hood should take care of the problem."

"Well, do it!" Winslow snapped. "And no witnesses this time around. You can't expect me to clean up any mistakes this time. I'm lucky to have one friend on the force."

The man tapped his hat once more in salute and vanished toward the street. Blaine never saw his face but she would guess that his eyes were gray.

She closed her eyes and tried to think herself invisible. They were talking about her, she knew it. If Winslow or the thin man saw her now she'd be as dead as they already seemed to think her to be.

# Four

"How are your pancakes, Mary?" the tiny bag lady beside Blaine asked.

Blaine carefully swallowed. She couldn't have eaten anything more solid than the mushy syrup-covered pancake. Her throat felt as if it had been rubbed with sandpaper. "I haven't had these in years," she managed to answer. "I forgot how good they taste."

The large bundle of rags from across the table nodded.

The little old woman, who'd shown her how to move through the line at the shelter, now lost interest in talking to anyone. She finished her plate and licked the plastic fork clean before sliding it into her pocket. When she saw Blaine watching her, she frowned. "They don't care if you take it. They got plenty more."

Blaine nodded and lowered her head. She needed time to think and for once she felt safer in a crowd. The conversation she'd overheard replayed itself over and over in her throbbing brain. She told herself they had to be talking about something else. Maybe the man had been Winslow's mechanic and Winslow had asked him to pick up his wife. The statement "You got the wife?" almost made sense. Almost.

But what about the rest!

Blaine glanced up and noticed a scarecrow of a man in his fifties stand and tap his glass with a real fork.

"Welcome," he shouted over the sound of a hundred hungry people eating. "If you'll bow your heads, I'll thank the Lord for our food."

Everyone but Blaine followed orders.

She stared at the man belting out his prayer. She resented the fact that he'd been given a proper fork. Not even pancakes were easy to cut with plastic. She watched the others at the head table. They didn't look as if they were homeless. Preachers maybe, or shelter workers. One, a young man of about twenty, sat at the corner of the table. He wrote in a notebook while he crammed food into his mouth. Sociology major, she'd bet. Probably writing a paper on the eating habits of the homeless.

She studied the head table more closely, as always, picking up details. They all had flatware, not plastic, and they all had little sausages.

The scarecrow announced showers would be available for anyone who wanted to stay and help clean up. Then he moved toward the door without taking his paper plate to the trash. He talked with the other members of his table as they prepared to leave.

Blaine almost laughed out loud. Even among the homeless, she worried over details. The people at the head table would never be invited to her home. But, if they were, she certainly wouldn't eat steak while serving them bologna.

"I got to go, Mary." The old woman beside Blaine stood, pulling a handful of napkins from the dispenser in the center of the table. "We got our place in the park." She nodded toward the other bag lady who stood without a word. "If we don't get there soon, someone will take it. You have to watch out for squatters around here, Mary, but you're welcome to come for a visit if you've nowhere else to go."

The large black woman across from Blaine nodded once in agreement then began collecting bags they'd stashed under the table.

"I think I'll stay here," Blaine answered then remembered the slippers the little bag woman had given her. "Thanks for your kindness."

Blaine hardly recognized her own voice. The smoke, or maybe her screams, had changed it somehow—made it rougher and deeper. It was time for her to go home. If Mark noticed she hadn't slept there, or if he'd seen the note, he would be worried. She had to face her problems, hiding wouldn't solve anything. She'd talk it out with Mark, even tell him what she'd heard his law partner whisper to a man who'd been about the same build as the man on the lawn mower.

Mark would know what to do. After they'd talked, she'd go see her regular doctor, as she should have done to begin with. Feeling as if she'd nearly died yesterday, the possibility of pregnancy or even cancer didn't seem the Everest it had been before.

"You're welcome, Mary." The tiny bag lady patted her on the shoulder. "You owe me one, girlie. Those are fine slippers. I got them from the hospital Dumpster and they don't even look like they were used at all." The woman shuffled off, picking up forks and unused napkins as she moved to the door where the preacher stood, his hands clasped firmly behind him now that all his "guests" had departed.

Blaine stood, wanting to take a bath more than she'd ever wanted to in her life. It was almost 8:00 a.m. Mark would be at his office by now. She'd give him a call and have him pick her up. He'd be bothered, but once he saw her clothes he'd be glad she didn't come by his office.

She walked toward the front. An old library-style partners desk was wedged between the front door and the beginning of the serving line. It sagged with stacks of files and pamphlets. As the last stragglers departed, a breeze from the open door ruffled papers across it as swiftly as nimble fingers run across a keyboard.

The scarecrow preacher flopped atop the piles, a human paperweight, until the door finally rattled closed.

Blaine stepped closer, picking up a few slips he had let escape.

When he didn't look up, she asked, "Mind if I borrow the phone?"

He stared at the door, frowning at an adversary he knew waited to strike again. "It's not for public use."

"I only need to call a local number. It won't cost you anything."

"It's not for public use."

Blaine tried not to let her frustration show. She was well aware she looked no better, and maybe even a little worse, than the homeless, but surely he would help her. That's what places like this did, after all.

"Is there a phone I can use?"

"There's a pay phone outside."

Blaine touched her pocket wishing she had change. "Would you mind calling someone for me?" She hated being nice to this creep, but he was the only one with a phone.

Finally, he looked up. "I'm sorry, it's against the rules."

She caught a glimpse of the tiredness in his face and turned away. The cold blue of his eyes told her he was dead. Oh, he might still be walking around, breathing, talking, eating pancakes with a real fork, but he was as dead inside as she'd ever known a person to be. It occurred to her that maybe he hadn't given up the fight, maybe he'd never got involved in the first place.

Blaine looked over at a lone woman starting the process of cleaning up after more than a hundred people. She could be only a few years older than Blaine, but life weighed heavy across her face. For a moment their gazes met, both feeling sorry for the other.

"Want some help?" Blaine asked out of kindness.

The woman shrugged. "It's my job. I get a room in the back for cleaning up. The shower Brother Ray offers ain't worth all the work."

Blaine threw plates into the huge trash. "I'll help anyway." She needed to keep busy while she thought of what to do. If worst came to worst, she could walk back to Mark's office and hope no one noticed her dirty clothes, scraped face and hospital slippers as she made a mad dash to his office. A shower would help to make her more presentable when she went to Mark.

An hour later the work was done. Except for introducing herself as Chipper, the lone woman didn't have much to say. Now she turned to Blaine with a face that had forgotten how to smile. "Want that shower?"

"You bet. I'll feel a lot better after I clean up." She realized how strange she sounded. Her voice reminded her of an old radio announcer who'd yelled out one too many football games in the cold air.

Without smiling, Chipper handed her two towels and soap as she pointed her toward a room off the kitchen. "There's supposed to be a fifteen-minute limit on the shower, but take the time you need. You earned it."

Blaine thanked her, wondering how such a sad woman

could have such a name. Chipper sounded as if it belonged to a small dog, not a woman.

Chipper pulled a tube of antiseptic cream from her pocket. "You might need this for those cuts on your hands and face. I'm sorry, I don't have any Band-Aids. They give me this in case I cut myself cooking or cleaning up. Wouldn't do to have the kitchen help serving with an infected wound showing. And if I don't work, I'm back on the streets."

Blaine had to ask, "Why this job?"

Shrugging, Chipper said, "I get food, a room and a TV that gets over sixty channels. If I worked anywhere else, I'd make money, and I don't do too well with that. Tend to spend it on the wrong things. You see, I got a problem. I'm one of those compulsive shoppers you hear about, only I never get to the mall. I can spend all I have at the first liquor store."

The woman could have been talking about the weather for all the emotion she used. Without another word, Chipper moved to the TV propped atop the refrigerator so that she could sit and watch both it and the front door.

Blaine walked into the tiny white bathroom realizing she'd forgotten about the cuts. She set the towels down and looked up at the mirror. The sight before her almost made her bolt. A monster with her eyes stared back. Her navy pants and shirt were dusty gray with rips and holes beyond repair. Her hair looked far worse than the preacher's did. Some sections were burned while others were matted with ash and dirt.

Walking into Mark's office like this would probably end his career. He'd never forgive her for such an act.

As she undressed, Blaine smiled. Bruises covered her body, her hair was ruined, her voice cracked with hoarseness, yet in a strange way she felt as if she was free. She knew it was only for a few hours, but she'd touched death last night and this morning she was amazed how good it felt to be alive. The possibility of pregnancy, the problems between her and Mark of late, the fear she could no longer be the kind of wife he needed, all floated somewhere outside this little world she had found.

Here, she was nobody. Here it felt good just to stand beneath hot water and let her problems wash away.

She took her time, even brushing her clothes with the damp towels, but in the end, she looked at her reflection and realized she could not embarrass Mark by walking into his office. With that option gone, she figured she had two choices. Walk the ten miles home to Cat Mountain, or charm the preacher into letting her use the phone.

She must know a hundred people in Austin, but calling them might put them in danger. Talking to Mark was the best move to make. He would know how best to proceed. He always knew the right move to make. Yet, the thought of calling him was dreadful. In the ten years they'd been married, they'd always practiced the "politeness of strangers" policy. Since both had lived alone for several years prior to their marriage, they'd learned to be independent and strived not to slip into the pitfalls of leaning on one other.

She'd had a flat tire once out by the airport. When she had called him on her cell, he'd said simply, "Call Triple A." Well, almost dying might be the one incident worth asking for a little help.

Her cell! Blaine tapped her pocket before remembering that, like her wallet, it was in her jacket.

She washed her scarf and used it to tie back her wet hair. If she walked down the center of the highway in rush-hour traffic, not one person would recognize her now.

Taking the time to clean the shower, Blaine practiced what she would say to the preacher. There must be some way to get through to the man. All she wanted was to use the phone.

Her planning was wasted, for when she stepped out of the bathroom Chipper was the only one left in the hall. She was mopping between the tables using long S strokes that missed as much floor as she cleaned. A tiny black-and-white television blared from the kitchen.

The phone rang on the preacher's desk, but Chipper showed no sign of noticing. After a few rings, it stopped. Evidently she wasn't one of the chosen ones allowed to use the phone either.

Blaine thanked her for the antiseptic cream and walked straight to the preacher's desk. With any luck, she could make her call and be gone before the preacher returned. If he caught her, what could he do? After all, borrowing a phone wasn't a crime.

Her broken nail dialed the private number to Mark's office.

Usually he answered on the first ring, or an answering machine picked up telling her where he was. Not this time. She leaned against the desk as ring after ring echoed in her ear.

Finally, someone picked up. Muffled tones. Then, almost as if he were far away, Mark answered, "Yes?"

"Mark!" Her voice cracked and she swallowed, trying to make her vocal cords work. The real world came crashing down as she tried to think of how to begin to tell Mark all that had happened.

"Who is this?" he snapped.

She tried again and, in a hoarse whisper managed two words. "It's me."

She heard him take a deep sigh then say in an icy voice, "I don't know who this is, but you can go to hell."

Too shocked to respond, she took the full blow as he slammed the phone down on the other end.

Something was wrong. He sounded like Mark, but where was the polite stranger she'd always known? Maybe he didn't recognize her voice? Maybe he thought she was some kind of crank caller? She couldn't picture her husband being so rude. It wasn't his nature. She'd always thought of Mark as a huge paper doll. Stiff, proper, shallow. The perfect man to stand beside a paper-doll wife.

Trembling fingers dialed again. Maybe it wasn't even Mark? She could have reached the wrong number.

As the phone rang once more, Blaine looked down at the morning paper piled atop the desk. There, spread across the front page was a photograph of the burned remains of the clinic.

Her hand absently unfolded the corners as the smell of the fire returned to her lungs. She remembered screaming, crying, hiding as the panic of the night returned. She'd been sleepwalking since before dawn, blocking the horror of yesterday from her mind. Now the paper brought it all back.

In a corner of the shot, framed in on top of the scene, was her picture. A bright professional Blaine Anderson stared back. She recognized the shot as one she'd had made for a passport that she and Mark had never gotten around to applying for.

The phone continued to ring as she read, "Prominent attorney's wife one of four killed in bombing."

Slowly, she unfolded the rest of the page. There, in a full-color shot, was Mark standing beside a body bag. The guard, Frank Parker, stood on one side of him, a policeman on the other. Words blurred as she tried to read. "Mark Anderson identifies his wife's body at the scene. 'My wife must have just started volunteering at the clinic,' he told reporters later."

Setting the phone back in its cradle, Blaine scanned the rest of the article. It was impossible. She knew the clinic had been bombed, but the night before had somehow been more dream than real, more about her than the world. Mark must have read her note, if he was at the scene. But how could he have identified the wrong person?

She stared at the photo once more. There, beside the body bag lay the rumpled remains of her leather coat. Her ID had been in the pocket. Her rings. Her cell phone. All were inside the coat or with the nurse, Sindi.

Realization dawned with cold certainty. The nurse must have tried them on a moment before the blast. She'd said her office was just beside Blaine's room.

"Terrible, ain't it?" Chipper said as she mopped around Blaine and the desk.

"Yes," Blaine whispered, thinking she had to get home. She had to find Mark. He must have thought her phone call was some kind of cruel joke. Her fingers trembled as she began to dial his private line again.

"Strange thing about that guard in the picture, that Frank Parker," Chipper mumbled as she worked.

"What about the guard?"

"They said this morning on the news that he reported seeing a man mowing the lawn at the clinic just before the bomb went off. Someone checked. The lawn-service guy claimed he left the mower out back the night before and was still in traffic trying to get to work when he heard the blast.''

"So the bomber used the mower and Frank Parker may be able to ID him?"

Chipper shook her head. "Nope." She shrugged. "Parker fell asleep on the way home after working all night. Missed his exit going seventy. They interrupted *The View* for a special report." Chipper plopped the mop in dirty water and began to wring out the strands. "I was enjoying their talk today, all about how women on the Pill are more likely to participate in extreme sports."

"About the guard?" Blaine fought the urge to grab Chipper by the neck and squeeze.

"Reporter said he was dead before they could cut him out of his car. Said he was going so fast he must not have touched the brake."

Angry gray eyes flashed in Blaine's mind. Absently, she lowered the phone a few inches. She'd seen the bomber too. Not once, but twice. He'd glanced up when he turned the mower around. He'd looked through the window at her as though she were already dead. Now she knew why. He knew that in a few moments the blast would strike.

"Hello! Hello!" Mark's angry voice shouted from the dangling phone. "Who is this?"

Blaine placed the phone back in place. She had to have time to think before they were both dead. The gray-eyed man had been willing to kill innocent folks in the clinic, then Parker. She had a feeling he wouldn't hesitate to murder her, and Mark, if he knew she was still alive.

Closing her eyes, she tried to remember what the guy speaking with Winslow had said. Something about making some adjustments under the hood to take care of a problem.

And Winslow had said something about Mark being watched. He'd indicated that if "the wife" wasn't taken care of then someone would get to Mark.

Blaine fought back tears. She had to stay dead. At least until she could think. If she didn't, they might get to Mark.

# *Five*

Mark Anderson plowed his fingers through his hair and leaned back in his leather chair. If the private line rang one more time, he would pull the phone from the wall and throw it out his third-floor window. No one called that line but Blaine, and he had seen his wife folded into a body bag last night. She would never call again.

When he took over the corner office, there were two phone lines. All business came through the main one, all friends knew his cell number, but Blaine liked using the private line as if it were a secret they shared. She didn't call needlessly, so he never hesitated to pick up. Until today.

Rubbing his forehead, Mark tried to concentrate on what he had to do. Plans to be made, people to call, details that must be addressed and soon. But it had been over twenty-four hours since he'd slept, and the crank call a few minutes ago rattled him more than he wanted to admit. The voice sounded nothing like Blaine's, but the caller had used the same words she might have said to him. "It's me." A coincidence that made his skin crawl.

Had it been only a day since he'd picked up the note Blaine had left by the phone and stuffed it in his pocket without reading? He'd worked all morning on a new case, barely aware of the sirens screaming through the streets of downtown Austin. At lunch he remembered one of the partners commenting on an explosion several streets away. They'd said the blast had probably been caused by faulty gas pipes, since the old clinic was in a building in need of repairs.

Mark had half listened to the conversation, as always his mind saturated with work. His only thought about the explosion had been that he hoped the emergency crews got the mess cleaned up so it didn't tie up traffic later.

That evening, he'd pulled his car keys out of his pocket and headed toward the parking lot, focused on working for a few more hours at home, when he noticed Blaine's crumpled message.

She had a habit of leaving notes for him. Shortened conversation, he always thought. Plus, she often said he never remembered anything unless it was written down, so even before they married, leaving notes became her habit.

As Mark unfolded the paper with one hand, he juggled his briefcase and laptop in the other. Expecting to see a reminder to pick up takeout, he was surprised when he read, "Gone to women's clinic to get a few answers. We need to talk tonight." She hadn't bothered to sign the page. The word *tonight* had been underlined twice.

He was at the car before it dawned on him that his wife might have been at the clinic that exploded. That would be a fluke, he thought, and slid into the seat of his BMW. She might have seen the accident or talked to someone who had. He smiled, thinking he might have to postpone work for a few hours tonight so she could tell him all about it over dinner.

He flipped to the news on the radio, then punched their home number on his phone.

No answer, but the local station blared away about the problems downtown. With trouble so close to the capitol, the National Guard was being pulled in as a precaution. The explosion had not been ruled a bombing, but early reports tended to verify that as the most likely explanation. Though hundreds in the area were questioned, only one man, a security guard at the clinic, had reported seeing anything unusual.

Collecting details from the news, he dialed home again. A breaking report verified earlier fears, the clinic had been bombed, at this point there was no possibility the explosion had happened by accident. Several casualties. Investigation continuing but no clues as to who, or why.

Blaine didn't pick up the phone at home. Mark tried her cell phone as he pulled out of the parking garage. Had she told him she'd be working late on one of her projects? He couldn't remember. He hadn't been listening. Had she talked about having plans when they'd had dinner last night... No, he corrected, it had been two nights, maybe three, since they'd eaten together.

No answer from her cell.

He turned his car north, trying to remember what street the clinic was on. Maybe Blaine was still there. She might be tied up giving a statement or helping out somehow. His wife was an eternal helper, always looking for something to do. He had no idea why she'd go to such a place. Probably one of her never-ending charity projects or, if the building were old enough, she might have been researching its history for her job. She was quiet, even shy, but if he encouraged her, Blaine liked to talk about her work.

Mark tried to remember how long it had been since he'd encouraged her.

Arriving near the clinic he pulled to the side when a roadblock prevented him from driving closer. Uniformed troops climbed out of an old army truck down the street, but they weren't organized enough to notice him. He locked the car and walked toward the fire trucks, angry that he was wasting time he needed to be spending on the case going to trial in two weeks. But if Blaine was in this mess, she'd probably need him. She wasn't good with strangers, she never had been. Since their dating days he had always taken the lead. She preferred being in the background.

As he moved closer, the street began to look like a war zone. Officers and firemen moved between trucks and ambulances. Trash and bricks littered the sidewalks. Mark headed toward the smoldering remains of a building, aware of a strange smell in the air. Tragedy, he thought. The odor of chaos.

The sun had slipped behind the buildings to the west, leaving the place in not quite light, not yet darkness. Men in huge plastic suits huddled around an open-sided Red Cross truck. The aroma of coffee flavored the smoky air. He noticed a camera crew from one of the local stations. All but a few of them appeared to be packing up, ready to move on to tomorrow's news.

"You're not supposed to be here, sir." A young cop, not out of his twenties, stepped in front of Mark. "Authorized personnel only."

The officer was respectful but firm.

"My wife may be somewhere in this mess." Mark almost pulled the note from his pocket, showing proof. "She was at the clinic and she isn't home." He wanted to add that if she was here, she'd be frightened. Things scared Blaine, things like talking in public or being the center of a conversation, or giving a statement. Even if she looked all calm, he knew how she squeezed his hand at times.

He glanced around. She would be frightened now. She would need him, even if she didn't admit it.

''They've taken most of the folks who were here to the station for questioning.'' The policeman pointed with an open hand in the direction Mark had come from. ''You could go there. It will be hours before we get everyone's statement.''

Mark shook his head, moving closer to the building, pulling the officer in his wake. ''No. If she were there, she would have called. She knows my cell-phone number.''

''They took seven injured to the hospital,'' the young man said. ''Maybe she's among them?''

Mark didn't bother to answer. She was here. He could feel it. If he kept looking, he'd run into her.

The officer reached for his arm. ''Sir.''

A security guard standing a few feet away glanced up from a clipboard and stepped toward them.

Mark twisted around the hood of a police car to avoid being touched. As he straightened, he saw two long, thin bags waiting to be loaded. He knew what they were—he'd seen them a hundred times on TV—but not like this, not real.

Body bags.

He shoved away from the officer, almost knocking the security guard off his feet as he hurried past them both.

Others became aware of him, an intruder in their midst, and closed in.

Mark kept moving, running now, determined to reach a scrap of coat crumpled on the sidewalk beside one of the bags. The dark leather, the color of the fur trim. It had to be Blaine's. Only, she would never leave her coat on the ground. She was always careful with her things.

"Hey!" a fireman yelled. "You can't…"

"Sir! I'm afraid you'll have to…" The policeman followed Mark.

"That's my wife's coat!" He stared down at the leather, now blackened and burned in places. "She's around here. That's her coat." He had proved his case. "Look, you can see her red wallet hanging out of the pocket."

The security guard knelt down and pulled out the wallet. The cop took a step backward.

"You'll only find her driver's license, a gas card and one credit card in there. She never carries cash." Mark took a deep breath as if he'd been running miles. "Is her cell phone in there? I've been trying to call her."

The guard flipped open the wallet. Blaine's picture stared up at them from her license. "This your wife?" he asked in a whisper.

Mark smiled. "See, I told you she was here." His gaze scanned the crowd.

The guard placed the wallet back beside the coat and stared down at his clipboard. "I think I saw her," he mumbled. "A half hour, maybe more, before the blast. I saw her go into the clinic. She smiled at me, you know, like folks do when they're smiling at the uniform and not me."

Mark looked back at the guard, noticing for the first time that his name tag read Frank Parker. "What time did you see her come out, Mr. Parker?" he snapped in a tone he used often in court when he wanted rapid-fire information.

Frank's tired gaze met his. "I wasn't really watching the door, we had some trouble in the waiting room and

I was in there telling everyone to keep calm.'' He let out a long breath. "I didn't see her come out.''

The words hung in the air like the toll of a bell.

A fireman and the young cop flanked Mark, but made no effort to touch him.

"You need to leave, sir.'' The policeman's voice lowered. "This isn't the place, or the time. You can identify the body later. They're moving them to the morgue now.''

Mark went cold, as if all the blood had seeped out of his body. It took him a while to process what the cop was trying to tell him. Mark had been talking about a coat, a wallet, a driver's license…not a body. He was just here to keep Blaine from being frightened. She wasn't good with strangers. She needed him to run interference for her.

He wished the two men would pull him away, but they just stood there letting reality rain down on him.

"Open the bag,'' Mark ordered.

"But…'' The young policeman paled.

The fireman shook his head. "You don't want to see.''

"Open the damn bag!'' Rage built in Mark. Vaguely he was aware others watched him. People had stopped moving about. Even the men getting coffee turned in his direction. The folks from the news crew circled in the distance.

The guard knelt to one knee between the body bags and laid his clipboard aside.

The fireman glanced over at an older man then nodded to the guard. The guard unzipped the bag a few inches.

The odor of death almost knocked Mark over. For a moment, he was relieved. The blackened body couldn't be Blaine. His beautiful wife couldn't be so twisted and

charred. Then he saw it. A tiny piece of her hair that
had somehow escaped the fire. Blond hair. And in her
hand, curled over her face, were the remains of the rings
he'd given her the day they'd married. Gold interlocking
bands with diamonds, a one-of-a-kind design.

The guard moved her hand slightly and the rings tumbled in the dirt.

Picking them up, Mark turned them over in his hand.
He could still make out the initials they'd had engraved
inside. When he glanced down at the guard, the man had
closed the bag once more.

"Are you all right?" Frank Parker's voice was kind,
but sounded tired, as though he'd spent a lifetime living
this nightmare. "Would you like to sit down for a minute?"

Mark stared at him. "That's my wife?"

"I'm sorry. We have to take her to the morgue now."

"That's my wife." Mark repeated, still feeling the
warmth of the ring as he closed his fingers into a fist.
"I'm going with her. She doesn't like to be alone in
strange places."

"But…"

The older fireman stepped near. "Let him go, Frank.
He's in no shape to drive. He can ride along."

Mark climbed into the ambulance, then jumped out
and grabbed Blaine's coat before rushing back. He rode
in silence with body bags on either side of him.

He sat in the hospital hallway most of the night, waiting. A policewoman took his statement. A nurse brought
him a cup of coffee. A few other people, clustered in
families, wandered down the hall to the swinging doors
where they'd taken the body bags. They'd return a few
minutes later crying, looking pale and hanging on to one

another as though, if they let go, another of their clan might disappear.

Mark didn't go behind the doors. He'd seen all he wanted to see. Neither Blaine nor he had anyone to hold onto. They'd been each other's family for years now. Her mother was dead, her father had disappeared years ago. Mark couldn't remember his own mother, and last he'd heard, his father had gone back into rehab to try to sober up one more time. But parents didn't matter, Blaine and he had one another.

About an hour after dawn, Harry Winslow, one of the older law partners, appeared, looking as if he'd just crawled from bed. He wore a suit, but he hadn't shaved or bothered to comb his hair. He was a bull of a man with a sunburned look about him even in winter.

"Jesus, Mark, why didn't you call me?" He sat down in the plastic chair next to Mark. "We talked about the clinic exploding at lunch and you didn't even mention anything about Blaine being there."

Mark stared at him, paying only passing notice to what he said. "How'd you find me?" he finally asked.

"The front desk here at the hospital called our office and left a message. Bettye Ruth had just called them back to see what was wrong, when I arrived at the office. I left her to man the ship and came straight over. They said you were down here alone and had been all night. The nurse apologized for not trying to reach someone earlier. It seems they're short-staffed along with the coroner's office because of this damn flu everyone has. Too late in the year for a flu to be hitting everyone. Far too late if you ask me."

"I'm not here alone," Mark corrected. "I'm here with Blaine."

A huge tear bubbled from Harry's eye and fought its

way past laugh lines to his chin. "Blaine's gone, Mark. She died in the fire."

Mark resented being talked to like a child. "I know." He wanted to hate Harry at that moment, but the poor man looked miserable, as if he'd had something to do with the tragedy.

"How about I drive you home?" Harry raised his hand to touch Mark's shoulder, then reconsidered. "They'll watch over Blaine for a while. That's what they do here."

Mark glanced at his watch. "All right. Time I get cleaned up, it's almost time for work."

For two men who could spend hours arguing a case in court, they had nothing to say to one another on the ride to Mark's town house. Harry stayed downstairs while Mark went up to the guest room to shower and shave. He thought he heard the phone ring while he was in the shower, but Harry didn't mention it. In less than an hour they were on their way back downtown to the office.

Bettye Ruth Moore, Mark's secretary, looked surprised when he walked in, but years of professionalism kept her silent. She brought him a cup of coffee and waited in front of his desk with her pad in hand for instructions. He'd gone through four secretaries before he found her, but Bettye Ruth could read him like a book and had the same emotional depth as a keyboard.

"I don't want to leave Blaine at the hospital morgue any longer than necessary," Mark said, thumbing through his mail without seeing any of it.

"I understand." Bettye made a note.

Years of checking his emotions kicked in, drawing Mark to action as he rattled off plans. He might be out of the office some this week and he wanted to make sure everything ran smoothly. Bettye Ruth was the best assistant he'd ever seen. She would keep the wheels turning.

Then with both Bettye and Harry in the room, the private line had rung. While the rings sounded, Bettye whispered to Harry that no one used that phone except Mark's wife.

Harry took a step toward the phone, but Mark held up his hand. They stared at it for a long while before Mark finally lifted the receiver. The dam broke and all control rushed out as he heard someone pretending to be Blaine.

A few minutes later, the private line sounded again. Then again. Bettye looked at him for any hint of what to do. Finally, Mark forced his hand to the phone once more.

But no one was on the line. No one at all.

# Six

Blaine walked down the steps of the shelter trying to clear her mind enough to think, but the throbbing in her head, along with an ache in her throat, muddled her brain. Reaching for the handrail, she hesitated before touching it. The pain shooting through her right leg with every other step seemed preferable to sliding her fingers along a metal bar used by hundreds of people who did not bathe regularly. She felt as if she had survived a train wreck only to hear the wheels of the locomotive shifting into reverse.

Mark thought she was dead and the haunting possibility that someone had planned it to be so, gnawed at the corners of her mind. Mark and Harry Winslow were close. More than once she'd heard Mark call the old partner "the father he wished he'd had." Could the man she'd seen outside the office doors talking to Harry be the bomber? Had she seen the wife he'd "taken care of"? Did Mark know anything? She had to call him and find out. She knew he wouldn't be involved. She just knew it. But somewhere, somehow, he was mixed up with men like Harry Winslow. And Harry Winslow knew men who killed and called it a job.

At the bottom of the stairs, Blaine crumbled, wishing she could crawl into her bed a few miles away and sleep until this nightmare was over. But she could not return, not yet, not until she knew what to do. Not until she believed both she and Mark would be safe.

The only answer she could come up with was that, no matter the cost to her, she had to disappear for a while. She drew up her knees and buried her head, curling into a human ball. A day ago she thought her world was falling apart with the possibility of a pregnancy or, even worse, cancer. Now, nothing mattered, she had no more world. The loss was too great for tears.

When she forced herself to look up, a littered vacant lot across the street was her only view. Between the road and the parking lot, one lone tree stood, fighting for space amid the concrete, struggling to live in a world where no one cared. The elm was crooked, bent and twisted beyond any beauty. Blaine guessed some city worker had chopped off the branches on one side, leaving stubs without leaves where the limbs might have ventured near the windshield of a passing car. The effect bowed the elm's shadow, deforming it in the morning sun.

In a strange, unexplained way, the elm gave her an ounce of hope.

"You need to keep moving if you don't want to be bothered."

Blaine noticed Chipper sweeping the steps with the same careless effort she used to mop. The woman's pale, almost colorless eyes watched first the front door of the shelter, then the walk beyond the steps.

"Keep moving?" Blaine asked, thinking it seemed pointless to walk when she had nowhere to go.

Chipper stopped sweeping and stared at Blaine as if she had just discovered an original life-form. "You're new at this, aren't you? I thought it was just an act when we was inside. But now I think you really don't know nothing."

Blaine saw no point in lying. "You're right, I really don't know nothing."

"Keep moving and you'll be safe enough during the day. Just walk down the streets like you got ever' right to be there. Stop anywhere, go in any store, and the next thing you knew you'll find yourself in trouble." She looked down at Blaine with sad eyes, as though watching something die. "There's a place down near Neches and Seventh that'll feed you lunch. They don't ask questions, just let you eat and use their bathroom. They even have phones for local calls, but the waiting lines are usually long. Keep walking 'til then. When you get there, watch who you sit by."

Chipper's advice almost made sense. Blaine stood and automatically dusted off the back of her trousers before realizing it was a wasted effort. She would walk while she thought. She needed a plan. Once she decided on that, the rest would be easy. She'd give Mark time to calm down, then she'd try again. He must be still in shock, running on adrenaline the way he always did.

"Thanks." Blaine turned back to Chipper, but the woman had gone inside, apparently believing that sweeping the first few steps was enough outdoor activity for the day.

Blaine walked east until she crossed Brazos Street, then turned south. She knew the way as well as she knew the creases in her palm. Anyone wanting to be lost in Austin for a few hours only had to find Sixth Street. It was like a vein running through downtown. A vein pumping with the heartbeat of the city.

When she reached the fine old Driskill Hotel with its proud pillars, Blaine turned onto the street made for midnight entertainment. Sixth Street. She hardly noticed how shabby it looked in sunlight. At night, music drifted from almost every door and the air smelled of beer and pizza. Within a few blocks you could stroll along after dinner and hear everything from bluegrass to jazz. At night, college students, businesspeople, panhandlers and druggies populated the sidelines, but in the daylight all she noticed were delivery people and shoppers.

Several people wearing matching orange shirts passed her, whispering the protest they planned to chant near the capitol steps. Blaine made out the words on one large woman's shirt: Our Children Are Eating Their Way to Early Graves. Then in smaller print: Healthier School Lunches Starting Today.

The soft soles of her slip-on shoes made no sound as she weaved between groups of strolling tourists and men with dollies hauling in liquor. Blaine felt like a ghost drifting through the real world.

Blaine walked. She'd have to find some way of getting in touch with Mark. He needed to know she was alive. But if telling him would endanger his life, she might be better off letting him believe a lie for a while longer. Mark might be a warrior in the courtroom, but he didn't even own a gun. She couldn't imagine him defending himself against an attack, much less protecting her. Not that he was weak. Never. Civilization had simply bred the instincts out of him.

If he knew she was alive, the first people he'd tell would be the partners and at least one of them wished her dead.

Maybe if she went to the police, she would be safe. The station house was only a few blocks away. But hadn't Frank Parker thought that same thing when he filed his report about the bombing? He had been a guard. He must have known something about protecting himself, and what good had telling done him?

Blaine took a deep breath. She didn't know any hard facts; she might just be paranoid. And Frank, it was pos-

sible no one had tampered with his car. He could have
simply fallen asleep at the wheel after being up all night.
Maybe he wasn't the "detail" the shadow talked of
"taking care of."

She could almost believe she imagined the conversation between the thin shadow in a cap and Harry Winslow. Almost.

If Mark thought she was dead, the bomber would too,
unless he'd been watching last night when she'd stumbled from the alley. And if he had, he would have told
Winslow. Maybe it was safest to stay dead a few hours
longer.

Mark had answered the phone both times. Only she
knew about the private line in his office.

Blaine crossed another intersection and entered a part
of town called the East End. Here the shops were trendy
and the bars were replaced by sandwich stops and bakeries. For the first time she noticed the people around
her. All kinds, from different walks of life, with one
thing in common. None of them seemed to see her.

She had become one of the invisible people no one
looked at on the street. Even when she tried to make eye
contact, it was impossible. The feeling was foreign to
Blaine. All her life, well, since high school anyway, she
had been one of those girls, then one of the women, that
people noticed. Men often smiled, not so much in greeting, but more in appreciation. Mark had once said she
was the kind of person people enjoyed watching move.
Perfection in motion, he had declared matter-of-factly,
in more of a statement than a compliment.

Their stares had usually made her uncomfortable, but
their choice not to see her bothered her more.

People never walked around Blaine Anderson. Or at
least they never had until now. She had just gone

through the worst twenty-four hours of her life and woke up invisible. How much darker could this nightmare get?

She purposely lined up in a direct path with the people on the street.

They walked around as if she were no more real than a lamppost. Two women even parted and moved past her without the slightest pause in conversation.

Blaine tried to do what her mother always harped on…think of the bright side. Well, at least she wouldn't have to worry about holding in her stomach or keeping her back straight. She'd eaten so many pancakes, she wasn't sure she could hold in her stomach. Here she was without a dime to her name but her belly was full.

I'm cracking up, she decided as she slowed in front of a coffeehouse. The aroma made her absently reach for her purse. One half-decaf latte, she almost said aloud.

Then she remembered. No wallet, no money…no coffee.

She glanced at her reflection in the shop window. The face staring back looked pale, frightened, almost transparent. Lowering her head, she continued walking until the crowds thinned. The wind whipped between buildings and passing cars circled dirt in the air, but Blaine hardly bothered to notice.

By the time she reached the cemetery, a thin layer of grime covered her face as if it had been spray-painted on. Blaine strolled through the limestone gates and into the quiet peace of the State Cemetery, welcoming the shade and the smell of spring. Walking through this place was like strolling through the history of Texas. She'd always loved it here. The silent marble beckoned her as before.

Here, her mind could stop worrying about being watched, for no one seemed to be around except those made of stone. She found the water fountain first, sur-

prised at how thirsty she was, then walked beside the
Confederate graves before circling back to Stephen F.
Austin's monument. This place of trees and grass and
headstones calmed her the way leafing through an old
album, when you already know all the pictures by heart,
might.

Here were the brave of generations. The thought gave
her a little hope.

Blaine relaxed on a bench and took deep breaths, willing her soul to soothe. Even if no one knew it, she was
alive. Things could only get better from here. Every cop
in the county must be working on this case, they'd catch
the bomber and she'd probably be one of many who
could identify him. In hours, maybe a day or two at the
most, she'd be back with Mark and they'd be laughing
at her worry over what Mark's old law partner said to
his mechanic outside the office.

A lecture she remembered finding interesting echoed
in her mind. Something about a pyramid and what things
were important to people. She recalled the teacher saying
humankind is only hours into civilization. Take away the
bottom of the pyramid…the food, water and shelter…and we all go right back to the primitive days.

Blaine smiled. For the first time in her life she stood
at the bottom of that pyramid. Forget love and accep-
tance and reaching one's potential, what she needed to
think about now, what she had to think about, was food
and water. Survival. She had no money, no credit cards.
But she would survive. An old saying about no matter
how bad things are they can always get worse crossed
her mind. Somehow the horror of the bombing had put
her fear of pregnancy in a new light.

A workman rattled past her, pushing a wheelbarrow
loaded down with gardening tools. His work clothes

were worn and had been patched in several places, but he still was dressed far better than she. For a moment she thought he might pass her unnoticed, but to her surprise, he smiled.

"*¿Cómo está?*" he said.

"*Bien,*" she answered, switching to Spanish easily. "Is it all right if I sit here for a while?"

"*Sí.*" The man nodded. "No sleeping." He glanced down at her filthy slipper shoes.

Blaine swung her feet beneath the bench.

"Are you all right?" he asked in a caring tone.

"Yes," she answered, wishing she could tell this man all her problems. He had a kind, weathered face. "I just need a place to rest for a while."

He nodded as if he understood and moved on down the path. An hour later, when he crossed the path once more, he lay half of a sandwich wrapped in a paper towel beside her on the bench. When she thanked him, he only smiled as if to say, "I've been where you are. I understand."

His simple kindness touched her deeply. He wasn't giving her charity, he was sharing.

As the day passed and the shadows in the cemetery deepened, Blaine felt a kind of exhaustion unlike she'd ever known blanket her. Clouds blocked the sun and the wind whirled in her hair, but she barely noticed. Finally, when rain splattered against her cheeks, she pulled from deep inside herself and moved.

At first she ran beneath an old cottonwood, but the wind shoved the rain into her hiding place. She tried to guess the time. Had she sat for an hour or all day? It was dark enough to be dusk, but storm clouds could be playing tricks with the time.

Blaine glanced toward the old rock offices of the cemetery. The lights were out in the main office building, but still on in the rock-walled offices. Blaine hurried to the second building. When she entered, she could hear voices in one of the rooms.

"Have you locked up yet?" a woman asked.

"I was just fixing to," a man answered.

Blaine moved between flag stands holding each of the six flags that had once flown over Texas.

A wiry man hurried from the office. He didn't bother to turn on the lights as he locked the door. "We'd better hurry if we plan to beat this storm." He didn't even look in her direction as he turned and retraced his steps.

Blaine glanced down and saw the shiny puddles of rain her steps had left on the floor. If he looked down, even in the shadowy room, he'd see them. She held her breath trying to think of what she'd say if he saw her.

"Hurry up if you still want that ride," the woman yelled.

The man rushed to the office and gathered his things. Blaine heard the couple bumping their way down the hall to the back door. Then the door opened and a moment later slammed closed.

She was alone.

Cautiously, she moved past the first few desks to the phone. The clock on the wall marked 5:15 p.m. Mark would still be in his office. She'd call. The need to talk to him overrode her fear.

She dialed the private line.

It rang once, twice, three times.

Blaine fought the urge to break the call. It was all she had. Mark was the one person she cared about…the one person who cared about her.

Someone lifted the receiver. She could hear breathing.

"Hello," a man said. "Who is this?"

It wasn't Mark. Blaine panicked. She knew the voice. She'd heard it outside the office just this morning.

"Is someone there?"

Winslow! Blaine lowered the phone. Winslow had answered Mark's phone. To do so he'd had to unlock Mark's door and cross the office.

She huddled down onto a leather couch, shaking with cold and fear. She wanted to go home but she couldn't.

The friends she knew in Austin were more acquaintances who would be shocked if she involved them in anything more than a luncheon invitation. She couldn't call them.

Tears fell silently though no one could have heard her sobs over the storm that raged outside. Blaine cried as she'd never cried in her life. She'd never been totally alone. Not when her mother died, not when she'd lived in a one-room apartment. There had never been such complete isolation. Until now.

Exhausted, she curled into herself and slept as the storm raged in the sky above Austin.

When she awoke, the world slept silently once more to the dull sounds of motors, air conditioners, cars and faraway trains. The half moon blinked between the blinds. Blaine slowly stood, stretching her cramped muscles like a colt learning to stand.

She glanced at the clock: 5:00 a.m. Mark would be home. His alarm would be close to sounding. Blaine moved to the phone and felt the numbers to dial.

She let it ring, knowing it would take him a while to answer.

One, two, five, ten rings. No answer. It took her a few more rings to realize not even the answering machine was picking up.

She lowered the phone and slipped outside.

The air smelled newborn and traffic rumbled like a heartbeat a few blocks away on the interstate.

Leaning against the wall of the old limestone building she stared out at the State's sleeping ancestors. Her head felt clearer than it had since the bombing, and the throbbing in her throat had dwindled to a dull ache. Blaine crossed her arms. She had survived the bombing and the storm, she would make it through this also. She would survive. Somehow she would get past this and return to her life.

Sadness swept through her as she realized she wasn't sure she wanted to return to where she had been a moment before the blast. Despite still loving Mark, she knew that she'd been standing at a crossroads even before the bomb exploded. The things she'd lost sleep over before she went to the clinic seemed trivial compared to staying alive on the streets. If she had a child, it wouldn't be the end of her world. It might be the end of her marriage, but it wouldn't kill her.

And if worst came to worst, she'd fight cancer maybe with more success than her mother and grandmother had.

A strength kindled in Blaine. The kind of strength that comes only when you've reached the bottom and can look up and say, "Bring it on. If I handled this, I can handle anything." Lifting her chin, testing her newborn power, Blaine took the morning's dare. She'd make it, no matter what.

A shadow moved from one headstone to another, pulling Blaine out of her thoughts.

She waited, not even breathing.

The shadow crossed again from grave to grave.

Blaine was no longer alone.

# *Seven*

Mark Anderson stared into the night, watching the lights of Austin flicker through the trees outside his condo window. He waited for sunrise, as if he thought the start of the day would change one thing in his life.

Yesterday he felt as though he'd walked underwater all day. He heard people mumbling around him, but what they said made little sense. When he'd finally made it back to the apartment complex, things were not much better. The phone rang repeatedly with co-workers and friends who mumbled comments like, "We'll all miss Blaine" and "We wish we'd known her better." Several offered to help, but what could they do? What could anyone do? She was gone.

Harry Winslow had been more help than anyone, ordering Mark to go home and turn the phone off, which Mark finally did after an hour of constant calls.

The old partner had even suggested that Mark think about not trying to run for office during this hard time in his life. He'd said he was only a few years away from retiring and if Mark would wait to run, he'd dedicate himself full-time to the campaign.

The old man's generosity stunned Mark. It was almost as if he felt he personally had to make up for Mark's loss of Blaine.

Mark didn't want to think about tomorrow much less

six months from now. In truth, he didn't want to think at all, but he told Winslow he would give the idea some thought.

"What will *I* do?" Mark whispered, his voice echoing in the empty room. Blaine was a constant in his life, like sunrise and cool fall days. He realized he'd spent little time thinking about her over the years. Until today, she had always just been there. She liked to tell him little details from the news she knew he didn't have time to listen to or all about a research project she'd been hired to do. Half the time he didn't really listen to the details she seemed to think were so important. More often than not her assignment was nothing but someone in another state needing family history pulled up.

Mark realized he never truly listened to her when she talked about her work. Her voice provided background music to his thoughts.

When the sun rose he would start his day, only there would be no music in his thoughts. The details of *his* life had slipped away with Blaine. He didn't know the location of the dry cleaners, or which grocer it was who knew just how thick to cut his steaks for grilling. She'd always taken care of all the little things he never thought he had time to worry about.

He fought down the lump he couldn't get out of his throat. The little things were the mortar, it appeared, holding his life together. He had no idea how to go on without her. All the times he'd thought she was simply talking to him because she hadn't talked to anyone else all day, the notes she left him by the phone, the messages on his machine, they were all far more important than he'd thought. They were the details that held his life in balance. They were what told him over and over that she was there in the background…that he wasn't alone.

Mark wanted to dress and go in to the office. Maybe he could get lost in work and forget the time. Maybe, for a while, he could forget the charred form he'd seen, the blackened fist holding her wedding rings. Forget the way mud splashed on the body bags as firemen stepped around them rolling up hoses. Mud shouldn't be on them, he'd wanted to scream. Blaine would hate'that.

He knew he couldn't go to work. Everyone, from the other partners to the cleaning lady, had hugged him and told him to take a few days off. Mark grinned, remembering the way Teresa almost tackled him when she saw him by the elevators. She'd smelled of cleaning supplies and dust, but that hadn't stopped her from pulling him against her ample chest. He might be a big-shot lawyer now, but she'd been there when he started and she felt that gave her rights to mother him from time to time.

"Go home and be with your family," she'd said. "Let the shock wear off. It will take time for you to heal."

Mark hadn't bothered to tell her he had no family. That was one thing Blaine and he had in common. He'd lost his mother to a car wreck when he'd been in the second grade. His father sat him down and told Mark his mother had died instantly, as if that somehow softened the blow. Then his old man had crawled into a bottle and never came out.

Blaine's dad was still alive as far as she knew, but he never bothered to keep in touch. Mark wasn't even sure how to locate him. Her parents divorced before she started school. Neither, it appeared, had wanted her in the settlement. Blaine said once that her father made sure he didn't leave a forwarding address so he couldn't be tracked for child support payments or her mother's doctor bills.

Her mother had tried being a single parent for a while

but she was fighting her own battle with depression. When the doctor found cancer, she found another reason to wish herself dead. Blaine had taken care of her for a time. She had left Blaine with a friend one morning, but Blaine never said more. Out of curiosity, Mark had looked up the record. A police report said it looked as if she'd turned her car into traffic, but her death was ruled an accident. Blaine never talked about where she'd gone after that, but he knew she never made bonds strong enough to carry into adulthood.

She had said that her mother hadn't bothered to say goodbye. Mark hadn't asked more, not wanting to bring up bad memories.

Blaine told him once that as soon as she realized she was on her own, she learned to work the system. Scholarships, grants, work study programs. By the time she was in her third year of college, no one noticed that, for her, there were no checks from home.

Mark realized he'd always been proud of her for what she'd done. He couldn't help but wonder if he'd ever bothered to tell her so. He'd had an old insurance policy of his mother's to help him through his first four years of college, but as far as he knew Blaine had no one.

Maybe being on her own so early was why she always did the volunteer work she did. Never with the symphony or the art guilds, but always with the underprivileged programs. Maybe she was looking for that kid who needed to find the ladder to a better life.

Blaine never talked about her past. A few times he thought about how it was as if her life started the day they met, and nothing else mattered enough to comment on. He had been about to start law school the summer they met in the library. She'd just graduated with a library science degree and was taking a few education courses. He'd fallen asleep on their first date. Any other girl would have been furious, but Blaine had covered him with a blanket and left him until dawn on her couch. When he awoke she had breakfast ready, and somehow they both knew that they'd become a couple.

By fall they were married and she worked so he could concentrate on law school. It was that simple with Blaine.

It always had been. Until now.

Mark had never thought about it before, but there were years of Blaine's life about which he knew nothing. He'd never heard her mention the people she lived with from the time her mother died until she moved into the college dorm at seventeen. She said once that she had to work her first few years until her grade point was high enough to apply for more scholarships, but she had never said what she'd done.

He should have asked, he realized. He should have cared.

The mangy old calico Blaine called Tres banged its way through the cat door. For years Mark had tolerated the animal, and she'd done the same to him, because of Blaine. Now the cat looked at him and meowed in what Mark would swear was cat-cussing. The cat seemed angry that, if one of them had to leave, it hadn't been Mark.

"I don't know where your food is," he grumbled. "We had this conversation last night."

Tres swore back at him.

Mark opened several cabinets, finally giving up his search and pouring Cheerios in the cat bowl. "Take it or leave it."

Tres glared at him as if promising to get even and then ran back out the cat door. He watched her for a while, wondering if the cat had another home. Blaine called herself momma to the cat, but he'd never once thought of the animal as related to him.

First light changed the sky. Mark turned away from the window. If he couldn't go to the office, what would he do with his time? Sit around and think of questions he should have asked his wife?

He flipped the phone back on, thinking his secretary would call him as soon as she got to work. He'd need to at least keep her working on his upcoming case if he planned to be ready in two weeks.

With sudden urgency, he pulled on his sweats, darted through the hallway to the stairs and headed north, running down the still-sleeping street of Cat Mountain. The neighborhood had winding paths and shadows so thick they looked like oil on the roads. He loved running. When he ran, he seldom noticed much around him. Sometimes he tried to match his steps in rhythm to his heartbeat. Sometimes he'd hum old songs. More often than not, he counted off the minutes, eventually making himself a clock so accurate that he rarely glanced at his watch.

He liked the feel of his heart pounding, the way his shoes thumped out each step, the rush of breath again and again as if he were a machine, the way his mind went blank with the beat of it all. Even the strain of his muscles tiring was welcomed, for when he ran, the world balanced for Mark.

Sweating, he hit the front door still running. Seconds ticked away in his brain. In less than twenty minutes he'd showered, shaved and dressed. He walked into the kitchen, flipped on the TV at the bar and reached for his orange juice. Breakfast was usually juice and a health bar on the drive to work. Anything else took too much time out of his day. Cereal had been his midnight snack of choice since law school, but he never bothered with it in the morning.

One glassful of juice left, he thought, I'll have to leave Blaine a note.

The clock in his mind stopped. The carton of juice hit the tile floor, sloshing an orange spray across the tile. Mark started shaking as if a blast of arctic air had shot through the room. Like a crippled-up old bull rider, he staggered to the couch and crumbled, too numb to cry.

In the dullness of routine, he'd forgotten for a moment that Blaine was gone. For a moment, the pain within him had stopped, only to slam back afresh, hard as the first time. Only this time his heart was already bruised when it took the blow.

He lay perfectly still, trying to remember to breathe.

When the phone rang three hours later, he hadn't moved. For the first few rings he wasn't sure what the noise was. Then slowly he reached across the arm of the couch and grabbed the receiver.

"Mr. Anderson?" a friendly voice shouted into his ear.

"Yes." Mark sat up and tried to pull himself together.

"I'm Herb Phillips at the morgue. We're sorry we haven't called earlier, but most of us have been down with the flu."

Mark couldn't think of anything to say. He didn't care about Herb Phillips's problem.

The man continued, more serious now. "We've got an order to release your wife's body to the crematorium, but we'd like to check dental records first. Just routine."

"But I identified her." Mark felt he didn't need this hassle.

"We know, but there is a missing person from the

bombing and the police have asked that we double-check. If you'll give us your wife's dentist's name, we can call and make the arrangements for the records.''

Mark thought for a moment. ''Brooks, I think.''

''Thank you. Sorry to have bothered you.''

Again Mark didn't say a word.

Herb continued, ''The crematorium will need your signature on a form, if you'd like to take care of that while you're waiting. Then once we release the body all will move along.''

Mark didn't see that it mattered, but he agreed and jotted down the address. ''I'll go right out.'' He didn't add that he had nothing else to do.

''Better hurry. They close for lunch between twelve and one, no matter what,'' Herb returned. ''I've been a few minutes late and had to sit out with a body in the back of the wagon and wait for them to open back up.'' He cleared his throat, realizing he may have sounded insensitive.

Mark hung up the phone.

When he opened the door a few minutes later, he almost collided with his neighbor, Lilly Crockett. The old woman was the only resident over fifty in the complex of expensive apartments and condos and Mark had found himself frustrated many times waiting for her to get on the elevator or pull out of a parking place. She was always in the way. Today was no exception.

''Oh,'' she said, holding her hand over her chest while she took a deep breath without moving a step. ''You startled me. I was just about to knock and offer you a casserole.''

''Sorry.'' Mark stared at the square of Pyrex and foil in her hand, assuming it was food. He hadn't had a casserole in years. ''I was just leaving.'' He felt as if he owed her some explanation. "The crematorium needs a signature."

Some of the residents had mumbled that Lilly Crockett needed to move to a home with people her own age, but Mark, despite the inconvenience, felt she had her rights to live wherever she wished, even if she was a human roadblock everyone in the building avoided. Her apartment was one of the smallest, her patio the most crowded, and from what he'd heard, all the suggestions ever stuffed into the box at the complex offices had been signed by her.

Lilly still didn't move away from the door. Mark waited.

She stared down at the food in her wrinkled hands. "I could heat it up and have it ready for you when you get back, or I could put it in the icebox and go with you if you need someone along for the ride."

Mark almost laughed. How old could this woman be if she called the refrigerator an icebox? The last thing he wanted was Miss Lilly, as Blaine always called her, going with him. The woman dressed as if she'd been working as a carnival gypsy. He guessed she'd been crazy for so many years she wore the condition like a second skin. But she was trying to be kind, which was more than he could say for any of his "first-name only" neighbors.

"Thank you, but I'm not sure when I'll be back. I have to fill out some forms. If I don't catch them before lunch, I'll have to wait an hour."

She smiled and finally stepped out of his path. "That's okay. You just knock on my door when you get home. I'll have a meal ready for you."

Mark didn't have time to argue. He just nodded and hurried toward the elevator.

He sprinted to his car, but luck wasn't with him. He dropped his keys and spent a few minutes fishing them out from between the seat and the console. Then it seemed as if he missed every light. A van filled with kids sat through a turning light before Mark gave the short honk all Austinites learn. Not laying on the horn, no double beeps, just a polite blast to remind someone in traffic to follow the rules and hurry.

Mark passed the entrance to the crematorium and had to double back. When he swung into the first parking spot, he saw a sign on the door: Be Back at One. Enjoy Your Lunch.

He had nowhere else to be and nothing to do for the rest of the day. Frustration boiled in him. Why couldn't they have waited? Or staggered their lunch schedules? Surely more than one person worked at the place. But then, this wasn't a business overly concerned with customer satisfaction.

He pulled back onto the highway and headed for a restaurant where he and other lawyers often went for drinks after work. It was usually dead before the dinner rush, so they would talk over drinks without having to shout. Often they'd talk, more business than social, for a few hours then call their spouses to join them for dinner.

The sign was the same, the entrance looked exactly as always, but when Mark walked inside, he would have sworn he was in the wrong place if it hadn't been for the waiters all dressed in white shirts, black pants and red bow ties, as always. The bar was empty except for an employee reading the paper at one end. The tables were occupied, not with young businesspeople, but with older women in red hats and scatterings of mothers with kids on either side of them.

The welcome board at the desk that usually read, Please Wait To Be Seated, now spelled out in chalk, All-You-Can-Eat Seafood Lunch.

Glancing around, Mark noticed several people who looked as if they planned to get their money's worth. One long table of women all had on bright colors with flowers in their hats. They seemed to be having some kind of party.

He couldn't resist glancing back at the name to make sure he was in the right place.

"May I help you?" a young man asked as he passed with a tray of tea glasses.

"I'd like a bourbon and water," Mark said. "Make it a double. I'll be at the bar."

The man paused. "The bar doesn't open until two, but you can order beer with your meal."

Shaking his head, Mark walked out of the noisy place where laughter and crying babies seemed piped in. He sat down on one of the dusty patio tables and concentrated on breathing the warm, humid air. It was just a different time of day, he told himself. If he came back at five this would be his restaurant once more. The world hadn't changed just because his wife died. He could come back with his friends and drink until they called the wives to join them. Only, his wife would no longer come to meet him for dinner.

Blaine always laughed as if he was asking her for a date when he called. Then she'd say something like, "Order us a couple of Cokes, double cherries in both, and I'll be right there."

Mark smiled. Her request was her kind way of telling him he'd probably had enough drinking for the night. They had an unwritten rule—she never nagged him about drinking and he always switched to Coke when she asked. They had a dozen little tags like that. Conversations only the two of them understood.

Mark rested his elbows on the table and pushed his palms against his eyes. How come in the ten years they'd been together she'd never once told him what to do? She was so good at planning out the details of a dinner party or a vacation. But there was no plan now. He wasn't sure she would want to be cremated. It just seemed like the thing to do since the body was far too burned already to have any kind of funeral. If he had a funeral, he'd have to have a grave and he wasn't sure he could bear to see her name on a stone.

Why hadn't she told him what to do? Why hadn't she planned?

"Can I get you something, sir?" the same young man from the restaurant asked from the door.

"A couple of Cokes," Mark answered. "With extra cherries in them."

He had an hour to wait and then he would have to make some decisions without any hints from Blaine. For a moment, he was angry with her. She'd let him down. She'd died without telling him what he should do.

For the first time in ten years he wanted to scream at her for not being there when he needed her.

Dear God now he needed her!

# *Eight*

Blaine pressed against the rock wall of the office building and watched. The shadow darted again as if playing a solitary game of tag.

Time passed. She heard the shadow making calls almost like those of a wild bird.

The wind circled over the damp lawn. Blaine shivered, wishing for the jacket she'd left at the clinic two mornings ago. She wished she were home and warm. She hated the thought of worrying Mark. No matter her reasons, he would probably be angry that she'd put him through such a hard time. They might even fight, something neither of them liked doing.

A highway patrol car stopped at the gate. The shadow in the cemetery vanished behind marble.

A tall figure of a man climbed from the car and put on his Stetson. His outline could almost have been one of an old-time cowboy as he leaned against the cemetery fence and lit a cigarette. A tiredness was reflected in his stance, she thought, yet something about him was still alert. She guessed by first light he'd be ending his shift. She had read somewhere that the highway patrol guarded what they called the Capitol Complex, and the State Cemetery was part of that complex.

The static of his radio broke the silence. The officer moved toward his car.

She thought of calling out to him. She wanted to go home. She wanted to feel Mark's arms around her and his steady voice telling her everything was all right. Even if he often slept in another room, she had always felt him near. Until now. Now he seemed a million miles away, in another world. If she yelled, the patrolman might take her home, back to Mark. Or he might take her to the police station and book her for being in the cemetery after hours. Or he might not believe her story and just tell her to move along. After all, her clothes were ragged, her hair several different lengths thanks to the fire, and her face was scratched to the point that, even if she had makeup, it would do no good. Anyone would have trouble believing she lived in one of the choice complexes in the city.

She knew she couldn't call out for help. The danger would be too great. No one had protected Frank Parker when he said he'd seen the bomber. What if no one protected her? She was safer here in the darkness. In a day, maybe two, the police would find the bomber and this would all be over. She could go home to Mark and pretend these few days never happened.

The patrolmen drove away. Within minutes the shadow moved again. Blaine could see the figure as the sky lightened. He moved from tombstone to tree and back in a strange dance of hide-and-seek.

Suddenly she realized that he was only a child. A boy of ten, or maybe twelve.

She didn't move. Though he seemed harmless, she wasn't sure she wanted him to know of her. As the day brightened, she picked out details. His clothes were ragged, layered. She knew, without asking, that he wasn't a child who simply stayed out all night. He was a child of the street. There was nowhere else for him to go.

Suddenly he ran toward the far side of the cemetery.

Blaine didn't really know why, but she followed. When he reached the fence, he was over it and on the street within seconds. Blaine struggled to keep up, thankful he didn't turn to look back.

He ran beneath the interstate and down first one street, then another, to where the path turned off into a wooded area running along the creek.

Blaine slowed, staring down at a section of Waller Creek that she'd never noticed before. The city had made the sides of the creeks near downtown beautiful, even building a walking track that wound along the creek's bank. But only the brave ventured there, and then only in full daylight.

She hesitated, worried about the child, then realized that he was much more in his element than she. Like a shadow she followed, through groves of trees and around picnic tables, along white rock paths that caught the first glow of daylight, down to the stream of water bloated from the rain.

He skipped across a rock and bounded from one side of the creek to the other.

Blaine watched as, once across, he scrambled up a muddy bank to huge pillars bracing up a hotel where the land had given way to the creek. The rocky ground beneath the supports provided a hiding place, with the underbelly of the hotel as a roof. She watched him disappear into the blackness.

Wishing she were brave enough to follow, Blaine squatted low in the brush between two trees. The hiding place beneath the building was perfect, but like sticking a hand down a dark hole to see if there was a snake inside, she couldn't make herself move. The fear of what waited in the total blackness was far greater than her fear of being out in the open. For the child, the shelter might offer safety, but Blaine wasn't so sure it would do the same for her.

In a few minutes it would be full light and she could walk the streets once more. Rubbing her hand across her middle, Blaine realized she was starving. It had been a long time since she'd downed her plate of pancakes and half a sandwich.

It was too early for the shelter to be serving breakfast, or "feeding breakfast," as the homeless called it, but she could move in that direction. She'd be safe in the crowd waiting outside for the shelter to open. Maybe she'd find the two old bag ladies she met yesterday and stand with them.

Traffic was already congested in the streets of downtown, probably cars driven by people like Mark who thought he had to start his day an hour ahead of anyone else. This morning the crowd running past her with briefcases and raincoats over their arms made her sad. They were in their own world. If they pushed a little too hard and she stepped off into the gutter to keep her balance, they wouldn't notice.

Some passersby carried small bags of doughnuts or rolls bought in one of the shops between the parking garages to their offices. Some juggled coffee. Blaine walked against the flow of traffic.

She weaved into the oncoming stream of people. They shifted and walked around her.

"They don't see you." An old man laughed from the doorway of a boarded-up building that looked as if it had been a coffee shop in better times.

Blaine jumped into the doorway as if she were a chess piece taken out of the game, hesitant to talk with a man who looked more like a character from *The Hobbit* than someone real, but glad someone finally spoke to her.

"Hi." She liked his friendly, wrinkled face. Weathered with life more than age, it was impossible for her to guess his age. His white beard seemed colored with whiskey at the corners of his mouth and his teeth were badly stained, but his smile was genuine.

She smiled back. "I'm surprised you can see me, no one else seems to. I'm a ghost, you know."

"I see you, child," he answered. "Ghost or real, makes no matter to me."

"How are you?" Blaine felt great saying the everyday greeting to him, realizing how important such nonsense words were when there are no words between people.

The whiskery man laughed. "'I seem destined to be wed to poverty, but I fear it is not a happy marriage.'"

Blaine laughed, surprised to hear him quote Oscar Wilde.

"You seem lost in your chosen profession of the street," he added. "May I give you a little advice?"

"Of course." Blaine would have never believed she'd have talked to a dusty old man probably wearing everything he owned. The layers were thick over him and she wondered if the dirtiest clothing was on top, or next to his skin.

"Walk between the crowds. People in cars or hurrying along on the sidewalk tend to bunch up in groups. Herd mentality, I fear. If you pace yourself, you can walk in the space between and be far safer. When you're one of the 'not people,' the others don't see you and they won't notice even if they harm you by pushing you out of the way."

"Thanks." Blaine felt the sadness of knowing what he said was true.

"I'd ask for a consulting fee, but you don't look like you could pay." He shrugged. "There was a time my advice was valuable."

"It still is." She smiled. "But I haven't a dime. If I did have money, I'd be drinking a cup of coffee right now."

To her total shock he handed her two quarters. "The place next to the drugstore offers a large coffee for fifty cents and he doesn't mind if you don't pay the tax."

Blaine started not to take the money, but he insisted. "A loan until you find better times."

"Thanks." She smiled. "What do I call you?"

"Most folks call me Shakespeare." The lie slipped too easy off his tongue to be new. "And you?"

Blaine raised her eyebrow, imitating him. "Call me Mary, everyone does."

# Nine

Blaine talked with Shakespeare as they strolled toward the shelter. The little man had a wealth of quotes and a hatred for any type of establishment. He complained about everything from Head Start to Social Security. He would quote Hemingway while he scratched head lice. She guessed he was happy to have found a listener.

The early sun melted the chill from her bones and the stiffness in her muscles as they walked. They were within sight of the shelter when the old man stopped and bowed low before her. "Good morrow, fair lady. Parting is such sweet sorrow."

"You're not going to breakfast?" It crossed her mind that he might be embarrassed to eat with her. After all, she looked soiled and wrinkled, with hair burned and matted.

Then she glanced at him and reconsidered. The cuffs of his pants and his jacket were ragged and soiled. His hair hadn't been combed in days and dark stains marred the already dirty front of his shirt.

"I prefer to drink my breakfast," he answered, a little embarrassed by his own honesty, "but I thank you for the invitation."

"I'll see you again?"

"Perhaps. I make a habit of never being predictable, my dear. The government will find out if I do and tax me for it." He raised his bushy eyebrow as mirth wiggled across his dirty face. "The question is, will you speak to me when you do see me?"

"Of course," she said before realizing she may have passed him many times without speaking. Austin was such a sea of people, homeless, students, government workers, tourists. It would be easy to miss one, or hundreds of faces. "You're my friend now, I hope."

"Friends," he echoed as others walked around them heading into the shelter for breakfast. "One last lesson. Free advice to a friend."

Blaine leaned closer, ignoring the smell of him.

"'Be careful who you sit with and call friend, lest you be marked by their dye. Stay silent, your speech gives too much of you away.'"

"Thanks." Blaine wasn't sure what he meant about the dye, but he was right about her speech. Mark had often told her he could guess a person's education by the choice of words he used to describe himself. If she planned to stay lost among the homeless, she would be wise to keep her mouth shut. Also, he was the second person to warn her about the company she kept. First Chipper, at the shelter, now Shakespeare.

Blaine moved down the street into the informal line outside the steps of the shelter. Someone near the front yelled that today they'd be feeding oatmeal. Several groaned, but nobody moved out of place.

The two old bag ladies she'd met yesterday shouted at her to join them. They patted her as if she were an old friend.

No one seemed to care when she cut a few places in line. The one who had given her shoes called her Mary again and asked why she'd stayed at the playground so long when it was getting dark. While the ragged little woman mumbled, she shoved her belongings further into bags and retied each knot as though preparing for a storm.

Blaine could think more clearly today and asked both their names.

The one busy tying her bag said, "I lost my name in a tornado in Lubbock thirty years ago. It's circling somewhere in the wind but is bound to land one of these days."

Her friend huffed and answered, "Her name's Anna, just like mine. Folks call me Chocolate Anna and her Vanilla Anna so they won't get us mixed up. People think because we hang around together that we're friends, but it ain't true. I don't even talk to her 'less I have too. She's crazy as they come, bore a person to tears, but at least she ain't mean to no one. That counts for something in this world. We just travel together. It's safer that way, you know. The streets are no place to be when you're all alone."

Chocolate Anna leaned closer, the smell of cough syrup thick in her breath. "It ain't her fault she's not right, miss. I figured out a long time ago she lost more than her name in that tornado over Lubbock. She lost her whole family in one night. Far as I know, she ain't slept in a building since. She'll stay in one just long enough to eat, then it's back to open sky."

"And you?" Blaine asked the stout black Anna.

"I never liked the smell of too many bodies in one place. If I have my choice, I'll be outside. Even the cold is better than a bad smell."

Vanilla Anna moved with the line, losing all interest in the conversation. A group of boys in their late teens passed by, hassling people as they made their way to the end of the line.

"Out of the way, old bag." One pushed Vanilla Anna into a man trying to light a cigarette. He swore and shoved her back where he thought she belonged.

Another thug mumbled, "Crazy old witch. World would be a better place without ya." He shoved Anna back toward the smoker just for fun, as though she were no more important than a ball being tossed around.

Blaine started to correct the bully, but a wrinkled black hand touched her arm. "Don't say nothing. You don't want to draw attention. They're mean all the way to their livers. No amount of talking or aging on their parts will change that. Not a place in town will even let them stay the night, fearing they'll find a body the next morning with his throat slit and ever'thing stolen including socks. They'd kill you for a dollar and not think nothing of it."

"But why don't the police…"

"Who's going to tell the cops? Everyone is afraid of that gang except maybe hairy old Miller. He ain't afraid of nothing. Plus, the police don't settle things between the likes of us. They expect us to do that among ourselves."

Blaine found the class system fascinating. "Is this Miller meaner than they are?" It was like stepping into a case study. Suddenly she wasn't learning from books and records, but from life.

The boys swore as they moved away.

She found it hard to believe they feared anyone. She wasn't sure she wanted to meet someone who had no fear of them.

Chocolate Anna snorted. "Miller ain't none too friendly, but he ain't mean the way those kind are. He just wants to be left alone. I've heard it said that he don't care if he lives or dies. When folks get like that they're dangerous to cross.''

The line moved again. Blaine watched the people around her as if she had been set down worlds away in an unknown world. Kids, runaways or throwaways. Families with nothing but one another.

She studied the line carefully. Mostly men, mostly much older then her. Blaine saw no women alone. This was not a world for a woman by herself.

''That's him,'' Chocolate Anna whispered. ''That's Miller. Hairy mess of a man, ain't he.''

Blaine saw a man in his late fifties standing by the door, hat pulled low, his hands in his pockets. Anna was right about the hair. A stubbly beard darkened his chin and a bush of salt-and-pepper curls poked from his hat. He was stout enough to give the impression that it would take a train to knock him down. He looked solid as a granite statue.

When he glanced toward the back of the line, she noticed a two-inch scar running just under his left eye. The skin was discolored along the scar and reminded her of a single brush of war paint riding high on his cheek. His eyes were alert, not bloodshot from cheap whiskey. He stood just over six feet, with the build of a man who'd worked hard all his life. His clothes were wrinkled and worn, but cleaner than most.

Somehow he didn't look like the others. He didn't belong. Yet Miller stood in line, so he must be homeless.

''He don't like to sit by nobody and we all give him his space. Some folks say he went crazy when his wife died years ago, tried to drink himself to death. Others say he killed a man over in Oklahoma and the police will pick him up as soon as they find all the body parts.''

Blaine studied the man, looking for any signs of a

drunk or a murderer. She'd seen a murderer, she thought, two days ago. He had ridden his mower up to the clinic wall and placed a bomb there, then stared straight at her before turning and riding away.

Blaine shivered.

She knew what a murderer looked like. He looked like everyone else.

The line moved and Miller disappeared inside. When she could see him once more in the food line, he'd removed his hat. His hair was graying, but still thick, with deep sideburns bushing out onto his cheeks. Despite his size, he didn't look at all frightening to her, only sad. Unkempt.

Blaine lost the Annas in the crowd for a few minutes. When she caught up, the two bag ladies stood several people ahead of her in line. She felt suddenly very vulnerable. The man in front of her looked at her as if he thought she might be on the menu.

He mumbled something and winked.

She was glad she hadn't heard. She wiggled her way back a few people in the line.

Another man, wearing army fatigues, shoved too close behind her.

When she looked back at him, he didn't appear to even see her, but as the line moved again, the lower part of his body brushed once more against her hip.

Blaine suddenly realized why there were no women here alone. It wasn't safe.

By the time she filled her tray, the table where the two Annas sat was crowded with people who talked like old friends.

Looking around, she saw several seats open near the boys and a few spots vacant near the head table where the preacher and his small flock sat. The back table with Miller held the only other open spots.

Blaine squared her shoulders and marched to the last table. "Mind if I sit here?" she asked as she put her tray down.

He didn't answer, but waved one huge hand as if shooing away a fly.

"I didn't think you would," she said as though he'd agreed. The feel of the man in line pressing against her hip made her shiver enough to lose any fear of Miller. A man who wanted to be alone was someone she understood, even if it didn't seem practical to grant his wish.

While eating, she talked to Miller as if he were contributing to the conversation. Finally, halfway through her oatmeal, he looked at her and said, "You bother me. Go away."

Anger welled within Blaine. She only had an inch of planet left to stand on, she could no longer budge. The only choice left to her was to fight. "Well, you bother me too, so don't think it's all one-sided." When he didn't swing at her, she added, "I can't go away. I've nowhere else to sit. I'm afraid of those hell-raising boys, and that guy in fatigues wants to rub against me, and I'm not sure I could keep down my oatmeal if I sat any closer to that preacher. So you are stuck with me and I'm stuck with putting up with you."

Miller glanced at her. "If you had any sense, you'd be afraid of me."

Blaine swallowed a lump of oatmeal. "Oh, I am. You frighten me half to death, but half to death is better than what might happen if I went near that gang of delinquents. I'm living in a state of half to death so it's nothing new to me at this point in my life." Her bravery surprised her. "If I get pushed much more maybe you'll be wise to be afraid of me for a change."

"Move close to the preacher," Miller grumbled. "You'll be safe enough there. He'd never hurt you."

Blaine knew Miller might be her only chance to be left alone. The Annas couldn't protect her, Shakespeare wouldn't. He might like her, but he cared far too much for his whiskey to stand by her. And the preacher's only world lay within these walls. He would be no help as a friend outside the door.

That just left Miller. She had to win him over. If folks thought they were friends she might be left alone. "The preacher gives me the willies. I can almost see them jumping off him and landing on me every time he gets within ten feet of me. Holy willies are the worst kind, nothing kills them."

Blaine grinned. It felt good to stretch the truth, something Mark never liked her to do. Just the facts, Blaine, he used to say. She never had the nerve to tell her husband that there was a time, when she was first alone after her mother died, that she lied about almost everything in her life.

She glared at Miller. "If I get them holy willies, I'm coming back here and giving them to you."

She thought she saw the hint of a smile crease the old man's lips.

Miller took a bite of his orange and wrinkled his forehead in thought. Finally, he said in a low, none-too-friendly voice. "All right, you can sit by me but be quiet. I don't like to talk to folks and you are downright chatty."

"I can do that. I'll sit right here, quiet as a mouse." Her voice still sounded scratchy to her ears. "You won't even know I'm around. I'll just eat and be on my way and you'll—''

''Shut up.''

He glared at her, but there was no anger burning in his dark eyes.

Blaine met his stare even though her fingers trembled so badly her spoon clamored into the bowl. ''Mary,'' she managed to say. ''Shut up, Mary. You might as well know my name if you're going to talk to me, Mr. Miller.''

''I'm not going to talk to you.''

The minister interrupted with staccato clapping to tell everyone that he had all the help he needed for cleanup today thanks to a group from the Goodwill Baptist Church who were breaking bread with them this morning.

Blaine glanced back at Miller, trying not to let her disappointment show at the knowledge that she wouldn't be taking a shower. This was not starting out to be her day, but then compared to yesterday, nothing seemed bad. ''Oh, all right,'' she grumbled at Miller. ''You don't have to talk to me, but thanks for letting me eat by you.''

To her surprise he answered, ''You're welcome.''

Blaine finished her meal in silence, watching the crowd, ignoring the announcements the preacher made. Everyone ate, but no one seemed to be enjoying the meal. Surviving. That was all they did. Just survive.

Suddenly she missed home. She missed Mark and her cat, and all the little things like a warm shower, the feel of clean clothes, the taste of oatmeal with cinnamon and sugar in it. She wished she could reach Mark without anyone knowing. He'd think of some way to protect her. What good was she doing wandering the streets? Maybe even getting killed by the gangs, or the cold, or a passing car? Even the problems that had driven her to the clinic two days ago seemed small.

Miller stood to leave, rattling the table as he bumped against it.

"Goodbye," she said softly, not really expecting him to answer. "See you tomorrow, Mr. Miller."

"All right," he mumbled so low no one else could hear.

Miller didn't speak to anyone as he left and she wondered if the man had a friend in the world. What kind of life must he have lived to be so alone?

She frowned and answered her own question. Right now Miller lived the same life she did. Maybe they weren't as different as she thought. A few days ago she would have died at the idea of confronting such a man, but apparently dying wasn't as easy as she'd once thought it would be. Surviving seemed to be the challenge.

As Miller shouldered his way through the door, Blaine watched a man in an old blue cap slip past, using the remaining space.

She forgot to breathe as the stranger removed his hat with oil-blackened fingers. She watched him survey the room, then turn toward the food line.

He couldn't be the guy who'd planted the bomb, she told herself, yet somehow the message didn't reach her pounding heart. He had the blue hat, the same body build, the identical way of moving as though calculating each turn. He moved like the man she'd seen at the clinic...like the man talking to Winslow about "taking care of the wife"

She stared, trying to see his eyes.

A hundred men in Austin could own old blue hats,

even more might have dirty fingers. But the killer's hands had not been just dirty, they'd been oily, just like the man in line who now pointed to what he wanted.

She stared at her empty bowl, trying to remember what the man riding the mower had been wearing. Work clothes. Plain, nondescript work clothes.

Just like those of the man in line.

The need to run pounded through her body, but she froze. She had to get a better look. She'd worry over what to do when she was positive. Right now she needed to make sure. She'd be laughed out of any police lineup if all she could identify was an old hat and a hand with greasy fingers.

Through her lashes, she watched as the stranger picked up his tray and walked toward the only empty seats by the preacher's table. Blaine felt sure she would explode if he turned in her direction. She told herself he wouldn't recognize her, he'd only seen her for a moment and he hadn't known she stood in the shadows and watched him the next morning.

As he sat down, the scarecrow of a preacher stood to deliver what he called his "nuggets of wisdom" to those dumb enough to stick around.

Hurrying toward the trash can with her paper dishes, Blaine figured she had just enough time to get away before the serving of preaching started.

But she couldn't walk away without knowing if the stranger's eyes were gray. She'd never forget those eyes. If this man's eyes were gray...

"Now this morning," the preacher shouted, "I'm going to ask you to come to the front and shake hands with the Lord." His words were slow, drawn out for effect. "I've got several of my church brethren here to welcome you to the Lord's family. All you have to do is walk the walk to our Lord.''

Blaine moved slowly toward the man sitting almost directly in front of the preacher. People passed back and forth blocking her view again and again. All she needed was one glance, she told herself, then she'd blend into the crowd. If he was the same man, she'd know to avoid him at all cost. She'd know he was walking the streets looking for her.

She glanced between two people. His dirty fingers smashed the white bread as he sopped up the last of his oatmeal. He paid no more attention to the scarecrow than if the sermon were blaring from a radio.

Everything she remembered about him matched, she told herself, but she had to be sure.

''Come on down, sister,'' the preacher boomed. ''Come on down and confess your sins. We're all children of the Almighty here.''

Not taking her gaze from the blue hat, she moved closer. If he'd only look up, she'd know if he was the man she'd seen outside the clinic window a few moments before the bombing…. A few moments before her world shifted.

If he wasn't, she could relax. If he was, she'd better be ready to run.

But the man kept eating, his head down, the tattered hat on the table beside his tray.

Ten feet away, she slowed as the crowd thinned until no one stood between her and the man with oily hands. She'd come too far to turn back now.

He couldn't be the one, she reasoned, but she had to be sure. The killer would have vanished moments after what he'd done. If he'd killed the guard as well, he wouldn't be walking the streets of Austin only blocks from where he'd murdered innocent people.

"The time is now, sister! Your salvation is at hand."

Blaine stared, willing the stranger to raise his head. One look was all she needed. One look at his eyes. She'd gone so long without sleep, maybe her mind was playing tricks on her. She might just think the hat was the same. But if he raised his head, she'd know. Blaine would never forget his eyes.

"Welcome the Lord into your heart!"

She moved closer, rounding the last table between her and the stranger. Nothing else mattered, not the room or the people or the yelling preacher. She had to know.

Five feet. Three feet.

Look up, she wanted to scream. Look up and have any color of eyes but gray.

"Bless you, sister." The preacher grabbed her hand but his smile was for those standing with him waiting to bring in the sinners. "Bless you for recognizing you are a lost soul in need of saving."

Blaine halfheartedly tried to free her hand as the stranger looked up from his food.

Their eyes met. Just as they had forty-eight hours ago. Angry gray eyes, cold as stone.

She jerked her hand from the preacher's grasp as she saw a question register in the stranger's stare.

The preacher grabbed for his one fish, but Blaine darted away as the bomber slowly stood.

"Don't be afraid to leave the life of sin!" the preacher yelled. "You'll find your home in eternal peace if you stay here with us."

Blaine ran for the door. She didn't have to turn around. She knew the stranger would follow. She'd seen it in his eyes. He had the look of someone trying to place her face. If he remembered, he'd have to finish the job he started.

When she reached the door, Blaine glanced back. The preacher had caught the stranger by the shoulder and shouted in his ear. But the man only put his cap on and stared toward the exit.

Darting outside, she hurried down the stairs, almost tumbling into Miller at the bottom.

He growled at her, but when she looked up at him, a hint of worry wrinkled his forehead. "What's the matter, pest?"

After seeing the bomber, Miller no longer frightened her. "I need help!" She grabbed his lapels and pulled his face closer to her own. "You have to help me!"

To her shock he didn't argue.

"There's a man following me. Blue cap. Stop him long enough for me to run, to hide." As an afterthought she whispered, "Please."

Miller nodded once and shoved her on her way as he turned to face the stairs.

# Ten

Mark Anderson parked his car and ran through the drizzling rain to the opening of his complex. He didn't bother stopping at the mailbox. He didn't want to communicate, even in writing, with anyone on the planet.

He'd waited around to sign the papers at the crematorium only to find that there was some question about identifying Blaine's body. It seemed the dentist sent the wrong X rays over. By the time he made it back to the morgue downtown, they'd closed for the day. He'd have to wait another day to take care of Blaine.

Frustrated, he called his secretary and filled her in on the delay, asking her to inform Harry Winslow he'd be late tomorrow and why. Harry seemed to be the only one who made sense lately. The older partner had offered to help out with Mark's latest case, taking some of the pressure off him until he could take care of Blaine's memorial service.

Mark didn't even want to think about that. The last thing he needed was a crowd of people surrounding him.

He shoved the half-completed form to cremate Blaine into his pocket and headed home. It bothered him more than he wanted to admit that he couldn't fill out all the details of his wife's life. He knew her dress size, her shoe size, her brand of perfume, even the flowers she liked during different seasons. She'd written down the details for him years ago on a slip of paper in the Rolodex on his home desk.

How could t be possible that he knew those facts but he didn't know her mother's full name? She sometimes talked of her work, but she never mentioned her past. When he thought about it he couldn't remember her boss's last name.

He rubbed his face as he waited for the elevator. How could he have lived with a woman, loved a woman for ten years and not know every detail of her life? She was shy, he reminded himself. Quiet. But was it possible that during ten years of marriage he'd never asked her all the little questions, like what she dreamed of being as a child, or how she felt about her father, or if her view of their future was the same as his.

One fact nagged him more than the others. If he knew Blaine, really knew her, why didn't he know the reason she'd been a the clinic? The lack of that one fact summed up his defense and said simply that he didn't know her at all.

Mark stormed down the long hall banked on either side by apartments as he made his way to the end where their large town house waited.

Halfway down the hall, Miss Lilly opened her door as he passed her apartment. Everyone knew where she lived. She was the only tenant who decorated her door for each holiday. This month's choice was a long-armed bunny hanging from the doorknob. It looked more like one of those cheap wraparound monkeys sold at the fair that someone had sewn ears on and spray-painted pink. The bunny's apron spelled out Hop Hop Hoppy Easter.

Mark glanced up at Miss Lilly, who, like the rabbit, also wore an apron, only this one said, Born O.K. the First Time. He was in no mood to be nice to the crazy old lady, even if Blaine always did take the time to talk to her. She reminded him of one of those boxes you turn over in a store and it rattles, or laughs, or moos. Only, Miss Lilly never seemed to stop rattling.

"I'm glad you're back," Lilly said as he tried to keep walking. "I've been keeping everything warm." She turned and headed back into her apartment without waiting for him to comment.

Mark had no choice but to follow.

"I guessed it would take you a while. I've been through what you're going through a few times myself." She pulled on an oven mitt shaped like a fish, and moved to the stove. "So I figured I would have time to cook something fresh, not just warmed-up leftovers from last week."

Mark stood in a room that was stuffed with Home Shopping Network's overflow of knickknacks. She had half a dozen afghans with Scottish-cottage scenes, a hundred candle holders made of everything from silver to mahogany, several ceramic birds and dozens of little butterfly wind chimes lining the top of the sliding glass door to her shelf balcony that was barely large enough to hold two lawn chairs.

He closed his eyes, not wanting to see more. The decor was "early garage sale," the color scheme "clutter." These apartments had been small when he and Blaine had looked at them five years ago. Though it had meant stretching their budget at the time they'd bought the larger town house at the end of the complex. Now, with all the stuff, the apartment looked even smaller than he remembered.

"I made chicken spaghetti!" Miss Lilly yelled as she pulled a huge dish out of the oven. "I hope you like it."

He didn't know what to do. What to say. Running

crossed his mind. The only thing that kept him in this room was the fact that Miss Lilly's conversation seemed preferable to being alone. For the first time in his life he wasn't sure he wanted to walk into his place. The all-modern design he and Blaine had decorated in seemed cold with all the steel blues and grays. She'd been the one who loved the balcony garden, he never bothered to open the door.

"I have a secret way I make it." Miss Lilly laughed. "I put green beans in it. It seems a more complete meal that way."

He glanced around the kitchen. Over her stove was a little sign that said, Eat More Beef, Chickens Are Sneaky.

Lilly didn't seem to notice he hadn't said a word. "I always enjoyed talking to your wife. She was doing some fascinating work. She loved volunteering to help out with that story time the library had at midday, even though it took up her lunch hour. Seemed like almost every Friday she would tap on my door and tell me something funny that happened during story time. More often than not it was the parents, not the kids, doing crazy things. I'll miss her dearly." She shoved a tear off her cheek with the oven mitt and motioned for him to take a seat at the tiny table crammed into a corner of the kitchen.

Mark looked to his left, knowing her apartment, like the others he'd seen, would have a dining room. He wasn't surprised to find the space had been turned into a study with books lining every wall and a collection of dolls strewn in one corner as if some child had been playing with them. He folded into the chair and brushed his hand over a plastic tablecloth decorated in a colorful fruit pattern.

"I don't remember Blaine telling me any stories about her volunteering at story time." In fact, he almost added, she never talked that much about her days. Only little things from time to time and he usually hadn't listened all that closely.

"You probably had something on your mind when she did. My second husband was like that. Said he did his best thinking when I was talking. I didn't find out until much later that the thinking he was doing was about another woman." Lilly handed him a plastic plate that matched her tablecloth and napkins as she continued talking. "She gave me a ride once to the doctor when I couldn't get my car started." Miss Lilly dropped a huge helping of spaghetti on the plate in front of Mark.

"Who? The other woman?"

"No, your wife. She gave me a ride."

Until that moment, Mark hadn't thought about what had happened to Blaine's car. It must have been parked by the clinic. Maybe it had been towed. Maybe it was still there. He'd have Bettye Ruth check tomorrow when he called in to the office. The police should be able to run a check on it. Vaguely, he remembered seeing the keys in her coat pocket.

"On the way back we decided to stop for ice cream just like I was a little kid who'd been brave at the doctor's." Lilly blew on her food before continuing. "It turns out we both loved the same flavor."

Mark didn't say a word. He had no idea what Blaine would order and it bothered him that this old woman knew more about his wife's preferences than he. As he always did when he didn't like the conversation, he changed the subject. "You love to read?" He glanced at the book room that should have been a dining room. Lilly poured them both a glass of iced tea and sat

down at her place. "I was a librarian's assistant before
I married my second husband. He talked me into moving
out to his farm promising I could buy fifty books a year
if I wanted." She giggled. "If he'd lived longer, my
whole house would be lined in bookshelves."

"You didn't go back to working in a library after he
died?" Mark asked then took a bite of food.

"No. I never went back to anything in my life. I was
a teacher's aide before I married the first time. When he
died I went back to school then worked in the library
until my second husband came along. When he died I
went back to school again and took enough journalism
courses to get a job writing columns for a small-town
newspaper. I owned that paper by the time I found my
third husband."

"When did he die?" Mark found Lilly's life story
interesting, like something they'd make a "for women
only" movie about.

"Oh, he didn't die that I know of. I just went for
cigarettes one day and I never went back home. You
would have thought he might have noticed something
was up, since I don't smoke. He was like that, lost in
himself."

"He was mean to you?" Mark felt sorry for her. He'd
seen dozens of women marry late in life to someone they
thought was worth having and the husband turned out to
be abusive. A few of the other partners in his office took
such cases, but Mark stayed away from them. He preferred his conflict to be over numbers matching in an
account book.

"No, he wasn't mean." Lilly downed half her iced
tea. "He just flat bored me senseless. I finally couldn't
take it."

"So you went back to school?"

She grinned. "You guessed it. Only this time I taught a few classes and I learned something I guess I'd known all along."

"What's that?" Mark stared at his empty plate, surprised he'd eaten every bite of the strange mixture while she had talked.

"If you can't go to bed with a good man, go to bed with a good book. It's much better company in the long run."

Despite his mood, Mark laughed and she scooped him another helping without asking if he wanted more. He could never remember talking to someone like her, and to his shock he found himself enjoying the meal. About the time he thought he had her figured out, she twisted the conversation into a new area he'd never considered talking to anyone, much less her, about.

She even asked why they'd never had children. Mark told her Blaine couldn't have any. He left out the fact that they'd never really looked into it. Blaine had made the question easy for him because if she'd been able to have children, he would have to consider it and the thought of parenting frightened him as few things did in the world. He liked feeling in control and most parents seemed to be sailing without a compass.

When they moved to the living area, Lilly handed him a bowl of popcorn and a can of root beer, then turned on the TV. "Do you watch *Survivor?*"

"I don't have time to watch much except the news. If we don't go out, I'm usually working on a case." He thought of telling her he needed to go and do just that, but she didn't give him a chance.

"Well, we've got to watch tonight. There's only two people left. It's the last night." The screen came to life with half-naked men and women running along a beach while drums beat in the background.

"I'm really not interested," he said honestly.

She wiggled into her recliner and popped the tab on her drink. "We can fix that. How much money do you have in your pocket?"

Mark reached for his wallet.

"Not your back pocket. I don't figure you for a sucker. In your front pocket, where you stuff the change from eating lunch out."

Mark pulled the bills from his left pocket and the change from his right. "Eleven dollars and forty-three cents."

"You a good judge of people?"

"I have to be to pick juries."

"Then I tell you what, you watch the opening where they show a little summary, and when they get down to the last two, you pick the one you think will win. I'll take the other. Even bet."

Mark smiled, almost feeling sorry for her. He'd bet his skill against hers any day. He'd always been able to read people. 'I hate to eat your food and take your money, Miss Lilly."

She grinned at him as if she knew a secret. "Are you trying to back out, chicken?"

He glanced at the plaque over her stove. "No way. You're on."

She dug in her purse until the exact amount of his bet was on the trunk that served as a coffee table.

Thirty minutes later the popcorn was gone and they were both on the edge of their seats. Mark thought the choice of who would win was obvious, but if so, why did she let him pick? Maybe the producers painted one guy in a bad light and then changed their tone about the time the viewer thought he knew who'd won.

Forty-five minutes into the game he decided she must have rigged the bet. His choice was turning out to be the jerk of the island. He yelled at the TV as if he could change what was happening.

Miss Lilly joined in and shouted for her pick not to listen to a thing Mark was saying. Then she laughed, as only a woman who loves to laugh can, with her whole body.

Five minutes to go and he found out her choice had a few secrets to tell and seemed determined to do so even as Miss Lilly yelled.

When the show went to commercial, Mark was up pacing the floor as if he was in a courtroom. Lilly was laughing at him, verbally poking him like a child toying with a chained dog. The thought crossed his mind that he should be thankful she hadn't gone to law school in her many returns to collect more education.

A few minutes more and the suspense was over. Mark yelled a football hoot he hadn't screamed in years. By chance his pick had pulled it off in a last-minute ploy. Lilly laughed until she had to use one of the afghans to wipe her face.

"That was great fun," Mark said before he caught himself.

How could he say such a thing after all he'd been through?

"It was fun." Lilly looked up at him as if reading his mind. The money lay forgotten on the table between them. "It's all right, Mark. It's all right to laugh and it's all right to cry. No matter what happens, as long as we're breathing, we've got to go on living."

Mark nodded, sat down on her ridiculous couch of many colors and did something he hadn't done since his mother passed on. He cried.

# *Eleven*

Blaine ran two blocks before she looked back to see if the man in the blue cap followed. To her relief, no one appeared. She turned a corner and hurried down another street, then another, then another, weaving her way to nowhere. She'd been a fool to walk so close to him, to think she had to see his eyes. Now, if he recognized her, he knew she was still alive. Now he'd be looking for her.

Desperately she sought safety in a town that suddenly seemed foreign to her. Austin was no longer home. No longer safe.

She ran down alleys, but the fear that the bomber might catch her alone in the shadows drove her back to the crowded streets. Here he might find her, but at least he couldn't kill her without someone noticing. She tried to guess if he'd recognized her, or simply hated the way she stared at him. She couldn't be sure. She had a feeling that if he wasn't sure who she was, he might still think it safer to kill her rather than take a chance at her causing him trouble.

A question lingered in her thoughts. Why had he stayed around only a few blocks from the bombing? Looking for a witness? Watching those suffer from the chaos he'd caused? Or was there a chance that he suspected she still breathed. The possibilities chilled Blaine's blood.

Could it be that somehow, when he'd bombed the back of the clinic, he hadn't accomplished his goal? Surely his one goal hadn't been to kill her. She tried to remember the exact word she'd heard Winslow and the thin man whisper in the shadows that first morning, but the conversation was blurred with memories of the throbbing in her head, the fire in her throat and the ache in her leg.

Blaine couldn't be sure that she hadn't been dreaming or out of her mind that morning. It all seemed smoky now, like a nightmare she couldn't shake. But the fear she felt was real and she had to think.

She tried to blend in with the crowd, but she was no longer one of them. People frowned if she moved too close, and a few turned around as though questioning why she might be following them. Women pulled their purses closer, men checked the wallets in their pockets. Blaine was afraid to stand too close, afraid to get too far away, for there was comfort among the strangers.

Blaine joined a group of schoolteachers protesting in front of the capitol, but with her ragged clothes, she stood out among the khaki skirts and white tennis shoes. She tried walking beside a group of tourists, all with cameras and fold-up hats and buttons that said, A Dozen Capitals in a Dozen Days. They didn't glare at her as the teachers had, but she knew she couldn't blend.

At the downtown library where she worked, she twisted around a corner and paused behind a dozen concrete steps leading to the back entrance. There, in the shadows between buildings, she tried to think. She had to be careful, very careful. The killer could be walking the streets only a block away, searching for her. Or maybe he had found a hiding place where he could watch everyone pass by. If she kept circling, she was bound to run into him. She had to have a plan.

As she gulped air, the door opened at the top of the stairs and one of the librarians hurried down and across the street to a coffeehouse. The girl didn't notice Blaine standing below the steps on the other side of the railing.

Blaine smiled. She was back to being one of the invisible people again. The question remained: was she invisible enough? She glanced at the door.

The staff, used to street people wandering through the library, would ignore her as long as she stayed in the public areas. What she needed, though, was not in the public areas.

She walked her fingers along the brick wall to the metal door. Just as she hoped, it had not closed completely. Probably left ajar because the staff worker would be returning in moments with coffees.

Blaine slipped inside so quickly the movement of the door could have been caused by a breeze. She hurried past stacks of boxes. The most likely place she would be seen was in this open area. An ancient camera blinked a red light from above the exit sign, but Blaine knew no one watched its recordings. She had seen the monitor near the circulation desk and never noticed anyone showing interest in the comings and goings at the back door. Below the exit sign was a huge cardboard poster demanding this door be kept locked at all times. For the library, that probably seemed security enough.

She moved with silent determination toward the stairs and the rooms below where desks were crammed into vacant corners amid old display cases and boxes labeled Book Sale. Hers was the only space not designated for volunteers. Since she usually spent only a few minutes each morning picking up assignments or dropping off books she wasn't ready to send back upstairs, Blaine didn't mind the drab almost-office.

The basement room was empty and lit only with faint strips of emergency lighting. Blaine didn't dare turn on a light and announce her arrival. It was still too early for volunteers to be there. Most came in around ten so they would have time to plan lunch before taking their break. Blaine let out a long-held breath and moved to an old typing table that served as her desk. Since she had no drawers for supplies, Blaine kept a box beneath the desk.

The phone looked so innocent, so unimportant on her desk. She lifted the receiver and dialed nine for an outside line, then her home number.

No answer. Mark had either turned off the answering machine, or it was full.

She dialed his private line.

Two, three, four rings.

"Anderson's office," a low voice said. "This is Harry Winslow." A long pause. "Hello. Hello, who is this?"

Harry still answered Mark's private line. Blaine pictured the stout man running across the space between his office and Mark's. He would have to pass Mark's secretary, so Mark must know he was answering the phone. But why? No one had ever answered the private line before except Mark.

It crossed her mind that Harry might be waiting for her to call in.

Blaine slowly lowered the phone. Twenty-four hours ago Mark had answered his own phone. If he wasn't home or at his office, where was he? Her mind crossed the possibilities. Driving to work? Out for coffee? She closed her eyes. Making funeral plans for his wife. Of course. Mark still thought she'd died in the bombing.

She had to reach him, but how? The last thing she planned to do was let Harry know she'd called.

Reaching through her belongings in the box, Blaine needed to connect with her life. Mark was safe, she told herself. He had to be. It would have been in the paper if someone had hurt him. He lived in a locked complex, worked in a public place, no one would hurt him. There would be no reason. He was a lawyer, thinking of running for railroad commissioner. No one would want to harm him. She was cracking up. Right now, he was far safer than her. She was the one who had to vanish and fast.

As she pulled out the box, her knee bumped against the slick nylon of her gym bag. She almost cried out in pure joy. How many times had she been angry with herself for forgetting to take the bag home? It was easy to work out at the gym a few blocks away before dropping by the library, but hard to remember the bag when she left the library with other things on her mind.

Blaine crawled under the desk and opened the bag, feeling her belongings in the darkness. Sweats, deodorant, a comb, one still-damp swimsuit wrapped in a towel and Nikes. Nikes. She jerked off the filthy hospital slippers and put on one of her tennis shoes. Heaven!

She continued her search.

Her favorite gold bracelet still remained zipped in a bottom pocket along with a ten in case she needed money for juice at the gym. She'd thought it such a crisis the day she'd broken the latch. Now the familiar feel of the chain made her smile as though she'd reclaimed a piece of her shattered life.

Within minutes she'd stripped to the skin and scrambled into her wrinkled sweats. When she pulled on her socks, she almost cried. Nothing had ever felt so good. She crammed her dirty clothes into the bag and tossed the slippers into a nearby trash can.

Blaine rummaged through her office-supply box for anything she thought she could use. It would be too risky to return again to the library. Anything she needed, she had to take now. Scissors, five quarters and two breakfast bars were all she thought might be useful.

With the sweatshirt's hood over her wild hair, she walked out the front door of the public library carrying her duffel bag with a Gold's Gym ID card dangling from the zipper.

The homeless Mary had been replaced by a jogger, but she wasn't safe yet. If the bomber got a look at her face, he'd still recognize her. She had to be careful until she knew she was out of danger.

Disappear, she decided. But with ten dollars and change in her pocket, it wouldn't be easy.

Blaine stayed on the move, watching for a tattered blue cap to appear from among the people passing. No one bothered her as she walked through hotel lobbies, for now in her jogging clothes, she looked very much like anyone else in the hotel on vacation. She could have easily been one of the many businesswomen who traveled but still went through a workout each morning.

In front of one hotel door with a Do Not Disturb sign hanging from the knob, Blaine picked up a paper. Now she could sit almost anywhere and read. Most hotel cafés would even bring her water. She made use of the hotel rest room to tie her hair back, then borrowed several of their soaps.

She devoured the paper for details about the bombing but learned little. The bomber had used dynamite and most of the damage to the clinic had come from the fire that followed the bombing. Two bodies were found, Blaine's and an office worker's. One nurse was still missing—a Sindi Richards, who had only been working in the clinic a few weeks.

On the back page she noticed a short article about upcoming political races. Mark's name was mentioned as still being considered in the running, but his law partner, Harry Winslow, had issued a statement that Mark might be reconsidering due to the recent tragedy.

Blaine's fingers twisted the paper. This race was so important to Mark. It was all he'd talked about for months. How could he be thinking about dropping out? The Railroad Commission held a great deal of power since they controlled oil production in Texas. Mark could make a real difference in such an office.

The coldness of reality moved through her blood. He was thinking of dropping out because of her. She'd done the one thing she'd sworn she'd never do. She'd interfered with his dreams. No, correction, she may have killed them.

It didn't matter if she could talk to him or not. If she wasn't dead, the press would be all over the story of how Mark Anderson's wife was almost killed at a clinic known for doing abortions. No matter how many times she told them she'd only gone to find out if she was pregnant, there would always be that shadow of doubt. Women don't have to see a doctor to find out about pregnancy…unless they fear cancer…unless they remember their mother thinking she was pregnant and finding out she had only months to live. In the end, her mother's cancer would be mentioned and then someone would find out about her mother's death. Blaine didn't want to think of her life spread across the headlines like some story out of a tabloid.

She closed the paper, folded it under her arm and began to walk. She kept her hood up and her head down as she passed block after block. One thought kept nagging at the back of her mind. What if? She didn't want to bring it to the forefront of her thoughts, but it wouldn't go away.

What if? kept whispering in her thoughts. What if *you* were the reason for the bombing? Not the clinic and its problems, but you.

She pushed the thought aside. Why would anyone want to kill her, Blaine Anderson, a part-time archivist who spent most of her time scanning old newspapers and articles?

The words Winslow had whispered in the dark that morning after the bombing drifted over her like icy rain. ''You got the wife,'' he'd said.

Blaine felt a sudden coldness even through the sweatshirt.

Why would anyone want to kill her, Mark Anderson's wife?

# Twelve

Blaine walked, trying to think. Yesterday she'd been in too much pain and shock to do more than breathe, but today she knew she'd better start to act, if she wanted to stay alive.

The worry over how she'd tell Mark about the baby if she turned out to be pregnant seemed so small today. They hadn't talked about kids for years. She'd told him she couldn't have them on their third date and he'd said he had goals in his life that were far more important than children. He wanted to change the world, make it a better place for the next generation, not just worry about his own children. She believed in his dreams and now, somehow when she wasn't looking, when she'd blinked, the world had changed and she might be the one who'd destroyed those dreams.

Despite all the worry and danger, a hollowness entered her. When she was young, she'd been afraid to dream or plan. She was organized, she remembered details, but no overwhelming need drove her other than the one to step out of the poverty her parents had lived in. When she'd met Mark, she'd found someone to help. He had enough dreams for them both. But lately, even before the fear that something was wrong inside her, she knew there should be *more* to her, but she had no idea how to find that *more*.

Now fate had slapped her back to poverty, but something had changed. She had changed. She had to figure out how to climb back to where she belonged, and somehow she had to do it without putting Mark in danger.

Late in the afternoon, she noticed the old man called Shakespeare slumped into a doorway of a boarded-up coffee shop. The smell of whiskey thickened the air around him. He clenched a bottle partly hidden in a brown bag. "Hello, my friend," he mumbled as though he didn't expect her to answer.

Blaine hesitated only a moment before grabbing his lapel and pulling the little man up to a sitting position. "Are you all right?"

"'Life doth drip from me as pure as frost's early thaw and just as coldly,'" he mumbled.

"Can I get you something?" She pulled one of the breakfast bars from her bag. "Have you had anything to eat today?"

Accepting the gift, he nodded his thank-you and placed it in his pocket, then patted a bag beside him. "'I've enough to drink my way into sleep. That's all I ask from the world this night.'" He glanced at the paper under her arm. "However, if you will loan me your paper, I would be grateful." His words tumbled over one another. His eyes were bloodshot and heavy.

With shaking fingers he took the paper from her grip. "I like to read my horoscope. Just to see if there is ever a good day coming." He closed his eyes and whispered, "'Would that morning dawned bright, for I'll not mourn the passing of this night.'"

"Oh, Shakespeare you need a place to sleep. You need help. You're not well." It suddenly occurred to her that the people passing wouldn't allow an animal to suffer so, but they didn't even see the shell of a man dying in front of them.

He nodded, "'Tis true, I'll be meat for the worms soon, but I'll breathe free air 'til I die, not the air of charity or prison. As for a hospital, the odds are not with you there. Better than ninety percent of folks die while in a hospital. Appears to be a place to avoid with all haste."

She almost laughed. She'd only been on the streets a few hours and already she was becoming as paranoid as Shakespeare, worrying that there might be a plot to kill her because she was the wife of someone thinking about running for office. Now that she'd probably been an idiot and let him know she was alive, he might try to get to her if he had another chance. After all, he got to Frank Parker. Or did he?

Blaine shook her head. She needed time. Every puzzle had an answer and she was good at puzzles. Only, in this game, her life balanced with the answer.

"You can't stay here in this doorway." Blaine wanted to help but knew of no way.

"Augh, but I can," the old man answered. "You see, I know the man who owns this establishment and he has given me permission to be in this passage anytime I like."

Blaine doubted his words, but guessed he thought they were true. The coffee shop had long wood-framed windows ten feet tall running across the street side, but the entrance was down a passage to a door set back several feet. The location offered Shakespeare not only a porch to watch the street traffic unnoticed, but also a square near the door that was covered and sheltered from the wind. No one passing would notice the space tucked away in the shadows of the passage.

A bedroll lined one corner, a few leaves had whirled in on the wind, but otherwise Shakespeare's home was orderly, no trash, no empty bottles.

"If you will pardon me, Mary, my dear, I think I'll have a nightcap and retire for the evening." He finished off the last of the whiskey in the bottle and laid back, using her paper as a pillow.

She heard his snoring before she left the passage, heading back to the street. "Good night," she whispered, wishing he'd been sober enough to talk to. He might have helped her find a place to hide. By now the shadows were long and the air had turned damp with rain.

She spent one dollar and change to buy a large juice when she neared the cemetery. Hurrying in before the gates closed, she placed the juice beside one of the headstones where she'd seen the boy playing. If the kid came back to the cemetery tonight, maybe he'd find the juice. Glancing at the offices, she thought of trying to sneak in there for another night, but the odds were not with her.

She needed to find somewhere that wouldn't get her arrested if she were discovered. Someplace where she didn't have to worry about the bomber finding her. She told herself one last time that he may not have recognized her, but she'd seen the truth in cold gray eyes.

She hurried out the cemetery and turned toward downtown. The library was a possibility, but again, there would be too many questions if someone stopped her.

When she passed the downtown gym, several people rushed past her obviously in a hurry to work out and go home. Blaine blended with them as they hurried through the door, down the stairs and into the lobby. She pulled out her card, holding it as though ready to swipe it across the scanner. But a man behind her pushed her forward and Blaine passed the desk without registering her name in the computer.

She kept her head down. The young people on duty were paying far too much attention to one another to notice only five of the six people passing had used the required ID card.

Blaine hurried to the dressing room thankful to find a rest room. Within minutes she'd slipped her swimsuit on and found a towel. A shower would be great, but Blaine wanted to relax her muscles in the pool first.

She floated alone in the pool for what seemed like hours. All the water-aerobics classes were over and it was too late for the mothers-with-tots swim. An old man came in, swam two laps, then climbed out without even saying hello. Blaine didn't care, she just drifted in the warm water, letting the chlorine sting slightly on the cuts that hadn't healed.

When Blaine finally made herself get out, she wrapped the towel around her and went back into the dressing room. Only the cleaning lady was there, picking up towels members couldn't bother to toss into a bin.

The cleaning lady couldn't have been many years older than Blaine, but with her fifty pounds of extra weight, she moved slowly. The woman took one look at Blaine's legs and cried out, "What happened to you, lady? You're black and bluer than I ever got when my first husband beat on me regular."

Blaine looked down at the bruises across the exposed flesh of her legs. "I fell," she said, trying to think of something that would explain away the marks. "I took a tumble down the stairs at home." She stood so that the scab from the cut on her left leg would not show.

"Are you sure you're all right? They got a first-aid

kit at the desk.'' The woman frowned. ''I'll go get it if you like.''

Blaine shook her head. ''No, but thanks. All I can do for bruises is to let them heal.'' She didn't dare lower the towel, for there were bound to be more marks she hadn't noticed.

The woman finished her cleaning as Blaine grabbed her bag and slipped into the shower stall. By the time Blaine had hot water, she heard the door close and knew she was alone. She used half the container of soap mounted on the wall to wash her body and hair.

Without any cream rinse or conditioner, her hair was beyond all help. She pulled the pair of scissors from her bag. They'd only been used to cut paper at the library, but they would have to do. As water steamed around her, Blaine cut handfuls of her hair and lay it across the soap dispenser. When most of the length was gone, she measured the section that had been burned to within two inches of her scalp, then slowly moved around her head cutting the remainder of her long blond strands to the same length as the burned spots. Inch by inch, her hair drifted atop the water and disappeared down a huge drain a few feet away.

Finished, she shampooed the short mop once more and then dried off, listening to make sure she was alone before venturing from the shower stall. It was late. On weekends people might work out after ten, but on weeknights few did. They were mostly the walkers or joggers and they didn't bother with the dressing rooms but went home to their own shower.

Blaine gathered up the long strands she feared might plug the drain and ran to the toilet. As she flushed them, she felt as if a part of her life was circling down. It had taken several tries for her to learn just how to color her hair. Somehow when she was blond, she was wearing a mask. Her father hadn't cared enough to stay around, her mother hadn't loved her enough to say goodbye, but even in her teens Blaine knew she was a survivor. She'd reinvented herself slowly, like a warrior of old preparing for battle. Blaine realized she'd prepared for life. She hadn't liked the person she'd started out to be, unwanted, unloved, so she'd molded herself to perfection. Blond hair, slender. She had pushed the world away until she thought nothing could hurt her. Until now. Until the bombing.

Blaine smiled. She had been a survivor then, and she would be now.

Pulling on her clothes, she stepped in front of the mirror with her comb. For a moment she wasn't sure who looked back. Some of the tiny scabs were gone, leaving her face blotchy. Her damp hair curled over her skull like a cap around her thin face.

She paid two hundred a month to keep her hair colored, straightened and styled. Brown roots showed and natural curl overpowered the straighteners she'd used. It had been time for her appointment two weeks ago, but Blaine had had other things on her mind. Now she was glad she had canceled the last appointment, for with the cut and the curl returning, she looked even younger.

She moved her fingers over her abdomen. Had it only been a few days ago when worry over whether she had a baby inside her had almost driven her mad?

The beginning of a plan began to form. Blaine glanced at the clock. If she moved quickly, she'd have enough time to get to the drugstore and back before the gym closed. She shoved her money in her pocket and hurried out, leaving her bag tucked out of sight beneath the sinks. If someone stopped her sneaking back in, she'd simply say she forgot her bag. Chances were, no one would ask, but if they did, she had the proof.

# *Thirteen*

Opening one eye, Mark glanced at the clock.

Eleven a.m.

He bolted upright, knocking Tres off the foot of the bed. He took another look at the time. Not since his college drinking days had he slept past seven. He was a morning person, often running in the foggy predawn light.

Today, it appeared, he had missed most of the morning. Briefly he wondered if Miss Lilly had put something in her chicken spaghetti besides green beans last night. Sleeping pills? Shots of tequila?

Mark smiled. Surely not. She was eccentric, but not crazy.

Like an old man, he rolled from bed and moved toward the bathroom. His bones ached from sleeping in one spot. When he reached the mirror, he wasn't sure he knew the man who looked back. His dark brown hair stood up in every direction like some kind of porcupine/human mutant. Three days' growth of stubble darkened his jaw and a thin layer of white stuff resembling watered-down Elmer's glue dripped from one corner of his mouth. He was a young man looking every bit as though he should be checking into the nearest nursing home.

Mark hit the shower without allowing time for the water to heat.

He thought he heard the phone ringing while soaping his hair for the second time. He almost yelled for Blaine to get it and tell the office he'd call them back. Then memory settled over him like lye soap, stinging his eyes, burning his nostrils, prickling him with a fact that wouldn't go away. Blaine wasn't there, she never would be again. She'd been a part of his life for forever and he wasn't sure he could go on now.

Bracing against the shower wall, he let the hot water run over him, trying to steady himself. He felt like an addict with the shakes. If he could just hold Blaine one more time. If she were alive and in his grip just for a moment, he'd hold tighter this time. Somehow he hadn't been watching. Somehow this was his fault. But if he had a second chance, he'd hold so tight she wouldn't slip away.

The water turned cold and a question gnawed at the corners of his mind. Why had she been at the clinic? He told everyone she was volunteering, but he couldn't lie to himself. She'd had a reason. Something she planned to talk to him about. But what? Though she talked about her volunteer work, she never felt the need to discuss with him what she did on her days off and lunch breaks. He knew she liked working with children and guessed most of the projects had something to do with literacy.

Mark swallowed hard. She loved children. Whenever she was around them, she couldn't stop watching them. He'd thought about asking her to go to a doctor once their income was stable. Maybe the reason she couldn't get pregnant could be fixed. If so, at some point, when they were ready, he had no objection to having maybe one child. Mark wasn't sure he knew how to be a father, but Blaine would be a good mother.

Would have been, he corrected his thoughts. Would have been a good mother.

He dried and rummaged though the junk on his desk until he found her note, trying to find a clue as to why she'd been at the clinic. He read the slip of paper once more, hoping he hadn't overlooked something in the two lines. *Gone to clinic for some answers.* What answers had she been looking for? He didn't even know the question. Then she had added, *We have to talk tonight.* As though there was a problem between them. Something he knew nothing about.

Mark folded the note, remembering what an old law professor had said about handling divorce cases. He'd commented that eighty percent of the time the husband didn't know there was anything wrong with the marriage until the wife told him.

Had there been something Blaine wasn't telling him? And why the clinic downtown? Why hadn't she gone to her usual doctor who was also a friend of theirs? Surely she could have talked to him. He would have worked her in between patients. Had her questions been so small that she'd just stopped by the clinic between her gym workout and her job? Or had they been so huge that she'd feared the answers and had not wanted anyone to know?

Mark dressed, deciding he would go crazy if he didn't get some resolution, but he wasn't sure where to look. The newspaper might be a start. The office had insisted he take the rest of the week off, which was probably for the best since he seemed to have lost track of time. He ran through the days in his mind. The bombing happened on Monday morning. Tuesday was a fog. He'd spent Wednesday trying to work out the details of getting Blaine cremated and then he'd had dinner with Miss

Lilly. This was Thursday and, thanks to sleeping, the day was already half gone.

He skipped shaving, but out of habit, Mark slipped on a tie. He was halfway through folding the knot when he realized he didn't need to wear a suit.

Turning toward the closet, Mark almost tripped over Tres spread out in his path like a rug. Stumbling, as he tried not to land on the cat, Mark hit his knee on the dresser and stubbed his toe on the corner of the bed frame.

Tres didn't bother to move. She simply stared at him as if he were doing some kind of strange dance she had no interest in learning.

Before either could swear at the other, the phone rang.

Mark winced and forced himself to walk toward the living room without limping. He didn't want to talk to anyone, but he hurried, thinking it might be the office and they needed him to come in. He had several cases waiting for trial and unpredictability ruled in a law office. Maybe if he could wrap his brain around a case, he could get a grip on what he would do with the rest of his life.

"Hello." He tossed his tie over the nearest chair and reached for a pen.

"Mark Anderson?"

Mark couldn't place the clipped, official voice. "That's right. Who is this?"

There was a pause before the man on the other end said, "This is Lieutenant Randell. I'm a detective with the Austin Police Department. I—"

"Has there been a break in the case?" If they had a suspect, Mark would be in his car within seconds driving toward the station. It was about time the police had something. A man couldn't simply bomb a building in downtown and walk away without leaving some clues.

"No, nothing yet," the policemen hurried to add. "I just need to ask you a few questions."

"Look, Randell." Mark didn't bother with the title. He had little patience with the police on a good day and this was not shaping up to be a good day. "I've already given you guys a statement. There is nothing else we have to talk about unless you have a lead on the bomber. I can't be of any help. I didn't even know my wife was at the clinic until I read her note when I left work about six."

"I know that, sir," Randell said. "But there's something I want to talk to you about. If you're going to be home for a while…"

"Can we do it on the phone? My time is limited," Mark lied. He tried to remember if he'd talked with a cop named Randell that night at the hospital, but the name didn't seem familiar. He had no desire to rehash every question. Blaine's death was already on constant rewind in the back of his mind.

"No, this better be face-to-face, Mr. Anderson," the cop insisted. "I'll be happy to come out."

The last thing Mark wanted was some stranger dropping by. No telling how long the man would stay, and cops had a way of making you feel as if they were rifling through your life even when they didn't touch a thing. Mark had learned a long time ago to hold all meetings on neutral ground. At his office or here, he'd be trapped. The police station would have too many distractions and it might take the man an hour to give out information. "How about we meet at the coffeehouse across from my office in about an hour? I've got to pick up some papers, so it's on my way," Mark lied again.

The lieutenant agreed. Mark gave him the address and they hung up without either one of them asking what the other looked like.

An hour later, Mark walked into the coffee shop and noticed one man sitting alone by the window watching people pass. His suit was wrinkled and was several wearings past needing to go to the cleaners.

Mark walked over to the table, put his cup down and offered his hand. "Randell?"

The cop smiled and shook Mark's hand in a strong grip. "Thanks for meeting me. I'll make this as quick as possible."

They were about the same age but the lines in Randell's face settled into a worried expression that in a few years would become permanently imprinted. His hair was thinning, his face too light for the Austin-tanned look, so Mark guessed he worked nights. Extra pounds pushed his belt out two or three notches farther than it should have been, but he didn't appear out of shape.

Mark sat across from the cop and ordered a doughnut, thinking that another time or place they might have been friends. "You need to ask me something more about my wife's death?" He got right to the point. "I assure you I would have called if I'd thought of anything new."

Randell shifted, his chair no longer comfortable. "I wanted to make sure you were the one who ID'd your wife. The report was signed by a fireman, Frank Parker, the clinic's guard, and you."

"I saw her." Mark tried to follow the reasoning. "Why?"

"Nothing probably. I'm just checking facts. The fireman didn't know your wife, and Frank is no longer here to answer questions."

Randell's intelligent stare met Mark's. The lawyer in

him didn't miss the worried look when Randell added, "You're sure it was her?"

"Of course. She was burned, but there was one part of her hair that the fire hadn't touched." He didn't want to think about this, but he forced himself to go through the details. "She must have covered her head with her arms." Mark took a deep breath before continuing. "No one had blond hair just the color of Blaine's. It had a touch of red in it." He swallowed the scalding coffee, trying to keep his voice steady as he continued. "Her rings were in her hand. She had a jacket I bought for her birthday a few years back. Her wallet was in the jacket pocket.'

"Are you sure they were her rings?"

Mark stared out the window remembering how they'd spent all day in Santa Fe looking for just the right rings for Blaine. She wanted something unusual, he'd mostly thought of finding something he could afford. In the end, he had been the one who talked her into the more expensive set. She'd jumped into his arms right in the middle of the store, surprising and embarrassing them both.

"They were her rings," Mark finally answered without emotion. "I could not be wrong about that."

"Did she know anyone at the clinic? I mean, as far as you know"

"No. Why?"

"I figured she might have gone to the clinic to see someone, or maybe she was tagging along with a friend who had an appointment. Most of the records were destroyed in the fire after the bomb went off."

Mark found the idea interesting, but had to answer, "No. Not that I know about." In truth, he knew Blaine had a few friends she went to lunch with from time to time. A few of the volunteers at the library and a couple of the partners' wives she sometimes worked on fund-raising with. He had never paid too much attention to any names. But it was a possibility. After all, Miss Lilly said Blaine had taken her to the doctor one day. Maybe Blaine was just along for the ride, but if so, why had she left the note?

Randell checked his notepad, then returned it to his pocket.

The silence was as thick as cold coffee between them. Finally, Mark said, "Why all the questions? Backtracking over the same ground usually means you guys don't think you got everything straight to start with."

Randell didn't look up from his drink. "Just making sure this time. You been around a lot of cops?"

Mark recognized the lie and the attempt to change the subject. He waited.

Finally, the cop added, "Half the coroner's staff is out this week with the flu. But they are trying to get your wife's body released for cremation as fast as they can. Problem is, the dental records the dentist sent over didn't match, and he swears he didn't make a mistake. We've got a nurse from the clinic that everyone reported seeing in the clinic Monday but we can't find her."

"What are you trying to tell me?"

Randell looked up, his worried gaze fixed on Mark, leaving no games between them. "We've sent for the missing nurse's dental records. It will take twenty-four hours to overnight them. She just moved here six months ago and hadn't used a local dentist as far as we know. She was the same height as your wife, almost the same build. Her friends said her hair color pretty much changed weekly but it was blond when she went to work Monday morning." Randell lowered his voice. "Blond with red highlights."

The hair rose on the back of Mark's neck. All the pieces weren't fitting together. "You think the body in the morgue might be the nurse?"

The cop shook his head. "I don't want to get you upset or anything. But it is something we have to check out."

"It's impossible!" Mark forced himself to lower his voice. "If it were her body…"

Randell ended his statement, "…then your wife is the one missing."

Mark stood suddenly and walked over to refill his coffee. Part of him wanted to demand why the detective was putting him through this. But the logical side of his brain had to know the facts, all the facts.

He sat back down. "What else?" he said, knowing there had to be more.

Randell spread his hands on the table. "An alcoholic who works at one of the shelters called in with a story of a woman who came to breakfast the morning after the bombing and maybe one time since. She claims this thin woman was scratched and bleeding from several cuts and acted half-crazy. She even said the lady had the smell of smoke on her before she took a shower. Right now, I'm thinking it could have been the nurse, or your wife."

"Do you believe this caller?"

Randell stared out the window. "This isn't the first time she's turned in what she thought was a clue. She watches far too much TV. Thinks she's working with us undercover some nights when she's heavy into the bottle. But from what details we got out of Chipper, this woman fits your wife's description. Five-seven, slender. She said her hair was pretty dirty, but it looked blond."

"Impossible. Blaine would have called. I work within

walking distance of the bombing. If she'd been simply hurt, she could have been at my office within minutes.''

Randell nodded. "Like I said, all we got is questions right now.'' He tossed his empty cup toward the trash. "Also said she thought she heard someone call the woman Mary, so the tip is probably nothing.'' The cop shook his head. "Old Chipper got her handle because she joined AA under half a dozen names in as many cities. She carries a pocket full of poker chips, but she can't manage to stay on the wagon long.''

Mark sighed and stood, wishing he hadn't wasted his time coming down to meet Randell. If Blaine had been alive she would have called, or gone home, or even rushed to his office. She wouldn't just wander around alone. And his wife, who always hurried to wash her hands when she touched a public railing, would never eat at a homeless shelter with people who only bathe monthly. He fought the urge to tell the man he was wasting his time. There was just a mix-up with the dental records, nothing more.

The two men walked out together. "Funny thing about this mystery lady.''

Mark fished out his keys. "What?'' he asked, just to be polite.

"Chipper said she was frantic to call someone that first morning. She wasn't close enough to hear what was said, but it appeared whoever she reached hung up on her.''

With a quick goodbye, Randell turned and headed toward his car with a backward wave.

Mark stared down at his keys. The crank call he'd gotten that first morning after Blaine died exploded in his mind.

It couldn't have been Blaine! He braced himself as

the crushing memory of her charred remains filled his thoughts.

The last moment on this earth that he'd ever see her, she'd disappeared under the zipper of a body bag.

It couldn't have been Blaine who called. It couldn't.

# *Fourteen*

Blaine slipped back into the gym ten minutes later, looking like someone who had chosen to do her run on the streets and not the indoor track. No one noticed her, or the small bag she carried in her sweat suit.

She washed out her underwear and hung it in an empty locker as she kept an eye on the huge silver clock on the wall of the dressing room. On tiptoe, she spread her towel on top of the last set of lockers. Carefully, soundlessly, she scooted the bench from along the wall in front of the lockers to use as a step stool.

The room was warm and humid as she climbed to her hiding place and lay down on her towel. She smelled the dust around her and heard the clanking of pipes above her, but dust seemed harmless to her now and the pipes only noise, nothing more. Here, in the women's locker room of a gym for members only, she would be safe from the man in the blue ball cap. Here, she could sleep.

It crossed her mind that Frank Parker must have thought he was safe when he filed his report with the police and headed home. She couldn't shake the thought that his death had not been an accident.

At 10:15 p.m. the door squeaked open to the ladies' dressing room. She didn't move, praying that whoever entered wasn't any taller than her five foot seven. Oth-

erwise, the intruder might be able to see Blaine stretched
out above the lockers. She pushed closer to the wall,
melting into the shadows.

"Anyone still here?" a girl yelled. She walked
through, banging open the stall doors. "All clear, all
gone," the employee said over the static of a walkie-
talkie. "Place looks clean."

Blaine waited. Five minutes later, the lights went out
and she relaxed for the first time since the bombing three
days ago. She was safe and warm. Closing her eyes, she
slept without moving.

Sometime during the night, the clanking pipes woke
her. Carefully, she slipped down from her perch and felt
her way through the room lit only by an exit sign over
the door. When she reached the hallway, even less light
greeted her, but she'd walked this path a hundred times.

Blaine moved toward the front desk. There, the light
was better thanks to windows facing the street. She could
see the clutter of membership forms and bins of dirty
towels scattered along the back counter. A phone sat on
one corner. Blaine moved her hand over it, longing to
call Mark. Not now, she told herself, maybe in a day or
two. If Winslow was close enough to Mark to answer
his phone, Mark might not be safe if he knew she was
still alive.

On impulse, she started dialing his private office number. Knowing he wouldn't be there this late. She reconsidered and dialed his public line. The answering machine would pick it up.

Two rings, then three. "I'm not in the office, but I'll
get back to you," his voice said. He sounded so good.
Almost here for a moment. Almost with her.

Blaine fought the need to whisper his name, but she
forced herself to end the connection. She couldn't put

his life in danger. Not tonight, when she knew the bomber was so near.

Pressing the receiver against her cheek, she tried to hold on for a moment to Mark, to her life before Monday morning when her world fell apart.

Moving like a ghost, Blaine carefully opened the low storage cabinets. Without much difficulty she found the first-aid kit and took out one half-used tube of antiseptic cream. Next she rummaged through the lost-and-found box, finding only an old pair of black-framed glasses that could have been a man's or a woman's, and a small bottle of conditioner. She thought of also taking an empty cosmetics bag, the kind given away at every sale in the mall, but she didn't want anyone to notice the box was missing items.

Though she knew it wasn't enough payment, she left three quarters on the counter and took several power bars and a juice from the display of healthy snacks. On her way out, she grabbed a few extra towels, then made her way back to her hiding place. There, in the darkness, she picnicked on the stolen food while she rubbed the ointment over her cuts. The one on her leg still felt raw, the wound more wide than deep. It would leave a scar.

Finally, she curled up on her towel and went back to sleep, breathing deep in the chlorine-scented air.

The lights flickered on just after 5:00 a.m. Blaine slipped down with the toiletries she'd bought at the all-night pharmacy the night before. With the shower running, she opened the bottle of hair dye and smeared it on her curls. By the time this brown wore off, the blond beneath could be cut off.

By six, the dressing room was a thriving ant bed of activity. Blaine lay on her back and listened to the conversations. She thought she recognized a few voices of women who'd been in her exercise classes. They talked of their aches and pains, as if such little things mattered. Once in a while someone would mention a bit of news they'd caught, making Blaine realize that her world had shrunk to one of survival. She knew nothing of what was happening anywhere but around her.

After half an hour of listening, someone below finally mentioned the bombing. They complained about having to go around the streets that were still barricaded and the traffic. Someone said she heard the police were close to a breakthrough in the case. It was agreed that, since the bomber used dynamite, it had to be a crazy and not some organized effort to bomb clinics. Then the conversation turned to cellulite.

At half-past seven there was a lull, and Blaine managed to slip off the top of the lockers. She retrieved her underwear and took a quick shower, not because she was dirty but simply because she could. Her hair felt so strange, short, curly, but to her surprise when she dried and brushed the mop, it didn't look so bad. With her face scrubbed clean of makeup and her hair no longer blond, she could almost pass for one of the college kids hanging out at the UT campus.

She packed her bag, afraid to leave anything behind, and slipped on the black-framed glasses. It was no wonder someone left them behind, she could barely tell they were prescription.

Pulling her hood over her hair, she passed the main desk and was back on the streets before eight. She jogged around businessmen and women hurrying to work, managing to reach the shelter just in time to slip inside before Chipper closed the door.

Chipper didn't even look up as she shuffled back to

the kitchen to begin her endless chore of restocking the food line.

Blaine weighed the risk of returning here against her hunger. The bomber could be back and, this time, he would be searching for her while he ate. She told herself she had changed her look so dramatically that he wouldn't recognize her. Still, she hung back in the doorway for a few minutes and watched the people.

The bomber wasn't there, and Chipper would be closing the line any minute. Hunger won out over fear.

Blaine grabbed a box of cold cereal, yogurt and an apple. She hated cold cereal, but this morning she felt like she could eat it, box and all. Despite the health bars last night, she was starving.

When she passed Chipper, the woman said only, "Coffee or milk?"

"Can I have both?" Blaine waited for Chipper to recognize her scratchy voice.

Chipper only nodded and passed her the cup of coffee and a carton of milk with shaking hands. "Move along," she mumbled with a slur in her voice.

Blaine smiled, realizing the woman didn't recognize her. This was going to work.

She found Miller at his usual back table and sat down across from him. If possible, the man's hair looked more like a bush than it had yesterday. His clothes were old and well worn but clean.

"'Morning, pest," he mumbled between bites.

"You recognized me?" Disappointment filled Blaine.

"You got new clothes, cut your hair too, but you're still dumb enough to sit by me. I figured there couldn't be two women in this town that stupid."

Blaine shrugged. "Maybe I like your company. Ever think of that?"

"No," he replied.

"Thanks for your help yesterday. How'd you stop the man in the hat?" She had no doubt that if Miller hadn't been there, the bomber would have caught her. With a chill, she realized that even if she had screamed for help, no one would have rushed to her aid. They would have thought it only trouble between the homeless.

Miller wiped his mouth on his napkin before he said, "Grabbed him by his scrawny neck. Told him he reminded me of a brother-in-law I had." Miller took another bite, using his spoon like a shovel.

"What did he do?"

"Nothing. I shook him a while. Then I turned him loose and he carted away. My guess is he won't be back here."

"How can you be sure?"

"I'm not.' Miller shrugged. "He's got coward eyes, though. I've seen his kind. Stab you in the back, or shoot from a hiding place, but he's not the type to face another man directly. He has a smell about him. Reminds me of the year I worked on the big oil rigs over in Odessa. A few of the fellows let sweat and crude oil blend so thick on their skin that ten showers wouldn't get it off."

"He'll kill me if he finds me." Blaine owed Miller information for the favor, but she couldn't tell him more without putting Miller's life in danger.

"You know him? He your husband? Your family?"

She shook her head. "No, but I saw him commit a crime a few days ago. The other person who could identify him is already dead."

Miller took the news without blinking. Apparently he'd heard more frightening stories. "You getting enough to eat, pest?"

Blaine nodded, realizing she'd devoured everything on her tray.

"You got a place where you're safe when you sleep?"

She nodded again. "All I have to do is be invisible for a few days. The police will catch this guy, then I can surface."

"Any family looking for you?"

"I have a husband, but he'll be all right. His work is very important. My guess is he'll get lost in it." She almost added that Mark never reacted to things. No highs, no lows. She could count on him always being the same. In the ten years they had been married, she'd never seen Mark show much emotion at all. Not anger or rage or frustration. Not passion or hurt or jealousy. Loving him was easy. Mark never snapped at her or got furious, but in turn he'd never made love to her as if he'd die if he couldn't have her.

Somehow, in his early years, his parents' coldness toward him had stunted his growth inside. She had no doubt he cared for her as much as he could and that had always been enough. His passion lay in his work and Blaine knew from the beginning she'd always be in the background.

"There's a place to get lunch on Neches. Mostly sandwiches and soup." Miller's voice lowered. His words sharpened—the words of a man who knew what he was talking about. "They don't ask questions. You'll be safe enough there, but stay off the streets as much as you can and be careful going anywhere not surrounded by people."

Miller stared at her as if sizing up her strength. "If he does see you and follows, the last thing you want to do is give him an opportunity to strike. He's stronger than most men his size. If he gets his hands on you, he wouldn't need a weapon to kill.''

"Are you trying to frighten me?"

Miller looked up from his food with steel-blue eyes. "Yes. This is no game out here and there may be no one to help you.''

Blaine studied Miller. "You will."

"Don't plan on it.''

She wished she could read his story in his eyes. Reasons hid behind his words, deep dark reasons that haunted him.

"You helped me yesterday. You're helping me now. Why?''

"You're nothing but a sparrow in a tornado. If someone doesn't give you a hand, you'll die circling in the wind." He tossed his napkin on his tray. "Eat regular and mind what I said. I'll ask around, maybe I can find out where the guy hangs out.''

"He's not a street person," Blaine volunteered.

"Neither are you.'' Miller stood and left without another word.

# *Fifteen*

"Anderson?" a male voice snapped before Mark had time to say a word.

Mark didn't have to guess the caller, he knew. "Randell, how can I help you?"

The detective didn't waste time with small talk. "We got the results back from the nurse's dental records."

"Yeah."

"There is no doubt. The woman you thought was your wife is a Sindi Richards. She didn't have any family here and no friends who knew her well enough to turn in an official missing persons the day after the bombing. The staff at the clinic hadn't gotten around to it. But the doc says there's no doubt about it being Richards's body, even if she was holding your wife's rings when she died."

There was a long pause, then Randell added, "You all right? I probably should have come over to tell you. It's not the kind of thing to just spring on someone." Another pause, then he added, "I'm sorry."

"I'm fine." Mark's voice was calm. No one could see the death grip he held on the phone. "You were right to call. I wanted to know the results as soon as possible."

What the detective wasn't saying rang in his head. If the body wasn't Blaine's, then where was his wife?

Finally, Randell said, "Do you want to file a missing persons?"

Mark closed his eyes. "No," he finally said. He needed time to think. Everyone in the police station would look at him as if he was just another one of those husbands whose wife runs out on him. He knew Blaine hadn't left him.

He didn't know where she was, or why she hadn't come home, but Mark refused to believe that she'd just left him. Blaine wasn't like that.

"How are you?" Randell asked as if they were friends. "Really?"

"I'm all right." He thought of adding that his world was collapsing in on itself. His wife had shifted from dead to missing. An hour ago Harry Winslow had distributed his caseload to the other lawyers as if handing out a dead man's clothes. He was suddenly swimming in an ocean of feelings he'd managed to keep locked away most of his life. He had no wife, no work and he felt as if his mind might snap at any moment.

"I'm fine. Really," Mark managed to say, wishing he could convince himself.

Randell would think he was cracking up if he talked about work after what he'd just learned, and he didn't know enough to ask what next to do about Blaine. For Mark, work was all that mattered. All that had ever mattered.

Until Blaine disappeared.

Mark hung up the phone and drove back to the office. He had no reason to go in now, but he didn't want to stay at the apartment. Maybe he could think more clearly sitting in the empty office.

Darkness settled over the city by the time he parked in one of the spaces out front of his building. He let himself in the main door and weaved through the outer office without bothering with the lights.

He was almost past Winslow's door when he heard voices. Winslow sounded angry, yelling about finishing a job that was sloppy from the beginning.

Another male voice almost whined as he promised to get the work done.

"This is your last job, Jimmy, don't screw it up."

Mark quietly retraced his steps to the front door and opened it just enough so that he could close it hard, then he flipped on the lights.

Winslow appeared in his door a moment later. "Mark!" he almost shouted. "What are you doing here? I thought you were taking the week off."

Mark didn't miss the redness in Harry's face.

"I just came in to pick up some papers," he said. "Bettye Ruth said she'd leave them on her desk."

As Mark moved across the room, he noticed Winslow blocked the door to his own office.

"You're working late," Mark said casually. "Hope taking on my extra load isn't too much."

"No. No." Winslow tried to look relaxed, but didn't quite pull it off. "I was just finishing up a few things." He stepped aside. "In fact, my mechanic just delivered my car, so I'll be heading out soon."

Mark looked past Winslow and saw a thin man wearing a baseball hat that had seen better days.

Harry waved his hand. "Mark Anderson, this is Jimmy, a guy who has worked for me off and on for forty years."

Mark nodded with the introduction, but Jimmy didn't look at him.

Winslow hurried to add, "We met out in West Texas during my wildcatting days in the oil business. There's not much old Jimmy can't do when the need arises.'' Winslow glared at Jimmy meaningfully.

Mark had heard a hundred of Harry's stories about his early days, but he wasn't in the mood to visit with this guy named Jimmy any more than Jimmy seemed to want to talk to him.

''Well—'' Mark grabbed the first file he saw on Bettye Ruth's desk '—I didn't mean to interrupt. I'll be in my office if you need me.''

Winslow nodded, but Jimmy seemed fascinated with the carpet. He didn't bother to look up when Mark disappeared.

Once alone, Mark tossed the file on his desk, emptied his pockets of cell phone and keys, then began to pace in front of his long row of windows. Harry Winslow had some shady people who came to him for counsel, everyone in the office knew about it. He was a lawyer who sometimes liked to work for trade and didn't always bill from the firm. No one said anything about it since he was a senior partner, but more than once Mark had wondered what had been on the table in the swap.

Mark plopped down in his chair and leaned back. More than likely Harry was getting engine work done for nothing while he handled talkative Jimmy's divorce papers. Mark would be willing to bet his pink slip that the mechanic wasn't just delivering Winslow's car.

For once in his life, Mark couldn't get everything to fall into place. He felt as if he was working with puzzle pieces to ten different puzzles. An hour passed and the lack of sleep caught up with him.

When he awoke it was after midnight. He grabbed his keys and forced himself to head home.

He was in his car before he realized he'd forgotten

his cell phone. No problem. He had no clients who'd be calling anyway.

Strange though, he thought, he usually picked it up with the keys. He didn't even remember seeing it on the desk. Mark scratched his head. He really had to get a grip.

# *Sixteen*

Mark drank his way through the next few days. Not bothering to shower or shave he waited, like an addict, until almost nine to venture out to restock his supply of alcohol. It didn't matter what he drank, as long as it would dull his mind. He worked his way through the liquor cabinet and then selected bottles at the liquor mart based on how close they were to the counter when he hurried in to buy more.

Several people called from the office wanting to know when Blaine's memorial service would be. Mark couldn't bring himself to tell them that there was no body, so he simply said they were waiting on family from out of town.

By Saturday, the alcohol had made him more sick than drunk. His message machine was full, and after listening to the first few, he erased them all. He read about Sindi Richards's funeral service and sobered up enough to dress and go. It was held at the funeral home, and the folded card he was handed when he walked in told him her body was being taken back to Jefferson, her hometown, to be buried in a family plot. For some reason, that made him feel better. After she'd lain in the morgue under someone else's name for days, at least she'd be among family now.

The smell of flowers greeted him as he walked in and

looked around the small chapel. Twenty people sat a few rows back from what had to be her family. A long blond-wood casket waited at the front. A picture of a young woman in a nurse's cap sat atop the casket.

Mark took a seat near the back. As the funeral started, he decided the older couple in the first row had to be the girl's parents but, of the younger couples, he couldn't tell which were siblings and which were just kin by marriage. Every one of the young couples had children.

The minister gave a canned sermon where he filled in the blanks with Sindi's name now and then. A man identifying himself as a brother gave a short history of the girl's life and how much she was loved. Several people began to sniffle. A woman, who said she was Sindi's boss, told of what a good worker she was and how greatly she'd be missed.

Slowly, Mark realized the very fact that had caused him hope had been a blow to this family. Until Randell called, Mark thought Blaine was dead, now he was searching for answers and the Richards family had found theirs.

Mark blinked hard and slipped out during the prayer. He hurt so badly, his chest heaved in pain. The girl had had so many people to cry for her, to miss her, to wonder how they'd go on without her. His wife had only him and he was a poor excuse for family.

He climbed into his car and pressed his palms into his eyes. "I'll find you, Blaine. I swear."

He drove home and called Bettye Ruth, asking her to find out who was the best private eye in Austin. As usual, his secretary made no comment about why. He then drank himself to sleep and dreamed of digging through ashes frantically searching for Blaine.

By Monday, the paper had the story of the mix-up in

bodies. By Tuesday, everyone Mark knew called, wanting to know more and to ask how he was holding up under all the pressure. A few invited him out to dinner, as if Blaine's disappearance might be an interesting topic of conversation.

Winslow called, suggesting Mark make sure all the correct papers were filed and all accounts were in Mark's name. He talked as if he was worried that Blaine might never be found, but he ended the conversation by making Mark promise to call the minute he had any news.

Mark was surprised and touched by his depth of concern.

Randell came by and together they made a list of places Blaine usually went, even asking her hairdresser and nail tech for information. The cop claimed that women will tell those people things they'd never tell even a husband. He also wanted a list of people who knew Blaine.

Mark realized no one knew his shy wife very well. No one had taken the time. Including him. Most of the research work she did was contracted and she worked at her own pace, then mailed the results. Though she had an office and a mailbox at the library, she didn't report to anyone there.

By Thursday, he'd sobered up enough to shower and pick up the bottles around the town house, which had the faint smell of a brewery about it. Tres still wasn't talking to him and Mark couldn't find the cat food. He'd bought her several different kinds, but she'd only stared at them as if to say, "You expect me to eat this?" He scrambled her an egg the way he knew Blaine did, and dropped it in her bowl on top of the one he'd scrambled a few days before. He didn't have any milk, and the fussy feline didn't seem to like watered-down coffee creamer. She circled the kitchen a few times and went out the pet door as if she couldn't stand to be in the same room with him.

"Leave me too," he yelled after the cat. "Why not? Leave me without a word."

When the cat door flapped back into place, Mark realized how foolish he sounded. He knew he needed to get a grip on his anger, but he wasn't sure how to do it. Blaine had always been the listener who helped him work through everything. Sometimes, when he'd had a hard day, she didn't have to say a word, just being with her made him feel better.

He went from worrying himself sick about what might have happened to her, to hating her for leaving him and hating himself for being the kind of person people never cared about. He wanted to stand on the balcony and scream that he was worth something, see all he'd done, see all he'd accumulated. He was worth something. He was worth someone caring about. He was worth being loved.

Friday, when he went down to check his mail, he ran into Miss Lilly painting daisies on her mail slot. The old woman was dressed in overalls embroidered with tiny purple frogs and wore a straw hat that looked as if it had once been wrapped around a potted plant.

Her smile was somehow sad as she asked how he'd been.

They talked about the weather, and the traffic, and the new neighbors who would be moving in next month, but Miss Lilly didn't mention Blaine. It was as if her name was on both their tongues but they had to talk around it.

Miss Lilly must have read the papers. She knew Blaine wasn't dead. Maybe she was afraid to think about what might have happened to her. Mark knew the possibilities were nightmares.

Just as he turned to say goodbye, Mark did something he'd never done before—he asked the old lady if she wanted to go to dinner. They had lived next door to one another for four years as polite strangers and now he was about to eat with her twice. He could attribute his insanity to the fact that the only calories he'd had in days had come from a bottle.

"You plan on shaving?" she asked with a lift of her eyebrow.

"No," he answered. Just to be ornery he added, "You?"

She set down the paintbrush and laughed with her whole body, taking no offense to his comment.

"You buying?"

"If you'll wash that paint off your face," he said, "I'll buy."

"I pick the place, though."

He agreed, relieved. He had no idea were one takes a little old neighbor to dinner. "Deal. How do I dress?"

"You're fine just the way you are. Pick me up in ten minutes." She waddled off with her paints in one hand and brushes in the other.

Mark almost ran after her and said he'd changed his mind, but the old woman had allowed his brain to think of something else besides Blaine. Maybe, if only for a few moments, he could relax and breathe. He felt as if he'd been holding his breath for days.

Ten minutes later he tapped on her door and wasn't surprised to see she hadn't bothered to change clothes. It crossed his mind that she might pick an expensive place but he doubted she even knew where the trendy spots were located. He had made the rounds, both with

Blaine and without her, when clients needed to talk. She never seemed to mind when he couldn't make dinner, and he wondered if she bothered to eat when she wasn't dining with him. No matter how late he might be, she usually managed to wait up for him, if only to say good-night.

"Where are we going?" he asked as he helped Miss Lilly into his car. Lilly and his BMW might both be built low to the ground, but she didn't fold inside easily.

"Subway," she answered as she fought with her seat belt. "I got a two-for-one coupon. You get two six-inch sandwiches for the price of one."

Subway wasn't what he'd had in mind, but it sounded as good as anywhere. She gave him a commercial on the place having all these sandwiches with less than six grams of fat, but made no comment about the six cookies and extra bag of chips she ordered with her meal.

To his surprise, after picking up their food, they were not eating at the plastic tables surrounding the counter. She wanted to drive out to Waterloo Park.

They talked of nothing while they ate. Mark picked at his sandwich, tossing most of it to the squirrels.

Lilly insisted they both have 7-Up to drink. She pulled a bottle from her suitcase-size purse and divided a few ounces of the red liquid into their drinks.

Mark thought it was cherry flavoring, but after one taste decided it had to be cherry vodka.

"Like red wine with beef and white with fish, this goes perfect with a sandwich," she announced.

Lilly took a long drink. "When you going back to work?"

"Monday," he answered in a flat tone. "I need to work. If I take any more time off, my brain will turn to mush. I hired a firm to search for Blaine, but they didn't seem to think they could do any more than the police.''

Lilly raised an eyebrow in question.

"She's just vanished. It's like she fell off the earth. The P.I. said most women clear the bank account, or pack. He said if she'd left with another man, she'd have taken everything she could. Blaine just disappeared. It's like she didn't go anywhere. She just left me.''

The park was quiet. A few joggers circled but no one glanced in their direction.

She studied him closely. "You got lots worrying your mind, but there's something more than Blaine missing. I've had enough husbands to recognize when something's gnawing at a man, and you look plum nibbled to death.''

"The police are doing all they can.''

"I know. ' Lilly added, "They called on me earlier this morning.''

Mark stared out toward the trees. "I've got to find her,'' he whispered more to himself than her. "I have to know.''

Lilly nodded.

Mark dug his fingers through his hair. "If something happened, she got hit in the head and doesn't know who she is, I'd never stop searching. I'm all she has.''

He raised his head and let the wind cool his face. "But it's more than that.'' He looked back at Lilly. "If she just left me, I have to know why.''

# Seventeen

Blaine developed a routine over the next few days. There would come a time when someone at the gym noticed her within the arriving crowds. She had to be prepared to vanish once more.

So far, her luck had held, but still, Blaine planned for the unexpected. She could feel herself changing, molding into someone stronger. Somehow the fear and panic hardened her.

She walked out of the gym each morning in time to eat breakfast, then stayed in crowded places until noon. Heeding Miller's advice, she ate lunch at the food line on Neches Street. The meal was hardy, so she usually managed to save back an apple and half a sandwich.

She took the food to the cemetery at closing time, leaving it near the headstone where she'd seen the little boy hiding. Blaine wondered if he lived in the homes bordering the cemetery and somehow played a game within the fence. Surely he wasn't on his own at such a young age.

One afternoon, she'd been a few minutes later than usual and barely made it through the gate. She turned in time to see the child dart from one stone to the other, pick up the food she left and hurry away.

Wherever he lived, she would bet that he wasn't eating regularly.

The next day, she placed the food a few stones closer to the fence. Again the child grabbed the food as soon as the guard was gone and disappeared among the headstones.

Blaine understood hunger. Constant hunger stayed with her. Each night the thought crossed her mind to rob the power-bar stand again, but she knew the staff would eventually notice the vanishing inventory. It went against the grain for her to steal anything. Her only other choice was to become more resourceful.

All her life Blaine had not been able to eat when she was nervous. Maybe it was something about being homeless and not knowing where the next meal would come from, but now she couldn't get enough food. The place that served lunch also gave away bread, fine-quality, day-old bread from the local bakeries. One afternoon she took a small loaf and, combined with the jelly she'd collected in small packets from breakfast, she had a feast for dinner atop her nest above the lockers.

She also learned that if she walked the halls of the Omni or Driskill Hotel just after nine, most of the breakfast trays sat outside doors. Carefully, she picked a different hotel, a different hall each morning. Surprised at all the things she could collect. Tea bags, small jars of jelly, untouched fruit, cereal boxes and sometimes muffins and butter wrapped inside cloth napkins. The napkins were a great luxury she allowed herself, then carefully returned them to the hotel when she made another round down their hallways.

Day by day, she began to feed the child in the cemetery more, each time leaving the food a little closer to the iron fence. Finally, she saw his frightened little face close up and he could not have been older than nine. His eyes were wild, but he nodded once in a thank-you.

That night, as she ate her bread long after lights-out, she laughed at herself. She and the child were somehow alike, both surviving. Reason told her she should call the authorities and turn him in so he could be put in a home or taken back to his parents or guardians, but deep down she knew he had no parents, and if he'd been in a home, it must have been bad if he preferred the cemetery.

She also knew he had no one but her. Maybe his parents both worked long hours, Blaine tried to reason. Surely if he'd been at the cemetery long enough someone besides her had seen him. They'd turn him in.

Blaine smiled. Mark would be proud of her. When this was over, she'd tell him all about feeding the boy. Mark was always fighting for the underdog, making a stand for a better world. That was one reason he wanted to run for office, to clean up some of the unfair practices.

She might still be a mouse in this world of lions, but mice survive. She was not only surviving, she was helping another.

She'd risked staying out after dark twice to try to catch Mark leaving his office. Both times all she'd seen was Winslow locking up…and both times the driver in the car that picked him up could have been the man who bombed the clinic. One night, Blaine thought she heard Winslow call him Jimmy again.

She studied the papers for any sign of the bomber being caught and several times tried to call Mark, but she only got machines. Each day, she became more desperate.

Eight days after the bombing, Blaine filled her plate at the shelter line and walked toward Miller without speaking to anyone. The Annas didn't seem to know her since she'd changed her look. The different clothes and short brown hair helped, but the glasses Blaine wore changed the look of her face. Vanilla Anna called her Mary once, but Elaine knew the old woman called everyone Mary. Several even called Vanilla Anna momma because she mothered them in her crazy way. When it rained she'd stand at the door of the shelter and warn everyone to stay dry or they'd catch their death of cold.

The cook, Chipper, had stared at Blaine a few times, but never said a word. When Chipper wasn't too far into the bottle, she watched people, always seeming to look for the evil that might be inside them. From the frown she usually wore, she'd found what she was searching for in most folks.

Chipper looked ill as Blaine passed her near the end of the serving line. But Blaine didn't want to ask questions for fear Chipper would remember her. The cook's eyes were bloodshot and she had given up on personal hygiene. It seemed it was all she could do to keep the food line stocked.

When Blaine set her tray across from Miller he looked up at her, worry wrinkling his forehead.

"You've found out something?"

Miller ate another bite before answering. "Not about the man in the cap. He must have fell off the earth. I've had Shakespeare watching for him. If he's still around, Shakespeare will see him. Problem is, I've got to get to the professor while he's still sober enough to keep the facts straight."

"If we have no clues, what's worrying you?" Blaine had the feeling Miller was wasting time, talking more than usual to avoid questions.

He hesitated for so long Blaine decided he wasn't going to answer.

"What?" She feared the worst.

Miller shook his head. "There's a cop asking questions about someone who disappeared after the bombing of that clinic last week, that's all. Persistent bastard."

"Is he looking for me?"

Miller corrected. "He keeps asking if anyone has seen a blond, thin woman with scratches on her face. The description is too close not to be you. You need to get away."

Blaine shoved her glasses up on her nose.

"I can't leave town."

She had never wanted to be standing next to Mark so much in her life. He'd always been the constant in her world. She needed him to hold her and tell her everything was going to be all right. Every time she awoke in the darkness above the lockers, she tried to imagine Mark holding her while she slept even though in truth he rarely did. She needed to be near him now.

But if she went to Mark, she would put his life in danger, she reminded herself for the hundredth time. As long as she was missing, there was a chance Winslow would still think she was dead.

"If the cops are looking and you run, you'll be out in the open. My guess is they're watching the bus station and the interstates."

"I don't know how much longer I can stay where I am at night."

"The gym?"

She wasn't surprised he knew.

"I watched you go in a few times just to make sure you're not being followed. Thought I saw a shadow trailing you, but it turned out to be just a kid playing in the alley."

Blaine wanted to cry. She'd been crazy to start this. Now if she went back to Mark, he'd probably have her committed. She'd thought she was protecting him as well as herself, but everything was a mess. She based all her fears on a conversation she'd heard the morning after the bombing when she'd been half out of her mind with pain.

But, she reminded herself, there were other clues. Somehow Winslow had cut her off from Mark. Maybe he'd sent the thin man out on the streets to find her. Maybe he was afraid to do anything until he knew she was really dead.

"Thanks for helping me," she said to Miller. The man never asked why. He helped her even knowing the police were looking for her.

Miller finished his breakfast and stood as if he hadn't heard her. He'd helped her once, but she wasn't sure he would again. He treated her as if she were as welcome at his table as fire ants.

Watching the crowd, Blaine tried not to catch anyone's eye. The Annas were sitting side by side, not talking, as always. Everyone else in the room seemed more occupied with the meal than with the people around them. Even the preacher had forgone his usual greeting and wandered off, showing a small group of women around.

She had to give the scarecrow credit. He managed to talk enough groups out of money to keep this place going. If he stopped, people would starve or resort to stealing. She might not like him, or his cold manner, but Blaine surprised herself by realizing she respected the man.

The young thugs had finished eating and, in the preacher's absence, were trying to carve something on one of the tables. The coarseness of their words blended easily with the scraping sound as they worked on the table.

Blaine leaned back in her chair and noticed Chipper slumped over the small table in the kitchen, her TV blaring the news. Chipper hadn't bothered clearing away the remains on the line today and Blaine wondered how long she would have this nothing job if she didn't stay on her feet.

The bottle was winning with Chipper, leaving the wreckage of a lonely woman behind. She was too young to be a bag lady, too old to work the streets as a prostitute. This place seemed her last stand.

Blaine had watched the hookers work one morning from the parking lot of a liquor store that faced Interstate 35. From what she could tell, the older ones took the scraps of the business, accepting offers none of the other girls wanted. The younger women stepped out when a newer car drove up. The older ones leaned against the old broken-down pickups that pulled in beside the store. They seemed willing to get in if the driver bought a six-pack.

Blaine knew she should take her tray to the trash and leave, but she couldn't ignore Chipper. It might have been in a small way, but Chipper had been kind the morning after the bombing. Blaine owed her.

Waiting for all the others to leave the dining room, Blaine kept her head down. Vanilla Anna was the last, collecting plastic forks on her way out.

Slipping into the kitchen, Blaine touched Chipper's shoulder. "Hello," she whispered. "Want some help with the cleanup?"

Chipper glanced around the room with bloodshot eyes as though she couldn't pinpoint where the question came from. "I could offer you a shower but it ain't worth the time." Her words were slurred.

"Don't worry about it. You rest, I'll clean up."

An hour later, Chipper slept with her head on the table while the small TV over the refrigerator blared. Blaine finished up, mopping the floor as she listened to the news. The floor didn't look as if it had been touched by broom or mop in days. It felt good to work, even at this mindless labor.

After one final wipe of the tables, Blaine set the last cup of coffee in front of Chipper and tapped her on the shoulder. "Is there anything else I can do for you?" In a small way she felt like a genie granting someone's wish.

Chipper rubbed her eyes like a waking child. She twisted around to look at Blaine.

Blaine kept her head down.

"You kind of look like the woman I told the cops about, but her hair was blond and her clothes ragged."

"You told the police about a woman?"

For a moment, Chipper looked as if she didn't want to talk, but the need to complain won over caution.

"Yeah. Lieutenant Randell said he ain't goin' to give me no more to drink if I don't see her again. You sure you don't know her? Tall and skinnier than you. Her face was all cut up. Her blond hair touches her shoulders. I gotta find her or things are goin' ta go bad for me."

Blaine touched her waist. All the pancakes and sandwiches seemed to have gone to her middle. She knew she had gained a few pounds, and thanks to the swims, all the scratches on her face were now faint blotches of pink.

"I think I may have seen that woman." Blaine chose her words carefully, trying to imitate the voices of those on the street. "She said she was taking the first bus out of town. Heading for Abilene, I think."

"Figures," Chipper snorted. "She's got so many people looking for her. I could make a little by spotting her."

"Who else is lookin' for her?" Blaine's body suddenly felt cold.

"You ain't planning on beating my time and passing on your bit about the bus alone, are you?"

Blaine shook her head. When Chipper didn't appear convinced, she added, "I got my reasons for staying away from cops even though they ain't been looking for me since I was fourteen and ran away from home." She smiled, loving the lie as she made it up. "My stepdad was a cop, used to beat me ever' payday for the hell of it."

Chipper nodded as if she understood the place Blaine came from. Same neighborhood as hers.

"I just like to know who is out there asking questions so I can avoid them." Blaine shrugged. "I gave up on keeping answers a long time ago." She leaned toward Chipper. "So, if you'll tell me who to avoid, I'd appreciate it."

Nodding, Chipper took the invisible hand of friendship. "Just the cop named Randell. Don't even know if he has any other name. Not that it matters. Maybe they issue them, one gun, one name. He's worked the downtown area for a few years, thinks he knows everyone on the streets."

She laughed at her own joke. "Oh, yeah, and some tall man came by a few days later asking the same questions. He didn't offer me a drink, so I didn't tell him nothing. My skill ain't for free, you know. I remember what I see and that is worth something around this place.''

''What did the other man look like? The one who offered nothing.'' Blaine forced herself to sit down and act as if she was just passing time. ''If you remember? Was he wearing a hat?''

''Of course I remember. Him, no, not any hat.'' Chipper closed her eyes. ''He was nice-looking. Early thirties. Tall. Hair black, or maybe a real dark brown. Kind of the color of my coffee.'' Chipper took a long drink. ''He had a beard, cut short. I remember thinking he could have be one of those models. There weren't a scar or tattoo on him that I could see.''

Chipper smiled. She'd proven her gift.

Except for the beard, Chipper had described Mark. But Mark would never grow a beard. He would never come to a place like this. ''You are good.'' Blaine guessed that a man without scars or tattoos would be the exception to the rule.

The cook straightened in her chair. ''You bet I am. If you don't mind, I'll pass along your information about the girl taking a bus to the cops. I work for them part-time, you know. Undercover. They tell me things they don't tell anyone else. They let me know when to be curious.''

Blaine took a chance. ''I heard something the other day that they might find interesting.'' She was about to take a big step, trust a person who didn't look as if she would be worth trusting. But Blaine had to do something. Her best chance at getting off the streets was to get the bomber arrested.

''What?'' Chipper leaned forward, seeing her chance for one more bottle.

''The man who blew up that clinic,'' Blaine began,

silently praying she was doing the right thing. "I heard someone say he had on a blue cap and had greasy fingers. The kind a man gets from working on an engine."

Chipper licked her lips, already tasting the whiskey. "Anything else?"

"I think I heard he had gray eyes. Cold gray eyes. The color of headstones."

Chipper leaned back and rubbed her face as though trying to wake all the parts up. "Was this someone sure? I've seen lots of true-detective profiles, no one ever remembers the eye color. Maybe this someone is just making up this man. Or maybe she's describing her boyfriend or pimp, hoping to get him into trouble. I've seen cases where someone does that. The police always figure it out, but the boyfriend is still locked up for a while."

Blaine had the uneasy feeling she'd already said too much. She had to tell Chipper enough to make Randell believe the information, but if she said too much the cop might start asking too many questions about where Chipper picked up the story.

"What you want for this tip?" In Chipper's world nothing came free.

"Milk." Blaine named the first thing she could think of. "Two cartons every morning, along with the coffee."

Chipper frowned at her.

Blaine decided she was no good at lying. She couldn't think of the answers fast enough. She had to make her lie believable or the information might not be passed on. "I could be pregnant." She said the words before she thought. It was the only answer she could think of as to why someone would need more milk. Somehow saying the words made it more of a possibility.

Chipper relaxed, accepting the answer, but still looked

as if she was considering the bargain. "Double the milk each morning if Randell takes any part of your story. Otherwise, you get the same as everyone else."

Blaine thought of reminding the woman that she'd agreed not to tell Randell about where she heard the story, but she didn't want to mention it again for fear Chipper would pick up on how important Blaine's secret was to her. She had an idea that if Chipper guessed, she'd be paying Chipper to keep her secret.

"You'll know Randell took the story if I set two cartons on your tray tomorrow morning."

"Deal."

"One other thing."

Chipper frowned.

"Would you let me know if the good-looking guy shows up again?"

Chipper nodded. "If you'll help with the cleanup."

Blaine agreed. "If you see him again and get word to me, I'll help you clean up this place again." She wouldn't put it past Chipper to lie just to get help.

Chipper raised an eyebrow, sobering up slightly. "How do I find you?"

"Just tell Miller," Blaine answered, not wanting to tell more.

"You with him?"

Blaine realized she might be putting Miller in danger. "No. But I see him around." She figured Miller could handle anything that came along. He might not like her and she wasn't all that sure she liked him, but she knew she could trust him.

She left feeling as if finally something might happen. She'd passed along the information without coming in the open, without putting herself or Mark in danger. Winslow didn't strike her as the type of man who did his own dirty work and if this Jimmy was a paid killer for Winslow, he would be the one who had to be arrested before Blaine was safe.

The TV announced a special report. The body found at the clinic was not that of Blaine Anderson, wife of attorney Mark Anderson. The police had not released the information pending further investigation until now.

Blaine moved closer to the TV trying not to act interested. She glanced at Chipper. The broadcast had drawn her full attention.

The report gave all of Sindi Richards's information.

They knew, Blaine realized. Everyone knew. Mark knew. The body in the fire hadn't been hers.

She closed her eyes and fought back tears. She had to get to Mark. She had put him through too much, no matter what the risk, it wasn't fair. Every time she'd tried to get to him something had stopped her, but not this time. She could feel what he must be feeling and the pain might kill them both before any crazy man with dynamite could.

She hurried out not even asking to use the phone.

Pulling the last of her money from her bag, Blaine ran to a pay phone in front of the shelter. She dropped the quarter twice before she managed to shove it into the phone.

She dialed home. No answer.

She tried Mark's office. Only a machine. She didn't dare leave a message. Winslow might get to the machine before Mark.

Digging for the last of her change, she tried to remember Mark's cell. He rarely left the thing on, telling everyone it was for outgoing calls, not incoming. But maybe she'd catch him. At the very least, he'd be the one who got the message.

She dialed a wrong number.

Think! What order were the numbers in? Remember the details, Blaine scolded herself. She dialed again.

One ring. Two

A machine's voice sounded in her ear. "You've reached the phone of Mark Anderson. Please leave a message."

Eventually he'd check his messages and when he did, she'd be waiting, she thought. Somehow they'd have to get through this hell together.

"Mark! It's Blaine. Meet me in front of the Driskill Hotel. No matter what time, I'll wait until you come."

# Eighteen

Mark went back to work a week after the bombing but couldn't keep his mind on the research he needed to do for his upcoming trial. He'd been moved to the second string on all cases where he should have been the lead, but at least he was still involved. He told himself that all he had to do was prove how good he was, as he had when he'd first come to work for the company. Only this time his heart wasn't in it.

His heart was missing!

He'd force himself to complete what he had to at the office, then go home to sleep the afternoon away, conserving energy so he could walk the streets of downtown Austin each night.

Feeling like a zombie, half dead, half alive, he roamed, hoping for a miracle his logical mind told him could never be. Mark wasn't sure how it had happened, but part of him had died when Blaine disappeared and he did not know if he was strong enough to survive both the loss of her and of himself.

He knew the police were looking for her, along with a P.I. firm, but he had to try something besides staying home waiting for them to call. So he walked, looking into the faces of strangers, hoping to see her. Though he knew it couldn't be true, in some primitive/fantasy way his heart told him that she was simply lost and waiting for him to find her.

The world changed that morning of the clinic bombing though he'd been too busy to notice. The earth simply flew out of orbit and by the time he realized what had happened, he could do nothing about it. He lost his footing. No balance remained in his life. Any minute he'd step beyond gravity and drift away. Any day, if he wasn't careful, if he left his vigil for even a second, there would be no big-bang ending to his world. There wouldn't even be time for a sigh. He would simply vanish, as Blaine had...as his life had.

He took ribbing from the other partners about his beard. They said little about the haphazard way he dressed. Forgetting his tie. Wearing the same suit three days in a row. They kept the hints kind, whispering he would need time to get over what everyone in the office called "the tragedy," as if Blaine's disappearance had been a flu to be recovered from.

The kindness eroded into a pity Mark couldn't stand. He wished the partners would complain, or be angry, even threaten to fire him. Anything would be better than them feeling sorry for him. He'd always been powerful, someone to respect, but times were changing...he was changing.

Bettye Ruth, with her eternal quiet charm, seemed to understand and kept all their conversations professional. She didn't just act like a southern lady, he realized, she *was* one. There was a strength about her that got him through emergencies at the office. She never bothered him with words of sympathy or questions about news. It was as if she knew they would fall on deaf ears.

When he told her he'd lost his cell phone, she simply ordered him a new one and programmed all the numbers.

She suggested he call his friends and give them his new number, but Mark didn't want anyone to call. He'd heard enough sympathy to last a lifetime. He did call Randell and the P.I. firm.

Lieutenant Randell offered to meet for coffee, and to Mark's surprise, the conversation was friendly. Though Randell had no news, he understood what Mark was going through and the thirty-minute meeting wasn't as strained as Mark feared it might be. The cop asked about the new cell number and Mark told him that he swore he'd left the cell phone on his desk one night. Randell seemed to think vanishing cell phones were routine.

Mark talked with no one else most days, avoiding conversation at work as well as the casual hellos around the complex. He gave up answering the door and usually turned off the phone so he could sleep afternoons. Tres even quit talking to him. She passed through the apartment obviously looking for the right cat food to appear in her bowl. The eggs he scrambled and tossed in her feeder were starting to resemble a modern-art project. The old cat looked like the poster pet for Weight Watchers.

The only peace he knew lay in the stillness of the streets. It didn't matter if it rained, or how late the hour grew, Mark walked, listening to the sound of his own steps as he looked for the woman who, supposedly, was his wife. A woman who had appeared the morning after the bombing, then vanished.

In his mind he planned what he'd say to her. He held little hope she could be Blaine, but if his wife had lost her memory, he'd have to talk to her as though he were a stranger. Even Blaine without memories would still be shy, he didn't want to frighten her away. Everyone seemed to think they'd find her body in the rubble of the building, but they hadn't. Maybe the woman could have been someone else who'd been at the clinic that morning. If so, she might have seen Blaine those last few minutes.

He spent hours thinking about what must have been Blaine's last thoughts. Did she have a problem? Or was she just looking for something to do? Questions seemed to be his specialty and he had no answers to match them with.

The one question never slipped from his mind but remained. What day, or week, or year had he stopped knowing her as well as he knew himself? When they'd been dating, when they were first married, he would swear he could hear her thoughts. But not lately. Not for a long while. Somewhere in the details of their lives and work they'd lost one another long before the bombing.

Once in a while, he let his mind believe that there was a slim chance the stranger who'd wandered into the shelter that morning could have been Blaine, out of her head, without any memory. He held a grain of hope that he'd find her, that she'd come back. Even if she had no memory of him and their life together, somehow they'd fall in love all over again.

After hours of walking, the panhandlers stopped bothering him for money and treated him more like one of their own than a stranger. In truth, he felt like one of them. They didn't care that he wore the same clothes and never shaved. Among them, his insanity seemed more of a character trait than an illness. They respected his space, moving no closer to him than necessary when passing. The few who greeted him only nodded.

As the night passed, he learned the people of the streets. Not by name, but he knew them just the same. The drunk who slept in the alley between Fourth and

Fifth always snored. The chubby woman who pulled a suitcase behind her filled with empty cans and who sang "Amazing Grace" when she was well into the bottle. The prostitutes who got cheaper as the night aged. The youths who ran in packs and who he knew he'd see again in the courts someday.

The young thugs bothered him more than anyone. They weren't like the panhandlers who begged for change or the college kids who held up signs that said, Will Work for Beer Money. The small gangs were unorganized and unruly. He'd seen them bother people for fun, as if they were playing some kind of game and the streets served as their playground. So far, they'd left him pretty much alone. Maybe he looked as though he might give as much trouble as he got. Maybe they thought he might be an undercover cop. Mark didn't know why they walked around him, but he was glad they did.

Mark picked a corner on Sixth Street and stood in the shadows watching the college kids passing in groups from one bar to another. Memories of the days he'd dated Blaine lingered thick in his head. He used to spend hours telling her his plans over beer and pizza at these cafés. He'd talked of someday practicing law. Of making big money. Of running for office. And Blaine would listen. She always listened. Then she'd say, "I'll be your rock, Mark. Climb as high as you like. I'll be the base you come home to when all the dragons are slain." Then he'd make fun of how she liked to talk in fairy tales and she'd smile the way she always did, as if it was him and not her who couldn't see reality.

He closed his eyes and pressed the back of his head against the cold damp brick of the building. How long had it been since he'd heard her say those words? How many days or months had passed since they'd talked? Really talked?

If he could have her back, he'd stop talking and try listening. Blaine must have had dreams she'd never told him. Was she afraid he'd laugh, or simply not listen? In the ten years they'd been together, he had always thought her dreams were his dreams. Now, when it was too late, he realized he'd never asked her.

Dear God, he almost yelled out, the loneliness felt as if it might swallow him whole any moment.

She couldn't be dead. She couldn't. Mark still needed her. He wanted her so deeply there were no words. If he could go back he would sleep beside her that last night. Maybe if he had held her one more night, all night, his arms wouldn't ache so badly.

"Blaine!" he shouted, startling the drunk sleeping twenty feet away "Damn it, Blaine, don't just leave me."

The drunk sat up. "Keep yelling, buddy, at nobody about your woman being gone and before you know it you'll be sleeping next to me."

"Sorry," Mark said without any interest in the old drunk, or his advice. "I didn't mean to yell."

The bum settled back down on his dirty mattress and dragged a section of cardboard box over him.

*Pull it together* Mark reminded himself. He had every symptom of a man falling completely apart. He'd gone through grief before, he'd lost his mother. Then he'd turned to his studies and for the most part acted as if his mom was still home waiting. Blaine became his family almost from their first date. She'd helped him get through the first Christmas when his father hadn't bothered to call and Mark hadn't been surprised. Being with

Blaine...being with one person...was a thousand miles away from being alone.

Mark made himself a promise that he would work harder tomorrow, but he knew when darkness fell he'd be back walking the streets. Hoping. Wishing. Praying for that one-in-a-million chance that he'd find her again.

# *Nineteen*

Blaine hung up the phone and left in a run. Finally, after over a week, she was making progress, she was doing something. She'd called Mark. It might take him all day to turn on his phone, but when he did, he'd find her message. In the meantime, Chipper would call the cop and relay the information. Maybe they would pick up the thin man in the blue cap quickly. Soon she'd be home.

All she had to do for the next few hours was stay out of sight and keep circling by the hotel until she spotted Mark.

Clouds hung like wet cotton above her. Blaine walked toward the cemetery, staying beneath awnings whenever possible. The rain settled, thickening the air like flour thickens gravy. Within an hour, it soaked her to the bone.

She looked for the little boy who played between the headstones, but he was nowhere to be seen. Maybe he had a home somewhere near and only played in the cemetery in the evenings? She hoped he had a home to go to even if he didn't have someone to take care of him and feed him.

A few prisoners in white clothes rode with a guard along one of the paths. They stopped now and then to pick up a branch or a piece of trash that had blown in from the street. They didn't seem to notice her.

She didn't like the idea of the kid being abandoned or being a runaway. He needed to have someone who made sure he had clean clothes and hot food. Once Mark picked her up, Blaine swore she'd come back to the cemetery and look for the child again.

She circled by the Driskill again and again, watching for Mark's little car, looking for his lean figure waiting for her. The old hotel entrance had a porchlike seating area where she could wait out of the rain, but she was afraid to stay too long.

Twice, she went into the gym and dried off, but few people were there and her safety lay in numbers. She could have climbed above the lockers and slept a few hours, but she was afraid she'd miss Mark. She slipped out into the rain once more.

Finally, the bus stop across the street from the Driskill drew her, with its tiny shelter. People usually stood around the benches, blocking space between the building and the street, but today they huddled together as they waited. The five o'clock commuters had long passed, leaving mostly shift workers, a few students and the homeless.

Blaine waited and watched. Why hadn't Mark checked his messages? Surely he'd be here any minute. In the restaurant across the street, she saw a woman eating soup and wished she could taste it, or even smell it.

That was how she felt in her skin lately. She knew she was living, breathing, but she couldn't quite feel it.

Running her hand over her abdomen, Blaine decided the questions of a baby didn't seem any more real than her life. She no longer owned the problem. She knew it existed but just like the soup, it seemed somehow out of her reach, out of her reality.

She found the two Annas in the midst of those waiting for the bus. Chocolate Anna cautiously watched the people, obviously bothered by having others so near. She gripped her bags with both fists while her black eyes darted around. This stop was like her living room and far too many people had come to call. Vanilla Anna opened one of her many sacks, placing her head inside the bag as she looked for something. Every few minutes, she pulled out and took a gulping breath, like a deep-sea diver going after buried treasure.

Sailor June joined them. She stood just behind the Annas so that anyone wanting to stay out of the rain had to walk the gauntlet between her and the bag ladies' clutter. She was a tiny woman with a wink crammed full of mischief. She was one of those few people who pass through life smiling no matter what their station.

Blaine couldn't hold back a smile. She knew Sailor June checked pockets. Blaine had asked Shakespeare about her, but all the old man knew was that every once in a while June's daughter would drive up and take her off. A few days later the little woman would show back up with a new set of clothes and complaining about being shanghaied by pirates again. Shakespeare said he thought she had a room down on the West End, but he wasn't sure.

In the blink of an eye, Sailor June could slip her fingers into someone's raincoat pocket and back out again. "Having any luck?" Blaine asked in a low voice meant only for June.

"A few bus tokens." The angelic face wrinkled. "And hundreds of dirty tissues. I hate cold season." She wiped her hand on her pants. "Wish folks wouldn't carry the dirty ones around in their pockets. What the blazes you think they're keeping them for? Posterity?''

Blaine laughed. Over the past week she had learned about these people. They weren't like mainstream society by any means, but they had their own set of rules. June, for example, never took more than change, or a few dollars people dropped into their pockets. In truth, most of her benefactors probably didn't even miss the money that slipped from their coats.

Vanilla Anna pulled her head from the bag and twisted around to stare at Blaine. Her curly gray hair was fuzzy with rain.

'''Evening.'' Blaine barely recognized the low tone in her own voice. She decided days ago that the bombing had permanently damaged her vocal cords.

Anna was in no mind to hear today.

Chocolate Anna looked up as her friend dived back inside her sack. '''Evening, Mary. Don't mind her. She's got something on her mind, squashing all else out right now. We should all be thankful for the silence. When she gets in her mothering mood, there ain't no peace to be had.''

Blaine nodded, then pulled the loaf of bread from her gym bag. ''I picked up this at the free-bread line today, but I've still got half a loaf left from yesterday. Would you like some? It's raisin cinnamon.''

Anna raised her eyebrow, waiting for the terms of the trade.

''You would be doing me a favor. I'm tired of carrying it.''

''Oh, all right. If it will help you out.'' She squeezed to test the freshness of the loaf. ''I usually only eat the whole wheat. It's better for you, you know. But I could take this off your hands this one time.''

Another unwritten rule, Blaine thought. Never be beholden.

The other Anna pulled up from her latest dive into the trash bag. "Hi, Mary, my child," she said as if she'd just noticed Blaine. "Did you forget your lessons? You know how you have to keep practicing if you want to play in the band."

"I didn't forget," Blaine answered, touching the old woman's shoulder. "I promise, I'll practice." The game was getting easier, she thought. Blaine no longer felt the need to try to pull the old woman into reality. It was easier just to step into her world. And in her world Anna was the mother to all that passed her way.

"Good." Anna went back to searching.

"What are you looking for?" Blaine asked.

"I had a Lego I found in the park. I thought it might be yours and I know how you are about keeping all your things together."

Blaine watched the crowd as Anna searched the bag. The press of people closed around them as the mass grew in anticipation of the next bus. Most of the people ignored the two homeless ladies, but Blaine had the feeling she was being watched.

Standing, she walked to the edge of the crowd and studied the front of the Driskill Hotel. No one waited at the hotel's entrance. She thought of going back over to the huge gold doors of the hotel, but was afraid if she stood there one of the sleepy hotel guards might notice her. It made more sense to wait here in the crowd at the bus stop and keep watching for Mark.

Blaine moved back to the bench. She could almost feel someone just beyond the light watching her. Staring. Waiting for her to make a move.

She huddled closer to Vanilla Anna.

The rain poured with a vengeance, straight down with waterfall force as though determined to drive all inside. Blaine wanted to leave, seek shelter elsewhere. Even wet, she could probably run into the gym, but she'd told Mark she'd be waiting.

Her best bet was to stay put.

A bus arrived, splashing its way against the curb. Several in the crowd huddled together and made a mad dash for the opening doors as if they'd spotted the way out of hell.

Though fewer people populated the stop, Blaine still huddled into a space on the bench next to the Annas and tried to be invisible. She pulled the hood of her sweat jacket over most of her face. With the clouds, it was impossible to tell how close to sunset it was, but she shouldn't have to wait much longer for Mark.

Blaine couldn't shake the feeling of someone watching her from the shadows just beyond the curtain of rain. Slowly, she positioned her gym bag between her feet, protecting her only belongings.

People came and went with the buses. A few had umbrellas and stood outside the huddle, but most pressed as close as they could, hoping to be shielded from the downpour.

Blaine slowly turned her head, watching the people. Most were students with backpacks, or workers with black lunch boxes. A few businessmen stood with a paper tented over their heads. Three of the thugs she'd seen harassing people at the shelter lurked a few feet away beneath the short storefront overhang. They mumbled among themselves. Their heads were out of the rain, but water splashed around their feet.

Another bus arrived. The rain continued. Occasionally, she heard a slice of conversation. Two men mentioned the baseball scores. A woman asking if the Windsor Point bus had already come. A mother scolded a child who outweighed her by thirty pounds but obviously hadn't achieved independence.

Blaine shivered. It wasn't that cold, but the wind whipped around the buses just enough to blow across her wet clothes. She closed her eyes and tried to think about going home.

In the storm she lost track of time. What if Mark didn't get her message?

Two of the thugs jumped from against the building to the small area covered by the bus-stop awning. They splashed water on already wet people as they stomped in step almost like a small army.

Blaine glanced around. Lost in her thoughts, she hadn't noticed that their numbers had grown.

A tall, thin boy a year or two away from adulthood and his stockier friend tried to start a conversation with a young girl toting a full backpack. The chorus of their buddies still leaned along the building's wall cheering them on as if watching a fight.

"What's your name?" The short one slicked back wet hair from his pimply face.

When the girl turned away, the other thug moved behind her and repeated the question. He stood taller than her by almost a head. A few years older than the other, he had a hardness about his face.

Blaine watched as the boys tried to get the girl to talk.

"Come on, baby," the shorter one begged. "Tell us your name." He glanced at his friend. "She's so hot she could make this rain sizzle."

"She could make me sizzle." The tall thug opened his hand within an inch of her breast. "Just my size."

The girl did her best to ignore them, but while one

talked the other tried to get into her backpack. Each time she twisted away from one, the other moved a little closer until she couldn't twist without bumping into one of them. They acted as if they were only teasing, but terror showed on the girl's face.

"What you reading?" The tall one tried to pull out a book. "Something interesting?"

The stout one laughed. "Not as interesting as what I got to show you, baby. Now, come on, tell us your name."

Blaine clenched her fingers into fists and prepared to fight if they pressed the girl any harder. She felt the tension in the crowd. Several obviously wanted to help but feared getting involved. The two boys were not alone. Several shadows moved outside the shelter and no telling how many of them were thugs waiting to step in if anyone tried to stop the game their friends played with the girl.

Vanilla Anna looked up from her bag, suddenly aware of her surroundings and the boys so near. "Stop teasing her!" she yelled, drawing everyone's attention. "Or I'll paddle you both."

For a moment the boys stopped, then they laughed. The shorter thug pointed his finger at Anna and acted as if he was pulling a trigger, then he blew imaginary smoke from his imaginary weapon.

"We're not teasing her. She loves it," one said, grabbing the girl's arm. "Don't you?"

"Let go!" The girl dropped her pack and fought to pull away.

The other boy gripped her free arm. "Why don't we go somewhere and talk about this? We got lots to talk about and you can catch a later bus."

Blaine had had enough. Just as she stood, a man in a

raincoat stepped in front of her, knocking her back in place beside Anna.

"That's enough." The man's cold, even voice echoed in the tiny space surrounded by walls of rain. "Leave her alone, gentlemen, or I'll do more than paddle your worthless behinds."

Both thugs turned, swelling for a fight.

Blaine watched the stranger's raincoat part and saw a badge clipped beside a gun on his belt. The boys saw it too, for they didn't make a move as a bus splashed to a stop a few feet behind them.

The girl grabbed the straps of her backpack and ran for the open door without glancing back.

"You boys want to know my name?" the officer added. "It's Randell. Lieutenant Randell. I'll be happy to talk to you. How about we go somewhere and do that? I know just the place."

The thugs' bravado melted like sugar armor in the rain. "We weren't doing nothing. Just having a little fun. We weren't hurting nobody." The boy's defenses mumbled together.

Randell looked more bothered than angry. "How old are you two juvenile delinquents? Not old enough to be on the streets, I'll wager."

"We're not on the street," the tall one said. "We were waiting for the bus to take us home from school."

"Yeah," the other one added. "We was just going home from school, minding our own business. We just asked the girl her name, ain't no crime in that, Detective."

Randell didn't appear to be listening. "Let me see some ID." When they hesitated, he added, "All I want is your name. You've got nothing to worry about unless you're wanted for something."

The boys looked at one another. Neither reached for any identification. Again it was the taller of the two who spoke first. "Why are you picking on us? We ain't doing nothing. We was just talking to a girl."

"Turn around and assume the position. My guess is you know the drill." Randell shoved the taller thug into the rain and toward the building. "Next time you say you're coming from school, you might think about what day of the week it is."

At once, Blaine felt as if they were all in a blender and someone had turned on the machine. She wanted to run to Randell and tell him who she was and ask for his protection. But what if he was the "one friend in the force" that Winslow had mentioned that first morning to Jimmy. That would explain why he kept asking questions. Blaine waited and watched.

The tall youth suddenly decided to fight, struggling against the detective who outweighed him by almost double. He swore as Randell tried to cuff him, jerking like a snake dancing on fire.

Randell fought both the boy and the wind flapping his raincoat.

In an instant, the boy was free, darting away.

Shadows of the thugs who watched from the sidelines jumped out of Randell's reach as the detective tried to grab his prey. They played a game of tag with the cop as the tall boy slipped from view.

Blaine rose, seeing her chance to melt into the rain. She had to get as far away from Randell as quickly as possible and do it without him noticing her. He might have no idea how close the woman he was asking questions about was to him, but thanks to Chipper, Blaine knew who he was. If he was Winslow's friend, she wanted nothing to do with him.

The stout thug, who'd been forgotten, crossed in front of her to get to Vanilla Anna, knocking Blaine back against the bench.

"This is all your fault, you old bag," he whispered, his gaze darting to make sure Randell couldn't hear. "If you hadn't yelled, no one would have noticed us." Rage won out over reason as he advanced.

Before Blaine could react, the kid pulled a knife and swung toward Anna, who still studied her bag unaware the boy was even talking to her. People scrambled in every direction.

Blaine opened her mouth to warn Anna as the blade swung wide. Someone shoved her hard from behind, knocking her into danger.

The steel dug into Blaine's side before she could move, cutting through her jacket and into her flesh.

She looked through tears of pain at the kid, seeing surprise and horror in his eyes. He pocketed the knife and stumbled backward into the traffic. A car clipped his right thigh, but he kept on running like a wounded animal until the rain swallowed him from view.

Blaine fought a scream and doubled forward, hiding her injury. Randell ran toward the boy, dodging cars in an effort to catch at least one of the troublemakers.

This was her chance, maybe her only chance. He'd been the one watching her, she was sure of it. If the boy's antics hadn't distracted him, she might be in Randell's grip, and if he was Winslow's friend, she might be dead before the rain stopped. She pressed her hand across the wound and willed herself to stand.

Vanilla Anna looked up at her with questioning eyes. "Leaving so soon, Mary? I was hoping you'd stay for pie."

Blaine nodded. "Watch my bag for me, will you?"

She couldn't hold her hand over the wound and lug the gym bag.

She made it to the phone booth a half block away and searched for her last few coins. Frantically, she dialed Mark's cell. She'd tried home and the office before. This number had to work. It had to.

It was picked up on the first ring. "Hello."

Blaine froze. It wasn't Mark.

"Hello! Is there someone on the line?"

She recognized Harry Winslow. Opening her mouth, she tried to get the words out to ask for Mark but couldn't manage a sound. If Winslow had the cell phone, he knew she was waiting.

"Who is this?" Harry said low as if he could somehow see through the phone line. "Blaine, is that you? Tell me where you are. I'll send someone for you."

Blaine glanced back toward the bus stop and thought she saw a thin man blink into sight with the lightning, then disappear once more into the blackness. He could have been standing just behind her. He could have pushed her toward the knife.

She hung up the phone, not knowing who to trust. She had no idea why they wanted her dead, but deep down she knew they did and she'd walked right into their hands.

But who to trust? She couldn't get to Mark, somehow Winslow had cut him off from her. Randell might be a good cop, but she couldn't be sure. After all, he gave Chipper liquor and that didn't seem right.

Miller.

She wasn't sure she had enough strength left to make it to Shakespeare's corner, but if she could, he'd know where to find Miller.

Blaine walked in the opposite direction from where

Randell and the boy had gone. Light-headed, she felt the wound in her side sting against her hand, as though the blade had been molten hot when it pressed into her.

Rain washed her face as she stumbled forward, making no effort to move below the overhangs. The rain no longer mattered. She had to get away.

"Keep moving," she whispered. "Keep moving." Not only her life, but Mark's, depended on it.

Glancing over her shoulder, Blaine thought she saw a lean shadow following her. She bit back the pain and tried to run. Her feet stumbled through low spots where water splashed over her shoes, but she didn't slow. Her body was hot and cold at the same time. Thick blood oozed its way through the fingers covering her side.

Run! she told herself. Run!

When she finally reached the corner with the boarded-up coffee shop, she turned and took a breath, listening for the sound of someone still following.

The rain and her heart pounding muffled all else. Blaine shoved away from the wall and moved toward Shakespeare's doorway.

She gathered the strength to look back. The outline of a man kept coming, closing the distance between them.

She waited for the blackness after the lightning. When it came, she vanished down the dark passageway to the shop's entrance where she knew Shakespeare slept.

# Twenty

Leaving the office, Mark pulled off his coat and tie before he reached his car. Stuffing the clothes in the back seat with what seemed like half of his wardrobe, he headed toward Subway. Since the night he'd gone with Lilly, Mark frequented the fast-food diner on a nightly basis. Not because he particularly liked it, but more because if he drove to the same place every night, that was one less decision he had to make.

He'd ordered straight down the menu. It didn't matter. He always said extra lettuce and olives more out of habit than any hunger or care.

Once home, he flipped on the TV, slid the old take-out wrappers off the coffee table into the pile of other leftovers and dropped onto the couch. Opening his sandwich, he noticed the cushions were starting to sag on the sofa. The one piece of furniture had become his pod. He sat there. Slept there. Ate there. At this rate he could sublet the other fifteen hundred square feet and just live on the couch. Rooms that had once been cool and stylish now only seemed cold and gray.

As he always did, he offered to share his supper with Blaine's finicky cat who jumped on the table within inches of the sandwich. Mark didn't know, or care, if it was close to the cat's lunchtime, or dinnertime, but he figured the cat didn't either. He passed a serving on a napkin.

To his surprise, Tres ate a small piece of roast beef and waited for more.

He tried an olive.

She waited.

Next came lettuce. Then bread.

She meowed in what he was sure was a swear word if he could only understand her language.

He offered another piece of beef.

She smelled it the way a connoisseur of wine smells the cork, then ate.

Mark tore off a few inches of his sandwich and passed it down the coffee table. "I should have guessed you'd never go for one of the ones under six grams of fat."

Tres ignored him.

"How about tomorrow, I buy you your own?" He smiled. For some strange reason walking into Subway and ordering two sandwiches didn't seem quite as lonely. "We'll be sure to hit the two-for-one deal."

He watched Tres pick around the cheese bread, licking the mayo and ketchup, ignoring the lettuce. "I don't think I can say hold the bread, but I could probably remember extra mayo."

An hour later, as he stretched on the couch realizing he'd been sleeping, Mark felt a heavy weight on his chest. In the first few moments of waking he thought he might be having a heart attack.

Then a paw pushed against his chin as if warning him not to move. The bothersome cat he didn't even like was spread out on top of him as if he was her own personal cushion. She seemed to have decided that if he could live in a few square feet of the town house, she would also.

Mark closed his eyes and went back to sleep without further disturbing Tres.

When he awoke again, it was well after dark and the cat had deserted him. Mark pulled on a navy jacket and headed out without noticing the weather.

Parking his car on a side street near the capitol, he began his trail through downtown. The rain didn't bother him. It kept most folks off the streets, making it easier to move from block to block. With each person he passed, Mark glanced up, sizing them up, hoping to see something, anything of the woman who'd fit Blaine's description. He knew his chances were shrinking by the day. But she might still be on the streets. If the woman was at the clinic, she might still remember Blaine.

He tried not to dwell on the possibility that the woman who'd been seen might be Blaine. How does a man walk up to his wife if she has no memory of him? He knew the only way she'd be on the streets would be if she'd lost her memory and if that was lost, were they lost?

Mark used his new cell to call Detective Randell and check in. He wasn't sure if they were becoming friends, or if Randell still considered him more a pest than a help, but it didn't matter. Mark had no plans of giving up. He knew the cop would be somewhere on the streets. Randell didn't seem to have much of a life other than his job. Mark could understand that.

After several questions, the officer admitted they had a new lead but wouldn't talk about it on the phone. Mark knew better than to push. Right now Randell was the only ally he had.

Harry Winslow had even used his contacts at the police force and he'd told Mark that since Blaine hadn't returned, there was a strong likelihood she'd left him. He suggested Mark begin the healing process of getting over her. File a missing persons report and make a public notice of a divorce action.

Mark refused. Blaine was alive, and somehow he'd find her.

Mark hung up from Randell agreeing to meet later for coffee. He cut the connection without bothering to say goodbye.

A few blocks later, when Mark turned the corner on Seventh, he spotted Randell climbing out of a beat-up Ford. He wore a tan raincoat that looked old and too small to button all the way down. Within seconds the detective was soaked, but like Mark, he didn't seem to mind. Randell walked at a steady pace toward a bus stop half a block away.

Mark followed, trying to think like a cop. If Randell were looking for someone, say, a thin blond woman, tonight would be a good night to search. Everyone, including the homeless, would be huddled waiting out the rain. She might be in a stairwell, or alley somewhere, then again, she might be in a crowd. If they were looking for a woman who wanted to be invisible, the rain might change her patterns. It might draw her out in the open as easily as pull her into the shadows.

He watched Randell circle the people at the bus stop. The cop was smart, he stayed in the rain where no one more than a few feet away from him was likely to notice him.

Following Randell's lead, Mark did the same, staying just close enough to Randell to make out the tan raincoat, just far enough away so that he could take a step backward if Randell turned his direction. Before the man could focus, Mark knew he could melt into the blackness of the downpour.

When Randell didn't turn around, Mark moved closer

to the shelter until he stood just outside the dry circle. Slowly, he began to make out the people. A few he'd seen before on the streets, a few looked familiar, like maybe he'd passed them ten times, or a hundred, and never really bothered to see them.

The two rounded piles of rags, who were always at the stop, were on the bench tonight. The bag ladies reminded him of a set of salt and pepper shakers. They didn't really match, but he'd never seen one without the other.

He noticed the drunk who usually slept in the alley nearby huddled among the others. Mark couldn't help but wonder if the man's bed was floating in two inches of water, thanks to the rain. He also felt sorry for anyone standing within three feet of the old drunk. The damp smell of him had to be bad.

Mark searched the crowd that grew and shrank with the coming and going of buses.

None looked like Blaine or the woman the shelter lady had told Randell about. There was a woman, knotted into a ball beside one of the old bag ladies, who looked as if she might be almost thin enough, but even in the pale streetlight Mark could tell the hair sticking up from her hood was brown, not blond and black-framed glasses hid her eyes. She had none of Blaine's posture, no straight back, no chin held high.

People talked, shuffled, waited. Then, unexpectedly, Mark heard Blaine's laughter blend amid the noise. More the echo of her laugh, he thought. That light giggle she used to do when something was funny just to her. A private joke.

He took a step forward trying to figure out if he'd really heard it or simply thought he had. The possibility of madness crossed his thoughts. All his life, everything down to the last detail had been thought out, planned. But no longer. Lately, he seemed to be drifting without a compass.

A bus pulled up. People blocked his path as they hurried from the shelter of the stop to the door of the bus. Mark heard Randell's voice over the noise, then others, but they didn't matter. He only listened for the laughter.

The voices grew as he pushed his way through the crowd to beneath the stop's covering. Slinging water from his face, he watched as Randell slammed a youth against a building. People jumped suddenly like popcorn dancing on one hot spot in a pan. They all seemed like shadows without faces no matter which direction he looked.

A kid of about fifteen ran into the street, drawing everyone's attention as cars honked and skidded on the wet road. Randell ran after him, shouting.

Mark followed for several steps before he realized he would be walking away from where he'd heard her laughter. He turned back to the crowd, but they'd scattered...hurrying to the buses, giving up on staying dry, frightened...he had no idea why. They ran just like roaches scared by the light.

Only the two old bag ladies remained on the bus-stop bench.

Mark moved toward them, listening to their voices as they questioned what had happened. The laugh had not come from one of them.

"The woman who was just sitting here..." He had no idea how to finish the sentence. He pointed to the place beside one of the women. "The woman in a hooded jacket?"

The rounded bag lady with warm brown skin glanced up at him. "I didn't see any woman," she mumbled between bites of bread. "Or maybe I've seen a hundred tonight and you want me to remember one. It's a waste of my time. Go away."

"The woman who was just here sitting next to you." Mark turned to the other bag lady, who didn't seem to be listening as she rummaged through one of her huge plastic bags.

He moved closer and spoke louder. "Do you know who the woman…"

The black bag lady answered again, louder this time. "I done told you we didn't see any woman sitting there. We ain't the population police. You want a woman, you'll have to go a few blocks over and just walk the street. If you're interested, it's like they can smell you. They'll come out of nowhere and find you."

"No. I'm not looking for any woman." Mark fought not to swear. "I'm just asking about the woman who was here only a minute ago. She had a hood pulled over her head. I couldn't see her face."

The other old lady pulled a Lego from her bag. "I found Mary's toy," she beamed as she showed it to Mark.

Her friend passed two slices of bread to her and said, "Keep it for her until later, would you, Momma."

"All right." She dropped the plastic block back into the cluttered bag and bit into her bread.

Mark knelt in front of her and asked in a low, slow tone, "Who was the woman sitting beside you?"

The pale gray-haired old lady stared at him blankly. "I didn't see anyone. It don't pay to see people."

"But I heard a woman laugh," Mark said more to himself than the two homeless women.

To his surprise, the pale old woman answered, "Yeah,

I heard that too. She does have an angel's laugh, don't she.''

Mark looked up into aging eyes long out of touch with any reality. "So, someone was sitting beside you?"

"No." The bag lady patted his hand as if he were a child. "I didn't see anybody. I never see anyone, even when I say I do."

Mark stood and walked into the rain, toward his car. He knew he'd be back tomorrow night and the night after that. Searching for the woman who someone thought looked like his wife. Listening for the sound of her laughter that he thought he'd heard.

By the time he reached his car he knew he wouldn't be telling anyone about what he thought he'd heard. They'd think he was crazy. A man wishing for something he'd lost. A man who wouldn't face facts. Now the people at the office would probably start whispering about how they could understand why his wife left him, after all, he wasn't quite right.

Yet, even as he drove away, the memory of her laughter still echoed in his mind. He'd find that woman no matter how many nights it took. Unless he finally snapped and started sitting at the bus stop, digging for Legos in a trash bag.

# Twenty-One

Blaine saw Shakespeare standing deep in the shadows of the abandoned café's threshold, watching people run along the walk. Every few seconds, almost as though he thought he might get caught, he raised a bottle wrapped in a paper bag to his lips and gulped once, then lowered it.

Ignoring the rain blurring her vision, she tried to focus on Shakespeare as she stumbled toward him. She bumped into one man and he mumbled an apology. When she collided with the next stranger, he muttered an oath. Blaine tried to concentrate on reaching the old man in the doorway before the blackness creeping over her mind as thick as ink covered all thought.

Car lights and stoplights reflected off the water that dripped from the building's roof like multicolored strands of beads blocking the entrance to the spot the old man called home.

She almost knocked Shakespeare over when she finally staggered in from the rain. She thought he'd seen her coming then realized too late that he hadn't.

Frightened, bloodshot eyes glared at her.

Shakespeare's bottle hit the concrete and shattered as he grabbed her, trying to steady her.

"Now hold on!" he yelled, then softened as recognition crossed his face. "What be this tragedy, my fair

Mary?'' His words slurred. ''Come through the depths of hell this wicked night.''

''Help me,'' she whispered. ''Please, help me. I need to find Miller.''

He looked down at his broken bottle, then at her.

''I'm sorry.'' She fought the urge to cry. Just when Blaine thought nothing in this world could make things worse, life proved her wrong. She'd broken the one thing Shakespeare cared about more than life and she did not even have the money to repay him. ''I may have been followed. I need a place to hide. Help me.''

To her surprise Shakespeare looked as if he cared. ''I've heard talk of your plight, my child. Gossip's cloth doth blow lightly in the wind.'' He pulled his hand away from her waist and stared at the blood that covered his dirty fingers.

''You're hurt.'' For once he forgot to color his words. ''How badly?''

Blaine lifted the end of her sweatshirt. Just above the band of her jogging pants ran a crimson line. The flesh gaped open for several inches. A thin waterfall of blood dripped down her flesh to soak into the thick cotton of her waistband.

The clouds grew darker. The world circled around her. She was hot and cold at the same time. She wanted to be home and all this to be only a dream.

She fought to clear her head, but the clouds moved in fast. ''Mark,'' she whispered as Shakespeare lowered her to the ground. ''Oh, Mark, I'm sorry, so sorry.''

She closed her eyes, feeling the broken pieces of the whiskey bottle cut into her back and the smell of cheap liquor pollute the air. But it didn't matter. Blaine no longer cared about anything but hiding in the darkness that closed in around her. She was a little girl again hiding in the closet, closing out everything.

Vaguely she heard Miller's angry voice yelling at the old drunk. Someone picked her up as if she were a child and carried her back out into the storm. Rain splashed over her. Powerful arms bound her in a tight grip. They plowed through the sheets of rain like a tiny boat in a storm, fighting to survive.

Blaine relaxed as her mind drifted back on feather pillows and unconsciousness dulled all feeling, all pain. The last thing she heard was a strong heart pounding, driving them faster and faster through the storm.

When she awoke, the rain was gone but Miller was still yelling. "You know why I didn't take her to the hospital. They'd need too many forms filled in! I don't know much about her, but I know she is in some kind of trouble and doesn't want folks asking too many questions."

Blaine opened her eyes a fraction. An elderly man with snow-white hair and long, thin hands leaned over her. Miller stood at her side, his silhouette twice that of the stranger's.

"I gave up medicine twenty years ago, Luke." The old man shook his head. "I'm not sure I remember enough to help her, and I'm not strong enough to do much good."

"You knew more than most to start with. You can afford to forget a little." Miller lowered his voice. "If it hadn't been for you, a great many of us wouldn't have come back from Nam and we both know it. So stop being modest and do what you were meant to do in this lifetime."

Blaine drifted, thinking the two looked like a pelican and a walrus having a conversation. A children's story threaded through her mind, a village where animals talked.

"That was a long time ago. My hands shake now," the doctor said, and in her mind the walrus echoed.

"I know, but you can still help."

"That was war," the doctor added as he pulled supplies from drawers.

"And this isn't?" Miller frowned. "If she had anywhere else to go, she wouldn't be on the streets, Doc. And she's not real bright as far as I can tell. Only friend she's made is me."

"Well, that's reason enough to feel sorry for her," the white-haired man mumbled more to himself than Miller. "Your friendship has been a cross I've had to bear for over thirty years. You won't even leave me alone and let me die in peace." He shooed Miller aside and pulled on a white apron, giving up the argument without another word.

The old doctor leaned closer and noticed Blaine watching him. "Hello there, young lady. I'm Dr. Early. Seth Early. Would you mind if I take a look at that side of yours? There appears to be a problem with blood dripping from it. I think we might be able to make that stop." She thought he looked a bit younger when he stopped talking about himself and started worrying about her.

He asked so politely. No harsh orders. No, I'm-important-and-in-a-hurry attitude. He could have been asking her to dance at the symphony ball.

"All right," Blaine answered and rolled to her unharmed side.

Dr. Early lifted her sweatshirt without any expression on his face, but Miller, standing just behind him, grimaced at what he saw. The old doctor motioned for the big man to hold her off the table while he removed her sweatshirt. As Miller gently lowered her back to the table, the doctor spread a sheet atop her chest.

"How did this happen?" He reached for a white towel and pressed it over the wound.

Blaine forced words. "I was at the bus stop. A kid pulled a knife. I got in the way." She noticed Miller's eyebrow lifted in doubt. "The kid wasn't trying to cut me, but someone pushed me forward," she said, more for Miller than the doctor. "I was just in the wrong place."

Dr. Early motioned with his head for Miller to press down on the bandage. When the big man followed his silent command, the doctor pulled another sheet across her and gently removed her shoes and pants. Then he hurried to the sink and began scrubbing his hands. "I can give you something for the pain and to fight infection but I need to ask you a few questions."

She nodded.

"Are you on any drugs, my dear?"

"No."

"Any medications, any health conditions I should know about?"

Blaine fought back tears. "Something is wrong inside me. I've been feeling sick in my stomach. But it has nothing to do with the wound. Something is just wrong with me deep inside and has been for weeks now."

The kind doctor replaced his hand where Miller's had been and asked the big man to leave.

Miller hesitated, weaving back and forth like a bull before finally heading toward the door.

The doctor waited.

Miller stopped, his hand on the knob as he turned back to them. "I'll go wash up," he mumbled as if it were his decision to leave. 'But I'll be within shouting distance if you need me''

"If you'll give the lady's clothes to Mrs. Bailey, she'll have them washed by the time our guest needs them again." The doctor said the words calmly, as though she had come in for a visit.

Blaine looked around the room for the first time. It was decorated like an old-time doctor's office from a hundred years ago, with strange smoke-colored bottles lining the walls and even stranger instruments displayed across the tops of the shelves. One wall was covered with old black-and-white pictures of a small western town.

Dr. Early smiled. "Don't worry. You weren't pulled back in time. This was my father's office seventy years ago."

The doctor's voice was tranquil as he prepared everything he would need. "I grew up watching him treat patients in this room. When he died, we closed it off, planning to move it intact to the museum. I live mostly on the second floor, and after I retired I never got around to calling the movers. I kind of like the feeling of home I get when I come in here. My father had a family practice in Austin for almost fifty years and though he updated the other rooms on the first floor, he never changed a thing in this first office."

Blaine was hardly aware of his touch as he talked. His low, kind voice calmed her nerves and his thin hands had a gentle touch. She had little doubt that, in his prime, he'd been a great doctor.

"Now, I'm going to touch from your shoulder to your legs. Let me know if you feel any pain anywhere besides where the wound is."

She tried not to jerk when his fingers moved over her

abdomen, pushing slightly in first one place than another. Without commenting, he slid his hands up to her breast. "Have your breasts been tender, my dear?"

"Yes." She hadn't really thought about it much, but they had been.

The doctor's hands moved slowly down along her ribs. She noticed he twisted both her arms slightly, probably looking for needle marks.

He talked as he worked. "A few years ago I decided to clean this place up and treat kids in the neighborhood with skinned knees and a few of the homeless who have nowhere else to go."

Blaine held her breath as he cleaned the wound.

"Why don't you tell me what you think is wrong inside you while I work. Maybe I could help. In my years I've seen about every illness you can think of and a few you can't."

A tear slid off the side of her face. Blaine realized she'd been trying to tell someone for weeks but had no one to talk to. "I haven't had a period for over three months, but that's not unusual. I've never been regular. But this time I've felt different. Sick to my stomach, tired, hungry. Something's wrong. My whole body feels strange."

She stared at the ceiling feeling her face warm with embarrassment.

"Is it possible you could be pregnant?"

"It's possible but unlikely. I did one of those home pregnancy tests and it showed that I was, but a doctor told me when I had my first pelvic that he doubted I'd ever be able to conceive or carry a child." She swallowed. She had to be honest about it all. "When my mother was my age, she thought she was pregnant and it turned out she had cancer." Blaine closed her eyes.

"She died." She wanted to tell him how her parents never got along, how they separated and tried to get back together a dozen times. When her mother thought she was pregnant, the fights were worse than ever. When she found out she had cancer, Blaine's father couldn't deal with her and finally left for good.

Dr. Early dropped a bloody towel into a pan beside the bed and continued to work.

He reached for a bottle inside the cabinet. Blaine noticed, though the outside of the furnishings looked like outdated equipment, the inside seemed to have all the necessary supplies. He handed her two pills and a glass of water

"I'd like you to close your eyes now. What I'm giving you won't do any harm to a baby if one grows inside, but it's going to make you feel sleepy."

She swallowed and tried to relax on the table. For some strange reason sharing the secret she'd carried made her feel like a weight had been lifted. Even with all the fear and trouble this past week, the thought that she might be pregnant still whispered in the back of her mind. Maybe the test had been right, maybe it was a baby and not some cancer growing inside her. But that still didn't solve the problem of Mark not wanting children. Maybe not ever, he'd once said, but definitely not now. Children weren't in his plan.

Closing her eyes, she remembered how Mark had told her once that his parents blamed him for all the bad luck they'd had in their life. He'd been unplanned and unwanted. He swore he'd never bring a child into this world until he was ready. A few times over the years Blaine had thought of going to a specialist who worked with women who had trouble conceiving, but other things got in the way.

Blaine hardly felt the needle slide into her skin just above the wound. She tried to think of being home with her cat curled up in her lap. As the doctor worked, she thought of how much fun it would be to watch an old movie and eat popcorn. Rainy days are for old movies, she told herself over and over. Rainy days are for staying inside.

Like an old-time radio broadcast, the doctor's velvet voice continued, telling her how Miller must have run ten blocks to get here. And how he would swear the man was as strong as he'd been thirty years ago in Vietnam. He told stories, but Blaine only half listened as, in her mind, she curled around her cat and slept the rain away.

When she awoke, the place where she'd been stabbed felt tight and warm. But when Blaine reached to touch it, bandages covered by soft flannel blocked her path.

Dr. Early sat a few feet away in a swivel chair. He'd propped his feet up on the bottom rail of the table she lay on and was reading a book. "You're awake." He smiled at her as he closed the book. "How do you feel?" He looked bone tired, as though he'd run a race all his life and now tried to keep going just a few more steps until he reached the end.

"Fine," she lied. In truth, she wasn't sure she could have stood if the building had been on fire. "Weak," she admitted when she realized he was waiting for another answer to his question.

"That's all right. You've been asleep for an hour. I finally sent Miller upstairs to one of the extra bedrooms. He threatened to kill me if I didn't call him with any changes."

The doctor's words didn't make sense. Blaine could

not pull the corners of her mind together enough to reason.

"If you feel up to it, I've got a couch in the other room. It would make good sleeping for the rest of the night and I'd be right upstairs if you needed anything."

Move, Blaine thought, that was an idea. She reached to pull the sheet up and encountered soft flannel once more.

"Sorry about the nightgown, but all Mrs. Bailey had was flannel. She helped me get it over your head after I pulled a few bits of glass out of your back. You slept like a baby, resting your head on her shoulder as I worked."

"I fell on a bottle," Blaine remembered.

"I figured that. Whiskey, I'd guess." He offered her his arm and she pulled up slowly. The gown covered her toes and could have wrapped around her twice.

"Mrs Bailey's a good-size woman. She goes home most nights, but she keeps clothes in a spare bedroom, just in case the weather's bad like it was tonight. Hates getting wet as bad as a cat. It was almost midnight when the rain lifted enough for her to head out."

The doctor laughed. "She'd make two of you, and if you eat her cooking a few days, you'll see why."

Carefully, he helped Blaine to stand up. "Mrs. Bailey made up the couch for you to sleep on. It's in the sitting room right between the bathroom and the kitchen, so you should be close to whatever you need. If I thought you could make it, I'd offer you a room upstairs."

"This will be fine. Thank you. You're very kind." He'd not only doctored her, he now offered her a place to sleep.

"Any friend of Miller's..." He paused, laughing.

"Actually, we may be the only two friends of Miller's. We should be kind to each other."

They shuffled through a door and into a little room with tall windows along one wall and heavy drapes that looked as if they could shut out the world.

When he lowered her to the makeshift bed, he knelt on one knee.

Blaine pulled a quilt over herself, ready to get back to sleep, but the doctor didn't move away.

"Tell me about your parents, child."

Blaine didn't want to answer, but she owed him too much to be unkind. "My father left sometime before my mom died. My mother dropped me with a neighbor who always felt she got stuck with me. Mom said she was going to the doctor and would pick me up soon."

"She died of cancer?"

Blaine shook her head. "She drove her car into a truck. They ruled it an accident but the neighbor told me she killed herself because she couldn't deal with her problems. The police told me she was dead and then for hours it seemed I had to listen to the neighbor calling her a coward for not thinking of anyone but herself."

Early's old eyes told Blaine he understood. "You're afraid if this thing wrong with you is cancer, you might not be brave."

Blaine swallowed. "I come from a line of cowards. My dad ran out when times got hard. My mother killed herself."

He smiled. "I think what you did tonight, running through the rain to find Miller, was very brave. Do you have any other family, child?"

Blaine shook her head.

The doctor patted her hand. "Times like these it's good to have family. I know how alone you feel, I've survived my wife and both my children dying. That's not the way God meant it to be.''

She closed her eyes, preparing for what she knew he was about to tell her. He was right, she could survive no matter what.

The old man coughed in his handkerchief.

She looked up at him, holding her breath.

''A baby grows inside you, my dear. I'm guessing you're almost four months along. So from now on you've got a family.''

''No cancer?''

''No cancer. It's a new life.''

''Are you sure?''

He smiled. ''It's a baby. I've gone through this with a few hundred women over the years, but it still leaves me with a sense of wonder.''

When she didn't answer, he patted her hand and whispered, 'You rest now. We'll talk more in the morning.''

# Twenty-Two

The morning after he thought he heard Blaine's laughter, Mark faced the day without interest. Life had leaked into his dreams. He'd listened for her most of the night. He woke thinking of the way she moved, the way her sunshine hair brushed her shoulders, the way she always smelled of spring. He smiled remembering how she jumped from bed in the mornings to brush her teeth and put on makeup as if he might love her less if she wasn't perfect.

He realized nothing would have made him love her less, but he could have loved her more. Dear God, he could have loved her more. The realization made him angry at himself and at her for accepting so little.

While he showered, Mark decided he must have imagined he heard her laugh near the bus stop. Or there had simply been someone who sounded a little like his wife among the crowd huddled in the rain. Even though he told himself another woman couldn't have laughed like her, he reasoned it was the only explanation.

Not impossible, he considered. But unlikely, his logical mind repeated.

Pulling on the only clean dress shirt left in his closet, Mark headed out of the front door. He took the stairs two at a time. He wasn't healing, he told himself, he was adjusting to the pain of losing her. Like a ballet dancer or a bull rider, he had learned to live with the ache deep inside and there was no use dwelling on it.

When he stopped for gas and his usual breakfast of coffee, he noticed a dry cleaner's sign on one of the doors of a strip mall across the street. Ten minutes later, he emptied the back seat of his car, leaving the lady in the cleaners sorting.

Walking into the office, he got the usual stares that silently said, "You're late" and "Why don't you pull it together," but Mark was becoming an expert at acting as if he didn't notice. In truth, he preferred those silent comments to the ones of pity a few kindhearted office workers sometimes allowed to show.

Pity was a punch in the gut. They felt sorry for him when they thought she was dead, but now they seemed to look more closely as if saying, "Poor man, he lost his wife. Wonder what was wrong with him?"

Or worse, he'd see in their eyes, "He's slipping, and to think he was almost ready to run for office." No one mentioned that cream now. No one had since Blaine disappeared.

Mark hurried into his private office, trying to remember if he had combed his hair after the shower. He ran his fingers through strands longer than he'd ever allowed them to be. No curl or wave ever appeared in his thick hair, making him look a little shaggy if he didn't keep it cut short. But he almost laughed, the hair went with the beard that framed his jawline.

"Mrs. Moore." He leaned his head around the wall separating his office from his secretary's. If Dell ever made a prototype of the perfect secretary, they'd model it after Bettye Ruth Moore. Efficient, calm and impersonal. She had to be about the same age as Mark, but she seemed like a thirty-year seasoned veteran of the office. When they retired years from now, Mark planned to ask her if she liked him, for she left no clue one way or the other.

"Yes, Mr. Anderson?"

She looked surprised and he tried to remember if he had bothered to speak to her for days.

"Would you make me a hair appointment?"

"Of course," she answered quickly. "Anything else?"

Mark knew there should be more. Before Blaine died he used to give Bettye Ruth a list of what had to be done each morning. "The case I'm working on..." he started.

"It was passed to Hodges last week," she answered.

"Oh." Mark realized he didn't care. He glanced at his clean desk, normally stacked with files. "And the other cases?"

She looked as if she didn't want to answer. Her words came out in almost a whisper. "The others have taken them over. They thought you might like to handle a few pro bono cases and the walk-ins until you're running full steam again."

Mark wanted to tell her he might never be running "full steam" again, but none of this was Bettye Ruth's fault. He walked back into his office and stared at his calendar, trying to remember how many days he'd bothered to come in last week. Two? Three? No wonder they'd passed his work along.

He leaned back in his chair, thinking about how long it had been since he'd handled walk-ins. With an old office downtown, his partners still hung on to some of the practices from their beginning years, like handling wills, and small legal problems for almost anyone who wandered in. They charged a base fee that would surprise most people. Mark figured the price hadn't been raised in twenty years. If he handled walk-ins, he'd be giving his time away.

It had been almost two weeks since Blaine's disappearance and he was the one who seemed to have died. Mark didn't need an analyst to tell him he was falling apart. He was well aware of the fact. She'd been the marrow of his life.

"Mr. Anderson?"

Mark swung away from the window. "Yes, Mrs. Moore." When had he stopped calling her Bettye Ruth? When had he become Mr. Anderson? He thought they'd been almost friends when he'd started, but now he wasn't so sure. Maybe she wanted no part of his grief and was afraid if she was too friendly he'd unload all his problems on her. Bettye Ruth might never think of shortening her name, but she was smart. Maybe she was simply distancing herself from him. No one in the office wanted to be tied too closely with a man on his way down.

"An admittance clerk from the hospital is on the phone. She's demanding to speak to you."

For a moment Mark couldn't move. All the memories of waiting outside the morgue for Blaine returned. It seemed as if he'd met the entire hospital staff that night. They'd all stopped by, asking him if he needed anything, hurrying on before he could think of an answer.

When Mark didn't respond, she moved closer to his desk.

"She was told to call you. It appears to be an emergency." Bettye Ruth picked up his phone and handed it to him as if he were a child.

"Hello," Mark managed to say.

"Hello," a voice finally returned, sounding busy and

bothered at the same time. "Is this Mark Anderson, attorney-at-law?"

"Yes." Mark straightened and reached for a pen. This was business of some kind. He could handle that. His blood rushed like a racehorse stepping into the gate.

"We have a client of yours here at the hospital. A Lilly Crockett, age sixty-eight. Just admitted with what looks like a broken leg. She says we can't touch her until you get here. She won't even fill out the paperwork without her attorney present."

"I'll be right there." Mark hung up the phone and laughed. It appeared his neighbor was expanding her territory.

He rounded his desk, wanting to get to the hospital as fast as possible. He didn't like the idea of Lilly being in pain and, he admitted to himself, he didn't like the attitude of the clerk who acted as if Lilly was a problem, not a person. If she was in trouble, they should be doing all they could, not complaining about her over the phone.

"Mrs. Moore!" he yelled, then realized she was three feet away. "I've got a client who needs me to come to the hospital. I'll be back as soon as I can."

She stood beside her desk, his briefcase in her hand as he passed. For the first time in over a week, she smiled. "I'll be here if you need me, Mr. Anderson. I stuffed in a few general forms that might be helpful in a hospital situation. Standard wills, power of attorney, living wills."

"Thank you." He nodded, not bothering to ask how she'd guessed he might need the briefcase.

"I may be calling with instructions when I know more details." It was a lie, but it felt so good.

Ten minutes later he entered Brackenridge Hospital's emergency room. Just inside the sliding glass doors, the place splintered into a maze with the smoky glass of a police office watching over the mayhem. Several people sat against one wall wrapped in white blankets, waiting their turn while staff rushed past. The double electric doors opened and closed with a swishing sound as steady as a heartbeat.

Before he could ask where to go, he heard Lilly yelling. He pushed his way past a crowd in the waiting room until he could see his neighbor.

She appeared even more determined than usual. She slapped at the hands of a nurse who kept trying to help her. "You're not giving me anything. I can't take shots. I can't. Hate the things. Always have."

When the nurse suggested she calm down, Lilly threatened her with bodily harm.

Mark pushed past the EMT worker and silently offered Miss Lilly his hand. No matter what state she was in, the old woman needed to know someone was there to stand at her side.

Everyone looked at him as if he'd just stuck his arm into the cage of a lion.

"'Morning, Lilly,'" he said as he wrapped his fingers around her chubby hand. "You having a little trouble with the world this morning?"

She took a deep breath and gripped his hand as tightly as a dockworker might. "I need a friend. Someone I can trust.' She made no apology.

"I'm here. And I'm not going anywhere for as long as you need me."

Suddenly the crowd turned to him for answers. No one questioned that he was next of kin. He moved through the system, staying right beside Lilly, answering questions, filling out paperwork.

She calmed with him near but wouldn't answer anyone's questions but his, and when he told her she had to do something, Lilly accepted the order.

Mark tried not to watch as they set the leg. He concentrated on talking to Lilly, finding out the details of how she fell coming back from her mailbox.

Lilly explained she was reading a letter while walking back into the building and hadn't noticed the steps until she was right at them. She blamed the whole thing on her third husband because the letter was from his lawyer. "Willard hired someone to find me and the first thing I hear from him in almost twenty years is that he wants a divorce." Lilly's face wrinkled with the pain, but she kept talking. "Imagine that. I told him when we married that I was in this 'til death do us part, so he'd have to die like the other two if he wanted out, but Willard never did listen."

A nurse interrupted them. "We'd like to admit her for the night," she said to Mark. "Though we expect no complications—it was a simple break—we'd just like to keep an eye on her. Her blood pressure is slightly elevated."

"Yours would be too," Lilly mumbled, "if your husband of twenty-seven years just up and filed for divorce. I haven't even been around him to give him one good reason. He broke my leg just as sure as if he'd been standing there." Lilly glanced at Mark. "We can file charges on him for battery, can't we?"

"About the room?" the nurse interrupted again.

Mark was about to agree, when Lilly said, "I'm not staying. These folks will wake me up every two hours to see if I'm asleep if I stay here. My plan for staying alive is to stay out of hospitals." She looked at Mark and added, "I'm ready to go home."

He glanced at the nurse. "Will she be able to get around on crutches?"

The nurse nodded. "If she takes it slow."

"Can you give her something for the pain?"

The nurse nodded again. "She's probably had enough meds to make it through the night, but I'll see you have a prescription."

"Then I'm taking her home."

Getting Miss Lilly home proved to be more of a challenge than he thought. There was no way she could fold into his car with her leg in a cast. Mark finally called a cab. It took her home while he followed, and between the driver and him, they got her carried into her apartment.

The driver returned a half hour later with two bags of groceries Lilly had asked him to pick up, claiming she couldn't recover without the right kind of foods. Mark tipped the driver a hundred, guessing Lilly must have made out a list on the ride home from the hospital.

It took him another hour to get all the neighbors, who had heard about the accident and who'd come to talk more than help, out of the apartment. Several promised to bring over food and two asked if he was her son. Mark found the question ridiculous since he'd lived in the end town house twice as long as Lilly had rented the apartment, even though it seemed everyone knew her and no one noticed him. Strange how you walk right past folks day after day and never really look at them.

While she dozed, Mark arranged her apartment so that she could maneuver on crutches without hitting anything. It wasn't easy. The woman had twice the furniture needed for her square footage.

Finally, he warmed a bowl of vegetable soup for her and sat at the end of her bed while she ate every bite and proclaimed it to be the best meal she'd had in months.

He wasn't sure if it was the pain medicine kicking in, or the fact she'd won the battle to come back home, but Lilly seemed content. To his shock, she showed no embarrassment when he helped her to the bathroom, acting as if they'd shared the experience many times.

The role of caretaker was new to Mark. He'd never even had a pet. The few times Blaine had been ill, his duties had consisted of calling the doctor. To his surprise, he didn't find the job all that distasteful with Lilly. She needed him and it felt good to be needed.

It was dark by the time he left her snoring and went back to his own place. She had a bottle of water, her crutches and the phone within easy reach with both his cell and apartment numbers programmed in. She also had two bags of cookies and the remote control. Surely she'd be all right until morning. He'd offered to sleep on her couch, but she'd insisted she would be fine.

He took her extra key, promising to be back to cook breakfast in the morning. "I'm somewhat of an expert on eggs," he bragged. After all, he'd been making eggs for Tres every morning for two weeks. Mark didn't bother to mention the cat had yet to try one.

The phone rang as he plugged it in. Mark's first thought was that Lilly might already need him.

But she hadn't had time to dial.

He answered impatiently. "Yes."

"Anderson? This is Lieutenant Randell." The cop's voice came through loud and clear. Randell didn't wait for Mark to answer. "I thought I'd try you one more time before I called it a night. I thought you'd want to know any news, even though it isn't much."

"What?" Mark leaned against the couch arm. He had

almost given up hope on anyone finding clues to the bombing.

"We found your wife's bag," Randell said. "It's got her ID from the gym dangling from the zipper." When Mark didn't comment, he added, "Someone probably stole the bag out of her car before you had it towed. Someone might be trying to impersonate your wife."

"But why?"

"The thief probably searched the bag for money and tossed it. Then a druggie or a street person may have found the bag and it took her a while to figure out how that ID to the gym might be useful. If she could pass into somewhere like a private-club gym, there is no telling what she could steal. We've had those kinds of crimes a few times in this area."

"Where did you find the bag?"

"An old bag lady had it. Said someone gave it to her last night. I just happened to notice the initials on the side of the bag and started asking questions."

"Can you show me who she was? I'd like to talk to her." Mark knew he was pushing the not-so-friendly friendship he'd developed with the cop, but he had to try.

"Now?"

"If you wouldn't mind. It's important." Mark wasn't sure why, but he had to follow this one clue to Blaine no matter how small. Every muscle and brain cell ached to do something, anything. "It's important to me," he added.

"All right," Randell finally answered. "There is no reason for us to keep the bag."

Thirty minutes later, Mark met Randell in front of the Driskill Hotel and they walked toward the bus stop together. Mark didn't tell the cop that he had followed him last night in the rain over this same path. Like all the others on the streets, Mark kept an eye on the cop. He didn't seem to have a home life. Mark had seen Randell working at all hours. If he were guessing, Mark knew Randell probably also watched him walking the streets.

Mark wasn't surprised when they reached the two old piles of rags he'd seen before. Salt and Pepper, he'd called them in his mind.

Randell explained to them that the bag belonged to a woman who had vanished and that this was her husband. If the two ladies could tell them anything about where they found the bag or who had it, they would be grateful.

Mark offered his hand, but neither took it, though Randell introduced them saying everyone called them Vanilla Anna and Chocolate Anna.

Chocolate Anna, an old black woman with weathered wrinkles cut deep into her face, clamped her lips closed and didn't look as if she planned to say a word.

But the gray-haired smaller one started crying. "I was afraid Mary would run off." She wiped her nose on her sleeve. "I heard her cry out when the knife sliced through her. She vanished. Sometimes folks do no matter how much you tell them to stay put."

Mark knelt down to the woman's level. "No, Mary didn't vanish. My wife did. She wasn't knifed. She was burned." Mark lifted the bag Randell had given him with Blaine's initials sewn into the fabric. "This was my wife's bag. Do you remember where you found it?"

Vanilla Anna pointed to the spot beneath the bench. "She left it right here when she ran. She asked me to watch over it for her."

Anna looked up at Mark with tear-filled eyes. "You

got to give it back to me. Mary told me to keep it for her.''

''I can't,'' he answered, feeling sorry for the old woman. ''This belonged to my wife.''

Randell moved in. ''This Mary, where is she now?'' He glanced at Mark, silently telling him they might get more information following Mary's trail. The old woman didn't make much sense, but if someone named Mary had left the bag, she might have been the one who'd stolen it.

Vanilla Anna pushed her tears aside. ''She went to take her lessons. She promised to practice or else she'll never make it into the band. She's a good girl. Always does what she's told. I'm proud of her.''

They talked to Anna for thirty more minutes but nothing made sense. She insisted that a woman named Mary gave her the bag but most of her comments made Mary seem like a child.

Chocolate Anna refused to say a word, even when Randell threatened to take her to the station. She seemed to have had her fill of questions in this life and no threat would change that fact.

Mark carried the bag home and dropped it on the coffee table. He sat on the couch to stare at it. Tres jumped up beside the bag and began rubbing against it, purring loudly.

''It's just her bag,'' Mark said as if the cat could understand. ''She was always leaving it places, her car, the gym. Who knows, she may have left it at the library or the clinic. It could have been missing for days before she disappeared.''

He pulled the zipper and looked inside. A towel, a damp bathing suit, a comb, half a loaf of bread and several tiny jars of jelly. Everything was neat and orderly almost as if it *had* been Blaine who packed it. More than likely, whoever had been using the bag hadn't bothered to toss Blaine's clothes out. Since the bread would not have been in there when Blaine had the bag, someone, probably homeless, had been using it.

He handled the bathing suit. The scent of chlorine stung his nose. Why would someone keep a damp suit? Were they wearing it or had the bag got wet in the rain? If not, how could the suit still be damp when everything else was dry? The suit made no sense.

Rummaging along the bottom of the bag, he found an inside pocket. Within were the earplugs Blaine always used when she swam laps, a quarter lodged in one corner, and the bracelet she usually wore on her left wrist.

Mark turned the gold chain in his hand. They'd bought it once on a whim when they'd been at Tiffany's at the Galleria in Houston. It had only cost a few hundred dollars, but she'd loved it, playing with both the blue box and the chain most of the ride home.

How many years had it been since they'd gotten away? Two, three? Blaine would talk about it sometimes, even plan a weekend, but something always came up. His work was never predictable.

Gripping the chain in his fist, Mark realized he had been the one to always change Blaine's plans. He thought there would be more time. There was always next week, next month, or even next summer.

The clasp was broken on the bracelet. Blaine must have been planning to take it in for repair, but she hadn't mentioned it and he couldn't remember the last time he'd seen the thin gold band on her wrist.

It crossed his mind that when someone stole the bag, they must have not noticed the small pocket inside, or else they would have hocked the chain. Blaine had been the one to put it in the pocket. She'd been the last one to touch the gold.

He gripped the chain in his hand as if he could somehow hold on to a part of Blaine for a moment longer.

"Why'd you leave?" he whispered. "Why don't you call or come back?"

He made a mental note to get the bracelet fixed, as if he could somehow start putting his life together if he could repair one small chain.

He leaned back and stared at the ceiling. "Why'd you leave me, Blaine?"

# Twenty-Three

Long after she heard the old doctor climb the creaky steps to the second floor, Blaine lay awake, letting his words echo in her head. The book-lined room was cool and smelled dusty. Blaine had the feeling she wasn't the first to crash for the night on this couch.

The doctor's words seemed to linger in the room lit by the twinkle of streetlights in the stained-glass windows above the overstuffed bookshelves.

Pregnant.

Before the bombing, the thought had dominated her mind. If she found out she had cancer, would she be strong enough to fight? If she was pregnant, would she have the guts to have an abortion, or would she risk ruining her marriage by keeping the baby? Mark didn't have time for her, how could he carve out time for a child? The possibility had only been part of their conversations a few times. She'd told him she couldn't have children and he had said that was fine. Once, just before they married, she'd asked him if he thought she should go to a specialist, but he'd only said someday, when we have time to think about a family.

He'd told her then how his mother used to yell when she was angry over something he'd done, or the world in general. She'd scream how she wished she'd had the guts to abort Mark. His parents had been free spirits, traveling with a band when he'd come along, and somehow a baby didn't fit in with their life. Mark's father had settled down and had taken a job he hated, his mother withered into a complainer never happy with anything. For a while, his father played at the local bar to pay off his tab, but that didn't last long. A man who lives on what-might-have-been doesn't eat well.

Blaine spread her fingers across her slightly rounded abdomen. There was no question in her mind. She loved Mark, and wanted the marriage, but she would not do anything to hurt the baby. This child had been with her through the bombing and all the problems of the past week. She hadn't been alone. Somehow, the baby had fought just as hard to survive as she had, and she'd fight to the death before she let anyone hurt him. The strength of her conviction rocked her almost as much as the knowledge that she carried a child within.

Finally, meek little Mary Blaine had found something worth fighting for.

"I'm here," she whispered to her unborn child. "I'm here and I'm going to see that nothing happens to you."

Tears flowed silently down her cheeks when she cupped her hands over her body, as if the baby would know she held him even now. Her life had changed once more and she knew nothing would ever be the same. A day ago, she wanted to hide from the bomber, hoping he wouldn't find her and kill her. Tonight, she felt she could easily kill him if he tried to harm her baby. She'd never felt so fiercely protective about anything in her life. She loved Mark and might die to keep him safe, but she'd kill to protect this child.

Blaine laughed. What a warrior she had become. Mark would be shocked that the mouse he'd married had learned to roar.

She fell asleep wondering how, when this was all over, she would tell Mark about the baby. Would he be happy? Or would he see her pregnancy as somehow a betrayal? For Mark, everything had to be part of the big plan so that all stayed balanced. He had his work. But now the impossible had happened and she would somehow find a way to tell Mark.

The thought still worried her at dawn when the doctor's housekeeper came in for work, loaded down heavier than the Annas with plastic bags.

"'Morning, Mary Sunshine," the large woman said as she closed the front door with her hip. "I'm Dr. Early's housekeeper, Jesse Lynn Bailey, but most folks just call me Mrs. B. We met last night, but I don't suppose you'd remember." She dropped the bags. "I brought you all kinds of things you might need."

She dumped her load in front of the couch and leaned back, stretching the muscles along her spine. "How are you feeling?" she asked when she finally straightened.

"Better." Blaine gently held her hand over her side as she sat up. "Thank you for the nightgown."

"Oh, you are more than welcome. I'd be staying here every night to keep an eye on the doc if I didn't still have a kid at home." She sat down beside Blaine and fanned herself with both her hands. "I tell the old fellow I work too late to head home some nights when he's real weak and I'm afraid to leave him."

"Dr. Early is ill?" Blaine felt like a fool for even asking. Of course he was ill. His skin barely covered his bones and his eyes looked tired, not just from the day, but from life.

"Wearing out a heartbeat at a time," Mrs. B. answered. "Some nights I don't think his heart will last 'til he gets up the stairs. But he thinks he's got to sleep in his own bed every night being he plans to die there. He says he was born in that big bed and that's where he'll leave to meet his maker."

"I didn't know he was ill. I shouldn't have come."

Mrs. B. patted her hand. "You are the best thing that's happened to him in a long time. Taking care of you last night, he forgot about dying for a few hours and remembered he was still breathing."

Mrs. Bailey rubbed a tear with the back of her hand and jerked clothes from one of the bags. "I brought you some of my daughter's things." Mrs. B. tried her best to smile as she changed the subject. "My Tuesday-girl got far too fat to wear them a few years ago but still dreams of dieting while she eats muffins on my couch and tells me how hard it is to get a job."

Blaine smiled, almost seeing the homely child that plain Mrs. B. would parent. Big bones must run in their family and the Bailey coloring had to be beige. Light brown hair, watered-down tan eyes and skin the color of sand. Mrs. B. was megasized monotone.

"Only good thing about her unemployment," the woman continued without pausing, "is that my daughter makes the best muffins in town thanks to a recipe Miller gave her that he said once belonged to his grandmother. They melt in your mouth. I brought you some for breakfast." She patted Blaine's arm. "Don't you worry none, they'll move you into a double-digit dress size in no time I'll warm you a muffin and bring it with a glass of milk. You can snack on Tuesday's blueberry-and-cream muffins while I cook breakfast."

The woman amazed Blaine. Like an underwater swimmer, she seemed to have the ability to go long periods without taking a breath. Pausing to inhale was an unknown rule to Mrs. B.

The housekeeper continued to yell from the kitchen. "Don't worry none about the doctor waking up this morning. He has his demons at night, but come dawn he'll sleep most of the day away." Mrs. B. returned with muffin and milk in hand.

"Miller says he'll help my Tuesday open a muffin shop when she gets the recipe down. Try this one, hon, and see if you think she's close."

Blaine took the plate. "I should go," she said to herself more than Mrs. Bailey. "Dr. Early doesn't need a houseguest if he's ill."

Mrs. B. sat down to watch Blaine eat. "Now, don't you even think of leaving. He liked helping you and I figure that helps him. Miller brought us a blessing to this house and there's no two ways about it. Since the doc's wife died five years ago, he hadn't had much interest in anything but reading all these old books. Dust catchers is all they are."

"But I can't just barge in."

Mrs. Bailey frowned. "You'd be doing us a big favor if you'd stay a few days. Miller said he'd vouch for you and I could really use a little help."

Blaine nodded. "With the housework?"

"No, with the doctor. I've been with him for over thirty years. He's outlived all his family and most of his friends. Miller says you got a way about you. Says you could talk to the doc."

"I have to go back home," Blaine said, thinking of the baby.

"We'll take whatever time you can spare. It wouldn't hurt you to stay still for one day."

Blaine nodded. She didn't know how to get to Mark, and if she wasn't very careful, he'd be in even more danger. She needed time to heal. And she needed a place to hide. Maybe she could spend one more night here.

She sat back and nibbled on the muffin, deciding she was the one who had found heaven.

One day melted into two, then three. The doctor was a wealth of information. He reminded her of a research book come to life. His body might be dying, but his mind sparkled. She could see the joy in his eyes as they talked. Pick a subject, he seemed to be saying. Pick a subject and let me tell you what I've learned. They talked of wars and presidents and fairy tales, of great books and modern trends. She couldn't find a subject or a classic he hadn't read.

For the first time, she ate all she wanted. Mrs. Bailey and Dr. Early treated her with loving care, insisting that she eat three huge meals a day and take both a morning and afternoon nap. On the fourth morning, Blaine hardly recognized herself in the mirror. Her skin had never looked better, her cheeks were rounded and her hair had grown slightly to a length that flattered her. The old, blond Blaine with a bit too much makeup had disappeared.

Dr. Early said she glowed as all mothers-to-be do. He slept most of the days away but always joined Blaine and Mrs. B. for an early supper. Then he loved to read aloud and Blaine found herself lost in his stories. She realized how much she had missed never having someone read to her. If she would join him, the doctor would have a midnight snack, then he'd climb the stairs and disappear into his rooms upstairs. She'd hear him walking the floor and coughing, sometimes even talking to himself, but she never bothered him. He must need his time alone or else he would have stayed downstairs.

The doctor might be a very private man, but Jesse

Lynn Bailey proved to be a wealth of gossip. She was a one-woman, twelve-hour-a-day, talk-radio personality on steroids. By the end of the first day, Blaine knew the names and life stories of all five of Mrs. B.'s children. None of whom seemed to have amounted to anything except trouble for their poor mother. She had a plan for all of them and her mission seemed to be to inform them of it daily.

After two days of listening to Mrs. B., Blaine decided the youngest child, the only one still living at home, must be deaf. After asking the doctor if it was all right, Blaine set out on a walk. She made it halfway to the cemetery before she realized she had to turn back. She might make it to the cemetery with the bag of food for the child, but she would never be able to make it back. Blaine rested on a bench for a while and returned home defeated. She left the bag of food on the porch and crumbled into her bed, asleep before her head settled into the pillow.

An hour later when Mrs. Bailey woke her for lunch, Blaine discovered the bag was missing. Someone had stolen it from the porch. Blaine shrugged, deciding she'd try again tomorrow.

The hand-me-down clothes from Mrs. B.'s youngest offspring took a little getting used to, but Blaine accepted them as a blessing. Having something to change into that felt clean was wonderful, even if it did have Winnie the Pooh stamped on it.

Blaine almost laughed aloud. Two weeks ago she wouldn't have worn a scarf that hadn't been picked especially for an outfit. Now she was blending nursery-rhyme tops with cartoon-character bottoms.

Blaine asked for a paper every morning, desperately needing to keep up with the ongoing investigation of the bombings. But other news filled the headlines. Everyone seemed to have forgotten about a bombing at a clinic that killed two people.

The act that had changed her life was little more than a footnote in the news.

She found a note on the third page about police investigating new leads, and twice there were new articles about possible people who would run for railroad commissioner now that Mark Anderson was no longer considering it. Blaine noticed that Mark never gave a statement to the press, but Harry Winslow did.

Once in a while, Blaine tried to reach Mark by phone, but he never picked up at home or on his cell, and Bettye Ruth always answered at the office.

Blaine was still almost within the shadow of the capitol, but somehow in Dr. Early's old rambling house with its overgrown trees hugging the brick, the headlines seemed a long way away. She could hear the traffic but it seemed more a hum than a roar of a city just beyond the thick walls of the doctor's yard.

She told herself she needed to step away from everything. She needed to think.

By the fourth day, Blaine felt as if she was strong enough to face Mark. Somehow he'd find a way out of this mess. They were a family now, they needed to be together.

She dialed his cell telling herself that this time Mark would get the message. The home phone might be broken or full of messages, his office phones might be picked up by someone else, but Mark always had his cell with him.

As usual, voice mail picked up.

She hadn't wanted to leave another message, but she had to. Maybe he hadn't heard the last one until after she'd been stabbed. Maybe he'd thought it was a prank. Maybe the rain had made it impossible for her to see him.

"Mark." Blaine fought down the panic as the phone beeped. "This is Blaine. I'm in danger. We're both in danger." She had to think of somewhere safe that they could meet. Someplace anyone listening to the message wouldn't understand. Somewhere she could walk to. The cemetery was still too far. "Meet me at sunup tomorrow where we used to eat pizza for breakfast when we were in college."

The message clicked off before she could say more.

Blaine tried to breathe. Tomorrow this would all be over. She'd find Mark and somehow he'd find a way out. If someone else, by chance, heard her message, they would have no idea where to meet her. Mark would be there this time. He had to be.

# Twenty-Four

Blaine blinked away the sun and rolled over. The pillows of the couch pressed against her face. For a moment, she thought it was Mark's back.

"Mark!"

She jumped up. How could she have slept past dawn? Not today!

Blaine ran to the bathroom, pulling off her gown and grabbing the first shirt and trousers from her pile of clothes. Both were too big, but she didn't have time to worry about it. Looping an old belt around her waist, she tied it off with a knot and stuffed the shirt in.

Pulling on an oversize windbreaker and her shoes, she silently slipped out the front door. Mrs. Bailey wouldn't come for an hour and the doc should sleep for hours yet. There was no one to explain her actions to.

That's why she'd overslept, Blaine realized, glancing up at the old man's draped window. In the few days she'd been in the house she'd come to dearly love Dr. Early. Each night she worried a little more, knowing he was one floor above her and in pain. Like Mrs. Bailey, Blaine watched him counting away his life, one step at a time, breath by breath.

Last night, about midnight, she'd tapped on his door asking if there was anything he needed. In his ever-kind way he said no, then hesitated and added, "Could you read just a few chapters to me. Just until I fall asleep."

He lay back amid a stack of pillows and smiled as she began to read *Treasure Island.*

When she took a break, she went down and got them both milk and cookies, then they talked while they picnicked in the middle of his huge old family bed. He told her how this house had been full of children once. He said distant cousins who'd never bothered to visit would probably inherit the place. The office complex next door had been trying to buy the land for years and would meet the cousins by the time he was put in the ground.

Blinking away the sunrise, Blaine hurried down the front steps. She couldn't help but glance back. It would be a shame to destroy this old home. Dr. Early said all the generations had left behind echoes of their laughter and their books for him to treasure. She'd spent her life trying to forget where she came from, while he lived with the richness of generations surrounding him. No wonder he didn't even want to leave the house to die.

The air blew cool, not yet warmed by the day as she walked the streets toward what all the college kids called the drag. It was a long line of restaurants, coffeehouses, bookstores and little shops that bordered the campus of the university.

When she left the neighborhood around Austin Community College, the old homes gave way to businesses, the silence to traffic. Blaine pushed on, thankful she'd walked at least once a day since she'd been injured, otherwise she'd never make it.

Blaine felt strong, light-headed almost. Finally, her nightmare away from Mark would end. The doctor had given her exactly the medicine she needed, time to think. She knew more was wrong between them than just her worry over the possibility of being sick or pregnant. She also knew she loved him, at least enough to try. Now she'd get her chance to talk to him away from their town house, where he might be watched, and away from his office, where others might hear.

Somehow they'd find a way out. There had to be a middle ground where they could stand together. She might not come from a family she could remember with pride, but Mark and she were strong, they could be the first generation to build on.

If they could live through this trouble, she thought. If he'd accept the pregnancy. If he'd be willing to bend. She wasn't sure he would. She'd never asked him to. Her whole future hung on a two-letter word. If.

As she rounded the corner, a block away from the all-night pizza parlor, two ambulances blinked into view.

Blaine slowed, noticing several police cars blocking the street. Something was wrong.

Half a block closer she blended in with the students who flowed endlessly like a river between the shops and the university. Yellow tape blocked off the sidewalk on either side of the pizza parlor that made a habit of selling all leftover pizza for half price at dawn. When Blaine and Mark had first dated, pizza for breakfast seemed like a good idea.

Blaine shoved closer until she stood among the watchers who'd forgotten classes or jobs in favor of curiosity.

"What's up?" someone in the crowd mumbled as he shifted his backpack.

"A drive-by shooting, can you believe that, man. A drive-by right here in downtown Austin."

An overweight man in his fifties shook his head. "Reminds me of the tower shooting back in sixty-six."

The crowd grew silent a moment. Most of them

weren't alive when Charles Whitman climbed the Texas Tower in the center of campus and shot fourteen people, but everyone had heard the stories.

"Was anyone hurt?" a girl shouted at a uniformed policemen directing traffic.

"Read about it in the news," he shouted back. "Move along. There's nothing to see. It's all over."

No one moved. Blaine stood just behind the plump man and watched a stretcher being loaded into an ambulance.

"That's the third," someone mumbled. "The other two were able to walk out."

The girl on the stretcher moved an arm and yelled something. One of the EMT tossed a backpack into the ambulance before closing the door.

Blaine waited. As the ambulance pulled away, the crowd began to move.

Blaine fell into step behind two students who barely looked old enough to shave.

"Do you know what happened?" one asked.

"Not much. I heard someone say a car raced by at dawn and blasted away at the pizza place. Shattered every window like some kind of gangland shooting or something. But everyone must have hit the floor. I heard a cop say into his radio that it was a miracle someone wasn't killed. From the looks of those who climbed into the ambulance I'd guess two students, both girls, and that old cook who works the night shift were the ones hit. I saw a few guys talking with the police, so I'm guessing they were in the shop at the time."

"Makes no sense," the other one mumbled. "The pizza wasn't that bad."

Blaine slowed, feeling suddenly sick to her stomach.

If Mark got her message, he might have been in there waiting for her.

People brushed against her as they passed. Finally, she made it to a side street and rounded the corner next to a line of Dumpsters. She folded over and threw up.

If she'd been in the pizza place on time, she might have been shot. She might be dead. Mark might be one of the two men who walked out, if she could believe the scraps of information she'd overheard.

She made her way back to the street and turned in to the first door she came to, a health food store and café. The girl who looked up from behind the counter couldn't have been more than eighteen.

"Mind if I use the phone," Blaine whispered. "I have to check and make sure my husband wasn't at the pizza place." She saw no reason to lie.

The girl nodded slowly.

Blaine dialed home. No answer. She tried the office. The office receptionist picked up on the first ring, rattling off the names of the law partners without pause.

"May I speak to Mark Anderson?" Blaine tried to keep her voice calm, businesslike.

"He's in a meeting. May I take a message?"

"Are you sure?"

"Yes," the woman sounded slightly annoyed. "I saw him go in ten minutes ago, but if you'd like me to interrupt the meeting..." She trailed off as if she had no intention of doing so.

Blaine hung up without answering. "He wasn't there," she whispered.

"Thank goodness." The girl behind the counter smiled.

Blaine thanked her and left before she started crying. She tried to walk with the crowd, but they were suddenly moving too fast. Gripping her side, she made it to an old wooden bench in front of what had once been a clothing store. Everyone around her seemed in a hurry just as Blaine's strength faded.

She didn't even want to think anymore much less be afraid. Closing her eyes, she fought to keep from throwing up or passing out.

It could have been half an hour, or a minute, she wasn't sure, but Blaine jerked as she felt something touch her shoulder.

Twisting around, she came face-to-face with the child she'd seen in the cemetery.

He held up a bottle of water.

As soon as she took it, he darted away, disappearing in the crowd as easily as he did between the headstones.

Blaine stared at the plastic bottle of cold water. She glanced around, noticing a bookstore with a side entrance that had a case of the same brand of bottles by the front door.

Blaine smiled. Her entire life was falling apart, but stolen water had never tasted so good. She didn't have to think too hard about how the child had found her. She'd been leaving food on the porch of Dr. Early's since that first day she'd tried to make it to the cemetery. The food kept disappearing.

It took her an hour to walk back to the doctor's house. She let herself in and sat down on the couch. "I'm safer here," she whispered, knowing she wouldn't be fool enough to leave a message on Mark's phone again. Deep down she knew if he'd gotten the message, nothing would have stopped him from being there.

"What did you say, Mary?" Mrs. Bailey asked without turning from the bookshelves.

"Where is Miller?" She thought it odd he'd brought

her here and then disappeared. "I have to talk to him."
Maybe Miller could help her.

"He's around. He's always around," the chubby
woman answered. "He and the doctor go way back."

"Back to Vietnam?" No one would know Miller, she
thought. Maybe he could deliver a message to Mark
without Winslow or anyone else noticing.

Blaine tried to plan and talk to Mrs. Bailey at the same
time.

"Yeah." Mrs. B was off on a monologue. "Miller
was Special Forces, you know. The kind of soldier who
goes deep behind the lines. Doc said once that Miller's
specialty was going in and bringing downed pilots out
alive. Said if they were wounded, Miller brought them
out on his back." Mrs. Bailey continued cleaning as she
talked. "Doc told me Miller served two tours over there,
living off the land most of the time. Then one night he
went in after the men in a downed helicopter. They must
have all been shot to bits when he found them, but he
started hauling their bodies out one at a time, crossing
under fire both directions. His captain ordered Miller to
stop, but Miller just turned around and went back for
the last man."

Mrs. Bailey didn't seem to notice that Blaine was lost
in her own problems and only half listening.

She wiped her eyes on her dust towel, then sneezed.
"Doc said Miller had four bullet holes in him when he
made it back that last time and the man he carried was
covered in blood, but somehow the guy was still
breathing. The doc went to work right there in the field
trying to save them both. Miller wouldn't let the doc
touch him until the pilot was seen to."

Blaine waited while Mrs. Bailey sipped from a forty-
four-ounce plastic cup she carried with her throughout

the house as if her journey might take her too far away from a water source. She wiggled into one of the wing-back chairs across from Blaine and continued, ''They shipped both men back that night as soon as they were stable. Within a matter of hours they were in the military hospital in San Antonio. Miller passed out half a world away and woke up an hour from home.''

Mrs. B. smiled knowing she had Blaine's full attention, then continued, ''The pilot lived, thanks to Miller and the doc. Miller had a hard time of it for a few months. He wouldn't even let them notify his wife for fear he wouldn't make it, even with her being right here close in Austin.

''Finally, he was getting out of the hospital about the time the doc got released from duty. Both men had spent many a night talking about when they got back to Austin, how they'd meet up and have a drink.'' Mrs. B. took another draw on her water.

''After several months, Doc went over to see him after Miller didn't return his calls. He found Miller sitting in his living room with a loaded .45 across his lap. Appears his wife got tired of waiting and left him. She even sold a little business that had been in his family for three generations. There he was, thirty-five with no wife, and thanks to getting shot up, no career.''

Miller's life changed suddenly, like hers. Blaine understood why he felt so lost.

''Apparently, Miller had never been too friendly a guy, even before he went to Nam. When he got back he was mostly bitter and mean. Only person he would have listened to that day was the doc.'' Mrs. Bailey took a bite of a poppy-seed muffin she'd left on the desk for the doctor in case he came down before lunch. ''Doc talked him into living, if you can call working heavy construction for twenty years living. Miller didn't spend a dime he didn't have to. He saved every penny until he bought his family's business back. It was just a little café but it wasn't cheap because it's on a prime downtown corner."

"Did he reopen?"

Mrs. Bailey shook her head. "No. He lives above it in a little apartment his grandparents once called home. He still doesn't spend a dime more than he has to. Eats at the free places when he can. He told the doc that those folks leave him alone and he doesn't have to put up with some waiter dropping by every few minutes asking him if he wants something."

Mrs. Bailey finished off the muffin and wandered off, mumbling about how she'd better call and wake Tuesday up or the girl would sleep all day.

Blaine paced, waiting for Miller, planning what she would say. The doc came down for dinner but seemed too tired to read. Blaine helped him upstairs and sat by his bed as he relaxed. Wordlessly, he reached for her hand.

She held his wrinkled fingers in hers until his breathing slowed in sleep, then she tucked a blanket around him and slipped from the room.

It was dark when Blaine walked out on the long front porch to watch the traffic from the college half a block away. She was surprised to find Miller sitting in the shadows, his big frame so still he could have been part of the mortar.

"'Evening," she said as if she saw him there every night.

"'Evening," he answered. "You feeling better, pest?"

"Yes, thank you." The thanks was for more than him asking about her health and they both knew it.

"How's the doc tonight?"

"Weaker," she answered.

Miller let out a long breath but didn't say anything.

Blaine leaned against one of the porch supports and waited for more questions. When he didn't ask, she said, "I guess you've got a right to know about me, but the stabbing that night was just an accident. The kid was trying to scare Anna. He looked as surprised as I felt when the knife sliced me."

"No questions," Miller answered.

She wasn't sure if he simply wasn't interested, or just hated talking. Blaine still didn't know why he'd helped her, or if he would again.

He was silent. They sat down on the porch in the metal chairs that creaked as they rocked…and thought.

Finally, he said in little more than a whisper, "The Annas told me a cop picked up the bag you left at the stop."

"Did you tell them where I am?"

He looked at her with a frown. "I'm not in the habit of telling anyone anything, pest."

"I figured that. I just didn't want the Annas to worry."

Miller huffed. "Vanilla Anna thinks you're at practice. I heard her tell someone the other morning that her Mary may give up the band and be a professional piano player and tour the world, maybe even go as far as Oklahoma City one day."

They were silent except for the sounds of the streets.

"My name is not Mary," Blaine had to tell the truth to this man who'd saved her life. "It's Blaine, Blaine Anderson."

"I figured that." He stared at her. "Anything else, Miss Mary Blaine, that you need to get off your chest?"

"I'm pregnant."

"I figured that too. You eat more than any skinny woman I've ever seen. Anything else?"

"I'm in big trouble." A tear rolled down her cheek. "I need your help."

When he didn't say no immediately, she rushed to tell him the whole story of the bombing, the morning after, when she'd overhead Winslow, the phone calls, everything. When she told of seeing the bomber, she whispered as if her voice might carry on the wind.

"I looked him in the eyes, Miller. I'll never forget his face and if he gets a good look at me, he might remember me."

Miller didn't say a word. She wasn't even sure he listened.

Blaine closed her eyes, remembering every detail. "That morning by Mark's office he was only a shadow, but I knew the other man, Harry Winslow. He said that as long as the wife was taken care of there was no reason to go after Anderson. I think he meant kill."

When she ended by saying that her husband first thought she was dead, Miller just rocked back in his chair, his face more in shadow than light. "Is your husband a tall guy with a beard?"

"No," Blaine answered, knowing Mark would never wear a beard. He usually had his hair cut every other week so it was never a fraction too long. "Why?" Miller had asked her once before about a man with a beard.

"Does your husband know there's a baby on the way?"

"No," she admitted. "Tell me why you asked about the beard."

"There's a man asking questions. He's not a weasel of a guy like the one you were running from that morning after breakfast and I'd guess he's not a cop. Shakespeare says he walks the streets at night, but if he's homeless he's not staying at any of the shelters."

Blaine didn't want to think of anyone else looking for her. The bomber, Detective Randell, probably Winslow and his friend were enough. Now a man with a beard was asking questions and drawing enough attention for Miller to get word of it.

"Do you want to go in…go home?" Miller broke into her thoughts.

"More than anything, but I don't want to endanger Mark. If the bomber found me, he might kill us both. The pizza shooting had to be meant for me."

"It might be a coincidence."

Blaine shook her head. "Not this morning. Not dawn. I left the message on Mark's cell. Winslow must have overheard it. Or intercepted it."

Miller stood. "Or…" He waited for her to finish.

Blaine stared up at him. "Or what?"

"If you want my help, you've got to consider one more possibility."

"All right," Blaine agreed.

"Or Mark knew."

# Twenty-Five

Blaine cried herself to sleep. She didn't want to consider Miller's suggestion. Mark could not be a part of this. He could not. He might have been distant, preoccupied, but he'd never think of killing her. Despite the fact that he was her husband and he loved her, Mark would never do anything illegal. He fought for the truth with every breath he took.

She didn't care what the evidence indicated; Blaine would never believe Mark had anything to do with the bombing of the clinic or the drive-by shooting at the pizza place. He might be in deep with Winslow, but not deep enough to plan the death of anyone, much less her.

At least Miller hadn't stayed around to point out the facts last night. The big man just got up and walked into the night, leaving her to think. If Mark wasn't part of this, why couldn't she reach him? Winslow could have gotten to Mark's phone at the office, but surely not his cell phone. Winslow would have had to have been in their house to turn off the answering machine and Mark had never invited him. If Mark had turned off the machine, then why? The chances of one of Winslow's men breaking in seemed slim what with the security around the complex.

Blaine knew the argument Miller could have named. Why was Mark never answering the phone? Surely he went home at night. Where else would he go if he wasn't in his office? Why would he give his cell to someone else? Or tell someone about the call? None of it made sense.

Why would Mark want her dead? He loved her.

Why would Winslow? He barely knew her name.

And the worst thing Miller hinted at already whispered in her mind. If it was Mark walking the streets, what did he plan to do when he found her?

"It's not Mark," she reminded herself a hundred times. "He doesn't know I'm trying to reach him, or he would come. I know he would."

Blaine fell asleep late into the night with shadows of angels dancing with devils amid the headstones.

She was still in bed when Mrs. Bailey's daughter made an appearance the next morning.

"There she is!" a woman shouted as she bumped her way into the house.

"Quiet, Tuesday!" Mrs. Bailey yelled just as loudly. "She's got a right to sleep, she's pregnant."

Blaine sat up in bed and watched the two Bailey women.

"Sorry," Tuesday said as she stared down at Blaine with open curiosity. "I just dropped by to pick up Mom. We're going to a movie and out to eat. Oh," she laughed and offered her hand. "I'm Tuesday Bailey and you've got to be the Mary who Mom talks about."

Blaine nodded, but wasn't sure if the girl offered friendship, or had simply grown tired of hearing about the pregnant woman living with the old doctor and decided to drop by for a look.

"Nice to meet you," Blaine whispered as she stood, but neither woman paid any attention to her.

Everything about Tuesday Bailey appeared to be supersized, from her clothes to her makeup. The only small thing about her colorful ensemble dangled from her wrist. A poodle-shaped purse. She carried an umbrella that banged against everything within three feet of her.

Tuesday Bailey spoke in a voice that could have easily distanced the block. "I just dropped by to make sure Mom leaves by noon today," she said to no one in particular. "We've got plans."

"Great." Mrs. Bailey clapped her hands. "Let me get my purse."

Tuesday lifted her nose. "I almost got a job today, but they'd just hired someone."

"You're getting close, sweetheart, just keep trying."

Tuesday pulled off a pair of white cat's-eye glasses and smiled at Blaine. "Would you like to come along with us?" Her smile appeared more genuine than the offer.

"No, thank you," Blaine answered, but Tuesday had already turned toward her mother.

"Maybe next time. Mom said you don't have any friends to run around with."

Blaine wasn't sure she liked the idea of the Baileys talking about her, but she remembered that Mrs. B.'s favorite activity seemed to be planning other people's lives, so why should she be surprised that the trait was inherited.

Mrs. B. shook her head. "She's like the doc, honey, keeps to herself all the time."

Before Blaine could join the conversation, Dr. Early started down the stairs.

All three women turned to watch his progress. He moved down slowly, crossed to the recliner in the corner and almost collapsed in exhaustion.

Blaine covered him with a blanket as Tuesday greeted him with honest warmth.

When he caught his breath, he told Tuesday she looked downright *parade* today.

"I came by to see if Mom, and Mary, will go out with me."

"Thanks, again," Blaine answered. "But I'll stay here with the doc. We're both a little under the weather."

The old man coughed in time to her comment.

Everyone in the room knew he was dying but Blaine didn't want to admit it. They'd become friends in an accepting way few people do. He'd opened his home to her, without asking any questions, almost as though he'd recognized one of his own kind. They shared far more than a love for reading. They were both the quiet watchers of life who fill in the background while the actors performed.

He'd given her hope in the statement of his life. A kind, quiet man who hadn't set out to change the world but who seemed content just to be alive in it and enjoy his time. She knew she could never pay him back for these days of peace, but she could make his time a little happier by sharing his books.

Blaine brushed the doctor's wrinkled hand as she looked up at Tuesday. "The doc is going to read me O. Henry tonight and I found a book of old nursery rhymes on the top shelf of his study. I thought I could read them after lunch. They'll probably put us both to sleep for a nap, then we'll have an early dinner. So we've got a great time planned."

Blaine swore she saw both Tuesday's and her mother's eyes roll back at the thought of their boring day.

"Fun evening," the girl mumbled. She motioned with tiny jerks of her head toward the door. "Well, we better be going. Wish we could stay."

Blaine and the doctor, fighting to hold back laughter, watched them hurry down the steps. Tuesday tried to be polite, but her moods were wrapped in see-through plastic.

Hours later, she watched the old man move slowly up the steps to his room. They'd read longer than usual, but he didn't seem to want to stop. When she finally closed the book, he patted her hand and thanked her as though she'd given him a gift.

Blaine poured herself a glass of milk and moved to the porch. She wasn't surprised to find Miller waiting for her. The open window told her he'd probably heard everything they'd read, even though he'd never admit to have been listening.

They sat for a long while beside one another in the cool metal chairs. Finally, Miller whispered, "You've been thinking?"

"I've been worrying," she answered without acting as if she didn't know what he was thinking about. Their conversation from the night before had weighed on her mind all day.

"I have to do something." Blaine's voice floated across the night air, hanging between them in the darkness. "No matter how dangerous. Saying nothing may end up getting more people killed. When the bombing happened at the clinic, I thought it was something that happened that had nothing to do with me personally. Then I heard Winslow and the thin man talking and wondered, but I still had no proof. If I'd have gone to the police with what I thought I heard they might not have even listened, but I would have ended Mark's career by pointing a finger at Winslow. Now the shooting.''

"You can't afford to risk your life. Not on one conversation you overheard in the dark the morning after you'd been hurt,'' Miller mumbled as if talking to himself. His big fists thumped the armrest, making the hollow metal sound like someone learning to blow a trumpet.

"I can't afford not to.''

Miller grunted.

"I thought when Frank Parker gave the police a description, they'd catch the culprit. But Frank's no longer around to make a positive ID. And the bomber is still out there, walking the streets, looking for me. I can almost feel him growing closer.'' Tears bubbled from her eyes. "If I step forward and talk to the police, he might go after Mark. What if he kills Mark before they catch him?''

She lowered her voice. "I think, from what I overheard that first morning, that if he hadn't killed me he planned to kill Mark. It makes no sense.''

"What were the words you heard?''

"Winslow asked the guy if he got the wife. I think he called the man Jimmy. When the guy nodded, Winslow added, 'Thank God we don't have to take out Anderson.'''

Suddenly the walk in front of the house was filled with students. A class at Austin College must have been released. Blaine and Miller watched them hurry to their cars and bikes, yelling goodbyes as they moved about all hunchbacked with their packs.

They seemed so carefree.

Blaine leaned closer. "I must have heard something wrong. Why would anyone want to kill me? At the clinic, I could have been at the wrong place at the wrong time. But not the pizza place.''

''Someone wants you dead.'' Miller stated the obvious.

''What about Parker?''

''If we assume the clinic guard's death wasn't an accident, I'd say Parker just got in his way. He put the killer in danger. Made him feel threatened.'' Miller steepled his fingers. ''Which might be a way to draw him out.''

''Got any ideas?''

''None that aren't risky.''

Miller walked to the porch railing in front of Blaine. He folded his arms and added, ''You could still go to the police.''

''No.'' She put her head in her hands. ''I wish I could corner the thin guy and hold him for the police. Then they'd have to believe me. Otherwise, all I've got is a description of a shadow.''

Blaine rested her hand on Miller's arm. ''We have to find him.''

Miller shook his head. ''Not me.''

''But you helped me. You saved me.''

''That was different. You didn't give me much choice. When you were running from the bomber, you ordered me to help you. There wasn't no asking about it. The other night it was either bring you to the doc or have you bleed all over the street.''

''How can I find him, then? With or without you, I've got to try. It won't be safe for me to go home until I do.''

Miller took a long breath. ''You're not giving me much choice again, are you, pest?''

''No.'' Blaine smiled. ''I need you.'' She didn't give

him time to think about what he might be getting into. "Where do we start?"

"Did he recognize you that morning at the shelter?"

"I think he thought I looked familiar." She didn't want to think about risking her life, but she had to try to stop this. She had been in an insane world since the morning of the bombing. Only the gray-eyed man could end this. "He knew I was staring at him."

"It's been more than a week since he saw you at the shelter." Miller added in almost a whisper, "If you remember his eyes, maybe he remembers yours."

"Possible, but unlikely."

Miller rocked in his chair. "He's not roaming the streets or someone would have noticed him. I've asked around and all I've got is a few maybes. Sounds more like he's holed up somewhere waiting for you to reappear."

"Which I would have done if I hadn't overslept."

Miller nodded. "We're lucky he's no better with a gun than he is with dynamite. You're right about one thing. The shooting was no coincidence. He knew you were planning to be there."

"So what do I do?"

"You'd better hope you see him first."

Silence crystallized between them. The sounds of the city drifted on the warm air. Cars, voices, music and the drone of air conditioners.

"You're saying I have to find him before he finds me." Blaine's voice blended in with the sounds of the night.

Reality corroded her will to end the charade she played. She no longer risked just her life and maybe Mark's. She risked her unborn child's. Part of her wanted to stay here in the safety of the doctor's house and be the meek little coward her mother always thought her to be.

Blaine touched her abdomen. Looking for the bomber might jeopardize the one thing she loved more than her own life—this baby that grew inside her.

She had to help, but she also had to be very, very careful.

"He's still on the streets," Miller reasoned. "I saw him twice, but he cuts wide around me. If I were guessing, I'm thinking he's figuring about now that he's invincible."

Blaine pulled her chair closer. "You sound like you know him."

Miller laughed. "At one point I spent a great deal of time learning how to read men like him. He's a coward to the core. My guess is he's doing this for money, or maybe as a favor owed. His heart's not in the killing, otherwise he would have stepped in close with a knife or shot point-blank to kill you."

"So, he's just doing Winslow's dirty work?" Blaine guessed.

"You got to ask yourself why a rich man like Harry Winslow wants you dead and is willing to pay, or call in a big favor to get the job done. He doesn't want his hands dirty on this, plus maybe he thinks the trail can't get back to him."

Blaine fought back tears. She didn't want to think about this. All she wanted was to go home to Mark, to tell him about the baby and beg him to still love her. He was a good man. Even if he didn't want children at this time in his life, he'd do the right thing by her.

"I wish—" she formed her thoughts into words "—I wish I could stand on a street corner and watch everyone in Austin walk by. I'd pick him out and scream at the top of my lungs. Then the police would arrest him and I'd be free to go home.'' A single tear rolled down her cheek. ''I'm so tired of being afraid.''

Miller pulled her from the chair and wrapped her in a big bear hug. It wasn't warm, or particularly friendly, but she knew he made a great sacrifice by holding another so close. He didn't say anything. After a few seconds, he sat her back down and straightened, looking proud of himself.

Blaine smiled. Sometimes Miller was a five-year-old inside a man of sixty. A six-foot dwarf named Grumpy. It crossed her mind that maybe Grumpy should have had his own story.

She shoved the thought away and concentrated on her problem. ''Maybe we could go to this Detective Randell and tell him my plan?''

''Might work.'' Miller didn't sound encouraging. ''If Randell can keep it quiet. Cops, even if they don't talk, they have a mountain of paperwork to fill out. If Winslow has a friend at the station, he might overhear conversations or read Randell's report.''

''Then how?''

Miller shrugged. ''My folks had a café not far from here. You wouldn't believe what we overheard. People don't seem to think someone waiting on the table has ears. Most folks can't describe the waitress or waiter the minute they walk out of a restaurant. How many times have you seen someone who has finished eating and, trying to get their bill, stops everyone who passes and says, 'Are you my waitress?' ''

Blaine couldn't argue. She'd seen Mark do just that a hundred times. ''So, I need to stand on the corner dressed as a waitress until the bomber passes.''

Miller stood. "Sounds like a plan to me, pest. We'll talk more tomorrow. Sit tight until I get back."

He walked off as if he was in a hurry to meet someone.

Blaine leaned back in the rocker. A huge puzzle spread before her and all she had to do was make the pieces fit together. She had to get home. She had to protect herself and the baby. She felt as if she had been living in the asylum so long the inmates were starting to make sense.

"Mark," she whispered, wanting him near more than she'd ever wanted him in her life. Closing her eyes, Blaine pretended they were in the still darkness of a movie theater. It didn't matter what movie they watched, she and Mark just loved going. If it stunk, he'd start to make fun of the actors, repeating whatever they said. If it was romantic, he'd always reach for her hand. And if it was sad, she'd start to cry and he'd throw popcorn at her, then swear so earnestly that it hadn't been him, she'd have to laugh.

As tears rolled down her cheeks, Blaine wished he could toss popcorn at her now. The sadness inside her drowned her heart.

The thought of going back to the streets made her chest tighten. For a while, she'd been safe. Here, she'd healed, but the problem wouldn't go away. She had to do something, no matter the danger.

She went inside, finished the warm muffin and curled into her tiny couch bed. As she fell asleep, Blaine pretended Mark's arms were wrapped around her.

# Twenty-Six

Twenty-four hours after Blaine confessed everything to Miller, he stood on the porch waiting for her to come out after dinner. She'd read every line in the *Statesman* looking for any news about the drive-by shooting. She found an article on the third page that said the police were inundated with call-in leads and were checking out each one as quickly as possible. All three people taken to the hospital had been released, but none were able to identify more than the color of the car.

"'Evenin', pest," Miller said without turning around to make sure Blaine stood behind him.

She sat down in the chair next to him. "I have to leave here. I'm getting fatter by the day."

He grunted. "You needed some meat on your bones."

"Thanks for the compliment." Blaine couldn't remember when someone had thought she looked better with a few extra pounds. Sometimes it seemed as if she'd been hungry all her life. Staying thin had crossed her mind each time she ate. But not now. Now, with the baby, she had a "get out of diets" free card and she took advantage of it.

"I think Mrs. B. has adopted me as her own because she's started organizing my life like I'm one of her children."

Miller fought to keep from laughing. "I like Mrs. Bailey. You never have to wonder what she's thinking."

"That's true. But I don't think 'finding me a working man before I get too fat to attract someone making more than minimum wage' is particularly good advice."

Miller rubbed his chin as if giving Mrs. Bailey's plan some thought.

Blaine leaned over and poked him.

"Seriously." Blaine lowered her voice. "I'm feeling better. I'm up for anything you can think of that might help us catch this killer."

"The doc could use you here. I can look for the thin man."

Blaine didn't pretend. "I know I'm helping. He told me I've made his past few days happy—loving books as much as he does—but I can do both."

"You probably can." Miller frowned. "But whatever we do, you have to promise me you'll come back here if needed. I don't want him to die alone. Mrs. B. and I will be close, but it's not the same. You're his kind of people. You understand him. I could see that in you from the first."

He didn't have to say more. They both knew Dr. Early grew weaker each day. Last night Blaine had had to help him up the stairs. "He wants to die at home," she whispered.

"He's got the right."

Blaine silently agreed. "I'll stay a little while longer." She couldn't bring herself to add, "Until the end." Part of her wanted to run from watching him growing weaker, but she'd done enough running lately.

"I've thought of a way you can help spot the bomber." Miller rocked back in his chair. "If we're careful."

Blaine had been through every possible plan. "How?"

"Standing downtown, being invisible, until you see him. Then we can catch him and you can go home to that husband named…"

"Mark," Blaine said, irritated that he thought her problem was that simple. Didn't he see she was doing the best she could? He acted as if all she had to do was pick up a bullhorn and start preaching on some corner and the bomber would pass by, repent, and turn himself in.

Before she could think of an answer, he added, "If I come up with a way, would you be interested?"

She answered slowly, "Yes."

"Then, walk with me."

He stood and started down the steps. Blaine followed. The night lingered, still hot from the day. Walking behind the big man she felt strange wearing her now too-tight jogging pants and one of Mrs. Bailey's daughter's shirts that no one but a drunken Hawaiian tourist would buy.

They crossed down streets lined with old homes, many remodeled into law offices and other small businesses. Commerce weaved like a root through what had once been a residential area, spreading from the lights of the capitol in all directions.

When Miller stopped at a corner for traffic, Blaine caught up to him and circled her arm around his. "Could you slow down a bit?"

"Afraid you might walk off a muffin?"

Blaine lifted her head. "No, I was thinking more how you're getting older and might lose your balance if I don't hang on to you."

He opened his mouth to object, then frowned. "I'd

hate to stumble and have to depend on you carrying me back.''

She patted his arm. "Then I'd better hang on to you.''

She couldn't help but wonder how many years it had been since anyone had teased Miller about anything. He might grumble, but she felt he loved it.

Evening settled over the streets, blending the light between day and night, stretching it out so people could enjoy it. Even though she'd grown up seeing the capitol, it still took her breath away. The history of Texas hung so thick here folks could taste it in the air.

Miller slowed as he crossed to the row of businesses lining Congress. When they reached the abandoned store where Shakespeare usually stood, he stopped.

The old drunk shuffled forward, already long into drink. "A pleasure to see you, fair lady,'' he mumbled. "'The dying light doth mellow sorrow o'er the land.'''

"Thank you for helping me the other night,'' Blaine said, though he'd done little. He'd tried to catch her as she fell, but he barely had the strength to keep himself from falling.

Blaine suddenly remembered something. "Someone followed me in the rain that night. I remember seeing a man behind me when I glanced back.''

Shakespeare shook his head, but Miller said, "I saw him too. He moved toward you as if he'd followed you from the bus stop.''

Shakespeare scratched the top of his head, sending hair flying. "Now that I think of it, a man was just behind you, Mary. He backed away when Miller stormed forward.''

"Did he have a beard?'' Miller stepped over a pile of trash.

Shakespeare shrugged.

"I didn't get a good look," Miller glanced at Blaine. "I had to get you to the doc. If it was the man with the cap, he was closing in for a better look. But the shadow seemed taller than the man I delayed at the shelter that morning."

As Miller talked he moved down the few steps to the walkway leading to the door of the abandoned business.

Blaine followed more to get out of range of Shakespeare's breath than for any other reason.

Long windows lined the building forming one wall of the entrance passageway. The other side of the walkway looked to be a solid brick wall painted over many times, with the peeling paint scattered like confetti along the brick path.

Blaine followed Miller while Shakespeare followed her into the tunnel-like darkness leading to the door.

To her surprise, Miller pulled a key from his pocket and opened the door. "This was my folks' place," he said without turning around. "They came to Austin after the First World War. Planned to open a chain of cafés across the West. Started here and never moved on." He reached inside and flipped on a light. "They must have loved this place, they never even took a vacation."

Blaine stepped into a small-town café from the fifties. Despite a layer of dust, everything remained in place. The furnishings were plain wooden tables, iron chairs, a long mahogany bar in front of a pass-through window that must lead to a kitchen area.

Little individual table lights were mounted along one wall, each giving a glow to the tables. The floors were brick, with paths worn smooth, and the huge ceiling fans threw shadows across the room. She saw how someone could settle here and never leave. The place was beautiful in its simplicity.

Miller watched her as she walked around. "I checked the kitchen," he said. "Everything works. The water and gas are on."

Blaine glanced at Shakespeare. The old man watched from the doorway as though afraid to come in. He looked haunted by ghosts of his own without going looking for more.

"I bought new coffeemakers and dishes. Other than that all we need is a good scrubbing and we could open the place."

"Are you suggesting…" Blaine couldn't even voice the words.

Miller nodded. "That you stand on a street corner in a waitress uniform and watch for the bomber?"

She understood.

He raised one bushy eyebrow. "Are you up for it, Mary Blaine?"

"Keep talking," she answered.

"At first I thought we could sell pizza, but every other café around here does that. The big chains have doughnuts and subs. I can only think of one thing not for sale along this street."

Shakespeare swore and stumbled backward.

Blaine watched him dart into the shadows a moment before Mrs. Bailey clomped down the passageway to the front door. She barged in, followed by a younger version of herself.

Tuesday was attired totally in purple—from her tennis shoes to her round glasses with tinted violet lenses.

Blaine smiled, thinking that even the girl's mood reflected her color choice.

"What was so important, Luke Miller, that I had to drag Tuesday away from her TV?" Mrs. B. looked tired and frustrated.

Miller frowned with this invasion of his space but he answered, "I wanted to offer your daughter a job."

The older woman brightened and marched forward. "Well, that's a different story entirely. She's been telling me for months that if she had a job, a friend would split expenses on an apartment. I would welcome having to do only my own laundry and being able to go to sleep now and then without Letterman talking in the next room."

Tuesday glanced around the dusty room. "I'm not cleaning this place," she mumbled. "I didn't go to college for a year to clean up old buildings."

Mrs. B. opened her mouth to begin a lecture, but Miller cut her off. "I need a cook. Someone who can make muffins."

He turned back to Blaine. "I thought we could call the place Midnight Muffins and be open every evening. We might even serve a few of the homeless folks free as the night wears on. There is no telling who you might see walk in that door."

Tuesday maneuvered closer, dusting one tabletop with her hip. "I can cook." Her voice sweetened so much it no longer seemed to belong to her. She lowered her glasses to the tip of her nose. "How much does it pay?"

Miller didn't take his gaze from Blaine. There was much more he wasn't saying in front of the Baileys.

"It could be dangerous," Blaine whispered.

"Oh, no. Cooking isn't dangerous. It's a gift. Mom says so." Tuesday continued though no one listened. "I'm like an artist with my muffins. I create new ones all the time."

"It's a risk within the boundaries you asked for." Miller watched Blaine. "From a stool in the back I can see the entire café."

Blaine nodded. He was right.

"I could provide my own chef's hat. I got it in a cooking class I took." Tuesday strained her neck to see into the tiny kitchen behind the counter.

"I'll be right here every minute you are," Miller said to Blaine. "If you spot him, he won't get away."

"Who won't get away?" Tuesday asked.

Blaine finally turned to the girl. "Customers." She glanced at Miller. "The pay is twelve dollars an hour and the clock starts as soon as we get this place cleaned up."

"Fifteen. After all, I'm the cook."

Miller nodded.

Tuesday pushed up her sleeves. "Well, we best get to work." She turned to her mother. "Mom, hand me your keys and I'll go get the cleaning supplies."

Mrs. Bailey shook her head. "I'll go get them. You stay and help move the tables. We can have this place cleaned and ready to open by tomorrow night. I'll help you clean, then if I'm not too tired, I'll help you move to an apartment this weekend."

Blaine doubted that they could be open so fast, but she didn't want to spoil the mood. Her muscles ached for a project almost as much as Tuesday wanted to escape her mother's house. Everyone set to work.

A half hour later when she helped Miller carry out trash, she whispered, "Can you afford to do this? We'll make some, but it will cost."

"I can afford it. I've been working on it since we last talked." He tossed a load of trash as if the bag were filled with leaves. "With the bomber out there, I can't afford not to."

By midnight, the windows sparkled and the floor shone. Mrs. B. and her daughter polished the kitchen.

They'd made a list of supplies they needed to order while Miller carried out more loads of trash. Shakespeare disappeared, but Blaine thought she heard him snoring behind the alley door.

Blaine polished the last tabletop and when she looked up, she saw faces staring back from beyond the glass. A few thugs, the Annas, and several more of the homeless.

"Come back tomorrow night," she yelled. "Everyone gets to test the muffins."

They all nodded and wandered away, but at dusk the next day they migrated back. A half-painted sign announced Midnight Muffins, and Miller unloaded stock at the back door. The homeless filtered in for their promised muffins and Tuesday had worked without sleep to make sure she had a selection for them.

The Annas were the first to step through the door. Blaine practiced on them. Tuesday made three dozen of each of four kinds of muffins. She'd also managed to figure out how to brew coffee in the huge pots Miller delivered.

Blaine brought the Annas a muffin and a cup of coffee, then left the bill in the center of the table that said, "No charge. Thank you. Come again."

She stood beside Tuesday and watched them eat, patting their lips with paper napkins between bites. The Annas didn't say a word to one another, but when Blaine returned to offer a refill, they both thanked her and stood. Both left a dime on the table as a tip.

The pattern continued until midnight. A few of the street people came in at a time, none were asked to pay, but most left a few cents. Students wandered in, some ordering only coffee as they sat and read at the little lighted tables, others splitting muffins and talking of things that only seem of great interest while one is in college.

The bill was the same each time. No charge. Students left folding money as tips and a businessman who ordered only coffee left a five as he stood and thanked Blaine for the atmosphere.

She looked around. The place wasn't like a bright, glaring diner, but more like a living room that invited conversation.

By the second night an Open sign hung over the door. The menu over the bar read, "Bottomless cup of coffee, one dollar. Muffins, three dollars if you have the money. If not, you're welcome to one and welcome to come back anytime."

"You'll go bankrupt in a week," Mrs. Bailey said as she frowned at the menu. "I should have been here to help you with that. But I can't be everywhere even though it seems my advice is needed everywhere I look."

"Maybe it will work." Blaine didn't want to argue.

When Miller walked her home, she'd asked him again about the operating costs and he'd mumbled something about having no reason to save. The doc had saved all his life and had no one to leave it to. Even Mrs. Bailey had sworn to haunt Early throughout the ages if he left her that huge old house she'd had to clean for years.

Tuesday made three dozen of six kinds of muffins the third night. They ran out by ten and had to close.

For the first time since the bombing, Blaine slept without dreaming. Exhaustion from honest work felt great. Also, since Tuesday had moved out of her mom's home, Mrs. B. claimed a bedroom upstairs beside the doctor's. If Dr. Early needed her, Mrs. B. would hear him and call her right away.

The old doctor's hours out of bed were dwindling. By the weekend they moved their reading times to afternoons for he was too weak to come downstairs for long. He still insisted on dressing, wearing a tie and jacket as if Blaine was important company and not someone crashing on his couch. When he tired, she'd help him climb the stairs and he'd say good-night even though the sun might still be bright.

When Blaine got home each night she'd check on him to find him waiting for her to sit on the corner of his bed and read him to sleep once more.

Every day, the moment Blaine awoke, she couldn't wait to get to the café. To her surprise, Tuesday felt the same way. The girl liked to bake early in the day, so by the time they opened she could be out front in her chef's hat taking orders—and then compliments. She had a great deal of her mother in her and talked naturally to everyone who came in. "What's your name, mister?" "You want the leaded or unleaded coffee?" "You look like a blueberry lover to me." "Welcome back. I got a chocolate chip muffin you'll like even more than that apple cinnamon you had last night."

Blaine couldn't be so friendly, but Miller had been right about how people talk as if no one stood beside them pouring coffee. She caught bits of conversations as she moved among the tables.

Each time the bell sounded, she looked up, searching for gray eyes beneath a blue cap. No matter how busy the hour, Blaine never forgot the reason she was there. Standing on the corner, she reminded herself, watching.

Three days passed. Business grew and nothing happened. Her life settled once more into the peace of routine.

Until the fourth night, a tall man in a beard stepped through the door and Blaine's heart stopped.

# Twenty-Seven

Mark stepped into the café along with the wind. The night had a chill. He thought a cup of coffee might warm him a little. He'd passed the place several times, but had never bothered to stop.

A huge man in the far corner read a newspaper. A few college students with books spread among their coffee cups argued over some theory. A waitress totaled up someone's bill at the cash register.

Mark took the first seat at the empty counter, deciding if any more people came in, he'd get his coffee to go. He was becoming a hermit.

"What can I get you?" a woman in a chef's hat asked. She sounded tired, but still made an effort to smile at him.

As he always did, he looked up, hoping to see a hint of the woman Randell had described. The one who'd appeared the morning after the bombing, then vanished. The one who might be his wife and have no memory of it.

No thin, blond woman hid inside this girl. "Coffee," he answered.

"How about a muffin?" The girl winked too boldly to be flirting. "You look like a man in need of a poppy seed with icing on top. No extra charge for the calories."

The waitress with brown curly hair finished at the register and passed him a cup of coffee while the chef tried to make a sale. She also passed him a tin of cream without bothering to ask if he needed any.

Mark mixed the cream in his cup and agreed to try a poppy-seed muffin. He looked over at the woman who'd handed him the coffee, but her head was down. The lights were low enough to almost make the place seem like a bar, but the few beams still caught highlights in her curls.

He waited for her to look up at him, but she didn't. She stood about the same height as Blaine, only maybe ten pounds heavier. A little thick in the waist, but not a bad figure.

She turned and lifted a pair of black-framed glasses from the shelf beside the pass-through to the kitchen. Her eyes disappeared behind the frames.

Mark sipped his coffee and studied the others in the room. When his gaze settled on the big man in the corner, he noticed the stranger had lowered his paper and was staring back. Mark looked away first. He had no argument with the man. Let him stare.

The chef returned with a warm muffin. She set it down in front of him, then leaned on the counter. She stood just tall enough that when she leaned toward him her ample breasts rested on the bar. It crossed Mark's mind that some take a load off other ways than getting off their feet.

He took a bite of the muffin.

"How do you like it?" she asked without waiting for him to finish chewing.

"Great," he mumbled.

"I make them fresh every morning. Secret recipe I have. We got some customers say they're addictive."

Mark took another bite so he wouldn't have to talk to the girl.

"You could stop by for one every night when you get off work. I'd save you one if I knew you were coming." When he didn't answer, she added, "That is if you get off work about the same time every night. Lots of folks do."

He didn't want to tell her why he walked the streets or where he worked, so he answered with a question. "You own this place?"

The cook shook her head. "No, Mary and I just work here."

Mark glanced at the woman with her back to him. She made coffee about five feet away. He noticed her hands were long like Blaine's, only her nails were short and damaged, not long and perfect like his wife's. He wanted to ask the waitress to turn around. Mary had been the name of the woman who had had Blaine's bag. Probably a long shot, but it could be the same person.

"You married?" the chef asked.

"Yes," he answered without thinking. He had no plan to open up to this chatty girl behind the counter. Wherever she might be right now, Blaine was still his wife.

The waitress stopped to clean up a spill she'd made. She still didn't look up, so Mark just watched the light dance in her hair.

"Oh." The cook sighed. "Figures. All the cute ones are nowadays. My mom says my chances of meeting a single, straight man shrink with every passing day. Not that I'm looking, mind you. I've got my career in full swing right now and haven't got the time to even date."

Mark downed the last of his hot coffee in one long gulp. He placed the cup in the saucer and smiled at the chef. "Great muffins. Would you mind putting one in a bag for me?"

"Be glad to. I'll get a hot one from the oven." The woman headed toward the kitchen. "For your wife?"

"No, my neighbor." Mark regretted it the minute he said the words. He knew the chubby chef would return with more questions. With luck, she hadn't heard his remark.

He watched the other woman put the lid on the coffeepot.

"Miss?"

She didn't look up.

"Could I have another cup?"

The shy woman lifted the coffeepot and moved toward him, keeping her head down. From the little he could see, she wore no makeup and her face seemed more rounded even with the black frames of her glasses slashing across, but for a moment, he thought she looked just a bit like Blaine.

Mark stared at the coffee as it dropped into his cup. He had to stop looking for Blaine in every woman he passed. Friends were starting to tell him to get on with his life. How could he tell them he no longer had one?

"Thanks." He reached for the cream.

"You're welcome," she answered in a low voice that reminded him of an old song about blue velvet.

He didn't look up, but realized she made no effort to move away. For some odd reason, he liked having her close and thought maybe if he didn't move, she'd stay.

The world turned a little slower and she leaned an inch closer. Out of the corner of his eye, he swore she raised a hand almost to his hair.

The bell over the door broke the moment. She stepped away and Mark heard Randell's voice behind him.

"What's up, copper?" Mark raised his cup without turning around. "Shot any bad guys lately?"

Randell slapped his shoulder as he moved into the empty seat. "Nope. How about you, chased any ambulances lately?"

"Nope. It's a slow night."

Randell's tone lowered. "I've been looking for you. I've got a theory I'd like to talk over with you."

The chef returned, greeting Randell like an old friend, even pouring coffee before he'd ordered. While Randell moved over to say something to the big hairy man in the corner, the cook gave Mark her full attention. She asked him what he did.

Mark glanced around, but the waitress had disappeared into the kitchen.

Mark answered simply, "I walk."

If the girl thought the answer strange, she made no comment. She just invited him to come back and handed him the bill. Randell held far more interest.

Mark dropped a ten and stood. "Finish your coffee," he mumbled low to Randell. "I'll be across the street when you finish."

Mark walked out without a backward glance. He stood across the street for a long while watching the people in the café through the painted glass. Every now and then he'd catch a glimpse of the silent woman. She worked hard, he thought, for she circled the chef several times a minute. The huge man in the corner never moved. He clearly wasn't in there for the coffee.

Finally, Randell joined him. The cop took his time to light a cigar.

Mark waited.

"I've been thinking," he began as they stood side by side. "What if your wife didn't just run off or have a memory loss? What if there's a reason she disappeared?''

''Like what?'' Mark doubted the cop could think of a theory he hadn't turned over a hundred times in his own mind.

''Like, someone kidnapped her and is holding her.''

''They would have called in with demands by now. Besides, anyone who knew my bank account wouldn't even take the cat.''

Randell took a long pull on his cigar and released a smoky cloud. ''What if the person who laid that dynamite was trying to kill Blaine? No one else, just Blaine. And somehow, she knew it. Then she'd run and she'd hide.''

Randell had named the one thing Mark hadn't thought of. ''But why? There's not a soul on earth who hates her. Why would anyone want to kill, or even hurt, her?''

''Maybe it wasn't her they wanted to hurt, but you.''

''Me!''

''I'm just thinking,'' Randell hurried to add. ''But every time I read about the clinic bombing in the paper, it seems you're being talked about on another page. Blaine's disappearance stopped you from running for office, didn't it?''

''Yes.'' Randell had Mark's full attention.

''Well, it just crossed my mind that the two could be linked.''

Mark's mind was already running ahead of the cop. If the events were linked, who was the one person from the beginning who'd suggested he might pull out of the race? Harry Winslow, at the hospital that night. And he'd mentioned it again the next morning at the office. In fact Winslow had been making it so easy on him, so easy he didn't even have to come into the office.

When Mark looked at Randell, the cop was watching him. "You know something?"

"No," Mark answered too quickly. "But I have an idea. Give me a few days to do some digging and I'll get back to you."

"Be careful. Anyone willing to try and kill Blaine would do the same to you if you get too close to something."

"I will." Mark knew the warning was not casual.

"One other thing." Randell tossed his cigar in the water of the gutter. "I think you're being tailed."

"You're kidding."

"Nope." Randell walked away without another word.

The café lights blinked off, and the big man Mark had noticed reading a paper in the back of the café walked both women to a car. The chubby girl removed her hat and bounced into the driver's seat. The huge guy seemed to take extra care helping the other waitress fold into the tiny car.

"See Mary gets home safe," Mark heard the big man say as he closed the car door.

"I always do," came the answer from the driver.

After they left, Mark walked the streets down on the West End for a while, needing to feel more alone than he did downtown. He thought through everything Randell had said, tearing every point apart, taking both sides. One name kept coming to mind, his partner, his mentor.

It was too late to do anything tonight, but tomorrow morning he planned to be on time to work for a change. Maybe even mention getting back into the race just to see Winslow's reaction. If the cop's hunch was right, he might be able to find out something that would help.

Mark turned toward home, forcing himself to relax. He couldn't get the waitress at the café off his mind.

How long would it take him before he could ask her if she knew anything about Blaine's bag? She might know nothing, but if he moved too fast, she probably wouldn't talk to him even if she had information.

He thought of calling Randell and mentioning Mary, but Mark wasn't sure he wanted the cop involved. After all, it wasn't as if he had a theory. He'd simply met a woman named Mary. There might be a connection. There might not.

Hell, Mark thought, he hadn't even really met her. He just knew her name.

When he got to the apartment, he let himself into Lilly's place, planning to leave the muffin he'd carried all over downtown on her breakfast tray, but he found Lilly watching old movies. She had her leg propped on a pillow atop the coffee table and seemed surrounded by food. Cookies to the left, chips to the right.

She motioned him in as if she didn't want to miss anything happening in the movie.

With one glance Mark recognized *Pillow Talk,* one of her favorites. He handed her the bag and plopped down beside her, jostling the bowl of chips. "I'll sit through this one more time with you, but I'm not singing the songs this time." He ate the chips that had escaped the bowl.

She laughed. "Hush, or I'll make you watch both versions of *An Affair to Remember.*"

Mark held up his hands.

She opened the sack. "A muffin!" Lilly squealed as if she'd been starving for days.

"I picked it up at a new little place downtown."

Lilly took a bite and mumbled, "Get us a couple of beers, will you." She rubbed the cast on her leg, silently explaining why she didn't move.

"Muffins and beer?" Mark raised an eyebrow. When she didn't comment, he added, "You don't keep beer in your refrigerator."

"I know." She grinned. "You do."

He didn't argue. He walked over to his place and returned with two beers. Opening one, he handed it to her, noticing that all that remained of the muffin was a few crumbs on her pajamas.

He sat back down. "I met a woman tonight."

Lilly clicked the mute button. "Oh?"

Mark smiled. "It's not what you think. She's a waitress in that new little café downtown. So shy, she wouldn't even look at me, but there was something about her. I guess she's pretty enough, but not the way I'd ever be interested in even if I was looking. Just something about her. Something that drew me."

"What did she smell like?"

"What?"

Lilly looked at him carefully, reading him as easily as she did one of her books. "Were you attracted to her?"

Mark shook his head, then decided not to lie. "Maybe a little. But not like I want to ask her out or anything. More like I just felt good being near her, even though we only said a few words." He leaned his head against the back of the couch. "Funny thing, I think she felt it too. There for a minute, she could have moved away, but she didn't."

"Were you close enough to smell her?"

"No," he admitted. "Why do you keep asking?" Mark had figured out days ago that Lilly usually had a reason for her questions.

Lilly picked muffin crumbs off her chest. "I read somewhere that we are attracted, and repulsed, by people according to how they smell. Not perfume or anything, but the base smell every human being has. Some say even with all the dating games we play that we still pick out partners by smell.''

Mark laughed. ''So, you're telling me I was drawn to her smell. If that were true, I should have gone ape over the chubby little cook who smelled of warm blueberry muffins and butter. In fact, the whole place smelled like muffins. Must be why they named it Midnight Muffins. Maybe the singles bars have it all wrong. We should just hang out at bakeries and sniff each other.'' He grinned, proud of his own joke. ''Like that kind of thing matters.''

Lilly pressed her lips together as she always did when sizing up how much money he had in his pocket for a bet. He showed no surprise when her next words were, ''Want to bet?''

Mark knew the drill by now. He emptied his pockets and counted out seven dollars and twenty-three cents. She rummaged in her bag and dropped the same on the table. They'd bet on everything from the weather to ball games. It might be a vice they both loved, but Lilly insisted they always limit the wager to change. The only time Mark won was the bet on how many olives were on his sandwich. He'd eaten enough subs to make an educated guess.

''All right, what exactly are we betting on?''

Lilly thought. ''I have to depend on you to be totally honest here.''

Mark agreed.

''You have to get close enough to this woman to smell her. Really smell her. If you're attracted, I win, if you feel nothing, you win.''

''Fair enough.'' He had no idea how he'd get that close but he'd try. ''I can tell you right now I won't fall for her because of her smell. I'm guessing all that will happen is that I'll want to order another muffin.''

''One sidebar, please.''

''Stop using my language.'' He laughed, deciding he'd talked far too much about his work in the dozen dinners they'd shared.

''Okay. One more point. I get a muffin every night until you get close enough to smell her.''

''That's black mail.''

''Have to set terms or you might drag this bet out indefinitely. I also have to factor in that beard of yours. She may not let you get close enough to her for a good smell if she thinks you're one of the homeless.''

Mark scratched his chin. ''Maybe she'll like it.''

''Slim chance, but I'm still willing to risk my money.''

They shook on the bet. Mark cleaned up the empty beer bottles and headed toward the door. ''I'll be by to cook breakfast tomorrow morning.''

''Sounds good.'' Just as he stepped into the hallway, she added, ''Thanks.''

Mark smiled as he walked to his door. He should be thanking her. Lilly kept him sane. She'd filled some lonely hours, and the trouble with her husband had given him something to work on at the office. He'd spent a week finding out all he could about her third husband. If she had to have a divorce, Lilly only wanted her money back on a car she'd left behind. Mark figured he could do better than that. Especially since the husband wanted out to marry a woman half his age.

He walked into his apartment and found Tres already claiming half the bed. Mark undressed in the dark and wondered why he hadn't mentioned to Lilly that the woman's name might be Mary. Lilly followed the progress of his nightly walks, knowing that he looked for clues he'd probably never find.

So, why hadn't he told Lilly about what Randell had suggested?

Simple, he decided. He didn't want anyone else near him in danger. Startled, Mark realized he was already buying into Randell's theory.

# Twenty-Eight

Riding home with Tuesday, Blaine didn't say a word. She didn't have to, Tuesday could carry on a conversation with herself.

Blaine kept asking herself why she hadn't run to Mark and held him to her. He was the only man she'd ever loved, the only person she had ever allowed herself to believe in. Everything she'd done since the bombing had been to protect him or to find him. And when he walked into the café, what had she done? She'd ignored him. She'd done everything she could to walk differently, talk differently, so that he wouldn't see his wife when he looked at the waitress.

Once, she'd almost got up her nerve enough to touch him, but Randell came in and fear won out.

Miller probably figured she wasn't sure of Mark. He may have thought she believed that somehow Mark and Winslow had planned her death, but that wasn't it at all. Despite all her talk and dreaming, a coward still lived in her skin. She wasn't ready to face what he'd say about her change, about the baby, about how she believed one of the partners was trying to kill her.

When she got home, Blaine sat beside the doctor's bed and told him a different kind of story. A true story.

In his kind way, the doctor took her hand and said, "If you love him, believe in him. I think in this life it must be better to be fooled by a dishonest man than doubt an honest one. In the first case, you are the only one who is hurt. In the second, it destroys you both.''

She smiled, loving the old doctor's logic.

Blaine worked the following three nights, listening for the bell over the door. Business grew, but the only person she wanted to see walk through the entrance was Mark.

He looked so different with a beard. Not like the powerful lawyer at all, more like a young college professor. He'd lost weight. His longer hair made him seem younger, almost as he had been when she'd first met him.

As Blaine scrubbed the tables an hour before opening, she wanted to cry. That was nothing new, she'd cried herself to sleep every night since she'd seen him and had said nothing. Fighting tears seemed a normal state for her lately. Dr. Early had assured her that it was nothing unusual during pregnancy but she knew it was far more.

She hadn't lost faith in Mark, she'd lost faith in herself. The father of her child had passed within a few feet of her without even knowing her. He'd tipped his wife of ten years for pouring him a cup of coffee and she'd taken the money.

But the memory of how sad Mark appeared saddened her most. As if he suffered deep inside. Her husband looked as though his heart was breaking.

Why had she thought he could take the punch of her death and then disappearance without feeling the blow? Maybe because he hadn't reacted to his parents not being there. Maybe because it hadn't seemed to matter to him if he saw her most nights. First school and then work had always been so much more important to him. She'd lived with that fact from the beginning. He'd canceled dates to study, broke dinner plans to work, backed out on vacations when an interesting case came up.

She always thought of herself as an extra in his life. He loved her, and only her, Blaine felt sure of that. But she saw their marriage as something that made Mark's life easier, not something necessary for his survival.

The Mark she saw three nights ago who sat at the bar and told Tuesday he was married hadn't been the same man she left the morning she headed for the clinic. He continued to wear his wedding ring and appeared to suffer from her absence in his life.

Blaine scrubbed the table harder until the wood shone. She'd always protected him, seen after him. Only this time she'd let him down. In protecting him, she hadn't been able to stop the hurt, the loneliness she heard in his voice. She'd made her choice the morning she'd decided not to go home. Now she realized that either way might destroy her husband. If she'd run home that first day, the bomber might have gotten to them as easily as he had Frank Parker. Now, alone, Mark didn't look to be thriving. She may only have traded a quick death for a slow one.

She stood, suddenly feeling a pressure in her side a few inches from her scar.

The odd pain came again, stronger.

"Miller!" she cried, folding over in pure joy. "Miller!"

The big man stormed out of the back at full speed. "What? Did you see the bomber?" He was around the bar and at her side in seconds. "Where?"

He looked from the windows to her. "Mary! Are you hurt?"

Blaine laughed. "No." She waved him away with one

hand while the other touched her middle. "I'm sorry to have panicked you."

He came close, clearly not believing her. "What is it?"

She reached for his hand and placed it over her stomach. "My baby moved."

Miller folded into a chair without removing his hand from her slightly rounded abdomen. "Really?" He looked worried and nervous at the same time. "Is that normal? Should I call the doc? What if it happens again?"

Blaine placed her hand over his. "Don't worry. I'm not asking you to deliver it. I just thought you'd want to feel it kick." She didn't add that she had to share the news with someone. The life growing inside her became more a part of her each day.

They both stood very still a moment, before Miller whispered, "I feel something. Like a little fist knocking from inside."

Tuesday rounded from the kitchen with the first load of muffins. "What's all the shouting about?"

"Miller thinks he felt my baby move."

Tuesday set down the muffins. She showed only a slight interest. After all, it related to nothing in her world. She pulled off a pair of dark-framed glasses she wore to accessorize her checked blouse and leaned on the counter to watch.

When nothing happened, she returned to her work, forgetting her glasses worn only because she thought she looked more intelligent in them.

"Should I talk to him?" Miller asked, still concentrating on Blaine's abdomen. "After all, he's pushing me."

The big man wrinkled up his face as if he were witnessing an alien invasion. "He must know I'm on the other side. Maybe he's trying to communicate."

"All right." Blaine smiled down at Miller. The man's wonder more than made up for Tuesday's indifference.

"Right there. He pushed against my hand again." Miller leaned closer to Blaine's middle and yelled, "Now, you behave yourself. Don't go giving your momma no trouble or I'll thump you a good one when you get out."

Tuesday squealed and came around the bar, her hips making tables wobble as she moved toward them. "Stop talking to the little guy like that. You want him to think he's going to be abused?" She shoved Miller aside and placed her hand on Blaine's tummy.

Blaine realized her abdomen had become public property.

"This is how you talk to babies." Tuesday leaned down to belly-button level. "Hi, you little darling. Goooo goo a byyyy byy, my little lovey-love. Gooo goo, my goochi goo."

"Stop that," Miller growled. "He'll think there's something wrong with his hearing."

Blaine laughed so hard tears ran down her cheeks. She didn't hear the door's bell but the sudden rush of hot air drew her attention.

"You folks open yet?"

Blaine could do no more than stare at the cop. Randell. He had given up his raincoat and suit jacket in favor of a short-sleeved shirt. Without the coat, his gun, radio and handcuffs on his belt were in plain view. Blaine fought the need to back away. She'd been as close as she ever wanted to be to the man that night in the rain.

Miller reacted much the same, but Tuesday played

hostess. She rushed toward the new customer, blocking Randell's view of the others.

"We're not open yet, but I've got some coffee made if you'd like a cup, Officer."

"It's detective, miss. Detective Randell." He tugged on his belt as he pulled in his stomach. "A cup of coffee would be mighty fine."

She motioned Randell over to the counter and pointed to a seat as she reached for the cups. "We were just talking about my friend's baby, trying to agree on how we should talk to the little fellow before he's born."

Randell accepted the coffee and glanced in Blaine's direction.

"You got any kids, Detective?" Tuesday drew him back. "Maybe you could give us a little advice."

"No kids, no wife." Randell lifted his cup to Blaine. "But wish you the best with yours, ma'am."

Blaine slipped on the black-framed glasses Miller handed her and tried to remember to breathe. Randell wouldn't recognize her. Chipper had told the cop about her the first time she'd gone to the shelter, but she'd changed a great deal since that day. He might have noticed her at the bus stop the night of the stabbing, but with the rain and her sweatshirt hood pulled up, he couldn't have had much of a look. He'd even been in once before for a coffee and hardly looked at her.

Miller glanced at Blaine with worried eyes as he vanished into the kitchen.

"Thank you, Detective." Blaine barely got out the words before Tuesday interrupted.

"No wife, huh? Well, you'll be wanting to try one of my homemade muffins. They flat melt in your mouth." She smiled. "I was hoping someone would drop by early. I've got a new one called strawberries and cream.

I could really use someone to sample it and tell me what they think.''

"I'm your man,'' Randell volunteered and they both laughed as if he was extremely witty.

Half an hour later the cop was still talking to Tuesday and she was giggling at everything he said. She'd patted him on the arm so many times Blaine wouldn't have been surprised to see a bruise. Randell had tried three muffins and claimed he'd have to taste the rest, taking it on as his personal quest.

Tuesday patted him again so hard his elbow knocked against the wood of the counter with a thud, but he didn't seem to mind.

He asked Tuesday all kinds of questions, but since the girl wasn't a watcher of people she didn't have many answers, which in no way stopped her from talking.

Blaine stayed close enough to listen. Chipper had been right, he still searched for the woman who'd stumbled into the shelter the day after the bombing. Thin, blond, tall, looking as if she'd been hurt. He seemed to think the person might have worked at the clinic and been there during the bombing. He told Tuesday that this was his first big case and even if he had to live on the streets he planned to find the man who'd killed those people at the clinic.

Blaine found it hard to believe that the woman he described had been her. With flat sneakers she wasn't so tall, and *thin* was no longer a word that fit with her, though she was far from fat. She knew her hair had changed her looks the most. When it had been long and blond that was all most folks saw when they looked her direction. Her stylish cut had always left bangs almost covering her eyes. Now her short brown curls made her eyes seem darker. Or maybe it was the lack of a tan. It had been a month since she'd spent time in the tanning salon where she'd been painted over in much the same way as if she'd been run through a car wash. The little time she'd spent in the sun these past weeks had freckled the bridge of her nose.

When Randell told Tuesday about a group of boys who were harassing businesses downtown, the girl acted terrified until he promised to keep a special eye on her place so nothing would happen.

Tuesday looked as if she would have kissed the man if the counter hadn't been between them.

Blaine glanced over at Miller who stood by the kitchen door, watching through the pass-through. The big man looked as though he might throw up. He didn't like the idea of her being this close to the cop any more than she did, but the idea Tuesday had settled in for a flirt probably bothered him more.

When Blaine squeezed past Miller, he mumbled, "It's like watching two water buffalo mate."

"Stop it." She giggled. "And work on making yourself look invisible."

"Like you do, Mary Blaine?" He frowned. "Think he won't see you behind your Clark Kent disguise?"

"It fooled Lois Lane." Blaine pulled off the glasses. "Oh, about that beard you keep asking me if my husband has? I was wrong. He does."

Miller grinned. "I already figured that one out." He moved back through the door and over to the corner table, which he'd claimed as his during the slow hours of the night. He lifted a newspaper, blocking his view of Tuesday and the cop talking, their heads almost touching across the counter. He might have to listen, but he showed no sign of wanting to watch.

Business picked up about dusk. Blaine didn't like

working after that for she could no longer see out the windows. Anyone on the street could observe those inside more clearly. If the bomber were watching for her, she'd be easy to see after dark.

But, as the days passed, she grew less nervous. The detective became a nightly guest, but he never noticed anyone but Tuesday. Mark stopped in now and then to buy a muffin and left without staying for coffee.

Each time she noticed him, he'd leave before she could build the courage to talk to him.

Shakespeare limped into the café an hour before closing one Friday night. To Blaine's surprise, he appeared sober.

He claimed some car had jumped the curb and run over him while he was on the sidewalk minding his own business. It frightened him so completely he planned to stay sober for a few days until he could have his eyes checked. He promised he'd get the license number if it ever happened again.

Blaine sat him at a small table by the window and brought him a cup of coffee. He refused the muffin saying that the cholesterol was bad for his heart. Every time she passed he listed a new ailment that might kill him any day. For him, sober was a gloomy world.

A group of tourists rushed in, apparently afraid they might not get a muffin before closing time. They walked the streets like some twenty-legged bug, huddled together for safety. They all claimed to love the atmosphere of the café and asked to take a picture first with Tuesday in her chef's cap and then with Shakespeare for color.

Tuesday was flattered. Shakespeare charged them a dollar a shot.

As they paid out, Blaine noticed a man fighting the current of tourists leaving the cafe.

Mark.

He held the door for the group. He looked tired with dark circles beneath his brown eyes and his shoulders bent forward. Blaine wondered why he wasn't home in bed, then guessed he couldn't sleep. Even when nothing was wrong, Mark had trouble sleeping. He often got up at night and worked an hour before returning to bed. That was one of the reasons he gave for moving into the guest room from time to time. He said he didn't want to bother her with his sleeping patterns.

"''Evening,'' he said as he slid into the first seat at the bar again. "Is it too late for me to get a cup of coffee?''

Blaine glanced around for Tuesday, but she must have been in the back closing up the kitchen for the night. The last dozen muffins were on the counter under glass. If no one claimed them soon, she planned to sack them up. Sometimes, one of the Annas would hurry over right at closing time to pick up the leftovers. Blaine guessed the women passed them out at the bus stop.

Reaching for the coffee and cream, Blaine forced herself not to look at Mark. She poured his coffee.

"You remembered,'' he said as he lifted the cream. "You wouldn't believe how I have to beg to get cream at some places.''

Yes I would, she thought. Only she would have never have used the term *beg*. Mark usually asked politely a few times and then demanded in a firm tone.

"Want a muffin?'' Blaine said in almost a whisper.

"Not to eat,'' Mark answered. "But if you've got a few left I'll take them to my neighbor. She's laid up with a broken leg. I've been taking care of her and she's mighty tired of my cooking.''

Blaine couldn't believe her ears, but she didn't say a word as she stuffed the two biggest muffins into a bag.

Watching him out of the corner of her eye, Blaine wished she could touch him. It would feel so good to push his hair back, or hold his hand even for just a moment. He looked so sad, so alone. She tried to picture how he would react if he knew she was so close. If he knew about the baby. Would he be happy? Or angry?

Dear God how she wanted to talk to him! But she knew him, he'd insist they go straight to the police. Everything legal. Everything out in the open. By morning her statement would be all over the papers. By noon they'd be the bomber's primary target.

Blaine closed her eyes. She couldn't tell Mark. If she did, she might get them all killed. She had to play the game a little longer.

Mark played with his spoon, turning it end to end with the fingers of one hand. He always twisted something, a pen, a paper clip, when he was trying to figure something out. Blaine couldn't help but wonder what troubled him tonight.

She didn't see how closely he watched her.

"Hello, stranger,'' Tuesday said as she rounded from the kitchen. "You want that coffee warmed? You got time before we close. It's not often you stop long enough for coffee, might as well enjoy it.''

Mark looked too deep in thought to pull out for a moment, then he shook his head and picked up the bag. Without a word to Tuesday, he walked over to Blaine. "How much do I owe you?''

"Seven bucks.'' She tried to sound like Tuesday, but

the tone in her voice was far too low to capture the girl's enthusiasm.

Mark handed her a ten. "Keep the change."

"Thanks."

"Mind if I ask you your name?" His request was so low, she wasn't sure she heard it until he added, "Just in case I come in again."

There was nothing flirty in his voice. Mark had probably never flirted in his life, he was a man of order, a man who liked to know names.

"Mary," she said.

"Well, thanks, Mary." The corners of his mouth lifted in almost a smile.

Her heart cracked. He sounded so lonely. Like he hadn't talked to anyone in days. Like he was trying to connect with her, with anyone, so that he could make sure he was still alive. He turned away from her but didn't move. She had the feeling that he had nowhere to go.

The bell above the door sounded and a moment later Tuesday yelled, "Sorry, we're closing up for the night."

The door rattled again and again as others entered.

Blaine pulled herself away from Mark's nearness and watched the new arrivals.

Four young thugs stood just inside the door, among them the two boys who had harassed the girl at the bus stop two weeks before. The kid who had cut her played with the folded knife in his left hand. In the time since that rainy night, he had developed an edge, a hardness about him. It crossed her mind that if he cut another he wouldn't show panic again.

"Looks like you're still waiting on people." The tall boy moved to the counter. "You got muffins left. So I guess you're still open."

Tuesday's voice shook as she said, "All right. You boys have a seat and I'll get you each a muffin."

"We heard we don't have to pay if we don't have any money." The leader straddled a chair next to the counter where Blaine stood behind the cash register. "Word on the street is that down-on-their-luck folks are welcome here."

The others followed suit, pulling chairs around the tiny table. "Yeah," one mumbled. "We ain't got no money."

While Tuesday handed each a muffin, Blaine moved to the window. She stared out at the night, wishing she could see Miller. He'd stepped out a half hour ago as he sometimes did to see if anyone watched the café from the shadows. She guessed he stood somewhere across the street watching now. He'd be in at the first sign of trouble.

Just before she turned back, Blaine thought she saw a man in a baseball cap walking between parked cars. His outline blinked only a moment when he stepped beneath the streetlight's circle, then he was gone. Miller must be watching him too, that's why he wasn't here. The bomber's whereabouts was far more urgent than the harassment from these thugs.

She saw Mark leaving and fought the need to scream for him to stay. The boys were probably only being boys, but she would have felt so much better if she knew he stood near.

Tuesday talked politely to the boys. They mumbled among themselves, but seemed content to eat.

Blaine scolded herself. As usual, she'd overreacted. Her emotions had been running wild for weeks. She cried at nothing and worried about things that she had no control over. Maybe the constant fear of the bomber finding her had filed her nerves raw. Maybe it was the pregnancy, but at this rate, she'd worry to death before she turned forty.

"Wish Detective Randell would come in about now," Tuesday whispered as she passed Blaine. "I'd be real glad to see him."

"You're always real glad to see him," Blaine answered with a wink. "And don't worry about the boys, they're just hungry."

Shakespeare, who had been sleeping at the corner table, woke up and made a grand show of saying goodnight.

The boys made fun of him, but he paid them no mind.

Blaine kept busy emptying the coffeepots and washing the last of the dishes while Tuesday took her nightly call from friends who always seemed to start their evenings about closing time.

Miller should be back any minute, she told herself. He was always there to lock up and walk her home if Tuesday had to run.

Blaine packed up two muffins for the Annas and poured two large coffees in paper cups. If neither of the women came tonight, maybe she could talk Tuesday into circling the block on the way home. Vanilla Anna had been coughing for days and Blaine worried about her. The nights could be cool and she knew the two old women would never consider going inside.

Blaine slipped the last muffin into a bag with a carton of milk. She'd leave it on the corner of the porch and by morning her little friend would have picked it up. She'd tried to watch for the child, but so far she hadn't seen him coming and going. But he'd thanked her once by bringing her water and that was enough. Miller had followed him once and learned the little boy lived with a mother working two jobs. A neighbor was paid to keep an eye on him, but mostly just watched the kid come and go.

Blaine dropped the two cold pills the doctor had given her for Anna into the larger bag with the muffins and coffee.

Before she could ask about driving by, Tuesday appeared at her side pulling her sweater on as she said, "Mind if I leave a few minutes early tonight? It's real important, or I wouldn't ask. My roomy says we can just catch the sneak preview if we hurry." She glanced at the boys. "Don't worry, I'll make sure Miller is out front before I dart away."

Blaine had learned that "real important" could be a movie starting at midnight or a party in full swing at the girls' apartment complex. "Sure," she said, wishing she had the guts to say no. "Miller can walk me home."

"Thanks." Tuesday rushed out before Blaine could say more.

Blaine walked to the door and held it open. "Sorry, gentlemen," she said to the thugs, "but it's closing time." She dimmed the lights to prove her point.

"How much we owe you?" one asked.

"Three dollars apiece if you have the money. If not, there is no charge."

Vanilla Anna suddenly blocked the door, breathing heavily as though she'd ran from the stop. "I'm sorry I'm late, Mary." She coughed into her hand. "I was at training union and must have fallen asleep."

Blaine knew Anna had been sleeping on the bus-stop bench as always, but she didn't say anything. She handed Anna the bag of leftover muffins. "I packed coffee too, with two sugars like you like it. When you down

about half of the muffin take those pills in the bottom
of the bag. They'll ease that cold.''

"Bless you, Mary. You make me so proud.'' Anna
whispered as she hurried away, "There will be diamonds
in your crown, child, I swear.''

The boys stood, but took their time moving toward
the exit. They didn't want anyone hurrying them.

"Well,'' the tall one said. "We ain't got no money
so I guess there will be no charge.''

Blaine couldn't make herself ask them back as she did
everyone else who passed through the place.

At the door the boy with the knife mumbled, "That
was sure a good muffin.''

"Yeah,'' another echoed. "I could eat another one but
it looks like they are fresh out.''

They were out the door when Blaine heard one say,
"I know where we can get another one. I seen her give
the old bag lady a whole sack of them.''

Blaine watched as they ran in the direction Anna had
gone. Panicking, Blaine rushed out the door and along
the passageway to the street. There, as she hoped he
would be, stood Miller watching the café from across
the street. Ten feet away from him, getting a paper out
of the machine, was Mark. Both men had been watching
the café from the street.

"Miller.'' Blaine shook so badly she could barely
force the word out. "The boys have gone after Anna!
They plan to take the muffins I handed her.''

Miller hurried toward her.

Mark tossed the paper in the trash and fell into step
beside the older man.

As soon as she saw Miller's face, she realized the
problem. He would have to leave her alone in order to
help Anna.

"Anna can take care of herself. She has for years," Miller reasoned.

"No," Blaine cried. "One of them has a knife and you know how they pick on her because she yells at them like they were children. She won't give them the sack willingly and she'll fight when they try to take it."

The big man didn't budge. "I'm not leaving you alone, Mary."

Mark stepped closer. "I'll watch over Mary." His voice rang out, commanding, as it often did in the courtroom. "Go after the kids."

She knew he didn't know what he'd walked into. If trouble happened while Miller was gone, could Mark handle it? Did they have a choice? The boys might have already reached Anna.

Miller glared at him. "See that you take care of Mary or I'll snap your neck." There was no hint that Miller might be kidding.

"Hurry!" Blaine begged. "They already hate Anna. I can't stand the thought of them hurting her."

Miller nodded once and turned away.

Mark took a step closer to Blaine, putting himself between her and the street. "Don't worry," he whispered. "Everything is going to be all right."

# Twenty-Nine

Blaine made it halfway down the passage to the café door before she turned her face to the wall, wishing she could melt into the brick. Mark had just said the words she'd longed to hear for months and he didn't even know he'd spoken them to his wife. Loneliness, fear and panic overwhelmed her. She pushed against the wall and tried to breathe.

She hadn't left him the day of the bombing—he'd left her long before that. The politeness, the shortened conversations, the courtesy of routine. He didn't know her. Maybe he never had. He'd never taken the time. All he'd ever witnessed was the outside of her and now that had changed, he saw her as only a stranger.

The hollowness of her life gripped her soul. The possibility that Mark felt it too doubled the pain. He must not only mourn his wife, but also the prospect of what could have been between them and never was. If she could blame him it would be so easy, but the crime rested with them both. He'd been right, they were a perfect match.

Blaine became aware of the heat of his body hovering just behind her and wished she could tell him how dearly she needed him, how deeply she'd always needed him. But she had never known how to tell him.

He would have no idea how to comfort her now. In

the darkness between the streetlight and the café it seemed safe to be so close to him, and she needed his nearness so desperately. She'd been adrift for so long.

"Don't worry about your friend." Mark placed his hand on her shoulder. "I'm sure that big guy won't let anything happen to the old woman." He rubbed his hand comfortingly across her shoulders. "Boys are more talk than action. I've seen them cry like babies when they get in front of a judge."

Blaine could no longer endure the distance between them. She turned into his chest, wrapping her arms around his neck and holding on as if her life depended on it.

For a few moments Mark didn't react. His hand just rested on her shoulder. He could feel her tears dampening his shirt. He took a deep breath.

And breathed in the scent of his wife, his mate.

A dam broke deep inside and he pulled her closer, needing the nearness to her as desperately as he needed air. He stopped thinking, analyzing and simply felt.

His mind floated while he held her, a woman reason told him he knew nothing about. He buried his face in her hair and breathed for what seemed like the first time in weeks. She smelled of cinnamon and Ivory soap and something else. She smelled like Blaine. Smiling, he thought of telling Lilly that he finally got close enough to the waitress.

She felt so good pressed against him. Her heart pounding, her breath on his throat, her breasts flattened against his chest. With instinct more than thought, he leaned her against the building, pressing her into the brick, needing the solidness of her, needing her softness.

He told himself he would pull away if she gave the slightest sign she didn't welcome his nearness, but to his amazement, she dug her fingers into his hair and held him just as tightly.

All thought vanished as his body moved with her breathing. He rubbed his beard against her cheek, and she turned her mouth to his, as if sensing what he wanted. His lips found hers before the idea of kissing her reached his brain, but he made no move to pull back.

The passion of their kiss rocked him. Her too, if he gauged her reaction correctly. She pulled back a moment and rubbed her cheek once more against his beard, then returned to his lips.

He felt as if they stood in deep water in the middle of a lightning storm not wanting to move. He wouldn't have pulled away even if they'd taken a direct hit.

He couldn't get enough of the taste of her, the smell of her, the feel of her body against his. His lips brushed over hers and she opened her mouth, begging him to take more as her hands moved across his chest, measuring, memorizing.

There was no world but here and now. No one else but the two of them. No past. No future.

His hand moved down the front of her blouse until he held her full breast. Moans of pleasure whispered between them as the kiss deepened and his touch grew bold.

Mark's sanity slipped and he didn't care. He pressed his open palm gently over her breast as though it belonged there as he kissed her with more passion than he thought he possessed.

Softening with his touch, she welcomed him with abandon. He couldn't kiss her deep enough or long enough to get his fill and she reacted the same way. Her hands moved over him, hungry for the feel of him.

They were not shy lovers stealing a kiss, but ageless lovers clinging to one another for survival.

He broke the kiss and listened to her rapid breathing as he slid his open mouth down her throat, then lower until the buttons of her blouse stopped him. With kisses he climbed back to her ear and whispered as his chest pressed lightly against hers, ''Unbutton it.'' He wasn't sure if the words were a command or a request. He didn't care. He simply needed to feel her skin.

Her hands trembled as she slipped her fingers between them and unbuttoned her blouse.

''Do you want me to stop?'' He tasted her flesh once more as words mingled between them.

''No,'' she whispered, already pulling his mouth to her.

The kiss was long and hungry. He broke it when she had no more breath left. As she gulped for air, his mouth moved along her throat and down. The material gave way and he savored the swell of creamy skin that rose above her bra. Then he pressed her against the wall once more and returned to her mouth.

Her body shook with desire. Absorbing the slight movements, Mark deepened the kiss.

His leg moved between her knees and pressed higher, trapping her with his weight while his hands spread across her hips. She moaned once more, a low sound of pure pleasure. He leaned against the side of her face loving the softness of her hair as her head rocked lightly back and forth to his touch.

Somewhere, in the frontier of his mind, he heard shouting. It took him a moment to gain reason enough to be aware of his surroundings.

Her hands pushed against his chest as the shouting grew louder.

Then she was gone. Running toward the street. Running away from him.

Mark hadn't had time to take a step when Detective Randell rounded the corner of the passageway and almost collided with her.

"Mary!" he said out of breath. "Call 911. Tell them we need an ambulance and backup. Now!"

Mary nodded and ran past Mark to the café.

"And don't worry about Miller, he's fine," Randell yelled after her as he kept an eye on the street. "Faring better than me in the fight," he mumbled as he ripped off the final few threads holding the pocket to his shirt.

Mark took a step toward the cop.

Randell noticed him in the shadows between the light from the café's doorway and the streetlight. "That you, Anderson?"

"It's me."

Randell put up his hand. "Stay out of this, Mark. Don't get involved. What's happening here tonight has nothing to do with you or your missing wife."

"But..."

Randell checked his gun. "If you want to help, get Mary home safely. A woman in her condition doesn't need to be on the streets this time of night. I'll tell Miller you're taking care of her. Tuesday told me the old man worries over her like a mother hen."

Without allowing Mark any time to argue, Randell turned and was gone.

Mark stared into the street. A woman in her condition? He absorbed the words one at a time, trying to make sense of it all. He knew he'd just held Blaine in his arms. She might have changed her hair and clothes, maybe gained a little weight, but a man could never forget the feel of his own wife against him. But Blaine wasn't pregnant.

Or was she? The reason for her clinic visit suddenly became clear. She'd gone to make sure before they talked. Of course! It was the only thing that made sense. But then something had happened and they hadn't been able to have that talk after all.

The bombing. She hadn't left him. Maybe his guess about her being hurt and losing her memory could be right. Or maybe Randell's theory of her having good reason to hide was correct. Otherwise why would she be here, only a few blocks away from his office, calling herself Mary?

Did she know who she was? Did she know he was her husband? He had to find out.

He'd discovered a few disturbing facts about Winslow over the past three days. The man had ties with a few big oil men and it looked as if he had been doing them favors for a while. The question was, what were they doing for him in return?

Every cell in his body wanted to run inside the café and demand answers, but he knew he'd frighten Blaine even more. There were reasons, there had to be. Blaine might be shy, but she had always been a logical person. For once in his life he needed to shut up and let her talk. Let her find her way back to him.

Mark knocked his head against the brick and groaned in pain. He was too dumb for a frontal lobotomy. How could he have acted this way with her? If she'd lost her memory, and didn't know who he was, she must be frightened to death. He had to slow down.

If she knew who'd tried to kill her, they had far more important things to talk about than whether she'd un-buttoned her blouse.

He wasn't some animal who went into heat—he had never been the kind of man to act before thinking. Even in college he was never drunk enough or dumb enough to go home with someone for a one-night stand. But, in his defense, he'd missed her so badly there were times he thought he was losing his mind.

Leaning against the wall, he decided she'd probably never come out of the café. If she had a memory loss, she'd lock the door and wait for help. She would probably think some kind of sex maniac waited for her in the darkness between the café and the streetlight.

He closed his eyes. Dear God, had he really asked her to unbutton her blouse?

He had to calm down, let her tell him. If she was hiding, playing the role of Mary, she might be lying about the pregnancy as well. He had to take conversation with her one step at a time.

Mark knew nothing of how to deal with someone with a memory loss, but attacking them probably wasn't the first plan. Maybe he should play along. Let her even call herself Mary if that made her happy.

He wasn't sure what to do, but one thing was sure, he didn't plan to lose her again. If he had to win her all over again, he would, and he planned to stand between her and whoever wanted her dead.

Blaine hung up the phone and stood in the stillness of the darkened café watching Mark's silhouette. By the time she felt brave enough to walk back outside, she heard the sirens answering Randell's call.

She had no idea what she would tell Mark, but the time for pretending was over. No matter how dangerous it was to bring him close she had to tell him everything. Part of him must already know who she was or he wouldn't have kissed her the way he did. Surely the moment he had touched her, he knew. She'd tell him every detail that had happened since the bombing and he'd figure something out. Whether planned or not, they were in this together now.

He stood among the shadows that crisscrossed in the entryway to the café. His hair was a mess and his eyes were closed, but she knew he heard her walking toward him.

Before she could say anything, or touch him again, as she dearly wanted to do, he pushed his body away from the wall. "I'm sorry, Mary. I don't know what came over me a few minutes ago." He plowed his hand through his hair, making it look more out of order than it already did. "Randell told me to see you home."

He could always talk faster than she could think, but all Blaine heard was one word. *Mary.* He still didn't know who she was. Her husband had kissed her with more passion than he'd ever shown and he thought he was kissing another woman.

She'd gone mad, Blaine decided. She was angry at Mark for kissing her. Angry that he hadn't known her when their bodies had been pressed together so closely. Angry that she was the other woman in a triangle of two.

Unexpectedly, Blaine laughed.

Mark joined her, first nervously, then truly. When they both calmed down, he added, "I love the way you laugh."

Blaine decided to play the game. She'd heard a librarian complain once that sometime in every marriage the wife realizes she married the village idiot and tonight must be Blaine's turn. "You loved her. This wife of yours?"

"She was my heart," he answered. "Trouble was, I didn't know it until my heart stopped."

She fought the knot in her throat as she folded away his words forever in her memory.

He glanced back at the open doorway. "If you'll lock up, I'll drive you home."

She pulled the door closed and checked the lock. "You don't have to drive me. We can walk."

"What about your purse?"

Blaine shrugged. "I don't have one. Don't need one."

They walked along in silence for a few blocks, enjoying the stillness of the city after midnight, enjoying being near one another. When they left the businesses and government buildings behind, the streets grew darker with streetlights spread farther apart.

Blaine took Mark's arm without saying a word. Usually, their strides matched in perfect rhythm as couples who walk side by side often do, but Blaine had shortened her stride as her center of gravity had begun to shift with the baby. Miller had told her one night that she was starting to walk like a duck.

She tried to think of where to start with Mark, but for the moment it felt good just being so close. After all the tension of the past weeks she'd found a peace by his side. She never realized how wonderful that felt until now.

"I'm sorry," Mark said again. "I didn't mean to walk so fast."

"It's all right, lately everyone seems to walk quickly. I'm pregnant, you know." She never dreamed she'd say the words so easily to Mark.

"I know. Randell mentioned it."

They continued in silence, both lost in their own thoughts. When she reached the steps of Dr. Early's house, Blaine turned without giving him any details as to why she was staying with the doctor. "Thank you."

"You're welcome." He hesitated, unwilling to leave her. "Are you safe here?"

"Yes," she answered.

She studied his face in the midnight light. "I don't know where to start, Mark. I don't know how to tell you all…" Frustrated, she felt the tears bubble in her eyes. All her bravery vanished.

He couldn't hold back any longer. He pulled her into his arms and held her against him. "It's all right, Blaine. Everything is going to be all right now."

She cried softly on his shoulder. When she tried to talk, he hushed her with light kisses. "Tomorrow, darling. We'll talk tomorrow. Right now it's enough that I found you."

# *Thirty*

Mark pushed the money on the coffee table toward Lilly as he delivered the old woman her breakfast.

She squealed with pleasure. "Tell me all about it. You did get close enough? You were attracted to her, right? I know it. I felt it in my bones just like my momma always could when she knew something was about to happen."

"That about sums it up. I got close and I was attracted," Mark answered. "Except the part about her being Blaine, my wife."

Mark leaned back in his chair and waited for the questions.

"You mean she reminds you of Blaine?"

"No. I mean I held Blaine in my arms last night. She'd done a good job of making herself into another person, but I seem blessed, or cursed, in this lifetime to be drawn to one woman."

Lilly raised an eyebrow. "Then why isn't she here?"

"We decided she's far safer where she is than with me right now." He leaned back in his chair and grew serious. "I may be way off, but I think someone is trying to kill her to get to me. The detective who is on this case came up with the idea and I thought he was crazy, but now I'm not so sure."

Lilly ate her breakfast as Mark filled her in on the

details. She asked questions between bites. "Does the detective know Mary is Blaine?"

"Not yet. I'm not sure he would go along with what I have planned. I've been trying to work out who would benefit the most by my not running for office or from not being active in the partnership. I can come up with only one person, but I can't get my hands on any proof. Blaine and I decided to tell no one, trust no one, until it's safe for her."

Lilly pointed her fork at me. "Then why are you telling me?"

Mark winked. "Because I need your help."

Lilly's grin made wrinkles appear all the way to her ears. "I'm in. This is better than any of my 'have to watch' shows."

"Can you manage to get dressed by ten?"

She slapped at her cast as if it were nothing. "No problem."

Mark told her what he needed her to do as quickly as he could. He wanted to be at the office as close to on time as possible this morning and he hadn't yet showered or shaved. "I'll need to borrow your car. You'll take a cab, but remember, timing is everything this morning."

Lilly took his arm as she rose. "I'll call Andy. Since you gave him that hundred-dollar tip he's at my door anytime I need a cab."

Mark wasn't surprised she knew the cabdriver's name. "Promise me you'll be careful. If anything goes wrong act like you're in pain and need to get out of there."

Lilly looked offended. "I can handle the man, Mark. Don't worry about me."

When he left her apartment she was already hopping around her bedroom trying to decide what to wear.

Blaine and he had agreed, for safety, to have no contact until tonight, but Mark had to keep fighting the urge to call her.

When he came out of the shower, he stumbled over Tres, but this morning he only smiled. "She's coming home," he whispered as if the cat could understand.

When he turned out of the driveway in Lilly's car, Mark looked for anyone tailing him. No one. Whoever the cop thought might be watching him must have gotten tired. Or, now that it was too late for him to step back into the race for the Railroad Commission, maybe there was no need.

Once in the office, Mark only had minutes to set up his plan. Bettye Ruth gave him one raised eyebrow as he used the copy machine without her help. He thought of including her on his idea, but since he'd be basically breaking and entering, he didn't figure she'd go along. If his plan failed, this would be his last day in this law office.

With a shock, he realized how little he cared.

He walked into Winslow's office as if just planning to say hello.

Harry Winslow looked busy, but he made time for Mark. "Glad to see you in so early."

Mark leaned on Winslow's massive desk. "I had to come in. We had a walk-in a few days ago who wants me to handle her divorce. I thought the case would be routine, but now I'm not so sure."

Winslow didn't look interested. "Glad to hear you're back at work. Walk-ins can be a pain, but they're one way to get back in the saddle."

"Yeah, this is a more interesting case than I first thought. Seems the husband has a folder full of old oil leases he wants kept out of the settlement. He probably could if she didn't have a copy of some of the documents."

"Really?"

Mark fought down a smile. He'd hooked Winslow's interest. "Trouble is, I don't know much about what she's talking about. I may be asking for help on this one since you played the oil game once. I don't think the woman has any idea what she has and, according to her, her husband is too interested in visiting the women in Vegas to keep up. They need someone to take over their books and from what the woman says neither have kin."

Winslow stood. "That does sound interesting. I'll be glad to help however I can."

Mark swore he saw the man lick his lips.

Winslow tapped his pencil on his calendar. "I could talk to the woman for you if you like. My schedule's not all that packed this morning."

Mark shrugged. "If you like. I'll bring her in here when she comes by."

"Mr Anderson?" Bettye Ruth stood at Winslow's open door. "A Mrs. Crockett is here to see you."

Mark stood. "Please ask her to come in here. Mr. Winslow will be sitting in on this one with me."

Winslow nodded.

Bettye Ruth looked uncomfortable. "I've already seated her in your office."

Mark knew she would have done just that before she went looking for him. Bettye Ruth was much too considerate to leave an old woman on crutches standing in the lobby.

"I'm not sure she can make it to this office. She looks exhausted."

Mark turned to Winslow. "Well, thanks for offering, but..."

"Nonsense." Winslow stood. "I can go into your office. I see no problem." He grabbed his notepad and led the parade back to Mark's office.

Within minutes, Lilly did exactly as Mark had instructed; she acted as if she trusted Winslow far more than Mark, even commenting on how younger folks don't always understand the problems.

Winslow agreed without giving Mark a glance. The man was at his best when dealing with older women. He knew just how to make them feel comfortable.

Mark talked down to Lilly the first chance he got, explaining something to her as if she were a child, which obviously irritated Winslow.

Miss Lilly leaned closer to Winslow and turned so that she left Mark out of the conversation.

When Mark asked Lilly exactly how many leases her husband held, Winslow clearly let it be known that he thought Mark was being too bold. He looked directly at Mark and reminded the younger partner that he had another appointment waiting.

This was the standard code for asking another to step out, but Mark still tried to look confused.

"You're welcome to use my office if you need to. I'll finish talking to Mrs. Crockett." Winslow glanced toward the door, leaving no doubt what he wanted Mark to do.

Without looking at Lilly, Mark stood, excused himself and went straight to Winslow's office. He'd left enough phony leases in Lilly's file to keep the old partner busy for an hour and Lilly could probably hold him longer if necessary.

Mark closed the office door and smiled as he saw Winslow's keys dangling from one of the files. Winslow was the only partner who kept locked files in his office.

He locked everything and never left without his keys. Not even his secretary was allowed to touch the files behind Winslow's desk. Only today, greed had made him forgetful.

Mark went to work. Within half an hour he found what he'd been looking for. Somehow, early on in his career, Winslow had found a way to skim twenty percent off the top of his clients' oil holdings. It was a tricky game best played with older clients and people who didn't really understand legal language. Ten minutes later he had copies. Winslow had made millions and all he had to do was make sure the files were never audited. If Mark had been elected into office as the railroad commissioner, all his papers and probably those of the partners would have been checked. Winslow's game would have been over.

With the new file under his arm, he walked back into his office and acted surprised that Winslow and Lilly were still there. Winslow looked frustrated as if he hadn't found what he'd been hoping for, and Miss Lilly looked tired.

"Walk me to my cab, young man" she said. "I've decided not to get a divorce today after all."

Mark helped her into the cab, kissed her on the cheek and said he'd tell her everything later. He had people to see and first on the list was Randell. He needed to tell the cop his theory might just be true, for Mark now had proof.

He had a hard day's work ahead of him. Everything had to be checked and double-checked. Mark wanted to ensure there were no loopholes Winslow could slip through.

"How'd I do?" Lilly asked as he put her crutches in the cab.

"Perfect. If I wasn't married, I'd propose to you right now."

She reddened, then waved her hand. "What makes you think you'd be man enough for me. I'm not an easy woman to please."

He grinned. "I never would have guessed." He closed the cab door before she had time to answer.

# Thirty-One

It was almost 11:00 p.m. when Mark walked into the café. Tuesday waited on him, forgetting the cream, but he was too tired to care. After he finished his second cup, he asked about Mary with what he hoped sounded like only mild interest.

"She went home early," Tuesday volunteered. "She reads to the doctor she lives with when he's feeling poorly and my mom called to say he was really having a hard time of it tonight. Sometimes Mary reads to him until dawn. Not that she ever complains. Not that she has to with Miller around."

Mark hid his surprise. Tuesday would have made a good witness on the stand, she gave ten times more information than necessary.

He started to ask another question, but Detective Randell walked in. In an odd way, they'd become friends. Kind of like the two kids in school who no one likes but who band together. The cop and the lawyer shared a desire to solve a crime. That mutual obsession connected them.

He'd tried to reach Randell several times during the day but all he got back was a message to meet him here. So, Mark had had to hold his news while he'd spent the day researching the law on oil rights and checking his facts.

Randell motioned Mark to bring his cup and join him at a table. It took several minutes for Tuesday to deliver Randell's coffee and run out of any reason to hang out at their table. Randell seemed to be a regular and no doubt the girl's favorite.

When they were finally alone, Mark asked first about the fight between the thugs and Miller. Since he hadn't read about it in the paper, he figured no one got hurt. He'd had Bettye Ruth check the arrest reports for any details but no one had been booked downtown except a few drunk drivers.

Randell finished chewing a bit of muffin before he answered. "The old man picked up a couple of the thugs who got too close to the bag lady and literally threw them out of the way. We rounded up some of the boys, but I couldn't see arresting Miller. From what I could figure, he stopped them before anything got ugly. Even so, little Vanilla Anna got so upset she thought a storm must be coming."

Randell leaned back and mumbled his way through another bite of muffin. "Miller took a little nick on the arm. He refused the ambulance saying he knew a doc who would sew it up, but I insisted on driving him to the emergency room."

"He gave them hell for a while before he finally let them patch him up. I ran a check on the old mountain of a man, and you're not going to believe this." Randell leaned closer. "Old Luke Miller got the Medal of Honor for what he did over in Vietnam. The old guy's a hero."

"Where does he live?" From his clothes, Mark would have guessed he slept on the streets, but Mary had said something about him staying above the café.

"Who knows, but he hangs out here. Seems to think his job is to watch over that waitress named Mary. Word on the street is they're friends, but he's none too friendly and she's shy as a mouse. An unlikely pair if you ask me.''

Randell finished off the muffin. ''I need to talk to you for another reason. I'm going to tell you something that I probably shouldn't.''

Mark leaned forward.

''We got a tip a few weeks ago as to what the clinic bomber looks like. It wasn't from the most reliable source, so we filed it away. But last week, with the pizza place drive-by, we got a dozen witnesses giving us the same description as the tip. They all claim our bomber was driving the car that slowed in front of the pizza place.''

''And?''

Randell took a drink. ''One of the uniforms spotted someone who fit the description two days ago. I'm thinking if I tell you the facts, you'd be another set of eyes watching for the guy. But I want you to swear to me that if you think you see him you just call, that's it. I don't want you confronting him. No citizen's arrest or anything like that.''

''I know the law,'' Mark said, ending Randell's rambling. ''I want this guy behind bars worse than you do.''

Randell agreed. ''Look for a man, slim build, blue baseball cap and dirty hands. The first informant said he had gray eyes, but the others didn't remember that.''

''Color of eyes is hard to see walking the streets at night. And anyone can change caps.'' Logic fired Mark's statements as if he were in court. ''He's probably washed his hands. Dirty hands on the streets are more the rule than the exception. Not much of a lead.''

''Right, but two witnesses to the shooting reported

how dirty his hands looked. They mentioned the cap and the build."

"If you two have had enough male bonding," Tuesday interrupted, "I thought I'd get you to try my new muffin recipe."

Randell grinned. "I'd love to, darling. Being your tester makes my night." He wiggled an eyebrow, indicating a few other things might "make his night" as well.

When Tuesday giggled and ran to get the muffins, Randell added in a whisper to Mark, "Another policeman walking the drag spotted him an hour before the drive-by shooting. He got a good look at him thanks to all the streetlights. He thought the guy might be a thief—there's quite a problem with burglary in that part of town. He tried to question the man, but said he ran like a rabbit. Since the cop didn't have anything hard on him, he figured he'd just keep an eye out and catch him next time. When he turned in the report, he also mentioned the same details, right down to hands covered in oil."

Tuesday fluttered back like a giant multicolored butterfly circling the table. She offered refills, then left, finally getting the hint that the men were talking.

Mark leaned back as he slid a folder across the table to Randell. He'd been waiting all day to tell Randell his news. "I found a man who would stand to lose a great deal of money if I got a seat on the Railroad Commission. In fact, Winslow knows me well enough to guess that if I got the job, I'd do it with a passion. And eventually, I'd discover the flaws in his legal dealings over oil leases."

Mark stared directly at Randell. "It was in his best interest to be my friend because I'm honest, but if I were in office, I wouldn't look the other way. Not even for a friend."

Randell was fascinated. He glanced at the first few pages, then looked up. 'But would he kill to protect himself?''

"Not me, it would cause too many questions. But he might have someone killed to stop me. If he were desperate and, from what I've been able to discover, Winslow is desperate. He's lost quite a bit of money in the market of late and with three ex-wives, two homes and half a dozen offspring bleeding him, he can't afford to let his extra income dry up. He's told me stories about the oil game fifty years ago when things were wild, like a poker game with too many aces. My guess is he's still playing the same game.''

Miller set down his muffin. "What are you trying to say, Anderson?''

"Your theory is right. Blaine was the target that morning at the clinic. He must have been at the end of his rope to come up with such a crazy plan. But maybe he knew the right people who'd do anything for a dollar. I think I may have met the man you just described in Winslow's office one night. I don't remember a hat, but I remember not wanting to shake hands with the man.''

"If we can tie the bomber to Winslow…''

Mark stopped him as two people passed them on their way to a back table. "If?''

As soon as Mark knew they wouldn't be overheard, he continued, "The morning after the bombing, one of the security guards at our town-house complex mentioned someone had tried to break into the parking garage. But, at the time, I was too lost in losing Blaine to care about my car. But what if that someone had been trying to get to Blaine's car? When he couldn't, he followed her to the clinic and somehow knew what part of the building she was in.''

"It's a stretch, but it might have happened." Randell leaned in closer. "Are you sure about Winslow?"

Mark nodded. "I've made copies of enough files to send him to jail for the rest of his life. First I went through all the partner documents. Nothing out of order. In fact the file was almost too clean. Then I remembered a locked file I'd seen Winslow close every time he left the office—even to go to lunch. All I had to do was get him to leave his office without thinking to lock the file."

"How'd you do that?"

"I used greed as bait and it worked. I had just enough time to copy the files so he won't suspect a thing until the moment he's arrested. The papers in the files are on standard office stationery so legally, since I didn't break and enter, we should be able to use them as evidence. I even have a witness who'll testify that Winslow told me to use his office. And if I know my secretary, she overheard the entire conversation between Winslow and me. She'll back me up."

Randell looked around. "If you're right and this partner, Winslow, hired someone to kill Blaine, you'd be wise to disappear. If he knows what you're up to, he will come after you."

"I'll take that gamble. Can you see these papers get to the right people?"

"I can, but you've got to come with me. We can put you in protective custody."

Mark shook his head. "Not now. I'm safe enough tonight. But as soon as you hand that file over, there is a possibility he will come looking for me."

Randell nodded. "Meet you here tomorrow night and I'll fill you in on the progress. It may take a few days to get the warrants. To link the clinic bombing and the pizza place drive-by to Winslow is going to take a little time.''

Mark agreed. He picked up two muffins for Lilly and left, heading home to sleep with the cat. Blaine was safe tonight and if he didn't get some sleep soon the mattress in the alley would start to look great. He wanted her, needed her near, but most of all, he wanted her safe.

On the drive home he tried to see if Randell had been right about him being tailed, but no one followed him. The cop was just being paranoid.

The next night Mark barely looked at Blaine when he walked into the café. He went straight to Randell. Mark decided that the fewer people who knew who she really was, the safer she would be. He might trust Randell with his life, but he didn't plan to trust anyone with Blaine's.

As Mark took a chair he noticed Miller was back on guard at the last table. The hairy old guy didn't look any the worse for wear after his fight with the thugs.

"Good news." Randell smiled. "We picked up a man over by your apartment complex and brought him in for questioning. He had a gun on him, violating his parole. A night in jail should make him more talkative, but I'd be willing to bet he's the man hired to watch you. Not much of a professional. Interesting fact though, he spent his youth working in the oil fields of West Texas.''

Mark smiled. "Just like Winslow." Mark glanced at Blaine. He wanted to talk to her, but keeping her safe was more important than ever. He didn't know how many others Winslow may have hired.

"If his gun was the one used in the drive-by, my guess is our watcher will spill his guts."

"Tomorrow?"

"I'm working on it." Randell raised his coffee. "We make a pretty good team."

Mark agreed and made Randell promise to call if there was any change. They said good-night as Miller locked the door behind them. Mark could see Blaine through the glass as she cleared the tables. She didn't look up, but he knew she was missing him as much as he missed her.

He walked to his car knowing he couldn't go the night without seeing Blaine. Driving down the back streets he decided he could have walked faster to the doc's place. He parked several houses away, got out of his car and waited. He'd drifted to almost in front of the doctor's house by the time Tuesday dropped Blaine off at the curb. Mark stood on the sidewalk between the circles of lights from the streetlights.

She walked past him as if he were no more than a tree root and headed up the path to the long front porch littered with old metal lawn chairs and broken-down wicker. When she reached the first step, she turned around. The porch light wasn't on, so he couldn't see her face. He didn't know if she smiled or frowned. She might even be angry.

He moved until he stood directly in front of her. "I—"

"You ignored me," she whispered in a voice he was still getting used to.

She was angry, he realized. Blaine was angry.

"You acted as if I wasn't there. As if I was of no importance."

Mark smiled. He'd never loved her more than right now. Right at this moment when she finally found fault with him. When she finally told him what she thought.

"You're right," he answered. "I didn't speak to you.

But not for one moment did I forget that you were there.'' He moved his fingers into her curly hair and said something he'd never said to her. ''I'm sorry. You'll never know how hard it was to keep from touching you, from watching you.''

She leaned off the step and into his waiting arms.

He tried to explain between kisses about Randell and keeping her safe, but nothing made sense but holding her. He'd worried about her from the moment he'd left her two nights ago, and the pleasure of holding her close once more was almost painful.

''I want to be with you,'' she whispered as he kissed her gently.

''I know, but you're safer here for tonight.''

''Then come in with me,'' she asked. ''We can sit on the couch like we did before and hold one another.''

He almost died with need for her, but he knew he couldn't stay. Not tonight. He needed to be ready if Winslow made a move. ''No one can know that you're my wife until we put a few men behind bars. With any luck you won't have long to wait. But I'll not put you in harm's way. Right now, standing too near to me might do just that.''

She nodded, unable to speak.

They stood in the shadows of the porch for a long while, neither able to let go even though they both knew they had to. Finally, he pulled away and walked into the night as she stepped inside.

Neither of them noticed the man sitting at the far corner of the porch, little more than a shadow among shadows.

Miller slowly stood, covered the sleeping child, hidden among the wicker benches and chairs, with an extra blanket and stepped over the back of the porch, leaving the same way he'd come.

# *Thirty-Two*

Blaine checked on the doctor, then curled into her makeshift bed on the couch and thought of the way Mark had kissed her. The taste of him lingered on her mouth. Familiar, newborn, addictive. He hadn't kissed her with so much hunger since…he'd never kissed her with so much hunger.

He seemed to be awakening before her eyes, evolving in her arms. The knowledge frightened Blaine almost as much as it excited her. She'd changed in the past few weeks, but so had he.

He had always been a good lover—when he scheduled the time into their lives. But spontaneity never altered their hours together. He usually asked politely if "tonight would be a good night" and all she had to say was "probably not" to discourage him. Occasionally, there had been lovemaking in the morning, but she always initiated those encounters, needing to keep him near her a few moments longer before his work claimed him once more each dawn.

Mark must be finding this sudden attraction to her as strange as she did. She felt as if they'd been calmly floating in their marriage for years and now suddenly faced a storm only to discover the water far deeper than either of them imagined.

He hadn't mentioned the baby. There hadn't been

time. Blaine knew they'd have to face it, but somehow they were both stronger than they had been.

She moved her hand over her middle, feeling the slight movements of her child. "We'll make it," she whispered. "We'll all make it."

Blaine got to work early the next afternoon. Tuesday was already there, baking up a new brand of muffin she claimed would be the "signature" Midnight Muffin.

They heard Miller stomping around upstairs, but neither had bothered to ask if he was moving in or simply dusting out the place. Since opening the café, Blaine noticed that his clothes were cleaner, and he'd even managed to find a barber who'd trimmed a few inches off the bush of hair he lived in. He hadn't changed his gruff attitude, though most of the regulars simply thought of him as part of the atmosphere of a café open so late.

Cleaning the tables, Blaine made a mental note of supplies needed, then counted out the cash for the register. The late sun sparkled through the windows when the first group of customers walked in.

Looking up, Blaine watched three women she had known for years. She had chaired several committees with Phyliss, and Alice worked with her on library fundraisers. The third was one of the partners' wives from Mark's firm. Though Jillian Winslow was probably twenty years older than Blaine, they'd shared many an evening while their husbands talked business. Jillian had been the one who'd introduced her to the world of volunteering. They usually worked on different projects, but ran into one another at the same places. Blaine preferred the hands-on work, Jillian the fund-raising.

"Oh, miss." Jillian looked straight at Blaine. "Do we sit anywhere?" There was a note of impatience about her as though she expected to be waited on immediately.

Blaine watched for the shock to move across their faces when they recognized her. It would only be a moment, she told herself, before all three rushed toward her, crying and shouting about how they all thought she was dead.

She could have been no more than a fixture for all the attention they paid her as they sized up the tiny café with its old furnishings and hand-painted signs.

"Oh, well," Alice said. "It smells good anyway. We need a break."

"Sit anywhere, ladies." Tuesday bumped Blaine with her hip as she passed. "I just finished writing the muffin choices on the board. While you decide, do you all want coffee? We make a mighty fine cup here."

"Decaf for me." Jillian moved from table to table as if looking for one clean enough to sit at.

Phyliss put on her glasses so she could see the list posted behind the counter. "Just water for me," she said to Tuesday. "With extra lemon."

"I'll have the same," Alice added. "It's far too hot for coffee."

Tuesday glanced over at Blaine. "Have you got it, Mary?" she mumbled. "I need to pull out the last batch of muffins."

Blaine nodded and began serving the table. She carefully put the drinks in front of the women, waiting for them to recognize her. Jillian and Phyliss acted as if she wasn't there and Alice moved her purse from the back of her chair to her lap, keeping her hand atop it.

"Would you like cream?" Blaine asked Jillian twice before the law partner's wife looked up.

"Heavens no," Jillian answered without smiling.

For a second their gazes locked. The older woman

looked away first, drawn back into conversation with her friends.

Blaine played the same game with the others. Asking them direct questions until they looked up at her. Waiting for someone to recognize her. How could they look at her and not see her? The sun shone on her face. She hadn't gained that much weight. Surely makeup didn't change her completely.

They said nothing to her. Phyliss even looked around her to follow what Jillian said more closely.

Blaine almost forgave Mark for not knowing her the moment he saw her. The café was shadowy after dark and the porch light at Dr. Early's even worse, but these women were looking at her in broad daylight. She wasn't going to keep her head down and speak softly, she would face each one. Surely, with one glance, they could see her. They had all spent hours talking to her over the years.

But none did. If anything, they seemed annoyed that she continued to interrupt their conversation. Blaine finally moved back to the counter to watch them. A month ago she had been one of them and now they didn't even know her. She'd worn the clothes, the expensive haircut, the makeup, the tan. She had talked of the next fundraiser, the next party, the new restaurants in town. But no more. She was no longer a part of them and she knew deep down that she never would be again. Maybe she never had been, maybe she'd only pretended.

The knowledge freed more than saddened her. In a way, she'd been wearing a mask with them and suddenly it felt good to breathe.

They chatted, lost in their own world with nothing around them of any importance. They asked for things, an extra plate, a bag to take half a muffin home, more water with extra lemon, but they didn't see Blaine as she waited on them.

It wasn't just the hair, clothes and makeup that had changed, Blaine realized. She had. Since that day in the clinic when she'd thought her world would end if she got bad news she'd grown and, more importantly, she'd survived.

"Will that be all?" Blaine placed the bill on the table.

"Yes," Alice said with a half smile as she reached for her purse. "Thank you, miss."

"You are welcome." Blaine returned her smile to the top of Alice's head. "Come again."

She held the door and they each walked past her and out of her life.

Blaine went back inside, cleaned the table and stuffed the dollar tip in her pocket. Tuesday spread out sandwiches and milk on the counter and waited. It had become a habit late in the day to eat a quick supper together. Mrs. Bailey always sent a meal to work with Blaine, afraid her youngest daughter wouldn't be eating right, now that she was out on her own.

Tuesday took a bite of her sandwich and mumbled. "How'd you like to be one of those rich ladies with nothing better to do in this world than shop?"

Blaine shrugged. "Seems like a nice life."

"Maybe. I haven't been able to shop in regular sizes since grade school. Kind of takes the fun out of going to the mall when all you can look for is purses and shoes."

Blaine nodded as she sampled one of the sandwiches.

"They're white bread though. Everything's all taken out of them. It must take generations of boring people breeding with even more boring people to make a woman like that. Give me whole-wheat, or banana-nut, anything but white-bread people." She giggled. "I like folks yelling, and feeling, and sometimes even messing it up. At least you know you're alive when you're hurting, or hungry, or lonely. Those women haven't felt anything in years."

Blaine didn't argue. Tuesday wouldn't believe her if she told her how easy it had been to slip into that lifestyle. More than just the money or education, there was something else. The fear of feeling drives people to eliminate all possibility of connecting with another. It's like thinking, "If I don't know you, you can't hurt me. If I don't step out of my safe little circle, no one can touch me."

Blaine fought to swallow around the lump in her throat. She couldn't go back to the nothingness of her life, no matter how much she loved Mark. She'd stepped too far out of the circle of safety.

The sadness in Mark's eyes came to mind. Maybe so had he. He didn't seem to be living the life he'd lived before she left. Even with all his worries last night, he'd remembered to get Miss Lilly's muffins, something he never would have thought about before. Maybe he'd changed.

Tuesday leaned back in her chair. "I love this job," she said honestly.

"You're good at it." Blaine pushed her thoughts aside. "What's your favorite part?"

Tuesday blushed. "When that detective comes in. Seems like I have to wait most of the evening before he comes blowing in, but it's worth the wait. He calls me hon, like he means it. He's not married or anything, I've asked him. When I suggested he might be late picking up his date last Friday, he laughed like I was making some kind of joke. He said he doesn't date much. Can you believe that?''

Blaine almost said yes before she realized she'd be hurting Tuesday's feelings.

''You think I should ask him over to my apartment and cook him a meal?''

Blaine smiled. ''Definitely.''

''What if he turns me down?''

''Then he's a fool,'' Blaine answered. ''But you're out there living, loving, fighting, mixing it up.'' Blaine turned Tuesday's words on her. ''You're living and who knows, maybe even loving.''

Tuesday reddened even more at the compliment.

Glancing past the girl, Blaine watched the street. For once she thought about other things. The man in the blue hat was almost at the door before it registered in her mind that she was staring at the bomber.

He came in, his head low, his left arm loaded down with a grocery bag. He took the first seat near the window.

Blaine could see the black oil on his hands from across the room. She swore she could smell it. He didn't look up, but she knew when he did she'd be staring into gray eyes.

Blaine dropped her sandwich and whispered to Tuesday. ''Get Miller!''

Tuesday opened her mouth to ask a question, then reconsidered and slipped off the seat. She hurried to the back.

Blaine was alone with the killer. She stared as he slowly raised his head and turned toward her.

Gray eyes looked at her as if she were already dead.

# Thirty-Three

**M**ark never walked the streets until long after sunset. The heat and the constant crowds around the capitol made it impractical. But when he left work a little after five his only destination was the café. He needed to see Blaine. All day he'd been pretending in the office that nothing was wrong.

He'd even passed Winslow in the hall and talked of nothing as they always did. As if he didn't know the partner would be arrested soon. As if he'd been able to sleep from worry. What if the paid killer got to Blaine before the police rounded him up? What if Winslow's "friend in the department" passed on news about the file? Winslow would have an easy guess as to who had turned him in, and Mark would be out in the open, a sitting duck. But, he reasoned, going into hiding would only cause questions. He didn't want Winslow to suspect a thing until the police walked in the door.

At this rate, Mark figured he might get in the *Guinness Book of World Records* for lack of sleep.

Mark walked to his car removing his tie and jacket and wishing Randell had called. Something must be going on. The wait was killing him.

A woman pushing a stroller walked past him.

Mark realized he'd had so much on his mind he hadn't given much thought to Blaine's pregnancy. Now a hundred questions formed. Was she sure? Did she want the baby? Did the thought of it frighten her half as much as it did him? He wasn't sure about how he felt about becoming a father, but he knew how he felt about Blaine, and nothing, not ten children, would stop him from needing her.

He glanced back at the stroller. The baby might as well have been an alien for all he knew of children. He had barely figured out how to keep the cat from starving, what luck would he have with a kid? A child would change them, change their marriage. Was it strong enough to survive?

The traffic fought his progress, but Mark finally managed to slide into a parking spot directly across the street from Midnight Muffins. The afternoon sun reflected off the glass, but he could see inside. Blaine stood by the counter and one man sat at a table near the door. Tuesday, the cook, and the guard dog Miller were nowhere in sight.

Crowds of people hurried down the street blocking his view again and again. Downtown Austin was a beehive about this time of day. Everyone hurried to get somewhere other than here, and the traffic crawled along bumper to bumper.

Mark watched Blaine work. For a few minutes he just enjoyed knowing that she was close. He'd always enjoyed watching her move and a change in hair color didn't alter his pleasure.

He couldn't see her very well through the glass, but he decided she wasn't any less beautiful than before. There was a grace about her movements and a glow in her cheeks that no amount of makeup could change.

Then he noticed she brushed her hand across her abdomen and then glanced toward the back door.

Nothing happened. She moved her hand once more over her middle, protectively this time, then looked from the one customer to the kitchen door as though waiting, or hoping, for something.

She was nervous, Mark thought. But why? There was only one man in the café, a thin guy with a blue cap on. Surely she didn't think it was too busy for her to handle the place alone.

A thin guy in a blue cap!

Even in the heat of the car, Mark felt a chill. A blue cap.

He tried to see the man's hands, but he was too far away. Mark told himself that a hundred people were probably walking the city wearing blue baseball-style hats, but it didn't stop the panic. He could be the one Randell and the police were searching for.

The only customer, alone with Blaine, could be the bomber.

Mark watched her move behind the counter. She felt uneasy, he decided, for except when she glanced quickly toward the back, she kept her eyes on the one stranger. She was in danger and no one stood near to help.

Climbing from the car, Mark waited for traffic to break enough for him to run across the street. He needed to get a closer look at the man. If his hands were oily, Mark would be on the phone to Randell within seconds. This could be the break everyone had been waiting for.

The two old bag ladies he'd seen at the bus stop neared the café. Chocolate Anna watched traffic, but the one called Vanilla Anna talked to the people passing by, wiggling her finger at first one and then another. Telling them to wait until the Walk sign before crossing or she would put them in the corner to think about their crimes.

Mark swore at the traffic that kept him from the café.

He didn't want to take the time to cross at the light. Blaine might need him now. She must be near panic. There was a phone in the kitchen she could use to call the cops, but to do so, she'd have to leave the stranger alone.

The constant flow of steel stopped his progress halfway across the street. Mark stood, cars passing on both sides of him, but all he could see was Blaine backed into a corner.

The Annas entered Midnight Muffins waving their hellos. They sat down at a table next to the man in the blue cap. Each arranged her bags around her legs so all would be in easy reach.

To Mark's horror, Blaine placed herself between the two old ladies and the man in the cap. As he darted across the street, he saw Miller storm from the kitchen with Tuesday a step behind.

The stranger grabbed the bag beside his chair and ran through the door before Miller rounded the corner of the counter. Mark was within five feet of the passageway only to have to weave through a crowd of grade-school children monopolizing the sidewalk. When he reached the entrance to the passageway, the bomber was gone, vanished.

"Did you see a man in a..." Miller shouted as he banged from the café.

"I saw him."

"Which way..."

"I don't know." The man had disappeared on the streets, too short to stand out in the horde of people.

Miller looked angry enough to beat the information out of Mark and frankly, if that would have helped, Mark wouldn't have minded.

"You go left, I'll go right," Miller ordered.

"If I spot him, I'll call Randell."

"You do that," Miller mumbled as he turned.

Mark turned to his left wishing he had on his running shoes or even more comfortable clothes. He didn't fit in as well in the crowd in a starched white shirt and custom-made trousers. Darting between the people, he fought his way as fast as he could, trying to look at every person on the street as he passed. He searched block after block, doubling back and taking a different path again and again. He walked into restaurants, hotels, bars, scanning every place for the sight of one man.

Shadows lengthened. Several times Mark thought he saw the cap only to find he'd followed the wrong person for a block. In the back of his mind he kept the hope that Miller was having better luck. They couldn't let the guy slip away. The thought that he'd been so close made Mark angry. The memory of him being almost within reach of Blaine made Mark sick to his stomach.

When he turned down the streets where bars lined both sides, he knew he'd gone too far, but he pushed on to the underpasses beneath Interstate 35. The sky was draped with heavy clouds, making it seem darker and later in the day. He walked past businesses with boarded-up windows and colored lights beckoning from shadowy doorways. Empty beer bottles clambered into the gutter as he stepped around a line of young people dressed in black waiting for one of the bars to open.

It was too late, Mark realized. The bomber could be standing ten feet away and he wouldn't be able to see the man. It was too dark. He'd let the man who tried to kill Blaine get away. Mark felt as if he'd failed her once again.

"You lost, Mr. Businessman?"

Several of the thugs he'd seen the other night had

fallen into step at his side. They bothered him more than frightened him, but he remembered one had knifed Miller that night the old man had tried to protect the bag ladies. Talking to them was like poking at a beehive. Mark reminded himself to take care.

"Look, fellows, I'm not hunting trouble. I'm just looking for someone." Mark walked faster, but they stayed right with him.

"Fellows!" one yelled and they all laughed. "He's just one of us fellows."

"We're his buddies," another one added. "His pals."

The thug closest to Mark held out his palm. "How about loaning me some money, pal?"

Mark moved faster, his runner's muscles responding to the challenge, but the boys stayed right in step.

"I could use a loan."

"Me too," another echoed.

Mark stopped and faced them, unable to see their faces clearly in the night. "Why don't you boys go away. I'm not going to give you any money and I've more important things to do than visit with you."

"Boys?" One giggled. "How you like this, *old* man?" He swung as if to land a blow on Mark's jaw.

Mark dodged it easily. "Look. I don't want to play. Leave me alone."

Another boy danced in front of him shadow fighting like a boxer. "How about we play?" He swung faster, harder, than the first.

Mark dodged once more.

The dancer continued, weaving back and forth as if only practicing. Then, without warning, he advanced.

Mark had never fought in his life, but his hands went up by instinct in defense of the blow.

The kid's knuckles connected at Mark's shoulder. Before he could dance away, Mark shoved him hard. ''Enough!''

Mark turned on the others. He knew if one made a move, they'd all storm toward him. In the darkness he couldn't even tell how many there were but his odds were not good.

One stepped closer, a bottle in his hand. He swung toward Mark's head like a baseball player preparing to make a home run.

Mark had no problem blocking the blow with one arm as he shoved his fist into the kid's middle and felt his release of air as he stumbled backward.

Another, shorter than the rest, ran at him like a bull. Mark jumped to the side, but the blow of the boy's head still plowed hard against his lower ribs. As he twisted, he raised his arm, swinging hard at anyone within range.

His fist connected with what felt like a face. He heard a cry and felt the warm rush of blood across the back of his hand. He swung again, blindly now.

The boys backed away.

Mark saw his chance. He ran into the total blackness between two buildings knowing that if he could make it five feet they'd have trouble following, for they wouldn't know if he stood a few feet down the alley waiting for them, or had gone on. The blackness would be his ally, not theirs.

He ran half a block toward the faint glow of a streetlight ahead. When he looked back, he heard no steps following and smiled. He'd escaped. A moment later as he turned back toward the light, something tripped him. He tumbled into a pile of trash that had dripped out of an overflowing Dumpster.

Boards tumbled from a stack of forgotten wooden delivery trays. One hit him hard across the head and he saw stars.

He lay back amid the trash and tried to keep from passing out. Every muscle in his body hurt. Rotted food clogged his senses. Warm blood dripped from his forehead. Mark took a deep breath as something crawled across his leg. Too large to be a cockroach, too small to be a cat. Mark forced himself not to guess what animal it might be.

He slowly stood and stumbled toward what he hoped was the direction of the café. He needed help, but he passed a dozen places that would have called an ambulance for him, or doctored his wounds and still he moved forward. He needed to reach Blaine and know that she was all right.

The thought crossed his mind that with Miller gone from the café the bomber might return.

Mark's head throbbed, his muscles hurt, but he ran on toward the café paying little notice of the people who stared as he passed. As soon as he knew she was all right, he'd worry about the bothersome cut that kept dripping blood in his eye.

When the café came into view, he saw Blaine serving coffee to a couple by the window. Miller stood at the counter. All looked calm. Mark slowed his steps and wiped his forehead with the sleeve of his shirt. Looking down, he realized his dress shirt was more red than white, with the blood of others more than his own, but he couldn't rush into the café and frighten everyone half to death.

He changed directions and took the alley. Finding Midnight Muffins's back door was easy, the old drunk everyone called Shakespeare slept on the steps as if it were his new flat. He mumbled when he saw Mark, but didn't stop him as Mark pulled the heavy door open and slipped into the back of the café.

A small bathroom stood just inside the door. Mark maneuvered around a stack of boxes and slipped in. He pulled off his shirt, and after rinsing it as best he could, used it to wash the blood off his body. The pesky cut above his eyebrow was just bad enough to continue to bleed. Mark rinsed the shirt once more and held it to his forehead hoping to stop the blood and wishing he'd paid more attention in health class years ago.

Just then, Tuesday reached for one of the boxes stacked beside the bathroom. A moment too late Mark realized he should have closed the bathroom door. He must have frightened her to death, for she screamed loud enough to wake Shakespeare outside. He poked his head around the back door as Miller hurried through the kitchen.

For a moment Tuesday and Miller danced amid the boxes, both trying to get past the other. Tuesday screaming. Miller swearing. The boxes toppling one by one as she bumped against them.

"It's all right!" Mark yelled, fighting down the spinning in his head. "I'm not hurt that badly and I didn't come in to murder anyone." He lowered the shirt from his forehead and the wound started dripping blood down his face again. The light around him was beginning to dim, as if someone was playing with a dimmer switch.

Blaine's face appeared from behind the others, her blue eyes full of worry and horror. Mark fought to focus.

The world dimmed. "Blaine," he whispered as he fell.

# Thirty-Four

When Mark came to, Miller knelt on one side of him and Detective Randell on the other. Despite the pain, he mumbled, "You two are the ugliest nurses I've ever seen." He managed to sit up, pushing away from one of the take-out boxes that dug into his left shoulder. "I'm suing this hospital."

"He's all right, or as good as lawyers get." The cop chuckled as he stood, taking up most of the space in the narrow hallway between the back door and the café's toilet. "He'd have to take a few more hits to the head to make him human." Randell glanced behind Mark. "Hope he didn't chip the sink with his hard head."

Miller poked at the bandage on Mark's forehead as if testing the doneness of a cake. "Bleeding's stopped, or at least it's not leaking through the gauze anymore."

"Stop that." Mark pulled away and banged the back of his skull against the sink's pipes. No one seemed to notice the ringing sound but him as he straightened and tried to sit up amid the clutter of boxes and brooms. "I've reached overload on my share of pain for the night."

Randell pulled out a notebook. "All right, let's get the facts down. Who beat you up?" He scribbled notes across the page. "Were you robbed?"

Mark stared straight at Miller, ignoring the detective's questions completely. "Any luck finding the guy?"

The old man shook his head. "You?"

"No. I never even saw a hint of him once he disappeared through the café door." Mark shifted to Randell. "I did run into the thugs you hang around with, Detective."

Randell's pen stopped. "Did they do this to you? Can you ID them? If you can give me a clean description of one, I can pretty much figure out who his friends were. They always run in packs like young wolves. But they've gone too far this time."

Mark laughed. "No, the kids didn't do anything." He pointed to his head. "I did this to myself. I ran over some trash in the alley."

Randell frowned. "How about the truth, Anderson? Miller's already told me you both ran after the suspect after I thought I was clear all I wanted you to do was phone if you saw him."

Mark was surprised by the hardness in Randell's tone. "Are you cross-examining me, Detective, or accusing me of lying?"

Randell pointed to the bruise along his ribs. "Unless I'm mistaken, those are knuckle bruises. I've seen the mark a fist makes too many times not to recognize it."

"You're right. I did spar with the boys. I gave more than I took. When I saw a way out, I darted down a dark alley, making a clean getaway until I fell over some trash someone had thoughtlessly left in the way."

This Randell believed. "You want to press charges on the boys? After all, I'm sure they started it. You wouldn't have been in that alley if they hadn't been bothering you."

"No." It crossed Mark's mind that they were probably underage. They could press charges on him if they wanted, but somehow he knew they wouldn't get close enough to anyone in authority to do so.

The cop still didn't look happy. "Miller tells me he had no luck tailing the guy after he left the café." Randell glanced at Miller, who looked as if he wasn't listening to the conversation.

Randell turned back to Mark. "You should have phoned. This guy is deadly, Anderson. He's not someone to play hide-and-seek with. You're a suit. You don't know the streets."

"I'm learning the hard way." Mark rubbed his hair away from the bandage covering most of his forehead. "I just wanted to make sure he was the right man before I called," Mark lied. He wasn't sure he wanted to tell Randell more. He'd done nothing with the information Mark had handed him so far. For all he knew, Randell might be the "good friend" Winslow had in the department.

While Randell made notes in his police version of a Big Chief tablet, Miller offered Mark a hand up. The grip felt as if it was shattering the bones in Mark's bruised knuckles. When he looked at Miller, he knew he'd been right to say nothing to Randell. Somehow the details were connected to Blaine, and Randell still called her Mary. The whole café seemed to be sheltering Blaine, protecting her.

"You had supper?" Miller asked with the tone of a drill sergeant.

Mark shook his throbbing head as he pulled on his wrinkled dress shirt. It was still wet and clung to his frame, but he didn't care.

"Mary grilled you a cheese sandwich before we talked her into going out front with Tuesday to close

up.'' Miller made the invitation sound like an order.
''We didn't know how many teeth were rattling around
in your head. Thought you might not be able to eat anything else.''

Mark nodded and pushed his way past the two men.
Even though the kitchen was closed for the night, all
clean and ready for another day, he found a plate of food
by a high desk built into a corner. Bills and receipts
covered the wall on three sides of the desk, but from the
stool where he sat, he could see through the passageway
into the café. Papers had been shoved back from the
center of the desk to make room for his place. He flipped
off the light above and relaxed, eating his sandwich more
by feel than sight.

Miller returned to his watch by the door and Detective
Randell went out front to ask Tuesday for another cup
of coffee. They were all waiting, like strangers trapped
in the same foxhole.

Mark needed time to try to reason through all that had
happened, but first he had to get past the drums pounding
in his head. In movies when guys take a fall there is
never any mention of how bad it hurts. Actors just jump
up and start fighting again. Mark wasn't sure he could
make it to his car. Like his bruised knuckles, his eyes
saw blue and purple clouds floating around in the shadowy room. He remembered an old joke about someone
saying to a drunk with bloodshot eyes, ''Those look terrible.'' The drunk replied, ''You should see them from
this side.''

He still sat on the stool when Blaine hurried through
the swinging door, her hands loaded down with coffee
cups.

She set them in the sink and turned to him. He could
see the need in her eyes, but she kept her distance.

"Sailor June just came in and said she'd talked to the Annas. They claim the stranger who was in here with them took one of their bags when he left."

"How'd they know? They each carry a dozen."

Blaine shrugged. "June said it was the one with a Lego in it."

"Strange," Mark said as he watched Blaine slowly inch her way toward him.

"You gave us a scare," she whispered in that low voice he thought belonged on a midnight radio show and not in a late-night restaurant.

"I'm sorry." He brushed her back, knowing that if anyone looked through the pass-through from the café they wouldn't see his hand. "It was my own damn fault. What kind of an idiot runs down a dark alley?"

He put his head in his hands and leaned into the desk, trying to stop the spinning.

A moment later, Blaine's fingers moved over his hands. She tugged them away and kissed the bandage on his forehead.

He started to push her away, but she whispered. "Randell's too busy with Tuesday to see us."

Mark closed his eyes as she leaned down and let her kisses drift along the side of his face. "I needed to talk to you," he mumbled when her mouth pressed gently over his. "I thought we should talk about..." He couldn't finish. She was doing the very thing that he thought they should discuss.

She moved between his knees and melted against him the way she did when he'd kissed her in the darkness. She'd never been so bold before, so sure of herself. All the pain of his cuts and bruises vanished. Mark kissed her as he had before, with a hunger that went all the way to his soul.

"I need to talk to you too," she whispered against his lips. "I need to tell you..."

He swallowed her words within the kiss. The longing for her drove him beyond all reason and Mark no longer cared. He slipped his hand beneath the loose blouse she wore and spread his fingers over her skin.

She swayed with him, leaning against his bent leg for support as his fingers moved over her. Starved for the feel of her, he no longer wanted to pretend. He was a man who needed his mate.

He wanted to drown in the familiar warmth and passion of her.

If Mark had been standing, his knees would have buckled at the softness of her flesh against his palm. He moved his hand down and felt the slight swell of her abdomen just above her waistband. Slowly, he pushed the elastic band down until his hand could move over the place where the baby grew. His baby.

If he'd been asked at any time before today, Mark would have sworn he'd have been repulsed by the feel of a pregnant woman. Any time before today. He spread his hand over her, loving that a part of him grew inside her. Loving her for carrying their child.

"I want you," he whispered against her ear, forgetting every other thing he wanted to tell her. "I need you."

"I know," she said against his lips. "I feel the same."

Tuesday entered the kitchen and flipped on the light. Blaine turned away. Mark felt as though if he fell off his stool he'd fall all the way to hell, because when she'd slipped away she'd taken his heart with her.

Tuesday, as always, was totally unaware of what went on outside her realm of concern. "Detective Randell has offered to take me to IHOP. You can drive my car back to the doc's and I'll pick it up later. I thought I heard it thunder a while ago and you don't want to be caught walking home in the rain.'' She laughed and whispered low so her date waiting in the café wouldn't hear. ''I may be much later, so don't wait up.''

Miller squeezed past her and deposited his cup in the sink. ''I've already locked up. It's time we call it a night. You want me to see you back to the doc's?''

''No, I'll take Tuesday's car and leave the keys where she can find them.''

For some odd reason, he didn't look at Mark, then Mark realized from his post by the door he probably had seen through the passageway—had seen everything that went on in the corner of the kitchen. It might have been too dark for details, but Miller could have noticed them leaning close. And Mark guessed Miller didn't miss very much.

Blaine moved about the kitchen, her head down as if she didn't notice anyone else in the room. He couldn't tell if she was waiting for them to leave, or was embarrassed at how far they might have gone if they'd had another minute.

He wasn't embarrassed, wouldn't have been if Miller had seen it all, heard it all. He was more amazed that he'd responded so deeply, so quickly. The thought that he'd let Blaine sleep alone so many nights amazed him. How could he have been such a fool?

Mark stood. ''How about I take Mary home?'' He tried to keep his tone casual when all he wanted to do was be alone with her. ''Then Tuesday can keep her keys and pick her car up here.''

Miller frowned and Mark didn't miss the way Blaine put her hand on the old man's forearm. ''It's all right,'' she whispered.

"Are you sure, pest?" Miller gave Mark a look that said he'd gladly kill him if she gave the word.

"I'm sure. I'll catch a ride with Mark tonight." She pulled on her sweater, picked up a bag of muffins and milk and walked through the swinging door to the café without even looking back.

Mark smiled, but Miller didn't bother to look in his direction. He wondered if Blaine had told this hairy friend of hers that he was her husband. Mark had a feeling she had or the big man wouldn't be allowing her to go home with him.

The thumping of the door closing blended with static from Randell's radio, which crackled in the café area. Everyone in the kitchen froze, trying to listen.

The only two words Mark could make out were *bus stop*. The rest was all in number codes. He glanced from Miller to Tuesday, but they didn't seem to understand any more than he had. Everyone waited as if to hear a translation being broadcast.

"Take a rain check on that breakfast, Tuesday," Randell yelled. "Bus stop across from the Driskill was just bombed." His words faded.

Miller moved first. As he headed out of the kitchen, he shot orders. "Tuesday, get Mary safely home and stay with her until I get there." He glared at the girl. "Do you understand?"

For once Tuesday didn't question. She nodded.

Miller moved on to Mark. "Maybe we can help the police spot the bomber. If he was at the bus stop, he can't be far." He opened the swinging door into the restaurant.

Mark agreed and they all rushed into the café.

"I hope the Annas weren't hurt," Tuesday said more to herself than the men. Then, addressing Randell, she asked, "Andrew, was anyone there when the bomb went off? Andrew?"

The door that Miller had locked only minutes before stood wide open. Randell had answered the radio's call. He was gone.

It took Mark a moment to realize what was wrong. The sack of muffins and milk sat on the counter. Blaine was gone.

Mark's heart rolled in his chest. "No!" he shouted and ran for the door with Miller a step behind. They were at a full run when they hit the corner and turned toward Sixth Street and the bus stop.

Mark tried to see her moving in the crowd in front of him. She couldn't be more than a few steps ahead of him! She couldn't already be in harm's way!

As they neared the bomb site, the smoke thickened the cloudy night. One of the buildings burned, splashing flames and smoke into the air. A fire truck screamed past them as people fled the scene at the same pace people were running to help.

Miller was at Mark's heels when they turned the corner. Men rushed to set up roadblocks and civilians directed traffic with flashlights.

The smoke, the screaming, people everywhere. Suddenly Mark was losing Blaine all over again.

"No!" he yelled and shoved his way past onlookers gathering. He stumbled over fire hoses and bumped into cars with windshields shattered from falling bricks.

He fought wildly toward the smoke. "Blaine's in there!" he screamed.

He'd been on the edge of sanity, balancing feelings he'd never allowed to surface. Now he was about to take the short step over and nothing would stop him. He ran, blinking away the smoke, yelling Blaine's name, listening for her answer.

Two uniformed policemen finally blocked him, forming an iron gate he couldn't seem to get around.

"I have to get past!" he yelled, feeling all reason slipping and no longer caring. Blaine, his baby, his future, his life were all just beyond the men holding him back.

"Hold on, buddy!" one yelled. "No one goes closer. It isn't safe."

"My wife's in there!" He shoved forward. "My wife's in there!"

The bandage came loose from his forehead and his wound started bleeding again, but still he fought. He heard one of the men holding him yell for help. A moment later strong hands felt as if they were pulling him apart. They shoved him into the back of a police car and slammed the door.

Mark pounded on the windows like a wild man. No one heard his cries. "Blaine!" he shouted. "God, Blaine don't leave me again." He'd let her slip from his grip one more time.

# Thirty-Five

Blaine took off running the instant she heard the radio report. She knew the Annas would be at their post at the bus stop as they were every night…as they had been the night she'd walked from the bombing and again the night she'd been knifed.

As she ran she pieced together what must have happened. The bomber had come into the café with a bomb and somehow left with the wrong bag. It was all her fault. She'd been the one he was trying to kill. Not the Annas.

Tears streamed down her face. If they were hurt it was all her fault. She'd been so worried about protecting herself, she hadn't found a way of stopping the madness. Blaine knew his face. She could have stopped him before now. She'd had one last chance earlier tonight when he'd been in the café. She should have thrown herself between him and the door. Maybe she could have slowed him for a few seconds, just long enough for Miller to run from the back.

Then he would have been caught and there would not be another report on a police radio of a bombing.

But she hadn't. She'd been afraid. She'd thought about when she should have acted and now the Annas, and others, might be hurt.

When she crossed the street at the hotel, she entered

a war zone with people lying everywhere. Most were crying, bleeding, asking for help. A few looked like broken toys tossed into traffic. Ambulances and police cars screamed from every direction and chaos whirled like smoke in the streets. Bricks, along with whole chunks of the building, littered the walk. Broken glass sparkled in car lights like diamonds amid the dust.

She ran past several cars damaged by debris, with injured people crawling out the doors while stoplights blinked off and on in double time above them. The smell of blood thickened the smoky air and flames from the roof of a building stretched into the sky.

Blaine moved, fighting her way as the cries of those around her blended with her own screams of panic.

When she reached the spot where the stop had been, nothing remained but rubble. If she hadn't known it to be a bus stop she would have thought it only a junk heap from a construction site. A fine dust thickened the air and settled over everything, turning the world to gray.

"Help me," a man whimpered from a few feet away. "Please, help me. I'm trapped. I can't move my leg."

Blaine took a step, but others rushed to the man beneath part of the wall that had stood behind the stop only minutes before. She spread her hands out, fingers wide as she searched in a broadening circle.

"Anna," she called. "Vanilla Anna, where are you? Chocolate Anna. It's Mary. Where are you?"

A fireman looked at her as though she'd lost her mind, but he had his hands full trying to help the injured tonight, so he didn't bother her.

Elaine's eyes burned from the smoke. The heat from the fire made it seem midday in July and not night. She knew she had only a few minutes before Miller caught up to her and he, or Randell, or even Mark would order her away, as if now that she was pregnant her brain must be leaking out and she no longer had the sense of a child. She had to know the Annas were safe before she left the scene.

Her circle almost reached the building now as she moved. Hope climbed into her thoughts. Maybe the Annas had gone to the bathroom, or for some reason were late to the stop. Maybe they hadn't been here at all and were safe.

Just as she breathed a sigh of relief, she saw two huddled mounds of rags in a doorway. Scattered, broken bags surrounded them, their treasures of plastic forks and sugar packets sprinkled around.

Blaine ran to the Annas as a white light scanned the area and a speaker somewhere yelled for everyone not authorized to move behind the barriers.

"Anna!" She hugged the old black bag lady. "Oh, Anna, I was so worried about you."

The hard old woman's face was wet with tears. "I'm all right," she said, holding herself away from Blaine's hug. "I got us as far as here, but she don't want to walk anymore. She keeps falling down. I told her we have to stay together, but she's not listening."

Blaine knelt beside Vanilla Anna. For a moment, she looked as if she was simply sleeping. But she was far too still.

"Anna?" Blaine tried, then remembered what a few of the homeless called the little bag lady. "Momma, are you all right?"

A dirty old hand reached out to cover hers.

"Momma." Blaine patted Anna's hand. "I'm home. I practiced, just like I promised."

Anna smiled. "I knew you'd come home, child." Her voice only a whisper now. "They said you was lost in that tornado, but I knew the wind would bring you back one day.''

Blaine glanced up at Chocolate Anna. The big woman nodded. ''She lost her three boys and one little girl thirty years ago when a twister hit Lubbock.'' She shoved tears away with her palm. ''A nurse at a clinic told me about it once. Said her daughter went to school with one of Anna's sons back then and she remembered the family, but I never let on like I knew.''

Vanilla Anna's grip relaxed around Blaine's fingers.

Blaine touched her face, begging Vanilla Anna to open her eyes.

The old bag lady had on several layers of clothes, but even in the heat of the fires burning so near, she wasn't sweating. It fact, she seemed cold.

''Anna!'' Blaine shouted. ''I need you to come with me. We're feedin' muffins, the best you ever ate, down at the café.'' Blaine pushed back tears. ''I figure I owe you another one for loaning me those good shoes. Get up now and go with us. This isn't anyplace for you to be.''

Blaine framed the old woman's face with her fingers. ''Come on, Momma, the kids need you.''

Vanilla Anna's head fell forward into Blaine's hands.

''Anna!'' Blaine screamed as blood soaked through the layers of clothing at the old woman's neck and spread across her fingers. ''No!''

She wanted to declare that this was all her fault. She was the one who should have died. But Anna wasn't listening.

Blaine grabbed her scarf and blotted at the blood as if it would go away if she pushed it back.

Chocolate Anna sobbed openly, her big body rocking from side to side as grief took control.

Miller's low voice told Blaine to step back as his big hands gripped her shoulders and he helped her to her feet.

"I tried to stop the bleeding, but I can't tell where it's coming from." Blaine shook so badly her words came out choppy. "I think she's hurt in the back of the neck. I'm afraid to move her."

He knelt in front of Anna, gently moving his hands to the sides of the woman's throat. A moment later he stood, his fingers now stained with blood. "I'll get help. Don't move her."

He ran toward the ambulances pulling up near the blockade. Men unloaded kits of supplies and stretchers, but the bleeding seemed to be everywhere. Firemen tried to get to the fire, now consuming an entire building, but they had to move the injured first.

Blaine knelt and closed her fingers around Anna's dirty hand. She gripped tightly as though she could somehow force the woman to hang on.

Great sobs broke from Chocolate Anna as she slid to the ground beside the doorway. Her cries could easily be heard all the way to heaven.

"Hang on, Anna," Blaine cried, wishing her arms were wide enough to hold both women. "Miller will get help. You'll see."

She leaned down, praying to feel Vanilla Anna's breath on her cheek.

But there was nothing.

# Thirty-Six

Mark watched the insanity around him from the silence of the inside of a police car. Adrenaline ran so thick in his veins he felt as if he might explode at any moment.

All his life everything had had an order, a logical path he could follow. Emotion was never a factor. He'd never loved, or hated, or cried, or felt until Blaine disappeared from his life, and now he was being driven crazy with feelings. The need to get to her had long ago transcended any reason and now overshadowed his basic survival instincts.

Detective Randell passed by, talking with a uniformed officer. The bumbling cop who had trouble talking to Tuesday without stammering was now in his element. Randell was snapping orders, displaying an authority and seasoned reason that surprised Mark.

When the cop was within five feet of the car, Mark hit the window with all the force he could manage, rocking the police car.

Randell looked up. A second later, he jerked the door open. "What the hell are you doing in there, Anderson? I thought you were back with the women at the café."

"Bl...Mary followed you here." Mark climbed from the back seat.

"Hell. I've got all I can handle without some pregnant

lady running around. Next thing you'll be telling me Tuesday's here passing out muffins.''

Mark shoved past Randell. He didn't have time to talk to the cop.

''Where do you think you're going?''

''I have to find her.''

Randell yelled. ''Then find her, Anderson, and get out of here. This is no place for either of you.''

The uniform policeman made a move toward Mark, but Randell waved him back as he ordered, ''Stay out of trouble, Counselor, or I swear I'll throw you in jail myself.''

Mark weaved his way through the police cars and fire trucks just as he'd done a month before. Then he hadn't known how death could rip a man's heart out. Then he hadn't understood about loss.

But now he did. He would not lose her again.

He spotted Miller at the edge of the crowd, watching the activity as he always did.

Mark hurried toward him, but he didn't have to say a word, Miller knew who he was looking for.

''She's straight ahead in a doorway with the Annas.'' Miller pointed twenty feet away. ''I've got a medic pulling out a stretcher right now. We'll be headed in that direction soon. He'll take care of Anna, but you need to get Mary out of here.''

''I've heard that before,'' Mark mumbled, wondering why everyone felt the need to tell him what he already knew he had to do.

Miller grabbed his arm. ''I mean it. Get her somewhere safe, fast. I saw the thin man moving among the crowd of onlookers.''

Mark stared at the old warrior's eyes and knew what

he was about to do. "You're going after the bomber, aren't you?"

"Just take care of your wife," Miller whispered. "I'm not your concern."

Mark was gone before Miller's words had registered. Mark glanced back. Miller knew.

Mark reached the crowded doorway just behind two paramedics.

"Everyone needs to step back," one medic shouted.

Blaine stood, sobbing as the two men knelt beside Vanilla Anna.

"No pulse," one said as the other pulled away clothes so that he could find where the bleeding was coming from.

They worked like a polished team, fighting to save a life as they'd been trained to do. Chocolate Anna huddled farther into the corner by the door. Sailor June stood guard above her, daring anyone to get too close. Blood dripped from the black woman's hand, but she wouldn't let anyone touch her.

Mark heard Blaine call his name from a few feet away. He turned, opening his arms, knowing she'd come. A moment later she slammed against him, almost knocking him off his feet. He took the blow like an electric shock and felt his heart kick into action once more. His wife was safe. He repeated Miller's words in his mind. "Take care of your wife."

She sobbed, crying his name over and over.

Mark put both arms around her and wished he could protect her from all the world. He took a deep breath, taking in the smell of her. How few times over the years they'd been married had he smelled the fragrance that was simply her.

"God, how I missed you, Blaine," he whispered as if they'd been parted for days and not minutes.

She rocked in his arms, putting her head on his shoulder as she calmed. The world had gone mad around them, but for a few seconds they held one another knowing that all was right between them.

He cradled her against him, digging his fingers into her soft hair. Not blond. Not straight, as it had always been. How he'd loved watching her blond hair move in the light. Mark laughed as he spread out his fingers and her curls caressed him. How he loved the feel of her hair now.

She felt so right in his arms.

He spread his hand over her abdomen and whispered, "Is our baby all right?"

She nodded against his shoulder. He knew she didn't want to watch the men work on Anna, so he tried to help her think of other things—of anything but the person laying a few feet away.

"How far along are you?" He tried to make his question casual, but others were already forming in his mind. "I haven't even asked."

"Almost five months, I think."

The men shifted Anna to the stretcher and one gave a thumbs-up sign. "We got a pulse. Faint, but we got one."

Blaine cried into his shoulder.

He pulled her close against him and whispered, "God, you're beautiful pregnant, Blaine."

The ambulance pulled close to the curb behind them. The medics lifted Vanilla Anna into the back without another word. Their grim faces told Mark they doubted the old woman would make it, but they'd done their best.

Chocolate Anna complained loudly when they tried to

help her into the back also. "I don't need no hospital. Just fix up my friend and we'll be on our way. We ain't used to breathing the air in those places. It's not good for us."

A man in a white lab coat worked on Vanilla Anna, frantically connecting her to life support. He glanced up and motioned the men to lift Chocolate Anna into the ambulance.

Chocolate Anna looked at Blaine. "Do I have to go?"

Blaine left Mark's arms and spoke to the men holding Chocolate Anna. "Turn her loose. She doesn't like to be touched."

They followed her orders.

She then looked at Anna. "Go with Momma. She might need you, and you know how the two of you have to stay together. I'll watch over your bags, don't worry."

Chocolate Anna nodded.

"Let them take care of your arm while you're there."

"All right," Anna said as she stepped up into the ambulance. "But I'm not taking off any of my clothes."

The medics closed the doors and slapped the back of the truck. A moment later they were on to the next injured person and Mark stood alone with Blaine.

He held her gently, feeling her pain in wave after wave of sorrow that racked her body. Part of him wanted to cry with her. Part wanted to pick her up and swing her around with pure joy. He'd found her, his mate, and nothing else mattered. All that counted was that she was near.

Finally, she stopped crying and he kissed away the last few tears.

With an ache in his heart, he tried to figure out why he hadn't seen how strong she was. He was a man who loved a woman who was far more than he thought her to be.

"We need to get out of here," he whispered as his hand moved to her back.

"I know." Blaine pointed toward the corner of the doorway. "Grab a few of Chocolate Anna's bags. She'll want them."

Mark reached into the corner and lifted two heavy shopping bags with handles that had been reinforced with plastic. One handle slipped and he had to pick up several pieces of clothing and stuff them back into the bag.

When he turned to leave, Blaine had vanished.

He glanced around. Expecting to see her only a few feet away.

Nowhere.

Only a blue cap lay by the curb where she'd stood.

# Thirty-Seven

Blaine fought the grip on her arm as the bomber dragged her down a side street away from all the people. Only a few inches taller than her, he could barely circle her shoulder with his arm and keep his hand over her mouth. All these weeks he'd been so much bigger in her nightmares. Now she realized he was simply a greasy little man.

She could taste the oil on his fingers. Jerking her head, she tried to break free enough to scream. His hand pushed into her teeth, splitting her lip in the corner.

"Cooperate, lady, or I'll kill you right here."

She had no intention of cooperating. Kicking at him, Blaine tried to trip him, but she couldn't even seem to slow him down. She thought of falling and letting him tumble on top of her, but that might hurt the baby. She had to wait for her chance, then she'd fight. She knew he planned to kill her, so she'd take her first opportunity to break free.

When they were a block from the bombing, he shoved her hard against a wall, releasing her grip on her mouth, but not her wrist. "Scream if you want to! No one will hear you."

Blaine knew he was right. Sirens sounded all around them. She'd only be wasting her breath. Everyone was watching the scene a block away. No one would notice her struggling with him.

"Let me go." She tried to reason with him. "I can do you no harm."

"Not a chance." He laughed. "You made a mistake. You should have died the first time." He pushed her once more, hard against the wall, allowing his anger to show. "You're the reason I'm not getting the money he promised."

"Who promised?"

"You don't need to know. You just got to die."

"Let me go. I won't tell anyone." Fear made her words choppy.

"You've already told one person too many." He glanced down the street in both directions, making sure they were alone. "I don't like the idea of killing face-to-face, but in your case I have to make an exception. If that old man in the café hadn't stormed toward me earlier, I wouldn't have grabbed the wrong bag. I'd have blown you all up instead of a few worthless old bag ladies."

Blaine knew her only chance might be to keep him talking. Every second that ticked by left more time for Miller or Mark to find her. "But, why kill me? I can't hurt you. I don't even know you."

He pulled a small pistol from his pocket and let go of her wrist long enough to jerk the weapon from its case.

Blaine hadn't taken two steps when he shoved her back against the wall. Miller was right about the man, he was stronger than he looked.

She tried to act as if he wasn't frightening her to death. "Why?" she repeated as she watched him point the gun toward her waist. He seemed to be searching for just the right spot to shoot her. ''I got a right to know before you kill me!''

He dug the point of the weapon into the material above her waistband and she heard her blouse rip slightly, giving the steel the right of way. When she would have inched away, he braced his arm on the other side of her, blocking her exit.

''I knew you didn't die that day. I could tell you were still around.'' He twisted the barrel of the gun against her skin. ''Laying that dynamite just below your window wasn't no harder than dropping it down a hole in the old days of drilling for oil. I was just doing my job, just like when I was the shooter in the oil fields. You should have had sense enough to disappear, but first thing I know, you're showing up at the shelter. Changed your look, but I could still see the fear in your eyes.''

''You don't have to kill me.'' Blaine grasped at anything. ''I will disappear.''

His smile turned her stomach. ''I can't trust you to stay dead.'' He leaned closer to her, fouling the air with his whiskey breath. ''I'm making sure this time.''

''But why?'' Blaine tried to ignore the gun barrel poking against her skin. ''You have to tell me.'' If he had to build his courage to kill her, maybe she could stall him a minute longer.

''I ain't got to do anything, lady.'' He swore. ''Once I kill you I'll be sitting pretty.''

He straightened with pride. ''For years I've been doing favors for them that don't want to get their hands dirty. Fitting their cars, making their problems go away. And I never got caught. Even if I did, they'd get me off.''

Blaine was too frightened to talk anymore. She wanted to scream, to beg for him not to kill her, but she knew nothing would change his mind. She was just a job he had to do.

She closed her eyes and waited.

A car went by, splashing water from the runoff of hoses near the fire. A couple ran, hand in hand, along the other side of the street. They didn't bother to look toward Blaine; they seemed afraid they might miss something if they didn't hurry.

The bomber jerked nervously and tried to push her into the alley, but she gripped a pole running along the wall behind her and held on with all her strength. If he planned to take her to her death, he would have to drag her, she would not make it easy for him.

The pole clanked against the wall, but held as he tried to tug her away with one hand while his other held the gun.

"Come on!" he ordered and poked her skin again.

"No."

"Come along, or you'll die right here."

She only widened her stance, preparing for the gunshots. If she was to die, better here in the street where someone would find her than in the alley where she wouldn't be found until dawn.

"Move!" The bomber's anger flared. "It's time to get this over with."

The barrel of the gun bruised her side, but she didn't budge.

"Wait!" Mark's voice rang with anger. "Stop right there!"

Blaine opened her eyes. Her husband, bloody and wrinkled, stood behind the bomber, looking nothing like the powerful lawyer he was, but sounding like one.

"Drop that weapon or you're a dead man," Mark yelled without a weapon in his hand.

The bomber tried to twist to see Mark without letting go of Blaine.

"I said drop it!"

"Come any closer and she's dead," the bomber threatened.

"No," Mark answered almost calmly.

"Stay out of this," he mumbled. "I got to kill her."

Mark took a step closer. The wound on his head was bleeding into his left eye but he didn't seem to notice. "Then you'll have to kill me too. Because I'm not going away, and if you kill her now I'm a witness."

The bomber heaved in frustration. Insanity settled in the depths of his grey eyes. "I might just do that," he answered.

"Then, kill me first!" Mark demanded, from a few steps away. "Kill me first because I'll not watch her die."

Without warning, the bomber whirled to face Mark and raised his gun.

Blaine crumpled to the ground, too frightened to breathe.

Mark stood perfectly still.

The bomber took aim.

Mark took a step forward, realizing he was too far away to reach the gun before the bomber could pull the trigger. In the second he had left in this life, Mark looked toward Blaine. He wanted her to be the last thing he saw on earth.

A shot rang out from the shadows, echoing off the buildings like a drumroll.

Mark rushed forward, knocking the bomber's gun away before he could fire.

The bomber stumbled backward, taking a shot high on his chest like a blow. Blood spread over his oily clothes as shock twisted his features. He tried to reach for his weapon, but Mark knocked his hand down.

Blaine scrambled out of the way so that he didn't fall on her. Without looking back, she ran to Mark. He lifted her off the ground and into his arms as footsteps ran toward them both.

Blaine cried out as she felt Mark, solid and alive, beside her.

Miller reached them first. He rested a hand on her shoulder long enough for her to nod and let him know she was all right, then he knelt beside the crumpled body of the bomber.

Detective Randell was only a few steps behind. "What happened here? I heard a shot."

Without a word, Miller handed the detective his weapon. A standard army-issue gun.

The cop knelt and rolled the bomber over. With care, he removed the small pistol from his fingers.

The thin man moaned in pain, blood dripping from him.

Randell looked at Miller. "You could have killed him with this cannon. Don't tell me you've been lugging this thing around for thirty years."

"If I'd wanted to kill him," Miller answered calmly, "he would be dead."

Randell radioed for a car. "I'm going to have to arrest you, Miller. You can't go around shooting people."

Mark didn't turn Blaine loose as he faced the detective. "If you're taking Miller in, I'm coming along as his legal counsel. I'll have him out in an hour."

Miller raised an eyebrow. Shooting a killer didn't seem to upset him near as much as the thought that he might need a lawyer.

The cop took a step back and stared at the three of

them. "You're a sorry-looking lot to be hauling in on a night like this. Anderson, you've got more blood on you than they have left at the hospital. No one will believe you're a lawyer. Mary has been frightened half out of her mind and that's not good for a lady in her condition. And you, Miller, who's going to believe a sixty-year-old man who owns a muffin shop can hit what he aims at from half a block away. Sounds like a stray bullet must have hit the guy."

The car swung to the curb and Randell motioned for the driver to help him with the bomber. "Why don't you three go home and we'll sort this all out in the morning. I'll see our troublemaker has full guard at the hospital tonight after I read him his rights."

He was gone before Blaine could think of anything to say. She moved from Mark's arms to Miller. When she hugged the big man, he almost hugged her back.

"Thanks," she whispered.

"I got used to having you around, pest. Besides, I couldn't let the little creep shoot my legal counsel, could I?"

Blaine laughed. "Help me one last time. We need to get Mark to the hospital for stitches."

Miller nodded. "Never knew lawyers had so much blood."

Two hours later, Blaine sat beside Vanilla Anna's bed when Mark walked into the room. His cut had been stitched and properly bandaged. Without a word, he waited at the door.

Blaine stood and touched Anna's arm knowing that she had little chance of making it and wondering if she really wanted to fight. Chocolate Anna slept in a recliner next to her friend. Miller had stretched out on a cot in the corner, his snoring louder than the pop machines, but no one complained. The staff had far too many problems tonight to worry about a few extras in the rooms.

Blaine kissed each one goodbye and joined her husband at the door. "I love them, you know."

"I know," Mark answered as he pulled her into the hallway. "Did you have someone look at the bruise on your side?"

"It was nothing," Blaine answered. "He didn't break the skin. But the doctor did insist on doing a full check including a sonogram."

"Everything all right?"

"Everything is just fine with me, and with little Luke."

She brushed her abdomen and walked down the hall.

It took Mark a few seconds to follow. "A boy? The baby's a boy?"

Blaine looped her arm around his. "Come on, Dad, let's go home. I'll explain it all after we get you cleaned up."

# Thirty-Eight

They rode home without saying a word. Mark reached for her hand and didn't let go until they pulled into the parking garage. He climbed from the car and hurried around to help her out.

"I can make it." She smiled up at him thinking that if she got much bigger she wouldn't be able to fold into his little car.

Mark waited to close her door. "I guess I'm just used to Lilly. She acts like she's being tortured every time she rides with me."

Blaine was surprised Lilly had been in his car. "How is Miss Lilly? I've missed her."

He put his arm around her waist as they moved toward the elevator. "Besides complaining, she's all right. Broke her leg on the steps by the mailbox, but after she turned me into her slave, she's been fine.

"Don't laugh," he said even though she hadn't made a sound. "I cook her breakfast every morning and deliver supper most nights."

"Really?" She did have a hard time picturing him cooking anything but coffee. Mark had never shown any interest in doing so.

Mark turned toward her as he pushed the button. "I've changed," he said almost apologetically. "I always thought I could handle everything, but I couldn't get a grip on the loss of you. If it hadn't been for Lilly needing me, I think I would have gone mad.''

She kissed him lightly a moment before the elevator opened and they rode up with strangers as they both tried to keep their hands off each other. When they finally stepped off the elevator, he took her hand in a firm grip and smiled as he gently pulled her down the hallway.

He didn't say more until they were alone in their home—a home that now seemed huge to Blaine. She walked around touching the things that had once meant so much to her. Things she hadn't missed at all.

Mark moved up behind her and held her for a long time, then slowly pulled away. ''We have to talk.''

''I know,'' she agreed. ''But let's clean up first.''

Without a word he walked to the guest bath and she crossed to the bedroom that had been theirs. Looking around, she felt as she knew she would. She no longer belonged here. This wasn't her world, her life anymore. The polished chrome and leather no longer suited her. Everything seemed sterile, like an expensive hospital waiting area decorated by a designer who would never know the patients. The bedroom looked like a hotel room where no one had ever lived.

She pulled an oversize sweatshirt and a pair of stretch pants from the back of her closet, tossed them on the bed and went into the shower.

Lined along the shelves were all her perfumes that had been a part of her daily routine. Her makeup and brushes. She'd half expected them to be gone, removed by one of their well-meaning friends who thought they were doing Mark a favor. But everything was exactly the same as it had been the day she left.

Only she had changed. All her things might be in the right place—but she no longer was. She felt as if she was moving through a stranger's home. But this was where Mark lived. The rooms were still a part of him. He'd been the one who'd wanted and planned for the expensive town house, not settling for one of the smaller apartments in the middle of the exclusive development.

Blaine closed her eyes, knowing that if she left this place she'd be leaving him too.

The warm shower felt great, washing away tension along with the smell of blood and fire and oily fingers.

Blaine stepped from the shower, wrapped in a thick towel that brushed her knees. She ran a comb through her hair and stepped out of the bathroom into the bedroom. It had to be after midnight. Mrs. Bailey would be worried about her if she wasn't home soon.

Mark sat in the chair by the window. He hadn't bothered to turn on a light, but she could see that he had dressed in clean clothes. The cream-colored slacks and cotton sweater fit his lean body. He was once more in his world.

She braced herself as she moved into the room. This wasn't a homecoming where she would crawl into bed and all would be forgotten. Mark would want answers. He'd want details. And in the end, no matter how much he said he'd missed her, or how he'd kissed her, he might not want her back.

Blaine couldn't blame him. She knew he still loved her, but she'd shattered his plans. When she'd disappeared, no matter how good her reason, she'd ended his chances of running for office. And she'd gotten pregnant. He'd never said he wanted the baby. All he'd said was they needed to talk.

Tres clanked through the cat door and walked past her, rubbing against her damp legs as if she'd only been gone a day.

Blaine wished Mark would say something. He must know that she saw him sitting there. Did he want her to say she was sorry? Did he want her to beg to come back home?

She didn't know where to start, but she knew there would be no begging, no apologizing. She'd done what she had to do and she felt strong enough to handle whatever happened. If she had to, she'd raise her son alone. She'd keep the café job. She'd survive.

Walking halfway across the room, she faced him directly. "What are you waiting for?"

Mark stood. "I'm waiting to see if you put on your nightgown, or those clothes you laid out." He took one step toward her, his words low. "I'm waiting to see if you're still my wife."

Blaine knew the time to be totally honest had come. "I'm not the woman who left this place a month ago." She raised her chin. "I can't go back to being that person."

"I'm not asking you to," he answered, almost angry. "I'm asking if you're still my wife." He took another step.

"I never stopped," she admitted. "But I'm pregnant and I'm not giving up this baby."

His fingers closed around her arms. He gently turned her to face him and waited until her eyes met his. "I'm not asking you to," he whispered as his mouth lowered to hers.

Blaine let the towel fall as she wrapped her arms around him.

His kiss was tender, gentle against her mouth as his hands moved down her body. In slow motion, he lifted her up and carried her to the bed, spreading out beside her while still kissing her. For a long while, he just touched her as if for the first time. Her changing body seemed to fascinate him as he examined it hesitantly.

Finally, he pulled away and removed his sweater. As he unbuttoned his shirt, he said, "When I saw the bomber holding you against that wall, I realized he had my life in his hands. He had my family."

Mark pulled his shirt off. "I meant it when I told him he'd better kill me first, for I had no plans to watch you die." The cream-colored, freshly pressed trousers tumbled atop his sweater.

He lowered, his chest pressing gently against her warm skin. "Make love to me, Mary Blaine."

He didn't give her time to answer, but covered her mouth with his. The need within them both set fire to their kiss and all thought of conversation vanished. He made love to her for the thousandth time, for the first time, all at once. She'd never known such hunger for him and he seemed to feel the same.

When she would have been shy, he shoved her hands away. He kissed her body, moving down until he came to the roundness of her belly. There, he took his time exploring, touching. He looked up and caught her watching him. "My son?" he whispered.

"Our son," she answered. "If it's all right with you."

"It's not all right with me," he answered. "It's perfect."

The world slipped away as they made love, then fell asleep wrapped in one another's arms.

Deep into the night, she felt his hands moving over her once more, needing her. They made love slowly as if both had dreamed the same dream.

At dawn, Blaine crawled from the bed and dressed. She had to get to the doc's house before Mrs. Bailey woke up. Blaine clicked off Mark's alarm. He needed to sleep. With luck, she would be back to have the talk he'd promised by the time he woke up.

In some ways they were still so far apart. She'd always known what he wanted, where he wanted to live, how he wanted their lives, but he'd never known her. Maybe she was just starting to know herself.

As she locked the door and started down the hallway, Mrs. Lilly's door opened. The chubby little lady maneuvered on crutches out the door.

Blaine looked up, but before she could say a word, Lilly smiled. "Welcome home," Lilly said. "I've been wondering when you'd be back."

"You recognized me?"

Lilly grinned. "I knew the minute Mark started telling me about this woman named Mary who you were. A kind woman who loves to read, he said. A woman who walks with grace." Lilly giggled. "I've read one too many mysteries not to be able to figure it out. Only question was why you weren't coming home."

Blaine hugged her. "Can I tell you all about it later? I've somewhere I have to be."

Lilly looked disappointed. "I guess I can wait, long as you bring muffins when you come."

Blaine promised and ran down the hallway. She stepped outside, walked half a block and caught the bus heading downtown. It crossed her mind that all the years she'd lived in Austin, she'd always fought the traffic and the parking downtown, when she could have stepped on a bus and been there quicker. Only, Blaine wouldn't have thought of riding a bus; Mary, on the other hand, with three dollars in her pocket, saw it as quite practical.

She walked the last few blocks to the doc's house and let herself in. The stillness of the old house welcomed her. The dark paneling, the overstuffed furniture, the

muted colors. Every few days the doc threatened to leave
the place to her, and though she always protested, in
truth, she wouldn't mind.

Blaine curled up on the couch and was almost asleep
when Mrs. B. came down the stairs.

"'Morning, Mary," she said as she opened a blind.
"You up?"

If Blaine hadn't been, she was now. "Yes." She
yawned. "How's the doc?"

"He slept well but he's sure up early this morning. I
told him if you were awake I'd get you to read to him
while I make him some oatmeal." She pointed her finger. "I promised not to wake you."

Blaine grinned. "You didn't. I'll go up."

Mrs. Bailey nodded. "I'll make you breakfast too. After he eats, he'll fall back asleep. Maybe you can tell me
what happened last night. Tuesday was worried about
you, but I told her you must have been with Miller."

Blaine grabbed a book and hurried up the stairs before
Mrs. Bailey asked any questions. As she climbed she
planned. She'd read, eat breakfast, then call Mark.

But the doctor was restless with pain and she read
longer than she'd planned. Finally, she tucked him in
and brushed his white hair back to make sure he didn't
have a fever.

"Thank you," he whispered, already half-asleep.

"You're welcome, Doc." Blaine could see seventy
years of goodness in this old man. She knew he could
double his pain medication, but his mind would slip
away with the pain and he wouldn't be able to follow
along with the stories she read. "Sleep now."

"You'll stay, Mary?"

"I'll stay until you fall asleep."

"No," he said. "You'll stay with me until the end."

"But you'll be better..."

"We've never lied to one another. Don't start now."
He patted her hand. "I only have a few weeks at the
most. I'd like my last hours to be filled with books. If
it's no trouble for you, I'd be grateful for the company."

Blaine gripped his wrinkled hand. She understood
him. He'd held the hands of all those he'd loved and
watched them die. Now it was his turn and there was no
family to stand by him. "I'll stay," she whispered.

He took a deep breath and relaxed into sleep.

# Thirty-Nine

**M**ark rolled over and reached for Blaine.

The sheets felt cold to his touch. He came awake in degrees of pain. His hand hurt with bruised knuckles, his head throbbed from the stitches, his ribs ached each time he took in a breath. But none of the pain mattered compared to the one in his heart.

Blaine had left him…again.

He sat up and tried to remember what he'd said to her. He'd told her it didn't matter about the baby, but had he told her he wanted it? He'd made love to her with more passion than he thought himself capable of, but had he said the words even once in the hours they'd been together?

Mark stood and pulled on his clothes knowing he had to go after her. At least this time he had a pretty good idea where she was. Only, was this how it would be between them? Never knowing when he'd wake beside her. Not understanding what she wanted him to do. What she wanted him to be.

Mark realized that for the past ten years it had always been what *he* wanted. He remembered talking about his plans for a career, for buying this place, for moving up in the firm. Had Blaine ever told him her plans?

He walked to the kitchen and stared at the empty refrigerator, remembering hoping, as if by magic, one morning food would appear.

Maybe Blaine's plans didn't include him. Maybe that was why she'd left without saying a word.

A banging at the door pulled him from his thoughts. Before he could hope that Blaine had returned, he heard Lilly yell, "Wake up. You can't sleep all day."

Mark opened the door and frowned at her. Her shoulders were almost to her ears as she leaned on her crutches with the top of a white bag wrapped around each handrest.

She smiled. "I brought doughnut holes and coffee. And news. Great news."

He managed a grin. "You shouldn't be up and about."

She didn't wait for him to invite her in. Handing him the bags, she swung over the threshold. "Don't tell me what to do. I'm not in the habit of listening."

Mark followed her. "No woman in my life seems to be these days."

"Stop complaining and come tell me why you look like something even Tres wouldn't bother to drag in."

Mark flipped the paper open. He wasn't surprised to see a picture of the bombing, but the headline below the lead story read Harry Winslow Arrested.

Mark reached for the phone and remembered he'd turned it off last night along with his cell phone. He dialed Randell and found out Shorty, a guy Winslow had hired to watch Mark, had spilled the entire plot. Winslow would never live long enough to get out of jail.

"I want to see you today," Randell snapped. "Why didn't you tell me Mary was Blaine? I didn't figure it out until I saw you holding her."

Mark didn't answer.

"As soon as we hang up, cut off your phone unless you want to talk to the press. I'll see you soon." Randell laughed. "I hear Winslow is looking for a good lawyer."

Mark swore, then laughed and hung up the phone. He drank coffee with Lilly and filled her in on the details. Then he retrieved his briefcase off the hall table. "I've got some papers for you to sign."

"I didn't come about me," she answered without interest.

"I know, but your husband's lawyer and I hammered out the details a few days ago. I noticed Bettye Ruth had the papers delivered here. Since Willard started his business with the sale of the car you left, legally you're a partner in his companies."

"I'm not interested in his companies."

"I know, that's why I agreed to a settlement. If you'll sign this he'll send you a check for two hundred and fifty thousand dollars."

Lilly dropped her half-eaten doughnut hole.

When she didn't answer, he asked, "Any plans for the money?"

Lilly winked. "I might go back to school. Looks like I'm single again. Or I might look for a bigger place, I'll think it over."

An hour later, Mark knocked on Dr. Early's door. He waited a long while before anyone answered. Finally, an older version of Tuesday Bailey jerked the door open and frowned at him.

"Whatever it is we ain't buying."

"Is Bla...is Mary here?"

"Who wants to know?" She crossed her arms and widened her stance.

"Her husband." Mark tried to decide whether to bully the woman or charm her. His charm hadn't had much luck lately, but she didn't look like the type who would bully easily. "I've got to see her."

Mrs. Bailey's head leaned over as she looked him up and down. "You got a job?"

Mark smiled. "Yes." Although he doubted he'd have one by this time next week.

"What do you make? Mary needs a man who can take care of her and a family, not some freeloader who looks like he's been in a bar fight."

"I make enough." Mark knew the women probably wouldn't believe him if he told her how much. "I need to talk to my wife."

"It'll have to wait. Come back later."

Mark held the door open with his foot. "It can't wait. Now, you can let me in, or I can stand here and yell her name. It's up to you, but I'm not leaving without talking to her."

The woman didn't look the least bit frightened. She raised an eyebrow as if debating how long it would take her to knock him out and toss him off the porch. "You sure you're married?"

He held up his left hand. The ring seemed to satisfy her. She stepped back.

"But be quiet, I got the boy asleep on the couch. Poor little fellow was so worried about Mary this morning he tapped on the door. I talked him into staying for breakfast."

Mark noticed a little boy in ragged clothes curled into a corner of the couch.

"You can see her, but she's upstairs sleeping with the doc."

Mark followed the tugboat of a woman up the stairs.

Maybe the old bag was simply trying to shock him, but he knew Blaine well enough to know she wouldn't be sleeping with another man.

He was wrong. When they reached the second floor, there was his wife, atop the covers of a massive bed, surrounded by books. A frail old man, tucked beneath blankets lay a few feet away, little more than skin over skeleton. Both were sound asleep.

"Whatever you do, don't wake the doc," the woman whispered and headed back down the stairs.

Mark moved to Blaine's side of the bed and brushed her cheek with his fingers. "God, you're beautiful."

She smiled and opened one eye, then rolled into his arms.

Mark lifted her gently and carried her down the stairs.

He sat her on the first chair he came to and knelt in front of her. "Are you leaving me, Blaine? There is no reason for you to run any longer, unless it's from me."

She rubbed her eye with her fist and yawned. "I don't belong there anymore."

"All right," he said as he stood and walked to the door.

She still sat in the chair when he returned a few minutes later. Tears sparkled in her eyes, but she didn't say a word as he dropped the suitcases on the floor.

He went out for another load and the cat carrier. When he returned, she said, "Try to understand, Mark. I can't go back to what I was. There is really no use in us talking about it."

He watched her closely.

"I can't be what I was, no matter how much I love you." She raised her chin as she stood. "Thank you for bringing my things. I don't know where I belong but it isn't in your town house world anymore with nothing to do. The doc needs me here and wants me to stay. I have to watch over Anna in case she makes it. Miller thinks he's all tough, but he needs someone to help him. And last night we finally got the little boy from the cemetery to talk to one of us. Tuesday couldn't manage the café without me to do the book work and—''

She stopped, realizing she was rambling.

''I agree,'' he finally managed to get in. ''But these are not your things, they're mine. I don't know where you belong, Mary Blaine, but I know where my world is.''

He stepped so close their bodies touched. ''It's here, with you. I know a woman who just came into some money who might buy our place. If you want to be here, I'll see if the house next door is for sale—I'll do whatever it takes.''

Blaine leaned near and rested her hand over the heart of the only man she'd ever loved. The baby moved and Mark's grin told her he felt his son.

''I love you,'' he whispered as he pulled her closer. ''By whatever name, in whatever world, I love you.''

Blaine sighed and breathed deeply. Finally, she'd found her way home.

Bestselling author Kate Wilhelm delivers another gripping story.

## A Barbara Holloway Novel

# KATE WILHELM

The Kelso/McIvey rehab center is a place of hope and healing for its patients—
and for the dedicated staff who volunteer there. But David McIvey, a brilliant
surgeon whose ego rivals his skill with a scalpel, plans to close the clinic and
replace it with a massive new surgery center—with himself at the helm.

Since he is poised to desecrate the dreams of so many, it's not surprising to
anyone, especially Oregon lawyer Barbara Holloway, that somebody dares to stop
him in cold blood. When David McIvey is murdered outside the clinic's doors
early one morning, Barbara once again uses her razor-sharp instincts and take-
no-prisoners attitude to create a defense for the two members of the clinic who
stand accused.

**"Wilhelm is a masterful storyteller whose novels have just the right
blend of solid plot, compelling mystery, and great courtroom drama."**
**—*Library Journal***

*Available in August 2004 wherever paperbacks are sold.*

# CLEAR AND
# CONVINCING
# PROOF

# JODI
# THOMAS

---

66715 THE WIDOWS OF
      WICHITA COUNTY      ___ $6.50 U.S. ___ $7.99 CAN.

*(limited quantities available)*

| | |
|---|---|
| TOTAL AMOUNT | $_____ |
| POSTAGE & HANDLING | $_____ |

($1.00 for one book; 50¢ for each additional)

| | |
|---|---|
| APPLICABLE TAXES* | $_____ |
| <u>TOTAL PAYABLE</u> | $_____ |

(check or money order—please do not send cash)

To order, complete this form and send it, along with a check
or money order for the total above, payable to MIRA Books®,
to: **In the U.S.:** 3010 Walden Avenue, P.O. Box 9077, Buffalo,
NY 14269-9077; **In Canada:** P.O. Box 636, Fort Erie, Ontario
L2A 5X3.

Name:_____
Address:_____ City:_____
State/Prov.:_____ Zip/Postal Code:_____
Account Number (if applicable):_____
075 CSAS

  *New York residents remit applicable sales taxes.
   Canadian residents remit applicable GST and provincial taxes.

**MIRA®**